1

THE
CASE
OF THE
MISSING
MAID

THE
CASE
OF THE
MISSING
MAID

ROB OSLER

KENSINGTON
PUBLISHING CORP.

kensingtonbooks.com

KENSINGTON BOOKS are published by

Kensington Publishing Corp.
900 Third Avenue
New York, NY 10022

Copyright © 2025 by Rob Osler

All Kensington titles, imprints, and distributed lines are available at special quantity discounts for bulk purchases for sales promotion, premiums, fund-raising, educational, or institutional use. Special book excerpts or customized printings can also be created to fit specific needs. For details, write or phone the office of the Kensington Special Sales Manager: Attn. Special Sales Department, Kensington Publishing Corp., 900 Third Avenue, New York, NY 10022. Phone: 1-800-221-2647.

Library of Congress Control Number: 2024943029

KENSINGTON and the K with book logo Reg. US Pat. & TM. Off.

ISBN: 978-1-4967-4948-2

First Kensington Hardcover Edition: January 2025

ISBN: 978-1-4967-4950-5 (ebook)

10 9 8 7 6 5 4 3 2 1

Printed in the United States of America

She who succeeds in gaining the mastery of the bicycle
will gain the mastery of life.
—Susan B. Anthony

THE
CASE
OF THE
MISSING
MAID

Chapter 1

Harriet Morrow considered the fashions of 1898 little improved over the year before. Long bell-shaped skirts and silly, frilly blouses with puffed shoulders continued to emphasize the distinction between the sexes—as if she or anyone else needed reminding who wore the pants. The popular silhouette, wide at top and bottom with a nipped waist, fit Harriet's midsection as well as a watermelon in a bread box. For reasons both practical and personal, she longed for the simplicity of men's straight-legged trousers and a white starched shirt. Although acquiescing to convention with a wardrobe of plain-fronted white shirtwaists and black bow tie, jacket, and skirt from the cheaper racks in Marshall Field's women's department, she'd rather paste grass clippings to a straw bonnet than pay two dollars for some ready-made women's frippery. Harriet tucked her wiry auburn hair beneath a man's black bowler—purchased from Sears, Roebuck and Company for a reasonable one dollar and ten cents.

Although an avid bicyclist, Harriet had left her prized Overman Victoria at home—today was not a day to risk dirtying the hem of her skirt. Grabbing the streetcar's last open seat, she sat wedged shoulder-to-shoulder between two fellow passengers on the hard wooden bench. Given the chilly March morning, she was grateful for the shared warmth of a body on either side. Anyone looking on might mistake her knees jittering beneath her handbag as shivers, when in truth she was anxious. In a quarter hour, she would meet her coworkers for the first time and didn't doubt that most, if not all, of them would think her entirely unsuitable for her new position. She'd do herself no favors by revealing her nervousness.

Three blocks from her final destination, Harriet hopped down from the streetcar and joined the throng of mostly men—all wearing nearly indistinguishable long dark woolen coats and hats—hurrying in all directions. In her twenty-one years of living in Chicago, the city had grown to become the nation's second largest. With miles of sidewalks swarming with pedestrians and a sprawling grid of congested streets, the midwestern metropolis throbbed with a dizzying cacophony of humanity. Not for the first time, she appreciated the city leaders' decision to elevate the passenger train serving downtown. The first full circuit of "the Loop" had been completed just the year before. Its structure of riveted steel plate resembled that of Paris's famed Eiffel Tower—or so Harriet had read in the pages of the *Chicago Tribune*.

Dodging several buggies and delivery wagons—and barely avoiding being run over by a new Duryea motorcar, a contraption that turned every head—Harriet crossed North LaSalle Street to Number 30, stepped inside the marbled lobby, and joined the huddle waiting for an elevator. Happy for the warmth, she glanced apprehensively at those around her, wondering if any of these men and women would soon be her colleagues. What might they think of her? Would they be welcoming? Incredulous? Or worse, might they be dismissive? Whatever reception she might receive, she couldn't allow it to affect her performance. She had taken a risk by quitting her bookkeeping job at Rock Island. Although the work had been mind-numbingly boring with no prospect for advancement—

and insufferably dusty from the grain elevators—it had been steady, providing just enough for both her and her brother. With scant savings to fall back on, she had no option but to make a go of it upstairs.

After stops on each ascending floor, the doors finally opened to the sixth and the offices of the Prescott Detective Agency. With a "pardon me" and "sorry, sir, but if I might just . . ." she wriggled her way out from the rear of the packed cabin. She had been to these offices once before. Last week, she shocked the agency's principal, Theodore Prescott, by presenting a clipping of his agency's ad seeking a junior field operative along with her application. Met with Prescott's furrowed brow, she had argued that Chicago's unsavory characters would be more inclined to let down their guard and reveal their secrets to a woman. Animated by her audacity, the diminutive Prescott had leaped from his chair, revealing his immaculately tailored gray worsted suit—the color matching his voluminous beard—and English-style shoes polished to a fine sheen. "Detective work is a man's work," he had lectured, adding that her boldness would surely dissolve when confronting the city's dark alleys, seedy pool halls, and nefarious gambling dens.

"With all due respect, sir," Harriet said, knowing she would not win him over by tucking her tail, "I may not wear trousers or whiskers, but history has shown both to be an unreliable indicator of either courage or intelligence."

As Prescott had sputtered in astonishment, she'd held his gaze.

"Raise up your skirt a few inches," he managed to say.

The demand was scandalous, but Harriet suspected Prescott wanted only to better see her shoes. Despite hers costing but a small fraction of his, they were of a remarkably similar style. After an awkward silence, Prescott surprised her by saying nothing about her men's footwear and instead declared her ankles to be "thick and sturdy," which would prove beneficial given the rigors of the job. He had then offered her employment as a junior field operative on a trial basis.

Despite Prescott offering her less than the salary advertised—he'd presumed he would be hiring a man—at nine dollars a week, she'd now earn fifty percent more than before. Struggling to contain her excitement, she had accepted the job on the spot.

"Who are you here to see?" the receptionist asked. That the young woman had no recollection of Harriet's visit the week before was unusual. Her bowler hat, conservative attire, and mannish features—a broad nose, thin lips, and square jaw—stood in opposition to the look common among women in downtown offices, exemplified by the petite receptionist's own stylish clothing, chorus-girl looks, and abundant blond curls pulled into a tidy knot atop her head. The woman would surely draw admiring looks from any man—or woman who, like Harriet, preferred a female's curves over a man's straight and uninspiring frame.

"I'm not sure who to ask for," Harriet admitted. "You see, I am a new employee. I'm to be a junior field operative."

The receptionist's tidy brows lifted. "Oh? Are you quite sure you haven't confused us with another firm? This is the Prescott Agency."

Over the puffed shoulder of the receptionist's white shirtwaist, Harriet could see the large PRESCOTT AGENCY sign. "Yes, I am quite aware."

"But we have no female detectives."

"Would you please notify Mr. Prescott of my arrival?" Harriet asked. "My name is Harriet Morrow."

The young woman glanced at the grandfather clock in the corner. "It's only eight o'clock. Mr. Prescott never arrives before nine."

"Then his secretary perhaps? Might she be available?" Harriet recalled meeting her when she applied for the job.

"Madelaine. We didn't have an occasion to speak, but I'm sure she will remember my interview with Mr. Prescott. Maybe she is expecting me?"

"Madelaine?" the woman said, looking like she'd been pinched.

"Yes. If you'd be so kind as to let Madelaine know that Harriet Morrow has arrived for her first day of work. I'm sure Mr. Prescott would prefer I begin straightaway than to sit on my hands for an hour until he arrives."

"If you insist," the receptionist said, "I'll relay the message." Heels clacking, she headed down the corridor to where the secretary's desk sat before the tall double doors leading to the principal's inner sanctum.

As Harriet waited, she took in the lobby. Someone had selected the spare furnishings—the receptionist's desk and chair, a small austere sofa for guests, and the imposing grandfather clock—with purpose in mind. The message: the Prescott Agency was a place of work and efficiency, not of frivolous comforts.

Hearing fast-approaching footsteps, Harriet looked up and immediately recognized the principal's secretary, who, easily two decades her senior, exuded self-importance based not on her own authority but rather on her proximity to it. Madelaine carried an excess of two dozen pounds and moved with the determination of a locomotive. With the receptionist racing to keep up, Madelaine started talking before reaching the lobby. "I'm afraid there's been a mistake. This is the Prescott Agency."

"Yes, I'm fully—"

"If you'd like to leave an application for a secretarial position, you're welcome to do so. But at present—"

"Madam," Harriet raised a hand, bringing Madelaine up short. "My name is Harriet Morrow. I was hired by Mr. Prescott last Thursday. Do you not recall my meeting with him?"

Madelaine waved an arm dismissively through the air,

wafting a cloying scent of talcum powder. "Then I'm sorry to say you misunderstood. We have no secretarial positions available at the moment."

The receptionist continued to observe the conversation as if watching two shoppers tussle over the last head of lettuce.

Harriet took a deep breath and expelled it silently, trying to project a cordial manner. This woman was her new boss's gatekeeper, after all. "Perhaps it's best then if I wait for Mr. Prescott to arrive."

"You shall do no such thing," Madelaine snapped, surprising Harriet with her abruptness. "Mr. Prescott is a very busy man. I keep his calendar. He has no time for interviews today. As I say, if you care to leave an application, we'll be in touch should you be qualified and something becomes available."

Harriet had expected to be tested by her colleagues, just not before she'd progressed beyond the lobby. She couldn't allow herself to be dismissed by the secretary. What would Prescott think? Standing her ground during the interview had won her the job. She hadn't wilted when confronting Theodore Prescott; she wasn't about to do so now because his blustery secretary was uninformed. If she were to last the first hour in the role, she would need to stay put.

"Madam, I am here because Mr. Prescott hired me"—Harriet paused just long enough for her next words to carry extra weight—"as a junior field operative. That you are unaware of my employment does not erase the fact. I was told to report here"—Harriet glanced at the clock—"precisely six minutes and fifteen seconds ago. I have no intention of not being present when Mr. Prescott arrives. I shall wait."

To Madelaine's sputtering dismay and the receptionist's stunned silence, Harriet lowered herself onto the sofa's thin cushion, maintaining eye contact with Madelaine.

"We shall see what Mr. Prescott has to say about this," Madelaine huffed.

Harriet gave a sharp nod. "I'm pleased we agree that it's his word that matters."

Accepting momentary defeat, the secretary threw her arms in the air—dispensing another whiff of powder—spun on her short heels, and retreated down the corridor. The receptionist wore an unreadable expression, which Harriet guessed was either admiration or pity—or perhaps a bit of both. Her accompanying words, "You've got nerve," did nothing to clarify her intent.

As Harriet awaited Prescott's arrival, she regretted that her parents weren't alive to have seen her off that morning. They had encouraged her bold ambitions. As a lawyer representing the interests of labor unions, her father had urged Harriet and her brother to pursue occupations engaged in righting wrongs instead of "*tsk-tsk*ing while reading the latest troubling headlines in the morning's *Tribune*." Her mother, who'd been an active member of the Illinois Equal Suffrage Association and supported the campaigns of women to serve on school boards, had told Harriet to pursue her dreams, despite what others might think of them. Harriet had taken her parents' advice to heart but knew that most jobs available to women in social justice were limited to secretaries, prison matrons, and cooks. The first two made her grimace. The third, given her discomfort in the kitchen, caused her to shudder. Then she heard about Kate Warne—America's first female detective. Hired by Allan Pinkerton right there in Chicago, Kate Warne had worked cases in the 1850s and 1860s, before Harriet had even been born. Harriet figured if Kate Warne could do it, why couldn't she? Sitting there, she realized the question had an answer—and it might come soon.

At ten minutes past nine, Harriet sensed her left buttock had fallen asleep when Theodore Prescott marched into the lobby. Seeing Harriet, he barked, "What in blazes are you doing there? I don't pay my employees to sit and gaze out the window."

Struggling to her feet, Harriet started to explain, but Prescott was already halfway down the hallway toward his office, still barking. "I suggest you follow me, Miss Morrow. Unless you want your first day as an operative at this agency to also be your last."

As Harriet hurried after her new boss, she caught the dumbfounded look on the receptionist's face. She couldn't help but return a smile. Theodore Prescott had just confirmed it.

She was now a detective.

Chapter 2

As Theodore Prescott approached his office, Madelaine sprang to her feet. He placed his hat and long coat into her outstretched arms. Then Madelaine saw Harriet.

"You!" she exclaimed. "Just where do you think you're going?"

From his doorway, Prescott turned back. His eyes darted from Madelaine to Harriet, then back again. "For heaven's sake, Madelaine. Miss Morrow works here."

"But, sir." Madelaine appeared suddenly distraught. "I was unaware that we needed another secretary. If only you'd said something, I would have happily—"

"You may bring my morning coffee." He turned to Harriet, who stood off to the side, hoping she didn't appear as uncomfortable as she felt. "Coffee, Miss Morrow? Tea?"

"Nothing, thank you." Harriet croaked out the words, so unexpected was the offer.

Prescott gave his secretary a confirming nod before entering his office. Stepping past Madelaine, Harriet couldn't avoid the woman's searing glare and imagined she heard a faint whistle of steam coming from her ears.

Inside the principal's private domain, Harriet was unnerved to see her boss had disappeared. A quick scan of the room revealed a strip of light beneath an interior door.

Before she had time to guess the room's purpose, the sound of active plumbing confirmed the unthinkable—Prescott had a private lavatory.

She had been so focused during her interview that she remembered little of her surroundings aside from Prescott's massive carved desk and his high-back, tufted leather chair that he'd occupied as if it were a throne. The light streaming in from tall windows framed by thick burgundy drapes had caused her to squint throughout the meeting. Now, with time to appreciate the entire room, she noticed that Prescott had decorated one wall with plaques and photographs of himself with various political leaders, including Illinois Governor John Riley Tanner and Chicago Mayor Carter Harrison Junior. Harriet didn't recognize the many important-looking men posing with Prescott in ritzy private libraries, dining rooms, and gentlemen's clubs—places that were either off-limits to women or inaccessible to someone of Harriet's station.

Prescott returned to the room. Seeing Harriet examining a particular pair of photographs, he said, "That's me with the architect Daniel Burnham and Charles Hutchinson, president of the Art Institute. The other is of me and George Pullman, who sadly passed last year, and Marshall Field, whose name is surely familiar to you."

Harriet chose a nod over any remark. Those men inhabited a world as foreign and distant to her as the moon. Besides being bound by gravity and mortality, she couldn't imagine they had anything in common.

"Now then, Miss Morrow . . ." Prescott sat and adjusted his gold-rimmed spectacles, ready for business. "As it happens, I have something for you."

"A case, sir?"

Prescott's brows shot up. "Case? Heavens no. A meeting. A favor really."

Harriet hadn't expected to be assigned a task so soon. But then, she had no idea what the first hours for an inexperienced junior operative might entail. Prescott began by telling her that his family residence was on Prairie Avenue, a street all of Chicago knew well, lined with stately mansions. She and her brother, as children, had made up stories about living fantastic lives within their walls—eating chocolate cake with silver forks, having their own rooms, and waking each morning to instantly hot water and freshly squeezed juice.

The matter at hand concerned Prescott's next-door neighbor, an older widow named Pearl Bartlett, whom he described as "harmless, but a doddering old biddy." Twice in the past twelve months, Pearl Bartlett had requested his help to find out who had absconded with first her silver and then her jewelry. Although doubtful that anyone had burgled the woman's home, Prescott nevertheless had dispatched Mr. Somer, his most junior operative at the time. "A neighborly courtesy," Prescott called it. After interviewing Mrs. Bartlett on several occasions and conducting multiple searches of her three-story mansion, Mr. Somer had reported his findings to Prescott: the woman had misplaced the items in question. He had found the silver in the pantry and the jewelry in a bureau drawer hidden beneath her late husband's toupee. Mrs. Bartlett's latest claim was not that something else had gone missing but rather some-one—specifically, her maid.

"Frankly, I wouldn't bother," Prescott said, reaching for a fountain pen and pad of paper. "The woman has proven herself to be entirely unreliable. But my wife . . ." He paused, apparently unable to speak and write at the same time. Scribbling finished, he looked up and handed Harriet a sheet of personalized stationery. "As I was saying, my wife is inexplicably fond of Pearl. She considers her something of an aunt. That's the address." He gestured toward the note she held in her hand. "You're not married, Miss Morrow."

"No, sir. I am not."

"It wasn't a question. One doesn't need to be a detective to see you have no ring. Had you worn one at your interview, your candidacy would have been impossible. I won't abide one of my operatives serving two masters. My experiment . . ." He stopped short, registering her frown. "Yes, you are my experiment, Miss Morrow. Oh, I know all about Allan's dabbling with a so-called Women's Detective Division. All that Kate Warne business. But I don't run the Prescott Agency like those fellows over at Pinkerton. This is a professional operation. And it will remain such."

Harriet bit her tongue. Was Prescott suggesting his agency's professionalism was at risk by employing a woman field operative? If that was how he felt, why hire her at all?

"You should speak with Mr. Somer before you depart for Mrs. Bartlett's. He can offer a few insights to save you time once you're there. You'll also need to become versed in how we issue reports and conduct operations around here. Protocols, Miss Morrow, are to be followed without exception. For that, ask Mr. McCabe. Like you, he is a junior, but McCabe has two years under his belt, more than ample experience to convey the fundamentals. I've yet to decide the best approach for your broader training—surveillance, undercover operations, criminal law, how we inform and conduct our work alongside the police. You've much to learn, but one step at a time. Unpreparedness in some lines of work might result in a paper cut or a twisted ankle, but for a detective, a wrong move might get your throat slit. Do I make myself clear, Miss Morrow?"

As Harriet nodded, Prescott opened a file on his desk and began to read, leaving her standing uncertainly in front of his desk for several seconds.

"That will be all," he said, eyes still fixed on the document before him.

As she reached for the door handle, he added, "Time is money, Miss Morrow. Don't dilly-dally with Mrs. Bartlett.

I'm sure it will amount to nothing. Do not prove me wrong."

Outside Prescott's office, with no sign of Madelaine, Harriet returned to the lobby.

"Hello, again," Harriet said to the receptionist. "I really could use your help. You don't happen to know where I might find Mr. Somer or Mr. McCabe?"

"Mr. Somer? Mr. McCabe?" The receptionist frowned.

Had Harriet not witnessed the woman's apprehension before, she might think her a halfwit.

"I can show you to the detectives' offices, but I must be quick about it. I shouldn't leave the lobby unattended."

Walking in the direction opposite Prescott's office, they first passed a room with three young men sitting at desks. "Clerks," the receptionist explained, tilting her blond head toward them. They then entered a long corridor with offices on either side. The doors' frosted panes had been stenciled with the name of each occupant along with titles ranging from junior field operative on the interior side to senior field operative on the window side.

"I trust you can find your way from here. I really must get back." And with that, she turned and left Harriet alone in the hallway.

Someone occupying one of the detectives' offices didn't consider it too early to smoke a pipe. Harriet fanned the air in front of her nose before considering how the gesture might appear to others. First impressions were indelible. She couldn't have anyone branding her as delicate or overly sensitive. Moving down the hallway, her head swiveled right to left, reading the names painted in simple black lettering on the doors. Charles was most common; there were three of them, along with two Josephs, one Walter, one Leonard, one Frank, and finally a name she was looking for: MATTHEW MCCABE, under which was stenciled, JUNIOR FIELD OPERATIVE. Harriet held back from knocking; she first wanted to find Carl Somer's office. She didn't have far to look; it was the next and last one in the corridor.

A knock on Carl's door met with silence. He was either late to arrive or had already come and gone. She stepped back to Matthew McCabe's door. As she raised a hand to knock, a voice said, "Come in. It's open."

Chapter 3

As Harriet entered the office, Matthew McCabe was already on his feet, a hand extended. "You must be Miss Morrow. Harriet Morrow, if I'm not mistaken."

Delighted that someone knew her name, she shook his hand with gusto, noting his soft, strong grip and that his shirt cuff was neatly pressed. "That's correct. How did you—"

"Your silhouette." He tilted his head toward the door. "The panes are frosted, not opaque. Prescott calls them semi-private. Frankly, I think he prefers that we not get too comfortable."

Matthew produced a winning smile, complementing his other features, notably pale blue eyes, a thatch of red hair, and a freckled complexion. She didn't doubt he would be a popular figure among the women in the office. Standing about six feet, he was six inches taller than Harriet and possessed a willowy frame similar to that of her brother Aubrey—a trait inherited from their father that had skipped over her by a wide margin.

"Actually," Harriet said, "I was wondering how you knew who I am?"

"Oh," he chuckled. "Every Friday, Prescott holds court with the detectives. You'll want to put that on your calendar. Every Friday, ten o'clock. Don't be late. Don't *ever* be late. That's when we all heard about you."

Harriet silently corrected his remark that "all" had heard the news of her hire, understanding that he meant all the detectives.

Matthew continued, "The announcement caused quite a stir." He smiled warmly, suggesting he was on her side. "In case you're unaware, we've never had a female detective before."

Not only was Harriet aware, but that morning's every encounter had affirmed the fact. "I'm sure it will take some getting used to," she said, her words applying as much to herself as to everyone else who worked there.

"Yes, well"—Matthew shifted his weight—"that's a fair way to put it."

Once Harriet relayed Prescott's instruction that she seek his assistance in issuing reports and other operational matters, Matthew cheerfully agreed to help her learn "The Prescott Way." He invited her to sit, gave her a pencil and tablet, and began by explaining the sixth-floor layout. Prescott's office, his private secretary, and the agency's chief accountant sat on the lake side of the building. On the opposite side of the lobby sat the clerks, men responsible for bookkeeping, routing mail, and cataloging case files. Past the clerks were offices for ten detectives. At the end of the hallway sat the secretaries.

Although Matthew McCabe seemed to take no personal interest in Harriet—no questions about why she wished to be a detective, where she was from, whether she lived with her family or alone—he was affable and unreserved in telling her what was where, and how this or that was done. She didn't mind his business focus; it saved her from a conversation about beaus and family that she found awkward and painful, respectively.

An hour later, her brain overflowed with information. Matthew apologized and said he must turn to other matters, and she slipped in a final question from his doorway, "Have you any idea when Mr. Somer may return?"

"Mr. Somer? Why are you looking for him, if I might ask?"

Harriet explained that Mr. Prescott's next-door neighbor claimed her maid was missing and she'd been told that Carl Somer had experience dealing with the neighbor. As she spoke, Matthew listened intently but lost his smile.

When Harriet finished, he said, "If Mr. Prescott asked that Mr. Somer assist you, I'm sure he will. As to his whereabouts, I can't say. You'll find that operatives keep irregular hours—aside from Fridays at ten o'clock, remember that." He wagged a finger for emphasis. "While Prescott will have some of us work together on larger or more complex investigations, we are most often assigned to our own cases."

After closing Matthew McCabe's door, Harriet tried Carl Somer's again. Like before, there was no answer. Returning once more to the receptionist, she learned that one Sandra Small typed Mr. Somer's reports and correspondence. Her desk would be among the others in the large open room beyond the operatives' offices.

Standing before the three secretaries, Harriet waited to catch someone's eye. When a woman glanced up from her typewriter, Harriet held her gaze while quickly approaching her desk. So closely did the woman resemble the pretty receptionist that Harriet wondered if they weren't sisters, both blond with little nubbin noses and tiny mouths shaped like valentines.

"I'm sorry to bother you," Harriet said, "but could you point me to Sandra Small?"

"Madelaine didn't say we were getting another"—the woman paused abruptly, seeming to notice Harriet's bowler hat, bow tie, and plain, unfashionable clothing for the first time—"girl."

Carefully choosing her words to avoid confirming the misunderstanding or a difficult conversation that a correction would invite, she said, "Yes, well, I'll leave it to others to make a proper announcement."

"I'm Sandra Small," she said matter-of-factly, tentatively extending her hand. "And you are . . . ?"

"Harriet Morrow, Miss Small. A pleasure to meet you. I'm hoping that you can tell me when Mr. Somer might return to the office."

The woman's tone shifted, becoming more wary. "What's your business with Carl? I handle all of his matters. I also assist Charles McKenna and Leonard Tusk. Both men are senior operatives."

First Madelaine, now Sandra. Were all these women territorial about their responsibilities? A new thought struck: would she be assigned a secretary? How would that woman feel about working for another woman who was both younger and inexperienced?

"Which operatives will you be assisting?" Sandra asked. "I was unaware we were shorthanded."

"I just need to pass along a question on behalf of Mr. Prescott." If seniority were a currency, Prescott's name would be the most valuable. By employing it, she hoped to cut short the woman's questioning. Not wanting to be the one to explain her role, she repeated, "So again, might you know when Mr. Somer is expected to return?"

Sandra's reluctance to help out "the new girl" was apparently outweighed by her desire to avoid any admonishment from a higher-up. "I don't really know," Sandra said with a shrug, calling attention to the perfect folds of her shirtwaist's puffed shoulders. "Friday is your best bet. All the detectives are here on Fridays." She smiled, albeit for only a second. "Now. Unless there's something else . . . ?"

"No. Thank you, Miss Small. You've been most kind."

Harriet now faced a quandary. Mr. Prescott had advised her to meet with Carl Somer before she visited Pearl Bartlett. But there was no telling when he might return. It could be any minute or not for days. She couldn't very well sit around twiddling her thumbs. Nor did she like the idea of asking Mr. Prescott what to do. The agency's principal was a busy man, and he didn't consider what he'd tasked her with even to be an investigation. "A favor," he had called it. Remembering something else he had said, "Time is money . . . Don't dilly-dally with Mrs. Bartlett," helped her decide. Initiative must surely be a quality valued among operatives.

Harriet would keep an eye out for Carl Somer, but she would not delay her meeting with Pearl Bartlett. If Prescott were right about her being "a doddering old biddy," the maid had probably already reappeared. But if she were truly missing, there was no time to waste.

Chapter 4

Stepping onto LaSalle Street, Harriet wished she had her bicycle. The southside residence of Pearl Bartlett, 1803 Prairie Avenue, was too far to walk in the chilly thirty-eight-degree temperature. Raising her coat's collar, she headed for the corner of Randolph and Wabash and the recently completed elevated train line serving the central business district. She cursed herself for leaving home without a scarf. Though just getting out the door each day on time was an accomplishment. Mornings at the North Side apartment she had inherited and now shared with her brother were frantic. Aubrey had grown more recalcitrant since their parents' passing. As the older sibling, she had laid claim to their parents' former bedroom—the larger of the two—an injustice Aubrey chose to protest anew each morning. Also on her brother's list of grievances: having to share a bathroom, Harriet's new kitten chewing his socks, the icebox's meager contents, and his sister's insistence that he not leave his used cereal bowl on the table. Yet, despite their constant bickering, they were family and had settled into a mostly comfortable coexistence.

The elevated train, boasting third-rail electric power first heralded five years earlier at the World's Columbian

Exposition, carried Harriet with efficiency to South Eighteenth Street, within several blocks of the Bartlett residence on Prairie Avenue.

Imposing as the three-story mansion was, Harriet marveled most at the home's tall, arched windows that would allow an expansive view of the property's front garden. With spring just around the corner, the large rhododendron bushes bordering the grounds promised a colorful display to anyone on either side of the home's thick redstone walls.

The bellowing door chime portended an intimidatingly grand interior. Considering the home's size, Harriet allowed extra time before ringing the bell again. She waited, shoulders squared, and clutched her handbag with hands now numb from the cold.

And waited.

From a spot on the walkway, halfway between the porch and the street, she raised a hand to shield her eyes from the sun's glare and looked up for any indication—the movement of a curtain, a shifting of light—that anyone was inside the massive house. There was none.

The idea of returning to the agency having learned nothing twisted her stomach. She had left the office as a detective—time to start acting like one.

Hiking her skirt a few inches, Harriet strode across the damp lawn to a black wrought-iron gate leading to the property's backyard. Were anyone to question her presence, she could say she was on official business of the Prescott Agency. Which home was his, anyway? Prescott had said Pearl was his next-door neighbor. Presuming the man chose his words precisely, she considered the houses to either side of Mrs. Bartlett's. To the north sat an enormous Queen Anne-style home with three corner turrets, each capped with a conical roof. To the south sat a symmetrical Italianate home, exquisitely maintained but half the size of Pearl's house, which was smaller than the Queen Anne. As a successful business owner, Prescott was surely a wealthy man. But not *that* wealthy. She guessed that given the choices, Prescott's family lived in the Italianate mansion, which like the man himself, was immaculate, refined, and inclined to be showy.

At the back of the house, Harriet found a rectangle of yard carved into a dozen furrows to form a sizable vegetable garden. Her attention was captured by music coming from the orangery. A woman's alto voice sang along to a phonograph recording of "Sweet Rosie O'Grady." Through the glass, Harriet saw that, in addition to singing with abandon, the woman was pruning a flowering bush of some kind. Was this Pearl Bartlett? She was uncommonly tall and looked to be in her mid-seventies, with gray hair—unusually short and wildly mussed. She had pushed the long sleeves of her pale pink housecoat up her thin arms to just below her elbows.

Harriet had been bold to enter the back of the property and didn't want to cause alarm. Might she be taken for a snoop? Worse yet, a burglar? The next instant, the woman looked up and saw her. To Harriet's relief, the woman didn't shriek or jump. Instead, she smiled amiably and waved for Harriet to come inside. Although pleased she hadn't frightened her, it seemed to Harriet unwise that Pearl Bartlett would readily admit a stranger into her home. Or had she expected Harriet? Had Prescott alerted the household that someone matching her description was coming? Harriet thought not. Prescott seemed too busy to bother, and he had said he didn't think the matter would amount to much anyway. The woman waved again, and Harriet stepped inside the glass-enclosed garden room.

"And who might you be?" the woman shouted over the music.

Harriet shouted back, "My name is Harriet Morrow. I was sent by your neighbor, Theodore Prescott. I've come to look into the matter of your missing maid."

"Prescott? Missing? Oh, dear!"

Harriet walked over to the phonograph and turned down the volume, hoping that would make conversation easier. She repeated the reason for her visit.

"And who are you then? The brother?"

Harriet's mind raced. Not only had she been misperceived as a man, but Theodore Prescott must be nearly fifty years old; hardly could anyone think of Harriet as his sibling. "I am not Mr. Prescott's brother, Mrs. Bartlett. Rather, I am his employee, Miss Harriet Morrow. I've come to inquire about your missing maid."

Pearl nodded emphatically. "Agnes. Agnes Wozniak. Lovely girl. The silver has never been so shiny." She paused momentarily as if lost in thought, then rhythmically shook her pruning shears in the air and sang, "When you need a good polish, you can rely on the Polish! Ha!"

Harriet smiled to hide her worry. Was Prescott right? Was Pearl Bartlett cuckoo?

Pearl stepped back, taking Harriet in from a different angle. "You don't look like a fella who would say no to a piece of cake."

Before Harriet could correct Pearl, she moved with surprising speed and disappeared into the adjoining kitchen, leaving Harriet standing in the orangery. "Milk?" she shouted.

Not hiding her grimace, Harriet followed Pearl into the next room, where her host sliced a generous piece of German chocolate cake and set it on a flowered porcelain plate.

"You can't solve a crime on an empty stomach," Pearl announced, sliding the cake across the counter toward Harriet. She then crossed the spacious kitchen and opened the icebox. "Drat. No milk. Agnes keeps the house stocked. But not if she's not here. Which she's not. It's been two days. *Two days.* Tell me that's not cause for concern."

A large white cat leaped onto the table, startling Harriet. Pearl chuckled proudly. "Meet Toby, king of the castle."

Harriet extended a hand to protect her cake from Toby's twitching nose.

"You don't mind cats, do you?" Pearl asked.

Happy to answer truthfully, Harriet said, "Oh, I love them. In fact, I just recently adopted a tortoiseshell kitten."

"This kitten of yours have a name?"

"Susan."

"Curious name for a cat."

"I named her for Susan B. Anthony. My mother was a great admirer of her work."

Pearl wagged a forkful of cake in the air. "That Hull House woman?"

"I think you're confusing her with Jane Addams," Harriet said, referring to the cofounder of the Chicago settlement house that served the immigrant community.

Pearl stared intently before nodding sharply. "Right you are. My mistake."

Eager to get the conversation back on track, she said, "You say Agnes has been missing for two days? When did you last expect her? Does she arrive each day at the same time?"

Pearl looked baffled. "Arrive? I do the arriving. I come down to the kitchen every morning and expect to see Agnes brewing a pot of tea, but not before I smell the bacon."

"I see. So Agnes arrives at the house before you awaken each day?"

Pearl returned the look Harriet had first given her when she thought her mad. "She's up before me, if that's what you're asking. Unless the girl's learned to fly, she comes down the stairs just as I do."

"Ah," Harriet drew out the word. "So Agnes lives here?"

"Where else would she live?" Pearl pointed a bony finger upward. "Third floor. She has it all to herself. I haven't attempted those stairs in years."

Suddenly, Harriet had a bad feeling. "You haven't been up to inspect her room?"

"Why would I bother? She's not up there. Like I told Teddy when I went next door to report her missing, she's not anywhere in the house."

"But, Mrs. Bartlett, how can you be sure?"

"I hollered up there from the second floor. Not a peep. And please, call me Pearl. Mrs. Bartlett was my mother. I need reminding of her like I need a hole in the head."

Harriet opened her mouth to speak, but Pearl continued, "I insisted Agnes call me Pearl. No reason for you to do any different." She pointed her chin at the counter. "That cake isn't going to eat itself."

Not only did Harriet not want the cake, but she couldn't eat it if she had. Pearl hadn't given her a fork. Toby, on the other hand, continued to probe her defenses.

"And the last time you saw Agnes? When was that?"

Pearl seemed to ponder the question for too long. Had she forgotten when she'd last seen her maid? Or had the question itself confused her?

After a shrug, she said, "We had stew."

As Harriet searched for the right words, Pearl continued, "Every Friday for supper. I turn in right after. Agnes would have stayed to clean up and put away the dishes. When the girl tucked herself in that night, I couldn't say. Next morning, no tea. No bacon. No Agnes."

That Pearl hadn't risked the stairs was understandable. But why had she waited so long before asking someone to go up and check? It was Monday. If Pearl was correct, it had been over two days since Agnes was last seen. Envisioning the discovery of a several-days-dead maid, Harriet shuddered. Still, despite fearing what she might find on the third floor, she said, "Mind if I take a look in her room?"

"You going to eat that cake or what? You can't let it sit out. Toby is partial to the frosting, but it doesn't sit well with him. With no maid, the cleanup will be mine to do."

"How about I try a bite after I look upstairs?"

Pearl gave an exasperated sigh. "Come on then." She covered the plate and led Harriet out of the kitchen and farther into the home's interior. "But I'm telling you, Agnes isn't here."

Passing through the mansion's main floor, Harriet was quite certain she had never been inside such a grand home. The high ceilings, thick carpets, and walls paneled in dark carved wood brought to mind the Palmer House hotel, where once, on a dare from her brother, she had stridden through the opulent lobby pretending to be a visiting prince. After ascending a sweeping staircase the width of Harriet's apartment, they arrived at a second, notably steeper staircase.

"You'll find Agnes's room up there, somewhere. As I say, I haven't been up to that floor in years. I told Agnes to take whichever accommodation suited her. Toby and I'll wait for you downstairs."

As Pearl departed for the first floor, Harriet made her way to the third. The ceiling was lower, the hallway narrower, and the quality of finishes, while still nicer than any home she had ever visited, let alone lived in, were more modest than the lower floors. Finding a hallway of doors, all closed, Harriet started opening them one by one. The first two rooms had once been used as bedrooms; the mattresses were gone, but bed frames and chests of drawers remained. Although clean, the long-unused rooms smelled musty. A door opened to a tiny lavatory. The hair tonic, soaps, toothbrush and powder, along with the towel hung on a rod—dry, so not recently used—told her this was Agnes's bathroom. Another small, windowless room filled with covered furniture preceded a final bedroom at the end of the hallway. Harriet took a deep breath and opened the door.

The whoosh of cold outside air startled her. Above the bed's headboard, the room's one window stood open. Thin curtains fluttered in the breeze. The bedclothes were a jumble. A lamp had been knocked off the nightstand and lay on the floor, its glass shade surprisingly intact. Quickly scanning the rest of the room, Harriet mentally cataloged its other features and furnishings. A family photograph sat beside some pale-yellow stationery on a small writing desk. A tall bureau's drawers revealed expected items: a hairbrush, undergarments, a half-corset, slips, and a night-gown. Hanging inside a wardrobe were two identical, well-pressed dresses of modest style—maid's uniforms?—two petticoats, and a blue cotton coat worn at the edges and much too lightweight to keep anyone warm during Chicago's frigid winters. Resting on a high shelf sat a shabbily made bonnet. On the lowest shelf, Agnes had stored a pair of inexpensive, low-heeled shoes, the laces frayed to threads.

Harriet turned a full circle, taking in the room. Agnes Wozniak appeared to possess the essentials, but nothing approached an item of value. What a contrast to everything in the house below her—rooms full of luxuries that Agnes was paid whatever small sum Pearl offered to scrub, polish, and iron.

Harriet rubbed her temples. "Don't dilly-dally," Prescott had told her. "I'm sure it will amount to nothing." She took another glance around the room, certain this visit would not be her last. She had given the maid's bedroom a cursory look; it deserved a painstaking examination. But that would have to wait. It had already been more than two days since someone had entered through the window and taken Agnes Wozniak.

Chapter 5

"Tarnation!" Pearl's voice echoed strangely. She was bent over, her head inside the open oven. Not wanting to startle her, Harriet stood in the kitchen doorway and waited for her to finish whatever she was doing. Standing, Pearl grumbled, "Dadgum ganache will be the end of me!" She slammed the oven door, then turned and saw Harriet. "Go on, then," she said casually as if Harriet were a familiar presence in the house, "tell me what I already know."

Harriet stepped farther into the kitchen. "Mrs. Bartlett, it would appear that Agnes might indeed be missing. I found her bedroom window open, a lamp overturned, and, from what I could ascertain upon a cursory inspection, her personal belongings have been left behind."

"Ha!" Pearl slapped her thigh with a dish towel. "Told you so. Teddy didn't believe me. The man squints at me as if I've gone batty. Do you know the meaning of the word *mollify*, Harry?"

As Harriet fumbled for words, Pearl continued, "It means to treat an old woman as if she has driftwood for brains." She tapped the side of her head. "Never confuse an unconventional thinker for a goof."

Pearl moved closer to Harriet; dismay washed across her face. "Land sakes, Harry. You're a girl. I wasn't sure when you first arrived. But with a name like Harry . . ." Pearl waved a hand before her face. "The distance, you understand . . . My eyes don't work like they used to. I didn't mean any disrespect. Though I must say it's uncommon for a lady to wear a bowler. That with the bow tie and shoes . . . And again, that's an unconventional name you have."

"But my name—"

"My father was a Harry. Him, I liked. That you share a name I take as a good omen. Now. What did you learn upstairs that will result in the prompt return of my maid? This house doesn't clean itself. Just because I bake doesn't mean I cook. Nor am I keen on going through the rigamarole to replace Agnes." She consulted the clock on the wall. "I'd appreciate it if you had Agnes back here before three o'clock. That will allow her time to put dinner on the table. I've lived far too long to eat another cold sandwich for my supper. Not even Toby shows interest in my evening meal. How's *that* for a sorry state of affairs!"

Harriet explained that before Agnes could be returned, she must be found. Since what transpired between Friday evening and Saturday morning to result in Agnes's disappearance was unknown, the odds of discovering her whereabouts in the next few hours seemed slim to none.

"With your permission," Harriet said, "I will conduct a more thorough search of the house and grounds. That completed, I shall return to the agency and compile my report. It will then be up to Mr. Prescott to take any next steps. But rest assured, I will convey my belief that your maid is indeed missing."

"Best get to it then." Pearl waved a hand through the air. "You have my blessing to open every cupboard and peek under every sofa cushion. Though I can save you the trouble of looking inside the oven. She's not there."

Harriet received Pearl's cheeky remark with a smile. The woman had gumption, a trait Harriet admired in other women—and liked to think she might have inherited a little of herself from her mother. She noted the time. A painstaking examination of so large a house could take hours. Prescott would disapprove of Harriet taking that much time. Still, she couldn't return to the agency without having conducted enough of a search to confidently rebut Prescott should he argue that Agnes must be hiding somewhere in the house. After a tour of the entire mansion, she would inspect the carriage house and take a final walk around the gardens.

Moving from room to room, Harriet was struck by the home's massive size. Pearl must be used to living in the grand space with only Toby and a maid for company, but Harriet imagined she'd feel like a child lost in the Field Museum after closing. Growing up, she and her brother complained to their parents that their apartment was too small for a family of four. With a wink, her father had said, "But you can only ever be in one room at a time. What good will the others do you?" To that, Harriet and Aubrey had argued that a shared bedroom allowed them no privacy. Harriet complained about her brother's messiness while he protested her habit of borrowing his clothes and baseball mitt. The issue became more fraught as they grew older. Having neither the means nor the space to create a third bedroom, their father had constructed from plywood a makeshift separation down the middle of the room. Only months after the siblings had decorated their sides of the wall—Harriet's with posters of the Chicago Colts baseball club and advertisements for the latest models of bicycles, and Aubrey's with flyers of boxing matches and the recent World's Columbian Exposition—their father, followed twenty-six days later by their mother, succumbed to pneumonia. Harriet had been seventeen at the time, Aubrey twelve. Too young to live on their own, they had been taken in by their father's second cousin, Roy, and his wife, Charlotte. The children had been too distraught to appreciate the accommodation that saved them from spending the rest of their adolescence in an orphanage. While their aunt and uncle had been hospitable, and they'd each been given their own bedroom, they would have returned to sharing in an instant if that would have brought back their parents.

Fifty-eight minutes and twenty-six rooms later, Harriet stood in the foyer next to a round table with a large porcelain vase adorned with an intricate Chinese motif.

"Agnes did that," Pearl said, appearing from nowhere and startling Harriet. "The girl is clever about such things. I would have let that ugly old thing sit empty until spring offered some color from the garden." Pearl flicked a finger toward the long boughs of greenery that Agnes, apparently, had artfully arranged in the vase.

Pearl had entered the room from a door that blended into the paneling beneath the staircase. "By now you must have seen most of the house. This monstrous pile was my mother's idea—more monument than home. There were only ever my parents and my sister, brother, and me living here. We could go for days without seeing one another, which was fine by me. My father was always away on business. What the man actually did, besides being anywhere but here, I never did understand. That left my mother to rule the first and second floors like Catherine the Great. 'I am an aristocrat. It is my profession.' If you don't already know, those words are attributed to the Russian empress but apply just as well to my mother. I had plenty reason to stick to the third floor and my workshop in the cellar."

"And you've just come from the cellar?" Harriet pointed her chin toward the hidden door.

Pearl nodded. "Oh, the things I used to make down there. Birdhouses, lacquered boxes for keepsakes. I once built a very fine cage for my sister's pet rabbit. I may not look it, Harry, but I'm handy. Or once was. There's no shame in a woman being handy. Don't let anyone tell you different."

Harriet decided she liked Pearl Bartlett and was grateful

for her soundness of mind—she might exhibit moments of odd behavior, but she wasn't, as Theodore Prescott believed, cuckoo. Harriet was also thankful that Pearl had made her aware of the cellar. So overwhelming was the mansion's size that it hadn't occurred to her that there could still be another unexplored level.

"Well?" Pearl said. "I've been listening to you clomp about my house in those big shoes of yours for the past hour. Did you find anything of interest?"

Harriet *had* found many curious objects—a tall alabaster statue of intertwined, contorted figures in the library, a tryptic mural of a European landscape in the sitting room, and a stout glass-fronted cabinet holding a dozen rifles in the hallway. But nothing suggested the presence or the absence of Agnes Wozniak. The only evidence that the young maid inhabited the home was relegated to the two modest third-floor rooms she occupied: her bedroom and the tiny lavatory.

After finding nothing of note in the cellar, the carriage house, or around the grounds, Harriet traded goodbyes with Pearl and Toby on the front porch. When Harriet was halfway down the pathway, Pearl shouted after her, "You tell Teddy I need my Agnes!"

The elevated train ride gave Harriet time to think. Mr. Prescott had sent her to Pearl Bartlett's as a neighborly favor, believing the visit would amount to nothing. Whether Harriet could convince her boss that Pearl's maid was indeed missing was a concern, but it was not the only one. She'd been fortunate that an opportunity to take on what seemed to be a genuine case coincided with her arrival. How long might she have waited before something else suitable for an untested young woman came along? If Prescott believed her, he would treat the matter as a bona fide investigation. Harriet hadn't been on the job for even a whole day. But still, she hated the idea of briefing another field operative so *he* could get on with making the inquiries she felt perfectly capable of doing. She needed only a little guidance along the way. Perhaps someone like Matthew McCabe could serve as her mentor. His involvement might sway Prescott to allow her to continue with the case. Recalling her mother's words, "Waiting patiently for men to give women their due will only result in another generation of women in aprons," Harriet began silently rehearsing her argument to Prescott. She felt it in her bones—this was her chance. Agnes needed to be found, and Harriet was determined to be the one to find her.

Chapter 6

Harriet returned to the agency exhilarated and eager to plead her case to Mr. Prescott, only to learn he had several client meetings outside the office and wouldn't return until three o'clock that afternoon. Madelaine seemed to take pleasure in telling Harriet that she had two hours to wait for an audience with the agency principal. Adding to Harriet's disappointment, Madelaine led her to the room where the secretaries sat and showed her to a desk nearest the women's lavatory. When Harriet pointed out that every other field operative had a private office, Madelaine curtly replied, "Those field operatives are men. You are a woman. You will sit with the other women." To ensure that Harriet gave up her argument, she added, "Unless you believe you are better than the rest of us?"

Sandra Small didn't hide her raised brows at seeing Harriet again. Would Prescott or Madelaine ever announce to everyone that Harriet was there not as a secretary? It didn't help that Madelaine appeared to be her supervisor. The other two women met her return with listless curiosity.

Aware that her fashion choices, if they could be called such, were unusual, Harriet was accustomed to drawing second glances from strangers. Her shoes mostly remained concealed by a long skirt, but her bowler hat and austere attire were conspicuous. With her attire already eliciting stares, she was tempted to exercise her true preference and wear a man's full suit of clothing. But the bold notion never lasted long. Her father had cautioned, "Society may allow a convention's bending, but never its breaking." Although he'd been referring to Harriet's "unladylike manner," covering a wide range of rough-and-tumble boyish behavior, she understood the remark's broader application. And so, as often as she tried on the much too tight clothing of her late father in the privacy of her bedroom, she always returned it to the back of the closet with a sigh of resignation.

Harriet took in the surroundings, which looked and sounded eerily similar to those at her previous bookkeeping job. The petite, pretty women clacked away at typewriters or scribbled into ledgers with the practiced efficiency of marching cavalry. Their day's work would never take them beyond this room or offer them more challenging tasks. Their roles were defined by men with no consideration of a woman's particular aptitude or ambition. Harriet suspected these women were capable of greater feats than tapping out fifty words a minute. Moreover, she didn't doubt that, given a chance, one of them might make an even better field operative than she. The difference between them was that Prescott had given her the opportunity. Squander her good fortune and she might ruin the chance for the next woman who came along.

Not content to sit and do nothing until Prescott arrived, Harriet made her way back to the operatives' offices. She was anxious to share what she had discovered at Pearl Bartlett's. Besides, she wanted to meet with Mr. Somer as Prescott had instructed—even if it was after the fact.

Approaching the last office in the corridor, Harriet saw the door was ajar. She stopped, suddenly nervous. According to Prescott, Carl Somer had twice visited the Bartlett mansion. He must have formed his own opinions of Pearl. Did he share Prescott's assessment that she was an old biddy?

Harriet stood straight, squared her shoulders, and tapped the frosted glass pane. Silence. She knocked again, then slowly pushed open the door.

"Can I help you?"

"Oh!" Harriet spun around. A man stood behind her. "I was looking for Mr. Somer."

"You've found him."

In an instant, Harriet recognized Carl Somer was the spitting image of Mike Tiernan, the New York Giants' handsome baseball player and the type of young man most every girl—Harriet being one exception—dreamed of marrying. Both men were nearly six feet tall, fit, with a short crop of neatly parted light brown hair. Harriet couldn't recall the right fielder's eye color, but she doubted they were the menacing hue of storm clouds. Both men also suited up in black and white; whereas Mike Tiernan wore a white uniform with *New York* arched across the front in black block letters, Carl Somer dressed in a simple black suit, white high-collared shirt, and black bow tie.

"And you are?" Carl asked.

Harriet extended her hand. "Harriet Morrow, Mr. Somer. I'm so very pleased to make your acquaintance. You see, I am the new field operative that Mr. Prescott mentioned this past Friday. Mr. Prescott said I should seek your advice on Mrs. Pearl Bartlett."

In response to Carl's blank look, Harriet added, "Mr. Prescott's neighbor."

The eye roll was immediate, as was his snort. "Oh, her. Missing silver and jewelry. As if I don't have better things to do."

"Might I take a moment of your time?" Harriet asked.

"I'm pressed as it is," Carl replied, brushing past her. "But if Prescott sent you, I can't say no, now can I?"

Were it not for the name on the door, Harriet might

think she had mistakenly stepped into Matthew McCabe's office—both were identical in size, minimally furnished, and without a single personal effect or decoration. The contrast between the operatives' offices and Prescott's corner suite was as stark as the Bartlett mansion's two main floors and Agnes's bare-bones third-floor room.

Carl Somer sat behind his desk, looking impatient. He didn't invite Harriet to sit.

"Unusual hat." Carl nodded toward her head.

"Is it?" she replied brightly, determined not to let herself be rattled. "Then I must have a word with the clerk at Sears Roebuck. He assured me it was a most popular style."

"For a man, yes."

"I appreciate a good hat, as do you." She glanced over her shoulder at the brown bowler resting on the coat stand.

"Hardly is that the same."

"Quite right. I prefer black." Harriet understood her quip might come across as impudent, but she didn't appreciate Carl's needling and wouldn't have him thinking her meek or undeserving of a modicum of respect.

Though not shifting his gaze, he appeared to appraise her from a different angle. "What is it you want, Miss . . . ?"

"Morrow." Harriet repeated what Mr. Prescott had told her, described her visit to the Bartlett mansion, and concluded with her determination that the maid, one Agnes Wozniak, had been snatched from her room sometime in the night.

"I see. And you find the old woman reliable, do you?"

Avoiding an unnecessary diversion about Pearl's soundness of mind, Harriet replied with facts. "What I found was an empty bedroom, an open window, and evidence of a disturbance."

Despite her confidence, Carl argued that the maid must be elsewhere in the house. When Harriet countered that she had searched the property, he suggested the maid had left of her own volition. When Harriet repeated that she'd found the open window, overturned lamp, and items left behind, he asserted that Agnes must be a figment of Pearl's imagination and her bedroom a scene staged to muster some intrigue in an old woman's uneventful life. Carl's obstinance was frustrating, and yet it might prove helpful. His arguments could be a precursor to Mr. Prescott's—better to be tested first by a junior operative than the agency principal.

"You should have come to me before racing off on a fool's errand," Carl said curtly. "I would have saved this agency the time and trouble."

Surprised that a junior operative would blatantly counter the principal's decision to send someone to the Bartlett mansion, Harriet repeated his instruction that she pay his neighbor a visit.

"I understood that the first time you said it," Carl snapped. "But had you done as instructed and spoken to me before dashing off to play detective, I would have spoken with Mr. Prescott and resolved the matter."

"I see. And how is that, Mr. Somer? Have you information that Mr. Prescott does not have?" Harriet squeezed her handbag, a minor outlet for her growing irritation. Carl hadn't been to the Bartlett mansion or inside Agnes's bedroom, yet he was so certain that he knew more—knew best. He manifested what she anticipated would be the job's greatest challenge: dismissal by a man for no reason other than that she wasn't one.

Had she any doubts about her correct reading of the situation, Carl continued, "I suppose it's natural that you became swept up in the woman's tall tale, but true operatives follow facts. You'll find Mr. Prescott values efficiency and quick results. Neither are products of hysterics."

"I see," Harriet said through gritted teeth.

"Good." He nodded sharply as if putting the matter to rest. "I'm glad that you do."

"So, despite your claim to follow facts, you would have ignored all observable evidence and dismissed Mrs. Bartlett's claim? I don't doubt Mr. Prescott values efficiency, but a speedy result hardly compensates for a wrong one."

"I don't appreciate your tone, Miss Morrow."

"And I don't appreciate your insinuation that I've gotten wrong something so obvious. The maid is not there. She hasn't been seen for over two days. As for not coming to you before, you were not in, and your return was unknown even to Miss Small, whom I understand performs your secretarial duties. Given that this case involves a missing person—not some misplaced cutlery or brooches—I did what I thought Mr. Prescott would have me do. If he finds fault with my actions, I will learn from his correction. But to be clear, Mr. Somer, regardless of which operative had been sent to the Bartlett residence, and specifically the maid's third-floor bedroom, the conclusion would be the same. Agnes Wozniak is missing."

"You will find, Miss Morrow, that self-certainty is not a valued characteristic among operatives. You have come to my office for no apparent reason other than for a pat on the head that you should now realize is not forthcoming— quite the contrary. I'm afraid this encounter has done nothing to benefit your position here at this agency. I will let Mr. Prescott know that we spoke, along with my thoughts on your manner of presentation. Good day, Miss Morrow."

Harriet locked eyes with Carl Somer as if looking away too quickly would signal fault or weakness. After a long moment, a tight smile replaced her pursed lips. "Thank you for your time, Mr. Somer. Although brief, this meeting has been most informative."

With a trembling hand, Harriet closed the door behind her. The encounter with Carl Somer couldn't have gone worse. But Theodore Prescott's opinion was the only one that mattered. She couldn't allow Carl Somer to get to him first.

An hour later, Harriet intercepted Prescott upon his return to the agency. She had just started to tell him about her visit to Pearl Bartlett's mansion when Madelaine ushered Carl Somer into the office. Carl justified his interruption as a service to the "agency's professional standing." His version of events tested Harriet's self-control to the limit. She stood before Prescott while Carl assailed her competence, her character, and her very presence. When he finished, Prescott shifted his penetrating gaze to her and said, "Well, Miss Morrow? I suspect you have something to say about all this?"

Harriet did have something to say. Citing pertinent details of her time at the mansion, she calmly and succinctly stated her case. When she completed her report, she turned to face Carl Somer directly. "As for your opinions on the matter, Mr. Somer, I can only say that your previous experience with Mrs. Bartlett does nothing to refute what I have seen and heard with my own eyes and ears earlier today. As for your disparaging of my character, I should like to think you would reserve judgment until you have evidence to form a fair opinion. As for myself, that is the professional courtesy I shall extend to you." Turning back to Prescott, she said, "I understand that you would have preferred Mrs. Bartlett's claim to have amounted to nothing, sir. I too would have preferred the maid to be safe and sound where she belongs."

In truth, Harriet would have been disappointed to find the maid there. She didn't wish Agnes Wozniak any harm, but discovering the open window and overturned lamp had been exciting. She added, "Were all in life as it should be, I don't suppose there would be much work for a detective agency."

Taken aback by her words, Prescott stared wide-eyed at her, then looked at Carl as if seeking confirmation that he had heard the same remark. Harriet readied herself to be fired. As devastating as the dismissal would be, the satisfaction sure to claim Carl's face would be unbearable.

"You are quite certain the maid is missing?" Prescott said, surprising both Harriet and Carl.

Harriet nodded emphatically. "Quite certain. And with

your permission, sir, I would very much like to pursue the matter."

Carl lurched forward, "Mr. Prescott, might I suggest that I pay a visit to the Bartlett residence tomorrow and—"

"I've heard quite enough, Mr. Somer." Prescott raised a hand; the late afternoon sun glinted off his ruby cufflink. "You are busy enough with your assigned case. I see no benefit to your duplicating the work that Miss Morrow has already done."

Harriet took no small amount of pleasure in watching Carl's face drop as Mr. Prescott agreed to let her continue inquiries into the whereabouts of Agnes Wozniak, adding the rationale that he wanted to avoid "the almighty fuss" his wife would throw if he didn't do something to help Pearl "find her dadgum girl." He then noted two conditions: first, Harriet must produce a daily written report of her activities, and second, she had one week to find the maid.

Figuring that Prescott would appreciate her desire for guidance, she asked if he would allow Mr. McCabe to mentor her during the investigation. Her momentary delight turned to dismay when he followed his words, "Excellent idea, Miss Morrow," with "I'm sure Mr. Somer, here, will make himself available to you."

Chapter 7

Standing before the stove, Harriet stared down at the potatoes, musing about their shared circumstance. One day they're both doing what's expected of them—the vegetables growing plump in the soil, herself balancing financial entries at her desk at Rock Island—when suddenly they find themselves uprooted and tossed into a pot of boiling water.

Recently reaching her majority by turning twenty-one, Harriet had come into her inheritance and taken possession of her parents' apartment. Although owned outright, the tax and related expenses depleted her weekly pay—there was little margin for overspending on nonessentials. To keep a roof over her and her brother's heads, she had to keep her job—even if she had little idea about how to do it.

Hearing Aubrey enter the apartment wrested Harriet's thoughts back to the present. She often marveled that such a skinny kid could have such loud footsteps. *You'd not make a very good cat burglar*, she'd once joked. In reply, Aubrey had rolled his eyes but said nothing. It was a response Harriet had come to expect from the sixteen-year-old. Their once close relationship had grown distant with their parents' passing. Often sullen, Aubrey refused hugs, met smiles with a grimace, and mainly inhabited a world to himself that remained largely impenetrable to Harriet no matter the angle of her approach. And so the siblings lived together in their family's old apartment like an aged couple that shared a home based primarily on mutual practical benefit.

"Potatoes again?" Aubrey complained. "That's all we ever have."

She spun around to face him. "That is not all we . . ." She dropped the wooden spoon in her hand. "Aubrey! What happened?"

"It's nothing." He turned his head quickly.

She hurried to where he stood in the kitchen doorway and gripped his chin. "Nothing? Hardly is this nothing. You've been in a fight. What happened? Who were you fighting with?"

Aubrey jerked free from her grasp. "I said it's nothing." He marched toward his bedroom, scooping up the kitten on the way; his heavy footfalls ended with the sound of the door slamming shut.

After turning off the gas flame beneath the pot, she wrapped a chunk of ice from the icebox in a dish towel. She tapped on the door as she opened it, not giving him a chance to tell her to go away. He was lying on his bed, facing the wall. Susan rolled around at his toes, nibbling on his stockinged feet.

"Geez, will you leave me alone?" he grumbled.

"She's just a kitten."

"I meant you!" he said, taking her bait.

Harriet lowered herself onto the edge of his bed. "You may as well save your breath, because you know I'm not about to do that. Like it or not, I'm your big sister. And like it or not, it's just you and me living here in this apartment. Part of living together is looking out for one another. I've brought some ice for your eye. I suspect it will stay black and blue for some days, but we can do something to bring down the swelling."

Intrigued by the block of ice, Susan bounded onto Harriet's lap. After several minutes of silence, she said, "The ice is melting, and there's only so much I can steal from the box before spoiling the milk and eggs. If you want breakfast and supper for the next week, I suggest you stop behaving like a child."

Aubrey rolled over with a groan. Harriet winced. Something about the lighting made his bruised face look worse. As she moved the ice wrap to his eye, he snatched it from her and did the job himself.

"You're welcome," she said.

He rolled the eye that wasn't covered.

"Now," she said, setting Susan on the floor and planting her hands on her knees to signal her intention to stay. "I'm ready to hear about your encounter with Gentleman Jim." Harriet hoped her reference to James J. Corbett, the most famous boxer of the decade, might pry a smile from her brother. Instead, he scowled and said, "He got beat last year by Bob Fitzsimmons."

An avid reader of the *Chicago Tribune*, including its sports pages, Harriet knew that—just as she knew the trick to get her brother to talk was to start with a topic in which he had an interest.

"So, were you more Corbett or Fitzsimmons?" she asked.

Over the next twenty minutes, Harriet learned that Aubrey had been bullied by a larger, older boy named Sherman Truss for the past several weeks. As Aubrey told it, Sherman didn't like that Louisa Klopsberger, a pretty girl in Aubrey's class, didn't return his attention. Aubrey didn't state it bluntly, but by listening to what he did and didn't say—combined with what she already knew about her brother—Harriet pieced together that Sherman was angry because Louisa took a shine to Aubrey, who was more handsome and far more intelligent. Even though Aubrey claimed to have done nothing to provoke the bully and had not shown any sign of returning Louisa's admiration—did he?—the simple fact that Louisa didn't like Sherman was reason enough for him to pummel her brother. In a fitting end to the story, Louisa had been the one to stop the beating. Seeing Sherman astride Aubrey in the dirt, she'd run up and kicked him hard in the head. Not seeing who'd struck him and acting impulsively, Sherman had swung at Louisa, barely missing her, just as her older twin brothers arrived. For an instant, Harriet almost felt sorry for Sherman.

Harriet hated violence and took no pleasure knowing that the bully Sherman had gotten what was coming to him; he'd started things by picking on someone smaller who'd done him no wrong. Even if Aubrey had somehow offended Sherman, there were better ways to solve their disagreement than throwing punches. Still, Harriet wasn't naïve. Her father's work for the unions had disabused her of the notion that men could always resolve conflict through debate and peaceful negotiation. To the contrary, she often wondered if nonviolent solutions were the aberration to men's natural inclination to impose their will by physically conquering one another. But not all men were like that. Her father, Uncle Roy, and Aubrey had never been aggressive; she was grateful for that. But now, looking down at Aubrey's bruised and swollen face, she worried. Was he too passive? Too gentle? Did he lack the strength to stick up for himself when the occasion demanded it? Did she?

Harriet had never fought anyone, but she'd once come close. Had her mother not intervened, she would have traded punches with her childhood nemesis, Bobby Carruthers, who had stolen her tennis racket, a cherished gift she'd received on her thirteenth birthday. When Harriet had discovered Bobby playing with her racket in the park, he'd refused to give it back even after she'd pointed to her name scratched onto the wood frame. Reflecting on that episode, Harriet understood her fury was as much—if not more—about the injustice of someone stronger taking from someone weaker as it was about the loss of the particular item.

Over a supper of boiled potatoes, braised cabbage, and pork chops—a once-a-week splurge—Harriet told Aubrey about her day. She wished her mother were there to hear about it but was grateful for her brother's interest.

"When you find the maid," Aubrey asked, his mouth full of potato, "what if you have to shoot the man who took her to get her back?"

"I doubt very much it will come to that."

"Why? Didn't Mr. Prescott give you a gun?"

"No, he did not."

"Don't the men detectives have guns?"

"They . . . I don't . . ." Harriet realized she didn't know the answer. Prescott's operatives must find themselves in dangerous situations. Some of the men must be armed, if only when necessary. Would Prescott consider issuing Harriet a pistol? The notion was both exciting and scary. It was one thing to carry a firearm and quite another to possess the skill and sound judgment to use it.

"You should have a gun," Aubrey decided as he stabbed another forkful of pork chop. "You may be strong for a girl, but you're still a girl. Though you'd have given Sherman a good match." He smiled for the first time that night.

Harriet returned the smile, but it didn't come easily. Her brother's bruised and swollen face was a stark reminder that every day in a city as large as Chicago, crimes—often involving severe injury and sometimes murder—occurred. Whoever had taken Agnes Wozniak had taken her by force. Provided Harriet could even find her, what then?

Would her abductor simply hand her over? The penalty for kidnapping must be many years behind bars. To what lengths might someone go to save themselves from such a fate?

Strong for a girl. Aubrey was right about that. But depending on where her search was to lead her, would that be enough to keep her safe?

Chapter 8

Given what had happened to Aubrey the day before, Harriet chose not to scold him for leaving the milk bottle out or breadcrumbs on the table—a sure way to attract more mice. Although Susan would one day help out with that, at just three months old she was outmatched and outnumbered by the rodents that pillaged the household's dry goods.

Despite his shiner and bruised cheek, Harriet was relieved that Aubrey appeared in good spirits—or no worse than usual. As on most mornings, she'd seen him off at the door with an apple and a peanut butter and jam sandwich, knowing any attempt at a hug would be rebuffed with a growl. Had Louisa Klopsberger's twin brothers not attended the same high school as Aubrey and Sherman Truss, Harriet would have accompanied Aubrey to school, marched into the principal's office, and given him a good scolding for having done nothing to prevent her brother's beating and to secure a promise for his safety.

Harriet was accustomed to arriving at work at eight o'clock sharp. But deciding it prudent not to arrive at Pearl Bartlett's before nine, she still had a few minutes to herself. Before the mirror, she pinned up her hair. Aubrey liked to joke that it looked like a bale of hay had been dumped on her head. Reaching for her bowler hat, she wriggled its crown over her unruly mane. The snug fit ensured that Harriet could ride her Victoria at top speed or directly into the city's notoriously strong winds without concern that her bowler would blow off her head. Another part of her system was the makeshift strap she could easily attach to or detach from her handbag. Once slung over her head and shoulder, the bag's security was assured, freeing her hands for the handlebars.

Pedaling toward Prairie Avenue and not her place of employment was an odd feeling. For the first time in her life, she was going to work but not to an office. As a junior operative, hardly was she her own boss, but the freedom to arrange her day was gratifying. Would it last? She had six days to find Agnes Wozniak. What would her experience at the Prescott Agency be like come Monday? Theodore Prescott had, of course, hired new operatives in the past, but never a woman. Would that make a difference? As much as she liked to think of herself as capable as any man, would Prescott? She hoped her training would be no different from that received by a new male operative. And what about case assignments? Would he treat her the same as if she were a Harry? Or would he seek to exploit her uniqueness as Harriet?

Grateful for the warmer morning temperature, she sped south on her Victoria. The black Boston-made bicycle featured two wheels of equal size, and its drop-frame style allowed her to pedal in a long skirt—though not without inconvenience. After crossing the Chicago River, she turned east on Madison and rode to Lake Park. From there, she traveled south again before cutting east a final two blocks to arrive at the Bartlett mansion on Prairie Avenue.

Harriet wheeled her bicycle up the pathway, climbed the stairs, and rang the bell. Pearl was quick to answer. "You're late!" she scolded, then turned and promptly disappeared back inside the house. Taken aback by Pearl's admonishment—they had set no time for a return visit—she stepped inside the house and followed a sauntering Toby and the sound of clattering pans to the kitchen. Pearl was spooning batter into a muffin tin. Seeing Harriet appear in the doorway, she waved a spatula in the air. "Harry, the situation is grim. Grimmer than grim."

Ignoring Pearl's insistence on calling her Harry, she said, "What's happened, Pearl? Has Agnes turned up? Has she been harmed?" Harriet stopped short of giving voice to her next question: had Agnes's body been discovered?

"What's *not* happened is a better question!" Pearl opened the oven door and plunked the muffin tin onto the rack.

"Tell me, please," Harriet asked cautiously, fearing the answer. "Is there news of Agnes? Has she been found?"

"Agnes? Found?" Pearl looked at Harriet as if she had ridden her bicycle into the kitchen. "If someone had found Agnes, would I be burning the bacon? Or making weak tea? Without milk! Last I checked, it was your job to find her. But you're here, and Agnes isn't. So what's happened is apparently nothing."

Harriet explained that Mr. Prescott had assigned her to the case and that for the next several days her sole focus would be discovering the maid's whereabouts.

"So you're saying Teddy is involved?"

"Mr. Prescott is aware, yes. Each day, I will report my progress. Also, another field operative, a Mr. Carl Somer, will be assisting behind the scenes. You may remember him. Mr. Somer was here on two previous—"

"Nincompoop! That young fellow did nothing but strut around here like he was king of the roost. I even made him a pie, pecan, to thank him for his trouble." Pearl narrowed her eyes and waved a bent finger. "Wouldn't touch it. Just stared down at the plate as if I'd served him molded cheese."

"I can assure you that Mr. Somer—"

"Please stop." Pearl batted the air. "I don't need you singing that fellow's praises. I only need you to—"

"Find Agnes. Yes, I know. I intend to do just that, Mrs. Bartlett." Seeing the woman wince, Harriet corrected herself, "Pearl."

Over scones and tea—Pearl refused to take "no" for an answer—Harriet learned all she could about Agnes Wozniak. An employment service, Lakeshore Domestic Help, used by many of Chicago's wealthy households, had sent five candidates to the Bartlett mansion before Pearl settled on Agnes. Pearl liked that the young woman was clean, polished her shoes despite them being ready to fall apart, and replied to questions with a simple yes or no. What had sealed the deal had been Toby's leap onto Agnes's lap and her reaction of petting the cat instead of shooing him away as the five previous candidates had done. The interview had lasted less than five minutes.

Curiously, Pearl had no interest in Agnes's previous employment or references, saying only, "The opinions of some rich old ladies hold no more interest than the Chicago Colts' season record." As for Pearl knowing anything about Agnes's circumstances before she'd moved into the mansion or her family, education, hobbies, and friends, it was all a blank slate. "Don't think I didn't try. That girl is tighter-lipped than a priest in a confessional box."

When Harriet had gone upstairs to retrieve the family photograph left behind on Agnes's writing desk and shown it to Pearl, it was clear she hadn't known Agnes had three brothers and a sister, the youngest and oldest appearing to be within ten years of age. According to Pearl, Agnes appeared the same age in the picture, suggesting the photograph was recent—all her siblings and parents were apparently alive and in one place. But where? Harriet suspected it was within the large Polish community on the city's northwest side.

As for visitors, Agnes never had any—or any that Pearl was aware of. Pearl had made clear from the beginning that Agnes was there to work. Personal matters could be conducted on the one day each week she had off: Wednesday, the day Pearl spent with her sister in nearby Evanston. Where Agnes went each Wednesday, if she went anywhere, was like every other aspect of her life: a mystery.

A loud *thud* from beneath them startled Harriet.

Pearl looked down at the floorboards. "That's just Gunther."

"Who is Gunther?"

"The handyman."

Learning that a man named Gunther Clausen had begun repairs to the house around the same time Agnes had started working for Pearl got Harriet thinking. "I'm sorry if this sounds onerous, Pearl, but I need to know everyone who has visited here in the three months since Agnes arrived."

A half hour later, Harriet had a list and description of eight individuals. As Pearl had described each person, Harriet had scribbled in her notebook and formed a mental profile of each individual. Four people frequented the property for typical reasons: the milkman, the gardener, the trashman, and the newspaper delivery boy. None of those workers had ever entered the house, and except for the twelve-year-old newspaper boy who was ten months into his route, all had been coming to the property for years. Although Harriet couldn't immediately clear them from suspicion, Pearl was certain of their innocence, referring to them by first names and recounting a surprising depth of knowledge about their families and personal lives. In that respect, Pearl reminded Harriet of her Aunt Charlotte, who, after residing in the same house for twenty years, knew everything about everyone within ten blocks in any direction.

Recommended by the woman across the street, Gunther Clausen had become a regular presence the past few months, repairing foundation cracks and leaking plumbing. According to Pearl, Gunther spoke little English with a thick German accent; she struggled to comprehend anything he said, making him the only other person besides Agnes whose life story she didn't seem to know. But Gunther was punctual, tidy, and polite. His work was primarily confined to the cellar, so he and Agnes rarely crossed each other's path. Harriet placed a question mark next to his name in her notebook.

Number six on the visitors' list was fellow operative Carl Somer, whose second visit to the Bartlett mansion had occurred one month ago. That left Pearl's two family members: her widowed sister-in-law, Esther, and Esther's adult grandson, Johnny Bartlett.

Five years older than Pearl and often stricken with headaches, Esther was the first person on the list Harriet decided could be safely eliminated as a suspect. The same could not be said for Esther's grandson, Johnny.

"A handsome charmer" was how Pearl described her grandnephew. Thirty-one-year-old Johnny Bartlett was unemployed but wanted for nothing. Pearl's deceased eldest brother had inherited much of their father's fortune, and his share had passed down to his eldest son and then to Johnny. Pearl smiled when speaking of her grandnephew's winsome features—wavy hair the color of chestnuts, gray eyes, and a lithe frame like a racehorse. As the older woman continued complimenting her grandnephew's good humor, refined taste, and generosity—never arriving without a gift—Harriet realized Pearl didn't simply like her Johnny; she adored him.

"Had Johnny ever met Agnes?" Harriet asked.

"Yes, of course. On many occasions. Although Johnny has a door key, he never just barges in. He rings the bell, polite as you please. Agnes answers the door and takes his overcoat. Johnny and I usually play cards. Then Agnes serves the tea and biscuits, clears the cups and plates."

"Did Johnny appear to take an interest in Agnes?"

Pearl snorted. "I know what you're asking. The answer is no. Johnny may not be as rich as Rockefeller, but he's got money, lots of it, and he's good-looking. Oh, he's a rascal, all right, but he understands the servants are off-limits—especially my maid. He may have held a gaze longer than usual, but that was to be expected. Agnes is beautiful." Pearl reached a heavily veined hand toward the Wozniak family photograph and tapped on the glass. "It's only natural that a man would take notice."

"I take it Johnny is unmarried," Harriet asked. "And yet he is thirty-one?"

Pearl batted the air. "Yes, yes. He should have a wife and children by now. That's the expectation, isn't it? But Johnny is a bon vivant. Quite frankly, the boy leads a life the rest of us wish we could. Envy causes others to look down their noses, complaining that he should settle down and stop sowing his wild oats. But it's his life. As long as he harms no one, why shouldn't he do as he pleases?"

It was precisely the *as long as he harms no one* that concerned Harriet. Although she doubted the key-holding young man would scale the outside of the house, enter through a third-floor window, and snatch his great-aunt's maid, Harriet had to gather the evidence to be sure.

"Does your grandnephew live nearby?"

"North of the river on Dearborn Avenue. But you're wasting your time."

"I understand that Johnny is a relation, Pearl, but no one is beyond suspicion until I discover what happened to Agnes. Even presuming your grandnephew's innocence, he might have knowledge about the crime. Or perhaps he saw or heard something during one of his visits here that might help me find her."

"It's not that. Johnny's never at home. If you want to

find him, try the Ali Baba Theater. He's there most nights. That's what he claims anyway."

Quite sure she'd never heard of the theater, Harriet asked, "And what type of performances are put on there? Symphonic? Plays? Operas?"

Pearl snorted again. "Nothing so above aboard. Quite the opposite. The Ali Baba is infamous for one thing, Harry. And that's hoochie-coochie dancers."

Chapter 9

Before departing the Bartlett mansion, Harriet descended into the dimly lighted cellar to speak with Gunther Clausen. The steeply pitched staircase groaned underfoot. Although in a mansion and not some murky cavern off a squalid alley, she felt the tiny hairs on the back of her neck bristle. The cold air smelled slightly pungent, as if a giant vat of pickles had spilled. Hearing a clang of metal on metal, she followed the sound around several stout timber pillars and found a set of thick legs protruding from beneath a fat, rusted pipe. A lantern and an assortment of tools sat beside them.

Harriet waited for a bout of hammering to cease and said, "Excuse me, sir. Might I have a brief word?"

A loud grunt was followed by the legs' owner scooting out from under the plumbing and clambering to his feet. Harriet's gaze rose higher than expected as his bald head came within an inch of the unfinished ceiling's joists. "Yah?" Holding a large wrench, Gunther Clausen stood six-and-a-half feet tall with the broad chest of a heavyweight boxer. It took no time for Harriet to confirm one element of Pearl's description of the man: what little English he spoke was coated in a nearly indecipherable German accent.

Understanding bits and pieces of what he said, Harriet learned that he had occasionally seen Agnes as he came and went from the house but that they only exchanged greetings—never a conversation. For the past few months, Pearl had assigned him various tasks across the property. His most significant work was in the cellar, where he was single-handedly replacing hundreds of feet of failing pipes. For the past two weeks, he had entered the mansion through a door at the back of the house and claimed to have not seen Agnes during that time.

When Harriet asked Gunther if he knew that Agnes was missing, he appeared genuinely surprised. "Pearl needs maid," he replied with a sorrowful shake of his large head. Harriet then asked if he'd seen or heard anyone or anything in his time at the house that seemed unusual or might provide a clue about what had happened to Agnes. Gunther shrugged his mountainous shoulders. "Work. Mind business."

Harriet would have liked to have learned something about Gunther's family life and personal history—he wore a wedding ring on a right-hand finger, a curious tradition common among Germans, and his middle age allowed for children—but he cut short the conversation by saying, "Work now," and crawling back beneath the pipes. Although too soon to rule the handyman out as Agnes's abductor, he didn't seem a likely suspect. Not only had he taken little notice of Agnes, but Harriet doubted the man could climb through the maid's bedroom window without becoming stuck.

Since it was too early in the day to visit the Ali Baba Theater, Harriet returned to the agency to start composing her report for Mr. Prescott. With luck, Carl Somer, her assigned mentor, would be out of the office, and she could instead ask the friendly Matthew McCabe for instructions on properly drafting a progress report for the agency's principal.

Whereas most of the Prescott Agency office was a comfortable temperature, the room where the secretaries sat was much too warm. Harriet narrowed her eyes at the formidable radiator below the window. She understood why all three women had removed their jackets and rolled up their sleeves—stopping midway up their forearms—and frequently paused their typing to wipe their brows and fan themselves with whatever was handy. Unlike the other women who had carefully coiffed their hair before leaving the house, Harriet felt hers unfurl with the subtlety of an avalanche when she removed her hat. The collar of her shirtwaist felt damp against her neck. Had she been alone in the room, she would have sought a solution—adjusting the radiator's valve or opening a window—but she didn't want such an early interaction with her female colleagues to be one of complaint. Besides, if there were an easy remedy, surely the women wouldn't continue to suffer unnecessarily.

When she finished the first page of the report, her stomach grumbled so loudly she worried the other women had heard. Thankfully, her empty belly's protest was no match for the clattering of so many typewriters. At her bookkeeping job, the eleven o'clock hour marked the beginning of a fifteen-minute coffee break, and Harriet would enjoy a light snack from her lunch pail. Having yet to establish a new routine, she'd not thought to bring along anything to eat.

With her mother's words in mind—"You can't do your best work on an empty stomach"—she restuffed her hair beneath her hat and set out to find a nearby grocer. As she passed the operatives' offices, Matthew McCabe stepped into the corridor, nearly bumping into her. Hearing where she was going, he offered to show her to a nearby sandwich shop. Harriet appreciated the company and the recommendation but was aghast to discover the least expensive item on the menu was a cheese and tomato on rye for fifteen cents. Hardly could she afford such exorbitant prices every day. Starting tomorrow, she'd pack a lunch.

Matthew sat beside her at the high counter facing the sidewalk. He did most of the talking as she ate, telling her he'd joined the Prescott Agency two years ago, shortly after arriving in Chicago from back east. His father, a judge in Philadelphia, was an acquaintance of Theodore Prescott's and had arranged an introduction. Matthew lived with a roommate in an apartment up north on Fullerton Avenue. He did not mention a sweetheart, and Harriet wasn't about to inquire because she disliked the question when it was asked of her.

As had happened the day before, Matthew showed no interest in learning anything about her personal life. Was he self-absorbed? Or respecting her privacy? Given the rarity of a woman operative, most people would wonder why she wanted the job and thought she could do it. Still, she enjoyed the cordial exchange.

Growing up, the girls Harriet wished to befriend hadn't returned her interest, so all her friends were boys. Then, nearing the end of high school, a new girl, Penny, arrived in the neighborhood from Milwaukee. Despite being unlike Harriet—Penny was conventionally pretty and slender and seemed contented to pursue activities common to girls—Penny liked her back, and they had become inseparable. As time progressed, so did Harriet's feelings toward Penny. She imagined holding Penny close and kissing her plump, red lips. However scandalous the thoughts, she was powerless to stop them. One spring afternoon, as they sat knees pressed together on a park bench, Penny shocked Harriet by squeezing her hand and saying, "My fondness for you shall be my undoing." Words that should have filled Harriet's heart with joy were instead met with ambivalence—she now feared Penny would be *her* undoing. Two days later, the first of Harriet's parents became ill, and within months, she and Aubrey moved in with relatives on the city's outskirts. Harriet hadn't seen Penny since and often wondered what had become of her. Had she remained in the neighborhood? Had she gone off to college or married? While many questions swirled, one overwhelmed the rest: if Harriet could find Penny, might they pick up where they left off? Perhaps the detective skills she would soon acquire could be used to find Penny and discover the answer.

The conversation with Matthew turned to work. Harriet informed him that Mr. Prescott had asked Mr. Somer to serve as her mentor during the investigation. Not wanting to come across as too forward, she didn't share the fact that she had been the first to raise the issue by asking Prescott if Mr. McCabe could serve in that role.

Matthew grimaced. "Mr. Somer is a knowledgeable and competent detective, I'll grant you that. There is much he can teach you. However, you'll find he's . . . he can be a bit abrupt. You shouldn't take it personally. He's like that with everyone."

Harriet took the opportunity to ask Matthew for pointers in formatting her first-ever progress report. After relaying the essentials and specifics about what Mr. Prescott did and didn't like, he said, "And what about your field training? Has Mr. Prescott or Mr. Somer mentioned anything about that?"

Harriet's blank stare apparently provided the answer.

"You do understand the agency has never had a lady detective before? That you're the first?"

"It has come to my attention."

"Typically, a junior operative works under a senior man for the first year. You learn by assisting him in his investigations. I'll tell you right now, it's the least glamorous detective work. Sifting through documents. Logging the precise times and places of people moving about their days. Standing in the shadows, waiting and watching for something to happen. But it's essential to the job. There are right and wrong ways to go about everything. I don't need to tell you that Mr. Prescott prefers his operatives to perform their tasks correctly. I imagine that when the week is up, whether or not you've found the maid, Mr. Prescott will assign you to someone."

Harriet had everything to learn, but Matthew's description of how she would soon be working—under a senior man's supervision—hardly matched her fantasy of roaming the streets on her bicycle and solving diabolical crimes independently as a detective. She'd been foolish to think Mr. Prescott might let her take on investigations by herself anytime soon. Allowing her to look for Agnes was nothing more than a way to placate his neighbor and wife at the lowest possible expense and exposure to the agency. But despite Prescott's motives, the maid *was* missing—giving her a chance to prove herself.

As if reading her mind, Matthew said, "It's highly unusual that you be sent out alone. Let's say you do discover what happened to the maid. What then? I don't suppose the culprit who snatched her will politely accompany you to the police station. How will you defend yourself if he decides to get rough? When I started, some men in the office invited me to accompany them to the boxing gym and gun club to practice shooting. Such skills are essential for an operative. Don't get the wrong idea; most of our time is spent in conversation and combing through stacks of documents, but occasionally we come across someone who doesn't like us poking around."

What *would* she do if she found Agnes and her abductor? Detective work wasn't without risk, but she'd pushed those thoughts aside, too thrilled at discovering Agnes's empty room and the signs of a disturbance. That harm might come to her was a sobering thought. Even more worrisome was the impact on Aubrey—he wouldn't bear the loss of her, too.

"The only detectives I've met are you and Mr. Somer," Harriet said. "I doubt anyone will be inviting me to join them at the gym or the shooting range."

"That's a clever way to twist my arm," Matthew said, grinning.

Harriet sputtered, "I was only saying—"

"The boxing gym is no place for a woman. Even for one with no qualms about"—he sat back on his stool to better take her in—"skirting convention. However, the gun club has seen women before. Not many, mind you. But you won't be the first. I shall take you."

Harriet hadn't considered handling a gun, let alone firing one. She found the notion exciting and a good bit scary.

Sensing her apprehension but mistaking the reason, Matthew said, "Don't worry. I'll speak with Mr. Prescott to gain his approval beforehand. You won't be kept from your inquiries for more than a couple of hours."

Harriet nodded but continued to fret. This time, Matthew guessed right about her concern. "As my guest, it will cost you nothing. However, when you feel ready, you should ask Mr. Prescott about a pistol of your own. As an operative, I can tell you we all wish we never needed a gun, but trust me, Miss Morrow, you will. And then you'll be glad to have it. Perhaps not today or tomorrow, but one day you will need to defend yourself."

"Have you had occasion to fire your gun, Mr. McCabe?" Harriet was ambivalent about the answer she wanted to hear. While she feared confirmation that the job would put her in peril, it had a strange allure, unlike anything she'd ever contemplated.

"Once. But the victim was a ceiling." He chuckled. "In breaking up a brawl in a saloon, I fired into the air. Once I had everyone's attention, I was able to keep the peace until the police arrived."

The mention of the saloon brought to mind her plan to seek out Johnny Bartlett at the Ali Baba Theater that evening. Hearing her intention, Matthew frowned. "Alone? I don't expect Mr. Prescott or Mr. Somer will be too keen on that. It's one thing to have you inquire about a missing servant, quite another to permit you to go unaccompanied to the Ali Baba. You do know what goes on there? Don't you?"

Repeating what Pearl Bartlett had told her, Harriet replied, "Hoochie-coochie dancers." Although she'd never been to that particular theater, she knew about such places. Her Uncle Roy, a Chicago police officer, had occasionally enthralled Harriet and Aubrey with stories of raiding similar establishments, where "all manner of vices are performed on stage and in back rooms." Her uncle never elaborated on those vices, but the *Chicago Tribune* wrote without restraint. The newspaper's accounts of female impersonators had made the greatest impression on Harriet. She could recall the exact description: "gregarious men who affect the mannerisms and speech of women, who lean to the fantastic in dress, and who have a cult with regard to sexual life." Harriet understood the men were queer, though the specific word hadn't been used. Had she ever met a sexual invert? The term used by the medical community bothered her intensely as it insinuated an abnormal condition. She felt a strange kinship with such men and knew there was nothing wrong with them— or her. Still, at all costs, they both must keep an essential aspect of themselves secret from the public.

Before Matthew entered his office, he said, "Presuming Mr. Prescott is unopposed to your accompanying me to the gun club, shall we meet here? Tomorrow, say eleven o'clock? Oh, and Miss Morrow, for what my counsel is worth, again, I strongly discourage you from visiting the Ali Baba Theater on your own. You are free to ask Mr. Somer and Mr. Prescott for their opinions, though I'd be surprised if either of them should disagree with me."

Harriet returned to her desk, pulled her report from a drawer, and retyped it based on Matthew's suggestions, eager to make a favorable impression on Mr. Prescott. Presuming he wouldn't be available to accept it personally, she would leave it with Madelaine. As for notifying Prescott of her plan to interview Johnny Bartlett at the Ali Baba Theater, Matthew had convinced her that neither Mr. Prescott nor Carl Somer would allow it. And yet she'd been charged with finding Agnes Wozniak with no limitations put on her activities. Were her first name Harry—as Pearl Bartlett seemed to think—would there even be a question? She'd been instructed only to issue a daily report and consult Mr. Somer as needed. And she would.

If all went according to plan, her next day's report would recount her time at the Ali Baba, but that was tomorrow. By then, she would already have proved there was nothing to worry about.

Chapter 10

Harriet knew her brother loved her, although he would never say it. Instead, it manifested in other ways, such as oiling her bicycle chain or giving in to her longing for a kitten. His current display of sibling affection was worry at hearing her intention to venture out after dark. She shared his concern for another reason: Aubrey had never been left alone in the apartment at night. His being sixteen was both a comfort—old enough to mind himself—and concern—old enough to stir up trouble. But she had no choice. As a detective, she now had irregular hours, and Aubrey had long passed the age of needing someone to watch over him.

Unused to riding her bicycle after sundown, Harriet stuck to streets illuminated by gas lamps rather than taking the most direct route. The *Chicago Tribune* had recently reported the city's decision to convert the lamps to electricity, but the lengthy process had yet to begin, much to Harriet's disgruntlement.

One aspect of her present mission satisfied a long-held desire. She had traded her skirt for the bloomers she'd bought on a lark and kept in a bureau drawer for the past year. When introduced years before, the Turkish-inspired pants had found some popularity among suffragettes.

However, as more women discovered the pleasures of bicycling, the full pants, gathered at the ankle and worn beneath a knee-length dress, had become acceptable attire for exercising and athletics. Harriet thought her visit to the Ali Baba Theater a serendipitous occasion to try them out for the first time.

After passing by the Haymarket and McVicker's, two of Chicago's largest vaudeville theaters, she found the much smaller Ali Baba around the corner on a dark, narrow street, its double-door entrance beneath a hand-painted sign in block letters evocative of ancient Egypt.

After chaining her bicycle to a post and tucking the padlock key into her handbag, she removed the long strap she used when riding and entered the burlesque theater. The abrupt shift of light, sounds, and smells was startling. Through thick clouds of cigar smoke, the stage stood ablaze in light at the far end of the cavernous room. An exotic-looking woman clad in yards of colorful silk danced seductively as two strangely dressed men sat cross-legged on large pillows, playing a drum and an odd-shaped stringed instrument she'd never seen before. Swiveling her hips and writhing her belly, the woman clapped finger cymbals in time to the music. The men in the audience huddled around tables littered with bottles and ashtrays. Their applause and hoots of pleasure filled the space with crackling energy. A quiver of excitement shot through Harriet. The theater's carnival-like atmosphere electrified the air.

Harriet needn't have worried she would be the only woman present—besides the performers, of course. Although outnumbered by the men, several women served drinks, sat on men's laps, or danced lasciviously among the tables. Were they all harlots? In her few minutes there, she'd already witnessed three different women escort men out through a side door of the theater. Wiping her eyes, teared from smoke, she headed for the bar.

Sensing her presence, the bartender said, "Yeah?" but kept his eyes lowered on the drink he was making.

Raising her voice to be heard over the din, she replied, "I'm looking for someone. His name is Johnny Bartlett. Might you point me to him? Presuming he's here."

The bartender glanced up. "Who wants to know?"

"A friend." Harriet hadn't intended to begin the evening with a lie, but announcing oneself as a detective in such a place would probably be met with disdain and, in her case, disbelief.

The bartender scoffed. "Is that so? Johnny is particular about his companions. Only a particular type appeals to him."

Harriet understood the implication. Rather than insulted, she was relieved there would be no need to fight Johnny off should he get the wrong idea about her. But then, Harriet wasn't the type of petite, doe-eyed blond that turned men's heads. She was grateful that men weren't typically interested in her—it went both ways.

Harriet repeated her question. The bartender shook his head, ignoring her. She had made an error in not asking Pearl Bartlett for a photograph of her grandnephew. But considering the dim, hazy room, it wouldn't have done her much good anyway. Presuming Johnny wouldn't appear on stage, the only place in the theater where a person could be seen clearly, she'd need to ask around.

A woman wearing a loose-fitting dress that exposed her shoulders and décolletage—one of the countless shocking displays at the Ali Baba—leaned against the wall. As she wasn't busy serving drinks or entertaining men, Harriet approached her.

"Hello, madam . . ." Harriet faltered. The dress, rouged and powdered face, and feminine carriage had fooled her. "I'm wondering if you have seen a friend of mine. His name is Johnny Bartlett."

The female impersonator gave Harriet a long appraising

look before saying, "Interesting," in an unexpectedly feminine voice. Whether referring to Harriet's unusual attire or a woman with her stout frame looking for Johnny Bartlett wasn't clear. She couldn't read his expression; he'd turned his gaze back to the crowd.

"Have you seen him here tonight?" Harriet asked. "Johnny Bartlett?"

The impersonator waited a moment before turning back to face Harriet. "I'm trying to make you out." He cocked his head as if her appearance might be better explained from another angle. "You're not one of Johnny's regulars . . . if he has any. And you don't look like a relation. So I wonder, why is a so-called 'friend' of Johnny's asking me, an enchanting stranger, where to find him?"

That the impersonator hadn't considered Harriet might be a policeman or a detective was expected, as none of the former and extremely few of the latter were women. Interviewing with Prescott, she'd argued that very advantage. Satisfied to be proven right, she must now make the most of it.

"Clever of you," Harriet said. "You're correct. I've never met Johnny Bartlett. But I've come to deliver a message just the same."

He raised a single brow.

Sensing his intrigue, she continued, "My roommate Scarlett *is* Johnny's type. The poor girl's besotted. I wish he had good intentions, but he clearly doesn't. I came to tell him she's off limits."

"Look around you, sweetie. You see a lot of good intentions?"

He returned his attention to the crowd and turned his shoulders slightly away from her, signaling the conversation's end. Harriet started to walk away when he abruptly flicked a finger toward the stage. "See that table up front? The handsome chap in the red tie and suspenders? That's him. That's Johnny Bartlett. But you didn't hear it from me."

Harriet started to thank the man?—woman?—but stopped. They'd already sauntered off into the crowd.

Now that Harriet had found Pearl's grandnephew, what next? Hardly was the atmosphere conducive for a serious conversation. After scribbling a note, she sacrificed two quarters for a tumbler of the bar's finest scotch, waved down a woman serving drinks, and gave her instructions along with a nickel tip.

Minutes later and holding the nearly empty glass of liquor, Johnny staggered up to her in the relative quiet of the entrance. "You're easy to spot." His slurred speech confirmed that the two fingers of whiskey she sent with a note to his table hadn't been his first drink of the night. Although he was disheveled, Pearl hadn't been overly generous in describing her grandnephew. Dashing, in his early thirties, he had auburn hair parted in the middle, oiled, combed flat, and just long enough to tuck behind his ears. His gray eyes matched the smoky background, and his slightly unbuttoned shirt hinted at a smooth, muscled chest.

"What's this business about my aunt?"

"I'll be brief and to the point so you may return to the entertainment, Mr. Bartlett. I've come to inquire about your great-aunt's maid, Agnes Wozniak."

"Agnes?" Johnny flinched with the exaggerated movement of someone in their cups. "You came *here* to ask me about *Agnes*? The maid Agnes?"

"Yes." Harriet wished the man were sober so she might better read his reaction. Then again, perhaps his inebriation might impair his ability to hide the truth by fabricating a story.

He shook his head like a wet dog. "I don't understand. Who are you? Why are you asking me about my aunt's maid?"

"Agnes is a beautiful girl, as I'm sure you must have noticed."

"Who wouldn't? But what's that got to do with anything?"

"Might you have a romantic interest in her?"

"What?" He squinted his eyes and blinked rapidly as if dust were bothering them.

"Agnes is missing, Mr. Bartlett. I'm quite certain someone took her from your great-aunt's home by force. My name is Harriet Morrow. I am a detective with the Prescott Agency. Pearl Bartlett asked for Theodore Prescott's help. I've been assigned the task of finding Agnes. As part of the investigation, I'm speaking with those who have recently been to Mrs. Bartlett's home to inquire whether they know of anyone or anything that might help explain what happened to Agnes. It was your great-aunt who told me that I might find you here."

While Harriet spoke, Johnny's eyes had grown larger. He was either an excellent actor or the news of Agnes's disappearance was a shock.

"Took Agnes? Is she hurt?"

"I certainly hope not, but until she's found, her condition can't be known. What can you tell me about Agnes? Please, any information you have might help me find her."

"She's Aunt Pearl's maid. She lives with her. What else is there to say?"

"Did Agnes ever speak about her family? Friends? A beau? She had Wednesdays free. Did she ever mention where she went on her days off? Anything like that?"

Johnny shrugged. "Listen, she's a maid. She knows her place. 'Hello, sir, goodbye, sir, more tea, sir?' "

"Did you ever go up to the third floor?"

Johnny blurted a laugh. "She's not my type. Besides, she's Aunt Pearl's servant. I wouldn't dare. She would spank me with a spatula." He laughed. "Look around"—he gestured toward the room—"plenty of others . . . who aren't the household help."

"Might I ask where you were last Friday, from the dinner hour to the next morning?"

A tolerable drunk until that moment, Johnny turned angry. "No. You may not inquire. I have nothing to do with Agnes being missing. That's all you need to know. Now . . ." Again, he shook his head roughly. "I'm done talking"—he stumbled away, then, as if forgetting, he turned back—"to you."

As Johnny weaved his way back to his seat, the female impersonator took the stage. He stood before a microphone illuminated by a single spotlight. A man at a piano had replaced the musicians on pillows. Hearing the first notes on the keyboard, Harriet recognized the popular song, "After the Ball." Fascinated, she listened and watched along with the enrapt audience, which joined in singing in the chorus.

> *After the ball is over*
> *After the break of morn*
> *After the dancers leaving*
> *After the stars are gone*
> *Many a heart is aching,*
> *If you could read them all*
> *Many the hopes that vanished*
> *After the ball.*

What a strange place, the Ali Baba Theater. Pearl Bartlett knew her grandnephew patronized the establishment, but would she still consider it harmless fun if she ever attended in person? Harriet had mixed feelings. While she understood that most women turned to prostitution in a desperate attempt to survive, she would never condone a job that so thoroughly subjugated women. Most fascinating was the female impersonator. The man not only dressed as a woman but also adopted a feminine voice and mannerisms. In a way, the female impersonator was the reverse of Harriet, who longed to dress fully as a man, though she had no interest in imitating the telltale cues of the opposite sex. What masculine traits she did possess—a stiff gait, husky stature, and voice at the deeper range of the scale—manifested naturally. Even the clothes to which she gravitated had nothing to do with a desire to resemble a man; they were a matter of taste, as simple as a person's liking sweets over salt or a preference for sunrises instead of sunsets.

Riding home on her Victoria, Harriet's figure cast a curious shadow in the lamplight. She pedaled faster. The chilly night air invigorated her. Her second day as a detective would end having made progress. She had a list of names from Pearl Bartlett, and two in particular deserved attention. The handyman Gunther Clausen seemed innocent, but crossing out his name in her notebook was premature. And Johnny Bartlett? She was less sure about him. But if Johnny had taken Agnes, Harriet had reason to hope—he spoke of Agnes in the present tense.

Chapter 11

Harriet marveled that a business such as Lakeshore Domestic Help had reason to exist. Catering to Chicago's wealthy households, the service supplied maids, cooks, valets, gardeners, buggy drivers, and whatever other servants might be needed for the proper running of a mansion. The employment agency had sent several candidates to Pearl before she'd settled on Agnes. Presuming they must have information on those they sent for interviews, Harriet climbed the three flights of stairs to their offices.

Behind identical desks sat two women, each considerably older than the secretaries at the Prescott Agency. The words *prim* and *proper* came to mind. On the other side of a glass wall worked a neatly attired man behind a large conference table. He glanced her way and, seemingly uninterested, promptly returned his attention to whatever he was doing.

Stepping up to the woman nearest the entrance, Harriet said, "Excuse me, madam, but I'm hoping you can help me. I'm seeking—"

"Please, take a seat." The woman pointed to a row of wooden chairs against the wall. "My colleague, Mrs. Dandridge, will take your information as soon as she's free." The woman appraised Harriet with a disapproving scowl.

That her men's shoes or unstylish attire might not meet the standards of the placement service didn't bother Harriet as much as the woman thinking she'd come for a job scrubbing floors or rubbing water spots from champagne flutes.

"I'm afraid you misunderstand. I'm not seeking employment. I'm looking for information on a woman you sent some months back to a local residence."

She pursed her lips, then replied, "That's an unusual request. Have you come on behalf of your employer?"

"Indeed, I have." Harriet smiled, proud to answer, "Mr. Theodore Prescott."

Frowning, the woman said, "Prescott? Doesn't ring a bell, I'm afraid."

"Allow me to explain. My name is Harriet Morrow. I am a detective with the Prescott Detective Agency. Mr. Prescott, the agency principal, is my employer. I've come on behalf of an agency client. A Mrs. Pearl Bartlett."

"Ah, Mrs. Bartlett." The woman drew out the words. "Her, I do remember. Maid, wasn't it?"

"That's right. Her name is Agnes Wozniak. I'm afraid she's gone missing."

"Missing?"

"Quite. Mrs. Bartlett is understandably concerned. I've come—"

"Yes, of course. While we pride ourselves on the reliability of those we place with our clients, on a rare occasion, a servant will leave without warning." She flicked her wrist as if dismissing an over-attentive waiter. "Not even the courtesy of a proper resignation. It can be most upsetting to the running of a household. Our clients are important people who shouldn't be burdened by any interruption in their domestic service. You'll need to have a word with Mr. Chauncey. Once you relay the particulars to him, Mrs. Dandridge or I will get to work straight away on sending other girls for Mrs. Bartlett to interview."

The woman, concerned only about the impact on the

homeowner, didn't consider that something frightful might have happened to Agnes. Were household staff so nameless and interchangeable? It struck Harriet that to these people Agnes was no more consequential than an empty milk bottle set on the porch for replacement.

"Madam, Agnes hasn't run away. If only it were that simple. It appears she was snatched from the Bartlett residence sometime during the night. Mrs. Bartlett's primary concern is not to replace Agnes but to find her." Saying the words aloud, Harriet realized that if she didn't locate Agnes soon, Pearl would, in fact, need the agency to send another maid. She hoped her efforts weren't delaying the inevitable.

"Snatched, you say? Is Mrs. Bartlett quite sure? Perhaps the woman stayed out longer than usual? Took a day off with asking?" She clucked a *tsk tsk*. "Young women these days . . ."

"I can assure you it's nothing like that. I inspected Agnes's room myself. All signs indicate she was taken by force."

"This is most unusual."

"As you've said." Harriet smiled again, tight-lipped. "Is there an employment file on Agnes Wozniak that I might review? I'm seeking information to help lead to her whereabouts. Her home address would be a fine start."

The woman raised a finger as she stood. "One moment." Crossing the room, her skirt's rough fabric rustled like leaves in a breeze; she entered the private office to speak with the man, presumably Mr. Chauncey. A minute later, Harriet was ushered inside his office.

"Now then"—he stood, smoothed his shirtfront, and tugged lightly at its cuffs—"what's this I hear about a missing maid?"

Harriet surmised Mr. Chauncey wouldn't abide a poorly ironed shirt, an improperly set table, or a joke of any kind. After hearing her story, he riffled through a stack of files on a shelf. "Aha," he said, extracting a folder, then handing it to Harriet, "I'll allow you ten minutes to jot down whatever it is you're looking for. Consider this a professional courtesy to the Prescott Agency. Please give Mr. Prescott my personal regards." With a slight bow, he handed Harriet a card with his name and business particulars. Seeing his name written in a script font, she couldn't help but smile. CHARLES CHESTER CHAUNCEY.

The woman hurried Harriet from the office to one of the chairs against the wall. Balancing the file on her lap, she scribbled into her notebook. Agnes Wozniak had listed her date of birth as November 21, 1878 making her only nineteen. Had Pearl wondered or asked the service bureau about Agnes's age? Surprisingly, Pearl Bartlett wasn't even Agnes's first employer. Beginning at the age of fifteen, she had served another household, the Schottenkirks, for four years, but only in the afternoons to help their cook prepare the evening meal. Was it legal to employ a servant so young? Harriet had read stories in the *Chicago Tribune* about children as young as eight years old working in coal mines, so she shouldn't have been surprised. Harriet learned from the documents that Lakeshore Domestic Help had placed Agnes in the Schottenkirks' home. Given its Erie Street address, Harriet imagined an impressive mansion similar to Pearl's and others lining Prairie Avenue.

The last page of the file was the most interesting. It listed Agnes's home address as 1218 Noble Street. Harriet wasn't familiar with that street. Still, she guessed it must be several miles northwest of downtown in the densely populated Polish neighborhood clustered around the six-point intersection of Division, Ashland, and Milwaukee avenues, known as Polish Downtown.

Harriet bounded down the steps, tingling with excitement. She had two addresses—two next steps in her investigation. She checked her watch: 9:20 a.m. She was to meet Matthew McCabe for shooting lessons at eleven o'clock, but the Erie Street address was nearby. Would the lady of the house, presumably Mrs. Schottenkirk, know more about Agnes than Pearl did?

Steering her bicycle through congested streets, Harriet wondered if there would soon come a day when movement of any kind would be forced to a standstill. Aubrey had recently brought home a fact learned at school—since his birth in 1882, the city's population had nearly tripled, to one and one-half million. Every year, taller buildings crowded the skyline and more immigrants poured into countless tenements. Chicago politicians crowed in the papers about the city's growth as if it were only a good thing, but how many more people could the city absorb before it burst?

Dismounting her bicycle in front of the Schottenkirks' home, Harriet gazed up at the four-story mansion's castle-like appearance with its intricately carved stone façade, massive arched portico, and corner turret. Whereas the Schottenkirk residence promised a splendid and massive interior, not ten blocks to the west a building of such size might house a dozen families, offering little heat, unreliable lighting, and a shared outhouse.

Harriet's knock was answered by a young maid with yellow hair pulled into a bun so tight her brows arched unnaturally. Her light blue dress, accented by white lace cuffs and collar, appeared so heavily starched that Harriet mused it would crack if the maid were ever allowed to sit. Inside the foyer, every surface appeared decorated in marble, alabaster, carved and inlaid wood, or patterned tile. Another woman, much older and dressed in black, emerged from the back of the house. Curiously, she wore her gray hair in a similar bun. She introduced herself as "the housekeeper."

After listening intently as Harriet explained who she was and why she was there, the housekeeper said, "My predecessor hired Agnes. Unlike myself, she kept no personal information on the servants. When I joined the household, Agnes reported to me, as do all staff. I found no fault with her performance, but I had no choice in the matter. I had to let her go. I can't allow the help to create a distraction. It upsets the smooth running of the household. And that I will not have."

Harriet started to remind the woman that she too was "the help" but kept the thought to herself. "Distraction? What do you mean exactly?"

"Harry and Robert are seventeen and eighteen, respectively." She nodded sharply as if that explained it.

"I take it Harry and Robert are also part of the household staff?" Harriet said.

"Heaven's no." The housekeeper reared back, affronted by the idea. "They are the Schottenkirks' eldest boys—the young masters of the house."

"I see." And suddenly Harriet did. Never had she considered that one's good looks could be a detriment, but Agnes's beauty had been too much of a distraction to the adolescent boys in the house. In truth, Agnes's physical charms weren't the problem; it was the boys' inability to look past them. Had they fought for her attention? Bothered her? Had they interfered with her? Harriet felt anger on behalf of the young maid. Doing her job well hadn't saved her from being dismissed. However, Agnes seemed lucky to have landed a position at the Bartlett mansion, where there was only Pearl and Toby to look after, and it wasn't run with the severity reflected in the appearance of the women servants here.

Harriet left the house with a shudder. Seldom did she consider herself fortunate, but her circumstances didn't force her to wear an uncomfortable-looking uniform and work in servitude from sunup to sundown. Her parents had instilled a belief that she needn't settle for a life as a homemaker, factory worker, or shop clerk. She was fortunate to have been hired by Mr. Prescott, but she had yet to prove herself. Screw it up, and she might find herself wearing a uniform before the month was out.

Harriet pedaled toward downtown. Although eager to begin her outing with Matthew McCabe, she was even more excited about the second address scribbled into her notebook: 1218 Noble Street. Surely Agnes's family must know something about her disappearance.

Chapter 12

Although eager to visit the Wozniak family in the Polish neighborhood, Harriet had not forgotten Matthew Mc-Cabe's offer to take her to his gun club. She couldn't stand him up, nor did she want to. So far, no part of her investigation had put her in a perilous situation. Not even at the ribald Ali Baba Theater had she felt unsafe. But Matthew was right: it was only a matter of time before she confronted danger. Better that she was prepared to defend herself.

At the agency, Harriet noticed Carl Somer's office door was ajar. She hadn't intended to seek him out, but Prescott had assigned him as her mentor on the case. She didn't expect her doubting colleague to impart something helpful, but still, she thought it better to do as Prescott asked and keep him informed. Her light knock was met with a clipped "Enter."

Carl looked up from a desk strewn with legal-looking documents. "Oh. I was expecting Miss Small."

"I'm sorry to disrupt your work, Mr. Somer. But seeing that you were in, I wondered if I might take the opportunity to recount my progress on the case thus far. If now is not a good time—"

"Ah, Miss Morrow. I trust your inquiries are progressing satisfactorily?"

Surprised by his friendly tone, she sputtered, "Why, yes, thank you."

"So tell me. Have you found the maid?"

"Found her? No. Not yet. But I am making progress. If I might share—"

"I'm sure it's not for lack of trying. Please. How may I assist you?"

"Oh . . ." Carl's change in disposition was so dramatic that she didn't know what to make of it. Had Mr. Prescott given him a talking-to? Or Matthew McCabe? Was he moody? Harriet's former boss at Rock Island had run hot and cold—one day, smiling and cordial, the next pounding his desk and shouting curses. She would be on guard until she figured out what influenced Carl Somer. She preferred this version of the man and didn't want to do anything that might cause him to revert to surliness.

"That's very kind of you, Mr. Somer."

Carl stared at her for a long moment before spreading his hands as an invitation for her to continue. With haste, Harriet recounted her return to Pearl's mansion, her conversation with the handyman Gunther Clausen, the encounter with Johnny Bartlett at the Ali Baba Theater, and that morning's discoveries at Lakeshore Domestic Help, subsequently leading her to the Schottenkirk residence.

"So you have the maid's home address?" Carl said. "Do you plan on going there?"

Choosing to skip over her upcoming outing with Matthew McCabe, she replied, "This afternoon, I should think."

"Presuming the parents know about the woman's disappearance, they'll be terribly worried. However, you can't be certain they already know. If they learn the news from you, they will likely become distraught. They'll want reassurance that their daughter is all right, that no harm has come to her, and that she'll be quickly found. I trust you have considered that possibility?"

Harriet opened her mouth to speak but then thought better of it—she had no ready reply. To those she'd spoken with so far, Agnes was either a servant or a stranger. Carl was correct that her family promised a very different reception. What would she say? What *could* she say?

"Am I interrupting?"

Harriet turned to see Sandra Small holding a stack of red leather-bound ledgers she knew from Matthew Mc-Cabe contained closed case files.

"Not at all, Miss Small," Carl said, his voice and expression still friendly. "Miss Morrow was just leaving. Good day, Miss Morrow. I appreciate you keeping me informed of your activities. Please give due consideration to what I said about the family."

Sandra's bewildered look reminded Harriet that, as far as she knew, the secretaries were still unaware that she had been hired as an operative.

As she raised a hand to Matthew McCabe's door, he opened it and bounded into the hallway in his hat and coat. "Right then! Shall we?"

He answered her unasked question once the elevator doors closed. "As I've said, the walls are thin. When I heard Miss Small arrive, I knew you were free to depart." He smiled, adding, "You are probably excited to get started."

"Thank you." She returned a smile. "I am, indeed."

Turning serious, he said, "Mr. Somer is not entirely wrong, you know. You'd do well to listen to him."

Harriet's stomach clenched. Matthew, too? Did everyone at the agency doubt her? Stepping into the lobby, she said, "Have I given you a reason to think I'm inclined to disregard sound advice?"

Matthew winced. "Miss Morrow, I believe you misunderstand me."

"You just said 'I'd do well to listen' as if I had a history of turning a deaf ear."

Hands raised in mock defense, he said, "I'm simply agreeing with Mr. Somer's concern about your visit to the family. You must tread carefully. You don't want to be the bearer of bad news if you can help it. You want the family to see you as someone who can bring about a resolution. I was going to share my thoughts on the topic after our shooting lesson, but since you apparently need to hear it now, so be it. Do not unduly alarm the family. You seem convinced that harm has befallen the daughter, but you can't be sure. Not yet. Trust me, Miss Morrow, unwarranted certainty leads to unnecessary failure. Simply tell the family that you're looking for Agnes. Ask when they last saw her. Ask if they might know her whereabouts. Find out whether she had plans to be away or if any of her family or friends recently visited her. Learn what you can. That's the job—to acquire information, not dispense it. Listen carefully to what they say and how they react."

"But if I don't announce myself as an operative with the Prescott Agency, who am I? What is the reason for my asking about Agnes?"

Matthew cocked his head. "Come now, Miss Morrow. Surely you are capable of fabricating a believable falsehood. Unlike shooting a pistol, that is something I cannot teach you."

Swallowing her shame at exposing her insecurity, she apologized to Matthew for overreacting. If she was to gain credibility among her male peers, she had to be twice as steady, smart, and courageous. To that end, she'd done herself no favors in the past five minutes.

Matthew grinned. "I suppose I am lucky that you're not yet armed."

Although she appreciated his effort to lighten the mood, the comment only compounded her mortification.

After traveling several miles south of downtown by hired buggy, they arrived at a large undeveloped parcel of land on the lakeshore. The driver halted the horses at a gate with a sign reading ROWLEY'S GUN CLUB. Harriet followed Matthew inside a small clapboard building. He exchanged greetings with a big-bellied man in suspenders behind the counter and introduced Harriet as his cousin from Wisconsin. Harriet shook Mr. Rowley's meaty, calloused hand, then silently stood to the side while the men conferred about a suitable firearm for "a woman stronger than most." Usually, Harriet would be rankled to be excluded from a discussion about which she was the focus, but she'd already misread one situation with Matthew; she would trust his approach. The men decided on a small silver pistol, which Mr. Rowley placed on the counter in front of them alongside a dozen bullets. Matthew pocketed the gun and cartridges, and Harriet followed him outside.

Walking across the wide, flat expanse toward the lake, Matthew said, "Thank you for remaining quiet back there. Rowley is a traditionalist, shall we say. Women must be accompanied by a club member—a man, of course— and a family member receives few questions. There is another lesson for you, Miss Morrow. A good operative draws as little attention to himself as possible. It's often the case that doing the job properly is to blend into the scene so thoroughly that no one recalls your presence."

Ignoring his use of "himself," she said, "I understand. But in this situation, what harm would come from Mr. Rowley knowing that I am your colleague? In fact, you said you were first brought here by other operatives."

Matthew wagged a finger as they walked. "Another assumption, Miss Morrow." The remark stopped Harriet in her tracks. He looked down his nose at her. "Do you not see your mistake?"

In an instant, she did. "Who does Mr. Rowley believe you to be?"

"Why, Miss Morrow, have you forgotten your cousin is a mild-mannered insurance salesman? I shoot merely for recreation."

Resuming their walk, she smiled slyly. "If fabricating your profession, why not something more . . ."

"Admirable? Exciting?"

"Quite. Why not a physician? Or a daredevil?"

Matthew led her to a tall, rough-hewn table with a number painted on its side. He pulled the pistol and bullets from his pocket. "You'll find there is great beauty in the ho-hum. Were I a physician, there would be much I must know about medicine. The same goes for any other role that might spark one's imagination. Most people won't be curious enough about the job of an insurance man to ask questions." He gave her a serious look. "As a detective, you want to be the one asking questions."

The shooting lesson began with Matthew explaining that he and Mr. Rowley had decided on a Remington Double Derringer pistol as a suitable weapon. "The gun fires two .41 copper rimfire cartridges filled with black powder." He demonstrated how to load the pistol by breaking open the barrels at a hinge at the top and sliding a cartridge into each chamber. He closed the barrels, cocked the hammer, and raised the gun in his outstretched hands. Aiming toward the lake, he pulled the trigger twice, firing two shots, each emitting a loud *pop* and puff of black powder. He extracted the spent cartridges, slipped two new cartridges into the barrel, and handed the weapon to Harriet. "Your turn."

After some back and forth to ensure she was holding the pistol properly and understood what to expect, she fired. "Oh!"

Chuckling, Matthew said, "It's a powerful little pistol. But keep in mind, and this is very important, this derringer is a close-range weapon, say five to six feet. At that distance, and with the proper aim, it's accurate enough to do the job quite effectively."

Half an hour later, Harriet had fired the weapon several times, increasing her comfort and confidence with each pull of the trigger.

"You're a natural," Matthew said. "I'll show you how

to clean the weapon properly. Then we should be getting back to the agency."

Returning to the clubhouse, Harriet said, "I almost hate giving up the pistol. I understand it's not a toy, but that was terrific fun."

"Whether you decide to carry a firearm is your choice, but you should know that on most occasions, other operatives do. For you, another benefit of this derringer is its compact size." He stopped abruptly as if struck by a curious thought. "Men find it easy to conceal their pistol in a holster affixed to a belt or shoulder harness. I'd not considered . . ."

"Then I shall do the same," Harriet said matter-of-factly. "Should that ever be cumbersome, I'll tuck the pistol in my handbag."

"First things first. We should consult Mr. Prescott before you acquire a gun of your own. He may not think you're ready."

"And what do you think?"

Nearing the building, he said, "There is the knowledge required to fire a weapon, and there is the judgment to know when you have no choice but to do so. I can vouch for your abilities on the first count. The second is up to Mr. Prescott." He let a moment pass before adding. "And ultimately up to you."

The excitement of the past hour dissolved with the sobering thought of aiming not at a target but at another human being at close range. Was she prepared to shoot someone? Even were her life at stake? There would likely come a day when she'd have to answer that question. She hoped it wouldn't be soon.

Chapter 13

Being aware of something's existence and experiencing it firsthand were very different things. Pedaling into Polish Downtown—the neighborhood centered at Ashland, Division, and Milwaukee avenues—Harriet thought, I never imagined all this! The observation was at once exhilarating and dismaying. Comprising some of Chicago's most densely populated blocks, Polish Downtown was an impossibly congested and frenetic world unto itself. Harriet steered around buggies and buckboards, merchants pulling carts, pedestrians darting back and forth while chattering in a language she didn't understand, and garbage spilled onto the street from overflowing sidewalk bins. After two near misses, one with a horse pulling a supply cart, the other with the Number 107 streetcar, she dismounted from her Victoria for fear of a collision. She walked her bicycle in the direction of the Wozniaks' home, marveling at the variety of businesses. Although most signs were in Polish, thanks to the window displays and other cues—the aroma of freshly baked bread, an illustration of a sewing machine painted on a door, a man dressed in a white coat holding open a door for a young man using crutches—Harriet discerned the purpose of many of them. Usually savvy with directions, she soon realized she was lost. She pulled a map from her basket, although it would do her no good without knowing her location on it. Seeing her confusion, a woman about her age approached.

"*Czy mog pomóc ci znaleźć drogę?*" The woman pointed to the map spread across the bicycle's handlebars. Registering Harriet's blank look, she smiled. "Can I help you find your way?" The woman's English tumbled out in a thick accent that Harriet found surprisingly beguiling.

"Oh, thank heavens. Yes, if you'd be so kind."

Hearing Harriet's destination, the woman tapped a spot on the map, traced her finger along several streets, and tapped again. "There. See? Holy Trinity Church is on Noble Street." She smiled proudly. "My parish. You will see a tall spire. The place you are looking for is down the block." Touching Harriet's sleeve lightly, she said, "God be with you," and melted into the crowd before Harriet could thank her.

When Harriet reached Division Street, she remounted her bicycle and pedaled east. Seeing a tall church spire in the distance, she turned left and soon arrived at the front of a large Catholic church named St. Stanislaus Kostka. She frowned. The angle at which she'd first seen the single spire had hidden a second one behind it. But Harriet had a mind for details. The woman had said, "A tall spire." Singular. Had she been mistaken? Or was the inaccuracy a slight error in translation?

Two young boys kicked a ball in the yard across the street. She waved and asked if she was on Noble Street. They shook their heads and pointed behind her, the whites of their blinking eyes a sharp contrast with their dark, dirt-stained faces. Their silence suggested they didn't speak English, but they'd understood her question well enough. She tried another. Pointing at the church's spires, she held up two fingers. "Two. Yes?"

The boys traded bewildered looks before nodding.

"Noble Street. Church. One spire?" She held up a single finger and looked to the street behind her. The boys nodded enthusiastically and pointed in the direction she'd just come. After rewarding them each with a hard candy from her handbag, she turned back and saw a single spire just two blocks ahead. How many large Catholic churches were there in Polish Downtown?

Just past Holy Trinity Church, she rested her bicycle against the porch of 1218 Noble Street. The three-floor wooden structure had been built right up to the street front and occupied all but a few feet of both sides of the lot. Having seen better days, its once dark green paint had weathered and peeled to reveal the underlying wood, giving the façade a mottled appearance. Only the street number was painted onto the side of the doorframe; the building kept secret the number of homes inside, yet if what Harriet had read in the newspapers was true, as many as a dozen families might occupy the front building. If, as was often the case, the property owner had crammed a rear cottage tenement between the back wall of the front building and the alley, another half dozen families might live on the lot.

Harriet climbed the four steps and knocked. After a long moment, she turned the knob and, finding it unlocked, entered a dark foyer. A narrow staircase was directly ahead, and identical doors to her right and left. She shrugged and rapped lightly on the door to her right. A stooped woman, hair covered with a black scarf, answered. The smell of cooking onions and other aromas Harriet couldn't identify spilled into the hallway. Whether the woman spoke any English didn't matter. She replied to Harriet's inquiry about the Wozniaks by pointing across the hallway before closing her door.

Moments later, Harriet faced a most striking woman. Although not conventionally beautiful, her proud carriage, beak-like nose, and dark angular features struck Harriet as arousing. Somewhere near thirty, she stood several inches taller than Harriet and would be considered slender were it not for a waistline appropriate for a woman with a healthy appetite. A long black braid fell over her shoulder. Harriet was instantly charmed.

Learning that Harriet had come to inquire about Agnes, the woman introduced herself in excellent English as her older sister, Barbara, and invited Harriet inside. Curiously, the tiny sitting room smelled like the woman's apartment across the hall, suggesting similar food cooking in both kitchens. Harriet tried to retain her smile, despite the grim surroundings. At various spots near the ceiling, paper peeled from the wall and the heavy, damp air reflected a lack of ventilation. Harriet and Aubrey lived modestly, but the Wozniaks' home lacked nearly everything. Someone had pushed together two ancient-looking steamer trunks to form a low table in front of a worn sofa. Although the three meager pieces were all that were in the room, they filled the tiny space, making it challenging to move around. Seeing Barbara lower herself onto one end, Harriet did the same.

"Who did you say you are? Why are you looking for Agnes?"

"My name is Harriet Morrow. I've come on behalf of Lakeshore Domestic Help. As a common practice, we like to check in with those we place and see how they're faring. I understand from Agnes's employer that she has each Wednesday free. This was the address in her file, so I assumed I'd find her here. I'm sorry to bother you if that's not the case." She smiled warmly, wishing Matthew were here to witness her artful fabrication.

Barbara nodded. "Usually Agnes would be. However, I'm afraid she's not here today."

"Perhaps I've come too early?"

"No, that's not it. Agnes arrives first thing, never later than eight."

"I see. And here it's nearly"—she lifted the cuff of her shirt to consult her watch—"one o'clock. Have you any idea where she might be? Or what might be keeping her?"

"No. She always spends the entire day, and we have dinner together." Suddenly a thought struck, pushing Barbara to her feet. "Forgive me. One moment." She rushed into the next room. Watching her go, Harriet appreciated her purposeful stride and sensible low-heeled shoes.

Alone, Harriet noticed the silence. Apart from Barbara's footsteps in the adjacent kitchen and a light clanging of pans, the house was otherwise silent. The other Wozniak family members were either asleep, out, or quiet as mice. Barbara returned, wiping her hands on a dish towel. She didn't sit. "When I see Agnes, I will tell her you came by."

Sensing her time was ending, Harriet said, "And the rest of the family? Have they any idea where Agnes might be?"

"They are at work."

"Of course." Harriet stood reluctantly. Although she'd learned little, she enjoyed being in the woman's company. "I do hope whatever is keeping Agnes is nothing of concern. Knowing my luck, I'll be not two minutes out the door, and she will arrive safe and sound."

"I would say you could wait, but—"

"That's kind of you. The ride here was far longer than I'd anticipated, and I don't mind saying that my legs could do with a short rest before commencing my return trip."

Barbara's curious expression drew Harriet's explanation. "I came by bicycle."

"A bicycle! How marvelous! I had a bicycle but left it behind when we came here. We could bring only what we could carry." She shrugged, appearing crestfallen. "It's one of many things I miss. Perhaps someday I will have one again."

"You're most welcome to give mine a spin if you like."

"Really?" Barbara's eyes sparked with excitement. "Could I?"

The woman's delight made Harriet's skin tingle. "As long as what's on the stove will keep, by all means."

"Oh! The beans." Barbara again hurried from the room, returning moments later, having shed her apron. "Okay. I'm ready."

Outside, Harriet unlocked her bicycle and set the coiled chain in the basket. "I'm sorry, Miss Wozniak, I don't have the proper tool to raise the seat, but it shouldn't be too uncomfortable."

Barbara waved away the concern and the formality. "It's perfect. And please call me Barbara."

"Then you must call me Harriet."

After a momentary wobble, Barbara set off down the street with a joyous hoot. Watching her pedal away, Harriet was reminded of her family's visit to the World's Columbian Exposition five years earlier. Aboard a new attraction called a Ferris wheel—her parents on one bench, she and Aubrey on another—the family had circled hundreds of feet in the air, exhausting themselves from giddy laughter.

Barbara returned minutes later, appearing years younger. Her glee triggered unexpected emotion in Harriet; her eyes welled at providing the woman a few moments of simple pleasure.

Back inside the apartment, Barbara surprised Harriet by inviting her into the kitchen, which was also small and dimly lit. Whereas the front room's sparse furnishings projected somberness, the kitchen at least felt homey. Pots and skillets hung from a makeshift rack of pipe and rope, and eight mismatched chairs in various states of disrepair encircled a table scratched and stained from years of heavy use. A cabinet, its door missing a glass pane, overflowed with books in Polish and English. Coats and hats, both women's and men's, hung on hooks, and against the wall lay a football, several pairs of boots, and a wooden crate of empty milk bottles. The Wozniak family didn't have much, but they had each other. The scene made Harriet wistful. She was grateful for her brother, but his laziness and surly moods sapped the possibility of regaining any of the happiness they'd enjoyed when their parents were alive. As he aged, would they grow farther apart? Never had she considered spending her adult years alone. But what had she envisioned? Although a husband didn't figure into her future, who did? As crazy as it was, gazing at the back of Agnes's sister standing at the kitchen sink, Harriet allowed herself a moment to imagine life with another woman—a woman like Barbara Wozniak.

As Barbara sliced carrots and peeled potatoes, she talked about her sister, Agnes, and the family's journey to America four years ago. The family patriarch Piotr Wozniak had chosen Chicago because his brother Witold had settled in the neighborhood years earlier and established a successful badge and banner works business on Milwaukee Avenue. Being a shop owner hardly made Witold rich, but he and his family of six, who lived in the next block, had more than most. Piotr and the family's twin sons Marek and Marcin worked for Witold at the banner shop. The eldest son, Tomasz, worked at a nearby sausage factory, while their mother, Ewa, worked at a garment factory on Ashland Avenue. Although Harriet didn't ask, Barbara explained, "My mother is an excellent seamstress, much better than me. She can earn twice as much. So here I am, doing what she would normally do, making the stew." Barbara went on to say that for the same reason—earning the highest possible income for the family—Agnes worked as a live-in maid for Pearl Bartlett. Harriet's sympathy for Agnes living apart from her family was lessened by learning that Pearl paid Agnes higher wages than anyone else in the family, which contributed to Pearl's popularity despite no one else in the family having met her.

"Your sister must miss living here with the rest of you," Harriet said.

"Yes. And we miss her. I miss her terribly. Agnes is my favorite." Barbara turned away from the stove to give Harriet a conspiratorial grin. "Though I don't miss sharing a bed with her in my mother's room." Registering Harriet's surprise, she added, "My three brothers share the other with my father." She turned back to her pot. "Agnes gets paid better dusting that old woman's house than she would working any job in the neighborhood. Plus she's not constantly pestered by Bogdan Nowak or Damian."

Harriet sat up straighter, preparing to mentally record the forthcoming information.

Barbara continued, "My sister is beautiful, yes?" Hearing no reply, she looked over her shoulder.

"Yes," Harriet blurted, presuming that as a representative of Lakeshore Domestic Help, she would have had reason to meet Agnes in person. "Most lovely. I'm sure she has her share of suitors."

Barbara waved a wooden spoon. "Damian isn't a bad fellow. Not handsome, but pleasant enough. He's a friend of my brother Tomasz, who works at Damian's family's business, Swiatek Sausage. I told Agnes she could do worse . . ." She spouted a laugh. "Not a ringing endorsement, is it? Still, Damian is decent and kind. But Agnes doesn't love him, so . . ."

"You mentioned another gentleman? A Bogdan Nowak?"

"Gentleman! Ha! He's a beast. A hairy beast!" Barbara mocked an ape by pressing her fists to her hips, slumping her shoulders, and stomping across the floor.

Harriet laughed. "I take it neither you nor Agnes is fond of him."

"My sister loathes the man, and for good reason. Bogdan Nowak is known to have a violent temper. Given that and his size, few people cross him. Those who do end up with broken skulls—and they're the lucky ones. Despite that, my father insists that Agnes accept him."

Harriet gasped. "But why? He sounds horrid."

"Bogdan Nowak is rich. He contributes a lot of money to the Polish Roman Catholic Union. That is the only reason my father needs. How Nowak makes his money is the subject of much talk, but none of us know for sure. My brothers think he is a loan shark and extorts money from local business owners for protection against theft." She turned back again, a brow raised. "Theft he would commit. Nowak conducts his business from the back of a pool hall in a walk-up on Blackhawk Street. I ask you, does that sound like any business that's aboveboard?"

"I don't understand. From how you describe Mr. Nowak, he seems an unlikely contributor to a religious organization."

Barbara dipped a ladle into a pot and tasted a bit of brown sauce. "You might think so, yes. But it's the way of things." She sprinkled three pinches of salt into the stew. "He gives money to the local political bosses to keep them out of his business. He gives money to the church to stay in the community's good graces. His cash ensures that everyone looks the other way. It's how it's always been done."

Harriet's thoughts jumped to her initial meeting with Theodore Prescott. When hearing her application, he'd replied that her boldness would dissolve when confronting "the city's dark alleys, seedy pool halls, and nefarious gambling dens." She never guessed how soon she'd be put to the test.

A clock's chime from a distant room told Harriet it was two o'clock. She had extended her stay a full hour and had been rewarded with two names for her efforts. "Well, I've imposed on you long enough, Barbara. I'm sorry your sister is late. I do hope she arrives soon." She stood to go.

"As it happens, I need to be going myself. I have a meeting. The Polish Women's Alliance." She appeared delighted to say the organization's name. "We help women become financially independent through education and employment. Isn't that marvelous?"

Words could not express how marvelous the Alliance sounded to Harriet or how enchanting she found this particular member.

Wiping her hands on her apron, Barbara escorted Harriet outside. As Harriet was about to set off, Barbara surprised her by pulling her into an embrace and whispering "*Jesteś piękna*" into her ear.

Beyond sight of the Wozniak home, Harriet stopped on the side of the road. Scribbling into her notebook, she recorded the names of Agnes's suitors, their places of work, and Barbara's particular thoughts about each man, lest she forget any details. Then turning to a fresh page, she wrote down *Yesh-tesh pee-enk-nah* in large block letters.

Chapter 14

Wearing a man's hat, tie, and shoes, Harriet was accustomed to curious looks, but the agency's receptionist and secretaries now appraised her differently. Although she couldn't know for sure, she sensed they had learned she'd been hired as an operative and were incredulous. No doubt Carl Somer had told Sandra Small, and from her, word had spread across the office. Harriet was relieved the truth was known, although, going forward, these women would scrutinize her every word and action.

She rolled a clean sheet of paper into the Underwood typewriter and began composing her report. Thirty minutes later, she pressed the period key a final time, nodded, and removed the page.

"I'm glad to see you can type."

Startled, Harriet slid her notebook into her top drawer and turned her report facedown on her desk before turning to Sandra Small. How long had the secretary been standing behind her?

"Years of practice," Harriet replied brightly, though annoyed by the intrusion.

"Something to fall back on then. That's fortunate. Though you'll have to pass muster with Madelaine. Prescott leaves the hiring of secretaries up to her. Last I heard, she had no shortage of qualified applicants. Most of them are quite experienced"—she smiled wryly—"from what I understand."

Harriet didn't want to say anything that might be construed as diminishing Sandra's job, but she didn't like the insinuation that she would fail as an operative. "I am simply tackling the task at hand. One step at a time."

Sandra continued to press her point. "Can't blame you for trying, I suppose. Still, those of us who work here understand what it takes to be an operative."

"Oh? And what is that exactly, Miss Small?"

The retort took the secretary off guard. "Well . . . to start, it requires one to be exceedingly clever."

Harriet forced a long breath. "Surely you're not arguing that cleverness is unique to men?"

"I'm simply saying . . . well, perhaps a better example is that there are occasions when physical strength is required for the job. I don't think *you* would argue that all women are as strong as men."

"No. You're quite correct. I wouldn't. Just as I wouldn't argue that all men are equally strong or all women are equally strong or that all men are stronger than all women."

"I don't think you understand my point," Sandra said, her voice hinting at irritation.

"Perhaps we can agree that each of us is unique and free to choose our own path."

Harriet must do what she could to avoid unnecessary spats with naysayers like Sandra, who puffed themselves up by belittling others. She wished all the Sandras in the world would just go away and leave her alone. But they never would. All Harriet could do was let Sandra know she wouldn't be daunted.

"As you can see, Miss Small, I am busy with my operative's report for Mr. Prescott. If you'll be so kind as to allow me to return to my work. I'm sure you have vital agency business of your own to attend to."

Sandra replied with a curious expression, then seeing the seriousness in Harriet's eyes, walked back to her desk. If Harriet had done something to earn Sandra's dislike or doubts, then Harriet would understand. But to denigrate her because she aspired to achieve more than was commonly expected was dispiriting. Harriet preferred to be friends with Sandra and the other women in the office, but that seemed increasingly unlikely. At her previous job, the other female bookkeepers talked about men and courtship, fashion and hairstyles, and having children—all topics about which Harriet could contribute nothing. She had kept to herself to be spared awkwardness. In time, the women decided she was aloof and spoke to her only when the work required. In truth, Harriet longed for friends and companionship. But finding other women with whom she shared common interests proved difficult, a problem compounded by moving, employment, and assuming responsibility for her brother and the apartment. The thoughts brought to mind Barbara Wozniak and her glee at riding Harriet's bicycle. It also reminded her that she needed to find someone who understood Polish.

Harriet expected to leave her report on Madelaine's desk, so she wasn't prepared to catch Mr. Prescott's eye through his open door and be waved inside.

"Ah. Miss Morrow. Day three on the job. Any sign of Mrs. Bartlett's maid?"

Handing over her report, she said, "No, sir. However, I have made solid progress."

"You have, have you?" He took the file, flipped open the cover, and began to read.

Had he not seen yesterday's update? She understood he was a busy man and that his neighbor's missing housekeeper figured low on his list of priorities, but why require daily reports if he wasn't going to read them?

"So," he said, turning to the second page, "the young Pole has two neighborhood men sniffing after her. What have they to say?" He looked up, not reading the final page.

Harriet shifted her weight, suddenly uncomfortable. "I've learned about the men only this afternoon. Tomorrow I intend to pay them each a visit."

Scowling, he closed the report and dropped it into a wooden box on his desk. "What you have planned for tomorrow could have been done today. How have you been spending your time, Miss Morrow? I thought I made myself quite clear. No dilly-dallying."

"But, sir, I was quite busy yesterday. All my activities were summarized in the report I left with Madelaine." She stopped short of asking whether he'd read it; she didn't want to appear impertinent.

Prescott furrowed his brow. "Is that so? When Madelaine returns, I'll ask her about it. Yours wasn't with the others."

Two different emotions competed to set Harriet's mood. She was angry with Madelaine for not passing along her report but relieved Prescott didn't doubt her claim of submitting it. She realized her good fortune in seeing Prescott in his office. Otherwise, she'd have left today's update with his secretary as she had the day before. Had Madelaine innocently misplaced it? Or had she purposefully withheld it?

Hearing Harriet recount her progress, Prescott seemed satisfied, though unimpressed. "I'll be interested to hear what you learn when interviewing the woman's suitors. Remember, Miss Morrow. One week. Today is Wednesday. You have two more days. Plus the weekend, if need be. But come Monday, I'll be assigning you to a senior operative to begin the agency's standard training program."

Harriet worried about which senior detective she'd be

assigned, how they would get along, and what he would allow her to do. She couldn't expect to avoid proper training and would be grateful to receive it. But she relished her independence and hated knowing it would soon end.

Approaching her bicycle, Harriet's eyes bugged. She trembled with anger. Someone had knifed both tires. How brazen! The sidewalk was constantly busy with pedestrians. Had the vandalism been a random act? Or had someone targeted her specifically? For the past few years, she had ridden her bicycle whenever the weather allowed, leaving it chained throughout the city without incident. Why now? Was it anything to do with her new job?

As the evening's temperature continued its steady drop, she raised the collar of her coat and grumbled a fresh curse. What was a twenty-minute ride home would be an hour-long walk with her limping bicycle.

"Aubrey!" she shouted, nearly tripping over her brother's boots. Once again, despite being told countless times, he'd kicked them off just inside the door. She leaned her bicycle against the wall and scooped up Susan. The wriggling kitten nuzzled her nose and chin. Harriet delighted in the tiny animal's abiding affection—the one constant in her day that never failed to give her pleasure.

An hour later, she pulled two baked potatoes from the oven and yelled, "Dinner!" at Aubrey's closed bedroom door. Several long minutes later, he shuffled from his room, heading straight for the kitchen.

"I'll thank you to go and wash your hands," Harriet scolded. "It's a rule in this house, not an option."

He rolled his head and groaned but turned toward the bathroom. He returned with hands raised for inspection. "Happy?"

"Yes, dear brother. Nothing pleases me more than you

doing the bare minimum. Now then, how was school?" She examined his face through the steam rising from their plates. "I take it there was no further fisticuffs with Sherman Truss?"

With a mouth half full of potato, he said, "He wasn't there today. I think he's scared of Louisa's big brothers."

"It's a shame everyone can't just keep to their own business. Why Sherman must bully you, and then Louisa's brothers do the same to him . . ." She shook her head. "You remember what Father used to say about corporations and unions?"

Aubrey swallowed a gulp of milk. "Those who possess power should use it to lift others, not just themselves."

"Quite right."

Silence settled over the table. She didn't regret mentioning her father, but thoughts of either parent never failed to sadden them. Their father's passing had been pure anguish, then less than a month later, their mother had started coughing and was struck with a fever. She died shortly thereafter. The following year had been a blur. Harriet didn't remember much apart from standing next to Aubrey, her Aunt Charlotte, and Uncle Roy when on two different but eerily similar occasions, snow fell gently onto a parent's casket as men lowered it into the earth. After moving in with their aunt and uncle, the children changed schools, losing their friends. When she inherited the apartment years later, Aubrey insisted on moving back with her, over the objections of Aunt Charlotte and Uncle Roy.

Now that Harriet worked as a detective, Aubrey showed more interest in her employment than when she'd been a bookkeeper. Although proud of her accomplishments, she knew her brother too well to provide much detail lest he brag a much-embellished version to his schoolmates. However, she was too excited not to tell him she'd fired a gun earlier that day.

Aubrey dropped his fork onto his plate with a clang.

"Please close your mouth when it's full," Harriet admonished.

"A real gun? With bullets? Who'd you shoot?"

She swallowed hard, nearly choking on a bite of food. "Good heavens, Aubrey. I didn't shoot anyone. I was merely practicing. A fellow operative allowed me to accompany him to his gun club south of downtown. I learned how to handle the weapon and fire it properly." She didn't deny herself a moment's pride. "I'm not half bad, as it turns out. Mr. McCabe, the other operative, said so himself."

Aubrey gave Harriet a look, the meaning of which she understood. He wanted to ask whether she might be sweet on this fellow, Mr. McCabe. The topic of Harriet and boys—now men—was fraught. Aubrey had learned not to ask, never to tease. Harriet didn't know how to explain her preference for women to a sixteen-year-old boy in a way he might understand. The dilemma was made worse when he'd recently confided that he looked forward to her having a beau because he missed their father and Uncle Roy, and it would be nice to have someone to take him to ball games and other sporting events. Any offers Harriet had made to accompany him to such entertainments had been rebuffed—she would forever be a sister to him, a girl—and that role had limits.

Talk returned to the outing at the gun club, and once they had exhausted that topic, Aubrey retreated to his room and homework while Harriet tended Susan's sandbox and washed the dishes. How often had she sat at the table and watched her mother stand before the sink, cleaning up after a family meal? Although her mother had performed most of the household duties, hardly had she relegated herself to a life as a homemaker. She had told Harriet, "When people tell you that because you're a woman, you can't do this or that, take that as a challenge to do precisely what they presume you're incapable of doing."

Grandiose ambitions aside, she needed a good night's sleep. Tomorrow she'd return to Polish Downtown by streetcar and seek out Bogdan Nowak and Damian Swiatek. According to Barbara, Agnes hadn't shown interest in either man. But had that stopped them? Or had desire for the beautiful young woman compelled one of them to have her, nonetheless?

Chapter 15

The morning wind off the lake was fierce. Striding briskly, Harriet crossed the river and headed for Milwaukee Avenue. The Number 104 streetcar would take her northwest of the city's business center and into the heart of Polish Downtown. Although she preferred to travel by bicycle, two flat tires were two too many. Although she had extra tubes, the tools, and the know-how to make the repair, her tires had been destroyed. A visit to the shop to replace them would have to wait, and she'd have to ask the shop's owner to allow her to postpone payment until she received her wages.

Earlier that morning, Harriet had found a North Cleaver Street address for the Swiatek Sausage Factory in a *Chicago Blue Book* advertisement. Ready to transcribe the information into her notebook, she recalled slipping it into her desk drawer when startled by Sandra Small the day before. And so she had scribbled the address on a loose sheet of paper pulled from the back of Aubrey's school binder. She knew from Barbara Wozniak that Agnes's other suitor, Bogdan Nowak, did his dubious business from the back of a pool hall on Blackhawk Street. Figuring it was too early for the pool hall to be open for business, she decided to visit the factory first.

North Cleaver Street lay directly behind Holy Trinity Church, a block away from the Wozniaks' home. It would take Tomasz, Agnes's brother who worked at the factory, no more than five minutes to walk from place to place; the neighborhood was indeed compact. Since her last visit, she'd learned its Polish residents called the area Stanislowowo-Trojcowo after St. Stanislaus Kostka and Holy Trinity, two of the world's largest Catholic parishes, located blocks apart.

She'd have doubted her destination were it not for the address clearly printed on the advertisement. A residential flat faced the street; the business was hidden behind, accessed by a narrow walkway with no sign to help anyone find it. Despite the cold temperature, the door was ajar. Stepping inside, Harriet understood why. The large open space was uncomfortably warm. She couldn't remain in the room for long without removing her coat and hat. The heat was hardly the worst of it. Taking in the gruesome sight and dreadful smell, she'd never look at a slab of bacon or a pork chop the same way again.

So diligently did the men perform their various duties that her arrival went unnoticed. Under other circumstances, she might venture farther into the factory to attract someone's attention, but the pools of pink liquid on the floor caused her to shudder. Until the moment required it, she would save herself from scrubbing blood and bits of offal from her shoes and skirt.

Her relief in catching a man's eye was short-lived; he waved her over to where he stood on the other side of the room. Hiking her skirt, she tiptoed toward him, carefully avoiding the largest pools of muck.

The man grinned, watching her approach. "*Czy mogę ci pomóc?*"

"I'm sorry, but I don't speak Polish."

Still grinning, he said, "Can I help you?" Despite his heavy accent, she understood him well enough.

"I am looking for Damian Swiatek."

He replied with an exaggerated formal bow. Harriet noted that Damian matched Barbara's description, not handsome but not unappealing—which, although nonspecific, suited him perfectly. His pale blue eyes conveyed kindness, and his lanky frame and ropy arm muscles likely found favor among a good number of women in the neighborhood.

"Is there someplace we can talk privately?" she asked.

The request for privacy might have elicited a serious expression, but Damian's smile was unrelenting—he seemed utterly delighted to see her. "Please say whatever you like. There are no secrets here. Besides, there is nowhere to go." He spread his arms in welcome. "Please."

Knowing that Agnes's brother, Tomasz, would likely be one of the other four men present, she lowered her voice. She didn't want to draw him into the conversation—not yet.

"My name is Harriet Morrow, Mr. Swiatek. I've come on behalf of Lakeshore Domestic Help. Our service placed Miss Agnes Wozniak into the household of Mrs. Pearl Bartlett. I understand you are an acquaintance of Miss Wozniak, and I'm wondering if you have recently seen her?"

Damian's reaction to hearing Agnes's name was unmistakable—he looked miserable.

"Whatever your reason for looking for Agnes, why come here?"

Repeating the fiction she'd told Barbara the day before, Harriet said, "I'm following up with Miss Wozniak about her present job as a maid with a private household. Miss Wozniak left the house some days ago and has yet to return. While I hope her absence proves to be merely a misunderstanding, our service owes her employer, Mrs. Bartlett, an explanation. Should we need to replace her with another maid, we'd prefer to do so sooner rather than later."

"Okay, I get that. But again, why come here?"

Realizing too late that she must do a better job suiting

her fiction to the individual she was interviewing, she said, "Yes, of course, a fair question. A fair question indeed."

"Did you mean to speak with her brother? Tomasz works here."

Grateful for being rescued, she said, "Yes. Precisely. But as a courtesy, I wanted first to ask your permission to have a word with him. He is, after all, an employee on the clock."

"So you're saying Agnes hasn't been at work either?"

Harriet smiled reassuringly. "Where she has gone remains to be seen, Mr. Swiatek. But Miss Wozniak is not where she ought to be, which is at work for our client, Mrs. Bartlett. Any information that might help me locate Agnes will be appreciated." Presuming Damian cared for Agnes, Harriet added, "I would hate for her to lose a good-paying job at a fine household if it can be helped."

Damian shook his head so vigorously that Harriet worried he might strain a neck muscle. "She should have been home yesterday. Tomasz will tell you. Her family doesn't know where she is. I was at the house yesterday and could tell they were worried. I argued that we should be doing something. Notify the police. Start looking for her." He scoffed. "The old man grew angry and told me to leave. Said it was none of my concern." He shook his head again, this time showing anger. "Tomasz walked me outside and promised to relay any news"—his eyes shifted to a fit, dark-haired young man across the room—"but there still hasn't been any. But go ask him yourself. I don't mind. Anything to help find Agnes."

Damian's distress appeared genuine. Could he be so good an actor to have abducted Agnes and now portray such convincing concern? Although doubtful, she needed to be sure.

"I appreciate that, Mr. Swiatek, and I will. But first, another question, if you don't mind."

He nodded. "If it helps bring Agnes home, ask anything you like."

"Mrs. Bartlett last saw Agnes in her kitchen last Friday night after supper and first noticed she was missing the following morning. I don't suppose you were anywhere near there? The home is on Prairie Avenue just south of downtown."

"I don't know where Agnes works. Just that it's a big fancy house somewhere south of here and near the lake. I don't leave the neighborhood much. No reason to."

"So I take it you were here from last Friday evening to the next morning?"

Damian winced. "You can't think I had something to do with Agnes being missing."

"I'm only trying to find her before we have no choice but to dismiss her. Not only will she never again work for Lakeshore, but all the leading domestic employment agencies trade information. I'm afraid the odds of Agnes ever finding good employment again as household help will be impossible."

"Don't get me wrong. I don't doubt Agnes does a fine job. But you seem to be going to an awful lot of trouble to find a maid."

Harriet nodded, thinking. "Quite right. While we would normally inquire with the family, that would be the extent of it. However, in this case, we're dealing with Agnes's employer, Mrs. Bartlett, who has become terribly attached to her maid. The woman isn't one to easily trust— or please. Agnes impressed on both counts. Frankly, doing a little leg work to find Agnes promises to save the service the considerable effort of finding a replacement that meets with Mrs. Bartlett's satisfaction." She smiled and leaned closer. "Trust me, it's a nearly impossible task. Agnes has a rare knack."

Assuaged that he wasn't under direct suspicion, he said, "Last Friday we had a concert at Holy Trinity Church. I sing in the Chopin Choir. My entire family was there. After the concert, we all went home. The next morning I was here, starting at five as usual."

"You all live in the same house?"

Damian beamed. "All thirteen of us. My parents, grand-parents, brothers, and sisters."

Returning a smile, Harriet said, "Must be a big house."

"If only it were. I share a room with my three brothers. Only two beds."

Harriet glanced across the factory to Agnes's brother. After thanking Damian for his time, she hiked her skirt and made her way to where Tomasz stood snipping casing ends. She introduced herself as a representative of the employment service.

From Tomasz, Harriet learned that Barbara had told the family about her visit to the house the day before. When she asked about his boss and Bogdan Nowak, he dismissed both men as possible husbands for his sister but for different reasons. He said Damian was "a good fellow, but Agnes wouldn't give him the time of day," adding, "he'd never do anything to harm anyone, especially not Agnes. He's mad for her." Of Nowak, he said, "Now, he's someone to steer clear of. Agnes finds him detestable. But Nowak's got money. He helps fund the Polish Roman Catholic Union. You don't know my father. That's all the reason he needs to give Nowak his blessing."

Harriet noted the consistency in the siblings' stories and asked if Nowak's wealth or his support of the Catholic Union earned his father's favor. Tomasz replied, "Both," then described the bitter rivalry between the Union, which espoused a strict view of Catholicism, and the Alliancists, represented by the Polish National Alliance, who sought to establish a Polish nation by reclaiming land from Germany, Russia, and Austria-Hungary. That there were two factions of Polish immigrants working against each other seemed to Harriet counterproductive. Were her father alive, she knew what he'd say: *The community should be united in fighting for better wages and working conditions!*

"And your boss, Mr. Swiatek," Harriet asked, "is he a supporter of the Unionists or the Alliancists?"

Tomasz chuckled. "Damian is a sausage maker, nothing more, nothing less. His father and brothers, however, are stanch Alliancists."

"I'm curious, Mr. Wozniak. Why has your father not gone to the police? Nearly a week has passed since Agnes was last seen. Surely he wants them to be searching for her?"

"Nowak." Tomasz spat the word like a curse. "He told my father not to involve them."

"But why?" Harriet's raised voice caused heads to turn in their direction.

As if compensating for Harriet's outburst, Tomasz lowered his voice. "It's well known that Nowak is a criminal. Gambling, extortion, lending money at impossible-to-repay interest rates, the list goes on. He keeps the police out of his business by contributing to our local ward boss."

Also as Barbara had explained.

"Yes, but that still doesn't answer my question—why not involve the police in Agnes's disappearance?"

"The last thing Nowak wants is the police sniffing around the neighborhood, asking questions. He pays a lot of money to keep them from doing just that. As for any worry about Agnes, my father thinks she's acting like a child, trying to prove her independence. He doesn't believe she's in any real danger."

In response, Harriet pointed out that by all indications, Agnes had been abducted.

"My father believes what is convenient. He is quick to dismiss any fact that conflicts with his convictions."

Harriet bristled with anger. His father's assertion seemed absurd, and he was doing nothing to find his daughter. Was his inaction intended to ingratiate himself with Agnes's wealthy suitor? Or was he scared of Nowak? Whatever the reason, Harriet wouldn't be crossing paths with the police in her search for the missing maid anytime soon. While she wouldn't have to explain herself or justify her actions to the authorities—who presumably would know what they were doing—the fact that she was Agnes's only hope was daunting.

Before leaving the factory, Harriet asked Tomasz a final question. Trying to recall the words she'd written her notebook, she said, "*Yesh-tesh pee-enk-nah*. It is Polish, yes? Can you tell me what it means?"

"*Jesteś piękna*," Tomasz said effortlessly, then smiled. "Are you flirting with me, Miss Morrow?"

"What?" She sputtered, worried she'd gotten the words embarrassingly wrong. "No. I'm sorry . . . I don't . . ."

"I'm just teasing." He chuckled. "*Jesteś piękna*. It means *you are beautiful*."

Chapter 16

Harriet walked the seven blocks from the Swiatek Sausage Factory to Blackhawk Street, strolling slowly while looking for a sign indicating a pool hall on an upper floor. Fortunately, a crude illustration of two crossed pool cues compensated for her understanding only two words of Polish—none of which she anticipated seeing in reference to her destination. She climbed the creaking staircase, passing yellowed posters depicting sporting events, boxing, basketball, and football mainly, the wording indecipherable and unpronounceable. Cigar and tobacco fumes stung her nose halfway up to the second-floor landing. Perhaps because of the word *hall*, she'd expected a larger room than the one she discovered when she reached the top landing. Light filtering through dusty street-facing windows spilled across four quiet green-felt-topped tables. Three unshaven men sat murmuring at a card table, playing a game she didn't recognize. At the opposite end of the room, deep in shadows, sat someone behind a desk. The newspaper before him hid everything but the top of his bushy black hair.

The men watched with curiosity as Harriet snaked her way between the tables toward the man sitting at the back. Hearing footsteps approach, he barked, "*Nie teraz.*"

While not wanting to antagonize the man, she had no intention of leaving—guessing at what he'd said. With only a few days to prove herself to Theodore Prescott, she squeezed her handbag, took a steadying breath, and said, "Good day, sir. I'm looking for Mr. Bogdan Nowak."

The man dropped the paper, revealing eyes wide with surprise. It seemed he hadn't expected a woman or someone who spoke in English—probably neither.

"Who the hell are you?" The man, presumably Bogdan Nowak, had a heavy accent like Damian Swiatek, but the similarities ended there. Whereas she'd understood Damian without effort, she struggled to comprehend Nowak's words through meaty red lips surrounded by a voluminous black beard. So long and unruly were his hair and whiskers that she imagined he hadn't seen a barber in many months.

"My name is Harriet Morrow. I've come on behalf . . ." She repeated the fictitious story of being with the domestic employment service and asked if he had seen Agnes recently. His cold stare caused Harriet to shift her weight uncomfortably. Barbara had said Bogdan Nowak was a beast, and Tomasz claimed he was a criminal. Still, Harriet hadn't anticipated a palpable hostility. Not only did the man exude violence, but she suspected it came easily to him. At that moment, she realized her previous good fortune—others she'd interviewed had been forthcoming and nonthreatening. How did experienced operatives deal with dangerous and uncooperative suspects? Perhaps working under the protective wing of a senior operative wasn't such a bad idea after all. Had Matthew or Carl been there, she could observe their approach and learn from their methods. On her own, she would need to make it up as she went and hope for the best.

Despite trembling knees, she set her shoulders and stood tall. "I asked if you have seen Agnes recently. Have you?"

When nearly another minute passed in silence, she exhaled the breath she'd been unconsciously holding and, trying for a confident tone, said, "Agnes's father, Mr. Wozniak, was enthusiastic when hearing of my plan to visit you. It would seem you have won his favor. I'm sure he'll be eager to hear the particulars of our meeting. Now then . . ." Harriet hoped the mention of Mr. Wozniak would shake loose Nowak's tongue, but he continued to sit and stare, though his expression had softened from fierce to unreadable.

As the seconds ticked by, her discomfort increased. With no claim to parry or argument to rebut, it was tantamount to facing a massive flat wall. If the man refused to speak with her, there was nothing she could do. As much as she hated to accept such an awkward and decisive defeat, she turned to leave.

"Tell me what you know," he commanded.

His abruptness startled her. She turned back.

"You come to my place of business, you should know that I ask the questions. You will tell me what you know. And you will do it now."

Swallowing hard and holding on to her nerve, she said, "I know Agnes has been unaccounted for for six days and that no one has come forward with any information about her whereabouts. That is the extent of my knowledge, Mr. Nowak. Perhaps if we worked together, we might make progress. Do you have any idea about what might have happened to her?"

Nowak lit a cigar, took three gentle puffs, and settled back in his chair, his muscular shoulders flexing beneath a tailored suit too expensive for the environs. His cold stare returned, apparently his natural expression.

Trying again, she said, "Is there not anything you would have me tell Mr. Wozniak?"

Nowak blew acrid smoke across the desk. She fought the urge to cough and turn away but couldn't stop her eyes from tearing. She waited, standing her ground, and was rewarded two puffs later. "That girl doesn't know what's good for her. She's lucky her father and I know better. This'll all be sorted out when she comes back." Like a locomotive put in motion, Nowak now conversed with little effort.

"You seem confident Agnes will return. Might I ask why that is?"

"The girl knows nothing about the way the world works. She thinks she has some say. But Piotr and I, we have an understanding." A sinister grin lifted the corners of Nowak's unkempt mustache. "The girl's pretty and young. Those are two things I happen to like. Because of that, I'm willing to put up with a bit of trouble. But only a bit. I'm not a patient man."

Harriet listened hard to understand Nowak's words and discern his meaning. Could Agnes be hiding from her father and Nowak to escape a forced marriage? She supposed it was possible, but that didn't account for the state of her bedroom. And why the window? Why not use the front door? Pearl Bartlett went to bed early and was hardly a sentry. But if what Nowak said was true—that Agnes would "come back"—that left a question: where had she gone? And for how long would she stay away? She couldn't hide forever. She had no money to speak of and would surely miss her family.

"And what if she doesn't return?" Harriet said. "Supposing you wanted to find her, where would you look?"

"Piotr invited me to join the family for dinner a few weeks back. It was a Wednesday. Agnes is there on Wednesdays. One of the twins, Marek or Marcin"—he snorted and shrugged again—"can't tell one from the other, teased Agnes about some man she'd liked the look of. Seems she'd seen this fella at the old lady's house she cleans. Agnes denied it. Got hopping mad, saying it wasn't true. But it didn't matter what she said. I saw the way she was acting."

"And how was that?"

"Like it was true. You don't know me, Miss Morrow, but I can spot a liar. It's one of my many talents." He grinned, displaying a set of teeth yellowed from tobacco.

"Did you ever learn who this other man was?"

Nowak stretched an arm across the desk and tapped his cigar on a tin tray. "Like I say, Agnes wouldn't admit it. But then, it doesn't much matter."

"Perhaps with Agnes missing, now it does."

"Should that be the case"—he took another long puff on his cigar—"you'd better find Agnes before I find that man." He raised the newspaper with the finality of a closing stage curtain. The conversation was over.

Approaching the men at the card table, Harriet again attracted curious looks. One of them, a redheaded man, said something in Polish, causing the others to snicker. Abruptly, the man pushed his chair into her path. She jumped back as he lunged for her. The other men hooted. She ran in the other direction, around a pool table toward the exit. Frantic, she raced down the steps, refusing to look back and risk tumbling down the staircase.

Safe on the sidewalk, Harriet gulped fresh air. *Damnation*, she cursed. She may never know how Mr. McCabe or Mr. Somer might have better handled the situation upstairs, but she knew for certain that they'd not have had to escape down a narrow set of stairs in a stupid skirt!

Adrenaline surging, she was already walking fast before deciding on a direction. Although she'd escaped any harm, she understood why operatives carried guns. Disgusted as she was by Bogdan Nowak and the other men, she was also angry with herself. What had she been thinking? Venturing into the pool hall alone had been reckless. Compounding the danger, no one at the agency even knew her whereabouts.

As an adolescent, Harriet had been intrepid, unafraid of attempting any feat performed by boys—sometimes besting them. On one occasion, when Harriet was thirteen, she joined the neighborhood boys in a mock bank robbery by Butch Cassidy and his Wild Bunch gang. As the only girl, Harriet was given the role of Ann Bassett and charged with protecting the hideout at Robber's Roost. Not about to be left behind in the neighbor's chicken coop while the gang stormed a recently burned building at the end of the block, she proclaimed herself Kid Curry and infuriated the boy playing Butch by outracing him to lead the attack. During the gang's bold heist, she was the only member of the gang brave enough to scramble on hands and knees into the charred and hollowed-out cellar to fill an empty burlap potato sack with make-believe cash from the vault.

Days of childish derring-do had been replaced by acts with real life-threatening consequences. Her boldness was an asset, but it could be her undoing if left unchecked. She knew that. And yet all evidence suggested Agnes Wozniak had been taken, and Harriet was the only person searching for her. Now Harriet had a new worry—nothing to do with her failing but her success. Would finding Agnes doom the young woman to a life with Bogdan Nowak?

Chapter 17

Another nickel—the streetcar fare was adding up. Harriet scolded herself for not thinking to raise the matter of expenses with Theodore Prescott. Until her bicycle tires were replaced, she'd need to ensure she had plenty of coins in her purse.

Entering the room of secretaries, Harriet attracted raised brows. She imagined their thoughts: *while we've been at work for hours, where have you been?* That none seemed to support her—another woman—trying to prove the role of operative could be performed by one of them was discouraging. If she were older, would they dismiss her as past her prime? If she were pretty, would they attribute her winning the role to good looks? Unproductive as her ruminations were, she couldn't shake them. She wanted to stomp her feet and shout, *Women will never get the vote or have any hope of achieving equal footing with men if you content yourselves with typing reports for men!* Harriet thought no less of Madelaine, Sandra, and the others for accepting jobs in front of typewriters. Instead, she felt frustrated that most women of her generation hadn't been encouraged to imagine more for themselves.

Vexed, she plopped onto her chair and opened a desk drawer. A long moment passed, and she opened another.

Then another, until she returned to where she started. Her notebook wasn't there. She sat back, mentally retracing her steps. Was she confused? Had she moved it without thinking? She snatched up her handbag and pawed its contents. She looked under her chair and desk, as silly as that was. Exhausting the possibilities was natural, but she'd known the truth when seeing the first drawer was empty. Someone had taken her notebook.

Harriet glanced around the room. Sandra Small had watched her put it in the drawer. Giving her the evil eye was one thing, but Harriet couldn't fathom the woman stealing from her. Madelaine? The receptionist? One of the other secretaries? The only two operatives she'd met were Matthew McCabe and Carl Somer. That Matthew would snatch her notebook was inconceivable, and while Carl had at first been rude and argumentative, she couldn't believe he would sneak into the room and rifle through her desk drawers. Her greatest concern now was what to do about it. Would Mr. Prescott believe her? Regardless, she didn't want an accusation of a thieving colleague to be her introduction to most of her fellow operatives. She might confide in Matthew McCabe but would otherwise keep silent. However, she'd be on guard and not leave anything valuable in her unlocked desk again. Not until she understood what was going on.

Harriet needn't have bothered removing her hat and coat. She was already back on the sidewalk, marching toward the elevated train to whisk her near Pearl Bartlett's mansion. Bogdan Nowak claimed to have witnessed an exchange between Agnes and one of her brothers, suggesting a man at Agnes's place of employment had won her admiration. Harriet had listed the names of four workers who frequented Pearl's property in her missing notebook, but Pearl had convinced her that none warranted suspicion. In addition, the handyman, Gunther Clausen, and Pearl's grandnephew, Johnny Bartlett, had drawn Harriet's interest, but after interviewing them, she became doubtful of their guilt. She now worried she had been too quick to dismiss them as suspects.

When the mansion's front doorbell went unanswered, Harriet didn't hesitate. She trudged across the lawn to the back of the house. Music could be heard from the garden, but the tune was unidentifiable. On the other side of the orangery's glass wall, Pearl, an orchid in her hair and wearing a man's flannel housecoat, sang with abandon and danced about the room.

Inside the house, Harriet immediately recognized the song, "Sweetheart May." When the recording—and Pearl— finally went quiet, Harriet said, "What a lovely voice you have."

"Pish-posh," Pearl replied, though her smile suggested she was flattered. "Once. Perhaps when I was young. But I do enjoy singing. This may sound silly, but I believe singing for a minimum of thirty minutes each day does wonders for one's health."

"Physically or spiritually?"

"Ha!" Pearl wagged a finger at Harriet. "Good point, Harry. Good point. Both, I should think. Had my husband been willing to sing a few bars instead of spending so much time in them, he might still be around. You don't look happy, Harry. What's bothering you?"

"Pearl, you do realize my name is Harriet?"

Pearl frowned, but the expression appeared to convey confusion, not displeasure. Fiddling with the phonograph, she said, "I am also Mrs. Bartlett, yet you call me Pearl."

Baffled, Harriet replied, "But both are your names, and you asked that I call you Pearl."

"Not my point, dear. Pearl suits me. Harry suits you." She perused a carton of records on a shelf, searching for her next musical selection. "Do you disagree?"

The remark surprised Harriet. Not only was it bold, but there was truth to it. On several previous occasions when Pearl had referred to her as Harry, she hadn't corrected her. Each was a rare moment when she imagined herself free from the assumptions that went with a female name and persona. In that instant, she was ever so slightly more herself—it was indescribably satisfying.

Slipping a record onto the phonograph's cylinder, Pearl said, "You're about the same size as my late husband. I never got rid of his clothes. Not because I was grief-ridden or nostalgic, nothing like that. I just never got around to the chore of packing them up and finding them a suitable home. For the entire twenty-seven years of our marriage, we had separate bedrooms. We never had children, which is to be expected when you never share a bed. We each had other interests. None of that is to say we weren't happy. But it was a happy arrangement more than a happy marriage. Remember that, Harry. There's more than the expected way to live your life. Be creative. It may not set you free, but it might provide you with enough freedom to be yourself. Anyhoo, his clothes are all still upstairs in his wardrobe. You're welcome to anything you like."

The phonograph's horn projected two seconds of sharp crackling before the sounds of an orchestra filled the orangery. Harriet stood frozen in place. She understood Pearl perfectly, and her meaning was shocking. She barely knew this woman, yet she knew Harriet better than her own brother did. She also thought she understood why.

When the music ended, Harriet cleared her throat. "I've come about Agnes."

"Who?"

Again Harriet sputtered to a stop, speechless.

Pearl burst out laughing. "Good lord, Harry. I'm not batty. Of course, you have. I figured you haven't found her since she's still not here."

Grateful that Pearl accepted the change of topic, Harriet recounted what she'd learned in the past two days. Pearl listened intently; her expression shifted from dismay to delight and back depending on the nature of the news.

"You're wasting your time," Pearl said, referring to the newspaper delivery boy and the three men who regularly visited the property. "As for Gunther"—she pointed toward the ceiling—"he's moved to the roof, replacing tired shingles now. The man is meticulous, but good lord is he ever slow. Seems harmless, but then I don't know much about him if I'm honest. You've met the man. I don't see him snatching Agnes from her bed. Do you?"

Harriet agreed, though her doubts rested primarily on Gunther not fitting through the third-floor bedroom window. Turning the conversation to Johnny, she said, "I know you doubt your grandnephew had anything to do with Agnes's disappearance, but I must ask, did they ever spend time alone together? As a maid, she answered the door, took his coat, served tea, etcetera. I understand that. But had they ever been alone? Perhaps occasionally when you stepped out or were somewhere else in the house?"

"You think my Johnny stole my maid from her bed in the middle of the night?"

Hearing Pearl say it so succinctly, it did sound farfetched. And yet, someone did just that. Why not Johnny? "I must presume everyone a suspect until I can rule them out with certainty. Before, you said he lived north of the river on Dearborn Avenue. Have you ever visited him there?"

"Ha! Dracaena, Parlor Palm, Golden Pothos, English Ivy. Every winter and summer."

"Aren't those all plants?"

"Of course they are. What else would they be?"

"I'm confused, Pearl. What are you saying?"

"Johnny hates the cold. Johnny hates the heat. He takes weeks-long vacations each season. I look after his plants while he's away. But now that I have Agnes, I sent her last time."

Harriet gasped. "Pearl!"

The older woman jumped at the outburst. "Good grief, Harry. What's got into you?"

"Why didn't you say anything about that? I asked you specifically about any encounters between Johnny and

Agnes. How could you have neglected to tell me you sent Agnes to Johnny's apartment?"

Looking stung, Pearl defended herself. "You did no such thing!"

Harriet pinched the bridge of her nose and sighed loudly, not caring that Pearl would notice.

"No, you did not! You asked whether Johnny and Agnes spent time here at my house. Not his."

"But surely . . ." She shook her head. "When was this? When did you send Agnes?"

"Two months ago. Johnny was in Charlotte. Or so he claimed. But Agnes never saw him. He never saw her. As far as I know, he doesn't even know it was Agnes who tended to the plants and not me."

"Did Agnes report anything unusual about the visits? Anything at all? It's important, Pearl. Try to remember."

"There's nothing wrong with my mind, Harry. I can re-member just fine, thank you. The answer is 'no.' She went once a week for one month. She watered the houseplants. The end."

"How did she get inside his apartment?"

"I have a key, of course. A ridiculously large skeleton key. You could use the thing for a hammer. I keep it with all the others on a pegboard by the back door."

"What is Johnny's exact address?"

"So my vouching for him isn't enough to satisfy you?"

"I understand the faith you have in Johnny's character. He's a relation, and you're fond of him. But I'm a detective charged with finding Agnes. I am inclined to doubt, not trust. It is expected we have different perspectives."

Pearl pursed her lips, stood quietly for a moment, then said, "As you should!" Further surprising Harriet, she strode from the room, shouting over her shoulder, "Come along, Harry. You and I have a wardrobe to clear."

Chapter 18

Harriet looked up from where she stood at the side of the three-story mansion. Gunther had propped one tall ladder against the house to access a stone awning over the dining room. From there, a second ladder reached the roof. Had Harriet not spent the past half hour selecting articles of men's clothing to pack into a large suitcase under Pearl's close supervision, she might have caught Gunther before he climbed to the roof to begin his repairs for the day. Harriet liked to think herself unafraid of most things, but regardless of the ladders' sturdiness, she was unnerved by heights.

Don't look down, she told herself, glad she wasn't in a race. To fortify her resolve, she imagined Sandra Small and the other secretaries watching her climb, incredulous and arms crossed; with every rung ascended, Harriet further disproved their doubts. Scrambling onto the roof, she crouched as if that would lessen the possibility or severity of a fall. Gunther was nearby, head down and on all fours, prying loose a worn shingle. Hearing someone, he turned and nodded as if expecting her. That he was naturally untalkative boded well; the encounter on the steeply pitched roof would at least be brief.

"I'm sorry to interrupt your work, Mr. Clausen. I've come again about Mrs. Bartlett's maid. I am speaking with everyone who has come into contact with Agnes since she began her work here. It's all quite standard to an investigation of this sort." Harriet didn't know if that were true, but she didn't want Gunther to feel as though he were being singled out. "It would be most helpful if you could tell me where you were at suppertime last Friday until the next morning?"

"Maid not found?"

Had she spoken any German beyond *danke* and *schnitzel*, she might risk a glib retort, but English was Gunther's second language, and he was doing an admirable job. After confirming that Agnes was still missing, she repeated her question.

His answer: "Home with wife."

"The entire time? Again, I am referring to the time between—"

"Home. With. Wife."

"Yes, of course. I mean no offense, Mr. Clausen. I'm simply making the necessary inquiries." Acting on reason and instinct alone, Harriet deduced that Agnes's abductor knew which room was hers and that it was accessible by the window. It further stood to reason that whoever it was had visited the house on at least one occasion.

Stepping down from the ladder, Harriet sighed in relief. It seemed Gunther had an alibi, but would his wife corroborate his story? To find out, she'd have to get to Mrs. Clausen before Mr. Clausen got home. However, that posed a problem: she didn't know where the Clausens lived and doubted Pearl knew.

Rounding the corner of the house, Harriet nearly tripped over Gunther's toolbox. He'd also shed his large, heavy coat and left it draped across the fence. She didn't hesitate.

An hour later, Harriet arrived at the Prescott Agency with a crumpled business card for Clausen Home Repairs she'd found in Gunther's coat pocket. The visit to the office was a time-consuming bother. Still, she needed to store the suitcase containing Pearl's late husband's clothing: two white shirts, the initials H.B. expertly stitched on the cuffs, a simple black suit crafted from quality wool, the label MARSHALL FIELD & COMPANY, four pairs of silk dress socks, three ties, and two coats, one for winter and another suitable for spring breezes. Regrettably, the case couldn't fit more; she'd had to leave behind Mr. Bartlett's collection of fine leather shoes. His hats, which required their own boxes, were too small for her head anyway.

Passing Matthew McCabe's office, she heard her name called. She pushed open the door and stuck her head inside. "How did you know it was me?"

Tapping his head, he grinned. "Yours is the only bowler traveling at that height and speed. You seem in a perpetual rush, Miss Morrow."

Despite being in a hurry, advice from an experienced operative could be helpful—she would be wise to spare the time. Besides, she liked Matthew and hoped they would become friends. After explaining that she had developed a list of suspects, but nothing pointed to just one person, she asked, "So, Mr. McCabe, I'm eager to know. Were you in my shoes, what would you do?"

Looking down at her feet, he said, "I've been meaning to ask . . ."

She chuckled. "I'll have you know, they're no less practical for a woman." She raised her long skirt a few inches and took a half step forward. "Hardly can I pedal properly or race down an alleyway in shoes with a woman's heel." Her smile added sparkle to her emerald green eyes. "Besides, you can't deny they're handsome."

"So you wouldn't mind if I were to purchase a pair of the same?"

She laughed outright. "Similar tastes, have we?"

He raised a brow, suddenly serious. "I've come to wonder, Miss Morrow, if we might not have something of greater significance in common."

"I'm afraid I don't take your meaning, Mr. McCabe." Her smile melted into concern.

"You are not married. Moreover, I don't think you are inclined to take a husband. That wouldn't suit you. Am I wrong?"

Harriet opened and closed her mouth, looking like a fish out of water. Although his comment conveyed no menace, it was bold, impolite. Never would she muster the audacity to say the same to him or any man—or woman, for that matter. Most alarming, could he possibly be referring to her most private secret? If so, why suspect her? She was only twenty-one; many women her age had yet to marry. She had no beau, but he didn't know that. He had never asked anything about her personal life. Obviously, she wore men's shoes and a man's hat, but from that alone, it was a mighty leap to assume she preferred women.

More shocking still, if she was right in reading his remark, was he insinuating that he was queer? Such an admission would be flabbergasting. She reassessed her colleague in light of the possibility. Did he seem the type who preferred men? Uncertain that she had ever crossed paths with a queer man, she drew upon her preconception of how such a man would present himself or give off signals of his secret nature: a feminine demeanor and perhaps a too-colorful attire. Matthew projected none of those qualities, making her wrong in either thinking he was queer or presuming all such men were the same. Were Harriet's secret revealed, she would be presumed to be involved in a romantic friendship considered a natural phase among upper- and middle-class women. But if a man were found out, he would be beaten and jailed.

After a long awkward moment, Matthew abruptly adopted a casual air. "I didn't intend to confound you, Miss Morrow. I was simply referring to our freedom from intimate entanglements. I am an operative, first and foremost. I've no time for competing interests. Your pursuit of this line of work led me to presume you were of the same disposition." He paused another long moment before filling the silence. "You thought I was speaking of another matter, perhaps?"

As much as she longed to divulge the part of herself she kept well hidden, it wouldn't be to a man she'd only just met. Besides, Mr. McCabe was a colleague. However he might explain his odd remarks, she sensed he was probing, testing her somehow. To determine if she were trustworthy? To lure her into a confession of some sort? For what reason? Despite knowing nothing was wrong with her, she knew physicians and psychologists would disagree. Calling same-sex attraction among women "lesbianism," medical authorities claimed the condition manifested primarily in two ways. Most common were sexual acts performed by prostitutes. The other was an abnormally masculine woman's dominance over a feeble-minded one. Harriet was none of those things. She simply liked women, and it infuriated her that men she'd never met presumed to know her heart. More maddening was that both explanations for lesbianism were predicated on the physical presence of a man or the strong suggestion of one. *The arrogance of men*, Harriet mused. *They think being lesbian is still about a man!*

To sidestep the topic, Harriet said, "We are indeed fortunate to be employed as operatives at the Prescott Agency. I'm looking forward to a long career here. But I'm getting ahead of myself. First, I must find the maid, Agnes Wozniak." She recounted her progress over the past twenty-four hours, concluding, "Given what you've just heard, I'd be interested to know where you would direct your energies. My time is running out. I must be efficient with every minute."

Matthew nodded, seeming to accept the change of subject. "You can hardly go wrong by following the passion, Miss Morrow. Love, lust, hatred, envy, greed, revenge . . . Those consumed by passion often lose control of their emotions. That's when most crimes occur. From what you say, the maid had two men vying for her affection. The sausage maker sounds harmless enough, but I don't much like the sound of that Bogdan Nowak character. I know you're eager to make your mark, Miss Morrow, but I don't think Mr. Prescott imagined you putting yourself in immediate danger."

"I'm simply making inquiries. I report my activities to Mr. Prescott daily. If he has any concerns, surely he will be the first to say so. To the contrary, he has urged me on, emphasizing my Monday deadline."

Matthew scratched his head, calling attention to the appealing waves of his thick red hair. "Yes, but when you ask questions of someone guilty of a crime such as kidnapping, they might react violently. You must be prepared."

"And you're saying I am not?"

"One outing to a gun range is hardly sufficient. Besides, you have no weapon."

Eager to change topics again, she told him about her vandalized bicycle and missing notebook.

Matthew appeared appropriately dismayed. "Nothing like that has ever happened to anyone here—not that I'm aware of, anyway. But still, believing what you say, you should think twice before leaving anything at your desk that you don't want taken."

"I'm keeping my new notebook with me from now on." She patted her handbag.

Matthew bunched his lips, showing concern. "The missing notebook is one thing, but the damage to your bicycle occurred outside these walls. The slashed tires could be unrelated to your investigation, but in this line of work, it's prudent to side with caution."

"I'm not averse to proceeding with care, Mr. McCabe."

"I would feel better if you had a pistol in that handbag alongside your notebook."

"But mustn't Mr. Prescott approve of my carrying a firearm? There's also the matter of the purchase. What should I buy and where?" While all she said was true, what most concerned Harriet was whether the agency or the operative was expected to pay for their own pistol. The five-dollar price she saw on the tag of a derringer at the gun club—the same model she had handled—was nearly the equivalent of two days' pay.

Matthew nodded. "You're correct. It's up to Mr. Prescott. But if you're free early tomorrow morning, we could return to the club for another round of shooting practice. Presuming you perform as well as last time, I will speak to Mr. Prescott on your behalf. The operatives' meeting is also tomorrow at ten o'clock. Afterward, we can discuss the matter with him."

No sooner had Harriet closed the door to Matthew's office than Carl Somer emerged from his. Wearing a coat and hat, he was apparently on his way out. Seeing Harriet, he winced, then put on a forced smile.

"Mr. Somer," she said, greeting him. "Having a good day, I trust?"

"Staying busy, are you?" he said, walking past her toward the lobby. She followed and hurried to his side; she would not be a woman who followed a step behind.

"I am making progress."

"You'll find Mr. Prescott values results."

Waiting for an elevator, they stood awkwardly, heads turned upward at the number indicating the floor. She said, "Surely progress is a requirement of a favorable result."

The doors opened, and despite the crowded compartment, Carl stepped in, causing a jostling among the ten occupants. Not to be left behind, Harriet squeezed in, too, eliciting a grumble from more than one stranger. When they reached the main lobby, and it became clear that Carl had no intention of speaking to her further, she hurried up beside him again. "Perhaps I can update you on my investigation after tomorrow's operatives meeting?" Harriet had no desire to impose herself on Carl, but if he were not current in his knowledge about her activities, it wouldn't be because of her lack of trying.

On the sidewalk, he stopped abruptly, seemingly irritated by her continued presence. "Shouldn't you be going the other way?"

Before she could respond, he strode off at twice his usual pace. *How odd*, she thought. Once again, Carl Somer proved to be pleasant at one encounter and surly the next. Harriet tried to shrug it off. It wasn't anything to do with her. Or was it?

An hour later, standing in front of a dilapidated five-story apartment building in the German neighborhood of Lakeview, Harriet searched the handwritten directory for the name Clausen. She found two—Apartments 5 and 9.

A plump woman in a housedress met her knock on the door of Number 5. "Yah?"

Harriet introduced herself and explained that she was looking for Mrs. Clausen, then remembering the other apartment, added, "the wife of Mr. Gunther Clausen." The woman's initial curiosity disappeared, replaced by disappointment. She pointed down the hall before shutting the door.

Harriet's second knock was answered by a woman so uncannily similar to the woman in the previous apartment that she wondered if a trick was being played on her. Her momentary confoundment was dispelled when the woman spoke with a deeper voice. Nodding when asked if she was Gunther's wife, she invited Harriet inside—but kept her close to the doorway. Sensing a short encounter, Harriet explained that she was with People's Gas Light and Coke Company and following up on a reported loss of service that started last Friday and continued to the following day. When Mrs. Clausen assured Harriet that there had been no disruption, Harriet asked, "And your husband? Perhaps he might have noticed something you didn't? Unless he was elsewhere at the time?"

"He was here," she said, attacking each word with determined, clipped precision.

"This past Friday night? You're quite sure?"

"It was my husband's brother's birthday. We had dinner here and stayed up late playing cards. Gunther and I went to bed when they left. Lights fine."

Harriet stepped onto the sidewalk, her mind conflicted. Had Mrs. Clausen not confirmed her husband's alibi, Harriet might have herself a prime suspect. On the other hand, she felt she'd made progress by finally crossing a name off her list. Considering her next step, Matthew had advised her to "follow the passion." Damian Swiatek's affection for Agnes seemed heartfelt, whereas Bogdan Nowak seemed more motivated by pride—proving he could get whatever he wanted, even a woman who loathed him. Then there was Johnny Bartlett. Although admiring Agnes's beauty, he denied taking an interest in her and turned angry when Harriet asked about his whereabouts at the time of her disappearance.

Follow the passion, she repeated to herself. But which was it? Love, pride, anger, or something else? Was one emotion more prone than another to evoke criminal behavior? Or could any passion run amok drive a person to abduct another?

Chapter 19

Gone. It couldn't be, and yet . . .

Harriet slowly lowered herself onto her chair. She needed a moment. *Breathe*, she told herself. There must be a reasonable explanation for why someone had taken the suitcase she had left beside her desk. Her gaze darted around the room. She had made fleeting eye contact with the secretaries when returning but hadn't detected any unusual looks, let alone a guilty one. As the day neared its end, the women appeared only listless. Unlike her notebook, which could be easily concealed, someone carrying the suitcase from the room couldn't have gone unseen.

Standing before the secretaries, Harriet raised a hand to gain their attention. Sandra Small and Marjorie Lancaster looked up. Head down and fingers tapping, Judith Middleton was too consumed in her work to notice. Harriet had admired Judith from the first moment she'd laid eyes on her. Tall and well-proportioned, Harriet imagined her comfortably spiking a volleyball or effortlessly stroking a backhand on a tennis court. It wasn't until Sandra called Judith's name, raising her voice above the sound of the clacking typewriter, that Judith raised her head.

Three sets of eyes fastened on Harriet. She said, "I'm

sorry to interrupt your work, ladies, but I left a suitcase sitting next to my desk. Perhaps one of you moved it for some reason?"

The women exchanged puzzled looks.

"Suitcase?" Marjorie's high-pitched, nasal voice suited her narrow face and bony frame. "That brown leather one you lugged in here earlier?"

Harriet's shoulders dropped, and she loosed a relieved sigh. "Thank heavens. You saw it then?"

"She just said she did," Sandra snapped. "We all did. Couldn't really miss it, now, could we? So what's the story? You between places? You don't seem like the kind of girl who'd move in with a fella."

There were two ways to read Sandra's remark, and Harriet chose to ignore them both. "I'm asking about afterward. Did you see anyone take the suitcase from the room?"

Marjorie shook her head. "No. But we all took our coffee break a half hour ago. I can't speak for the other girls, but I left the building and went for a walk around the block."

"And you?" Harriet looked at Sandra and Judith. "Did you leave the room?"

"Interrogating us now, are you?" Sandra scoffed, folding her arms.

"I went to the kitchen for a coffee," Judith answered, pronouncing *kaw-fee* like someone hailing from Boston. Harriet realized it was the first time she'd ever heard Judith speak.

Harriet's eyes fell on Sandra.

"Not that I owe you any explanation," Sandra said, "but I had an errand to run. Does that satisfy you?"

"I see," Harriet said, "so you all stepped out, leaving the room unattended. And when you returned? Did you see anyone? Did you notice the suitcase was missing?"

Sandra stood abruptly, the affront apparently too much

to take while seated. "I certainly hope you know better than to accuse someone who works here at the agency of stealing?"

"Of course I do," Harriet said, although that was precisely her thought. But arguing wouldn't help recover her missing belongings. Moreover, it might jeopardize the possibility of a cordial relationship with Marjorie or Judith, who, unlike Sandra, hadn't made it clear from the start that she was doomed to failure.

Judith said, "I'm *shore* it'll turn up. I once misplaced my gloves. Found them later that same day at the receptionist's desk."

Harriet forced a smile, appreciating Judith's attempt to reduce the tension and swallowing an urge to argue the difference. She returned to her desk, feeling wronged and outnumbered.

Twenty minutes later, her daily report in hand, Harriet approached Mr. Prescott's office. As much as she wished she could leave the file for Madelaine to pass along, the secretary couldn't be trusted. Harriet needed to speak with the agency's principal directly. True to form, Madelaine huffed and puffed about Mr. Prescott's busy schedule, insisting Harriet was better off leaving the report in her custody. To Madelaine's apparent bother, Harriet refused and stood waiting by Prescott's closed door.

Nearly an hour passed, during which Madelaine tried several more times to shoo Harriet away. Harriet was impressed by how seriously Madelaine took every facet of her job. The principal's secretary approached what might seem like perfunctory tasks with admirable zeal. Even the opening of a letter appeared to deserve unwavering precision. Harriet recalled Madelaine's clipped remark when showing her to a desk among the secretaries: *unless you think you're too good for the rest of us.* Harriet hadn't fully understood how those few words revealed Madelaine's reason for not wanting her there. Before her arrival, Madelaine had claimed the highest position attainable for a woman at the Prescott Agency. But the advent of a woman detective upset the established order. Still, Harriet didn't think personal rivalry stirred Madelaine's animosity. Instead, Harriet's presence signaled broader progress that some women found threatening.

Eventually, Prescott's door opened, and despite his surprise at seeing his most junior operative standing in the hallway, he ushered her inside. His welcoming demeanor didn't last long.

"Preposterous!" he replied, hearing about Harriet's missing notebook and suitcase. "You do realize, Miss Morrow, that your claim is tantamount to accusing an employee of this agency of thievery. Or do I misunderstand your claim?" He peered at her over his spectacles.

Harriet understood perfectly: this was her chance to withdraw the accusation. She'd do no such thing. Prescott might not like learning that someone on his payroll was meddling with her, but the fact remained. Moreover, he needed to do something about it. The challenges of succeeding in the job were steep enough without a colleague secretly working against her.

Taking a step closer to his desk, she suppressed the desire to raise her voice. While a man's vehemence reflected his fervent belief, such passion from a woman would be dismissed as histrionics. "My sincerest hope is that my possessions are returned along with an explanation that proves their taking was an innocent mistake. However, I don't see how a person mistakenly rummages through another's desk or removes a large suitcase that is not theirs."

She locked eyes with Prescott, refusing to wilt under his penetrating gaze. Had she gone too far? Was she about to be fired? Just last week, she was one of a dozen bookkeepers whose name was unknown to the business's owner. Now she was standing before the esteemed Theodore Prescott, principal of the famed Prescott Agency. What was she thinking by challenging the man in the first week of her employment? Yet what was the alternative? Pretend nothing had happened? Whoever had snatched her belongings would be emboldened. While she couldn't link the in-office thefts to the vandalism of her bicycle, she had her suspicions. If the culprit weren't found out, it was only a matter of time until his—or her?—undermining would lose her the job. She must stand up for herself. Everyone at the agency had to know she wouldn't be driven away so easily. She only hoped Mr. Prescott would respect her for it—just as he would were she one of his male operatives.

Prescott harumphed. Casually removing his spectacles, he raised them to the window's light and cleaned them with a small cloth. "Your items will reappear in good time, Miss Morrow. And when they do, you'll realize you misplaced them or another equally innocent explanation will come to light. Now, concerning Pearl Bartlett's missing maid, as curious as I am about how you've spent your day, you've exhausted what time I have. You may leave your report there." He pointed to the teak inbox on the corner of his desk. "And I'll remind you that tomorrow is our weekly operatives' meeting."

"Yes, sir. Ten o'clock. I won't be late."

"No, Miss Morrow. No, you will not."

On her way home, Harriet stopped by the bicycle shop— a place that never failed to make her heart beat faster. Although she adored her Victoria, admiring the newer Overman models and various accessories was a thrill. She described to Billy, the store's owner and her longtime friend, the damage someone had done to her bicycle. He pulled two new tires from a high shelf. Although Harriet told him she had extra tubes at home, he added a couple free of charge. She had long suspected he might harbor something of a crush; while she didn't want to encourage it, she saw no reason to make more of it as long he never acted on it.

Harriet had been without her bicycle for only a day, but she missed the freedom of going anywhere at a moment's notice. Never content to sit still for long, she reveled in the movement, the breeze on her face, and the reassuring grip of the handlebars. But there was another reason she was anxious to get her bicycle fixed. Since Harriet's visit the day before, the Wozniak family might have received news about Agnes. When Harriet returned, she was eager to offer Barbara Wozniak another ride on her bicycle as an excuse to spend more time with her.

Yesh-tesh pee-enk-nah. The words had knocked around in Harriet's brain nonstop since Barbara had whispered them in her ear. Harriet's attraction to the woman had been immediate and powerful. That it might turn into something was far-fetched. What could that something even be? In addition to the seeming impossibility of a romantic relationship with a woman, Barbara was of a different culture—not to mention Agnes's sister. She ought to banish such thoughts from her head. But whenever she tried, the image of Barbara's sky-blue eyes and the sound of her laughter crept back with unstoppable force.

Harriet's fingers felt fat as sausages as she fumbled with the second tire tube. She was excited but also in a hurry. The day wasn't over yet. With time ticking down, she'd make a quick supper for herself and Aubrey before returning to the Ali Baba Theater. Could anyone corroborate Johnny Bartlett's whereabouts on the night of Agnes's disappearance? Johnny, Damian Swiatek, and Bogdan Nowak remained on her list of suspects. While there could be others she didn't know about, with a Monday deadline looming, she had to play the hand she held. And although none of the three men had given anything away to suggest their guilt, she felt it in her bones: one of them had taken Agnes.

Chapter 20

"Surprised to see you here again." The female impersonator's sultry voice startled Harriet just as it had when they'd first met two days before. Unlike her initial visit to the Ali Baba Theater, Harriet didn't intend to seek out Johnny Bartlett. Instead, she wanted to learn whether anyone could confirm his presence there last Friday night, how long he'd stayed, and where he'd gone afterwards.

Harriet thrust out a hand. "I'm Harriet."

The impersonator stared at her hand for a long moment before extending his drooped fingers. "Gloria."

"A pleasure to meet you, Gloria."

"Is it? You don't seem . . . I wouldn't think the Ali Baba is your kind of place. I'm afraid you won't find what you're looking for here."

"I don't take your meaning." What *did* Gloria mean? One interpretation was obvious: the club catered to a boisterous working-class male crowd, who, if they desired, could slip away with a prostitute. Another—which she sensed was more on the mark—was that while the male clientele could find a variety of sexual companions, a woman desiring to meet a woman would end the night disappointed.

"I think you understand me perfectly," Gloria said, not

unkindly. "Mind you, here me and the other girls only perform on stage or sell drinks and cigarettes. Just part of the
front-of-house entertainment." As if a thought struck,
he added, "Johnny Bartlett. Weren't you looking for him
the other night?"

"That's right."

He chuckled, "Johnny, Johnny, Johnny. Most men who
come here work factory jobs and the like, but you do get
a few fancy men like him that get their kicks slumming."
He smiled wryly. "The bawdiness is titillating, but these
men here aren't really interested in girls like me. Not in
that way. Not most of them, anyway. We save that for the
rabbit."

Before Harriet could ask him to explain his remark, he
said, "He's here if you haven't already noticed. Usual
table."

"Yes, I see him. But what about last Friday night? Do
you recall seeing him then?"

Gloria narrowed his eyes. "Why not ask him yourself?"

Having no ready or compelling reason, Harriet tried,
"It's just a question from one woman to another."

The corners of Gloria's mouth twitched. The hint of a
smile? "When on Friday?"

"From the dinner hour on? What time does the club
close?"

Gloria snorted. "Close? You really are a babe in the
woods, aren't you? On the nights we're open, the Ali Baba
never sleeps. Sure, the theater dies down come one or two
in the morning, but that's when the basement booths are
most busy."

A jolt of adrenaline shot through Harriet. She had seen
women leading men through a side door. Prostitution was
not kidnapping, but might not one crime be proximate to
another? In that instant, Harriet knew she had to find a
way into the Ali Baba's basement—and better to do it before it grew late and more active. Something else hung in
the space between them. Gloria had said, "Here we only

perform on stage . . . most men aren't interested. We save that for the rabbit." Although he hadn't stated it explicitly, he suggested there was another place where he did more with men who were interested. Harriet wanted very much to know where that place was; a place where men met men might also be a place where women met women. And what had Gloria meant by "the rabbit"?

"So you work at another theater?" Harriet asked, hiding the excited quiver in her voice. "Where might that be?"

Gloria looked into Harriet's eyes, seeming to search for her honest intention. After a long moment, he shook his head. "Listen, you seem harmless enough, Harriet. But I can't help you. As for Johnny, Fridays are the one night of the week he doesn't come here. On the other nights the club is open, Wednesday through Saturday, he usually shows up around nine and drinks with his mates for a few hours." Gloria squeezed Harriet's arm gently and smiled, showing a bit of red lipstick on an upper tooth. "I do hope you find whatever it is you're looking for, Harriet." He then strolled off toward the bar, hips swaying, leaving her standing alone against the wall.

Harriet was determined to find Gloria's other haunt, but first things first. Was Agnes's abduction connected to the business that went on in the basement? She bought a cheap drink from a waitress working the crowd—reminding her again to ask Mr. Prescott about reimbursement for expenses—and sidled up to the door she presumed led to the basement. And waited.

Two musical numbers later, a woman appeared on stage to thunderous applause and hoots of approval. Lila Lola, as introduced by the master of ceremonies, was joined by the two exotically dressed musicians she had seen during her first visit. One carried a drum, the other, that oddly shaped stringed instrument. The musicians began to play. Lila Lola jutted her hips seductively from side to side, adding an occasional forward thrust that caused the audience to whistle and pound the tables, sloshing alcohol over the rims of their glasses. The music crescendoed, and Lila Lola spun in a dizzying circle; her knee-length skirt fanning out and calling attention to a sheer black underskirt and shapely calves hugged by white silk stockings. Equally scandalous was the flowered necklace, which she shook provocatively, arms held out to her sides, drawing attention to her ample bosom. Several men at tables nearest the stage leaped from their chairs and cheered, hands cupped to their mouths.

Sensing her moment, Harriet slipped through the side door.

The abruptly dampened sound and dimly lit corridor felt like she'd entered a secret and sinister realm. She stood, getting her bearings. The door at one end of the long hallway must lead to the alley behind the theater. The other end was enveloped in darkness. She headed toward it.

With her handbag over her shoulder, she extended a hand to avoid walking into a wall. Ten steps later, her fingers met soft, tacky fabric. A curtain. She found the opening and stepped through. Just ahead of her, a staircase descended to a pool of dull yellow light. Down she went. The explosion of claps and shouts in the theater erased any worry she might have had about squeaking steps. Lila Lola had apparently finished her number.

A room the size of her apartment lay at the bottom of the steps, illuminated by two gas lamp sconces on opposite walls. Several sofas were positioned against the walls. A patchwork quilt of threadbare oriental rugs further dampened the sound and created a bohemian feel. Beyond the room was another corridor lined with doorways occluded by more curtains. Harriet shuddered. That women worked here was nearly impossible to fathom, yet, for many, this was their reality, day in, day out.

"You lost?"

Harriet spun around. A woman about her age stared back with large brown eyes, her lids painted a thick charcoal gray.

"I was looking for my friend," Harriet sputtered.

"And what kind of friend is that?" The woman tilted her head, stepped closer, and smiled mischievously. Her sweet musky scent filled Harriet's nostrils.

Harriet jerked back. "Just a friend . . . Billy. I lost sight of him in the theater some time ago. I thought he might have come down here."

"And what if Billy did come down? What business is that of yours?"

Harriet realized she hadn't thought this through. She had acted impulsively and now needed to improvise, hoping she didn't spin a tale too wild. Her mind raced. Sister? Sweetheart? Friend? None of those associations would pander to the woman. Trading on her subtle offer, she surprised herself by saying, "Billy enjoys unconventional entertainments. On occasion, he enjoys my participation. Sometimes, he prefers to observe."

The effect of Harriet's remark was instantaneous; the woman's smile widened. "Well, well, well. I'd like to meet this Billy of yours. Your unusual clothing made me wonder about you. But never did I imagine *your* interests. You said Billy came down to the Depths."

Now it was Harriet's turn to show surprise.

"That's what we call this place. Once you end up here, you can't go any lower." She chuckled ruefully.

Having a moment to collect her thoughts, Harriet said, "Billy's favorite is a Polish girl. Pretty. Petite. About twenty years of age. I recall him calling her Agnes, though I can't be certain she always goes by that name. I don't suppose you've seen her?"

"Polish?" The woman shook her head. "There's a couple of German girls, but they're both older, and I doubt anyone has called them *petite* since elementary school."

The door at the top of the staircase opened, momentarily admitting the cacophony from the theater. Harriet had little time left before someone arrived. "What about Johnny? Have you seen him?" Registering the woman's blank look, she added, "Bartlett."

"Mr. Money Bags?" The woman scoffed. "Never to the Depths. Too bad. He's good-looking. And it's well known he's loaded. He can afford whatever suits him. We don't."

Against the sound of several pairs of descending footsteps, Harriet said in a rush, "Johnny *never* comes down here? Or just infrequently?"

The woman's expression slid from playful to suspicious. "If you really knew Johnny, you wouldn't have to ask that."

Harriet thanked the woman and turned to leave just as a woman and man entered the room. Harriet couldn't help but notice the woman's young age and beauty. In another circumstance, she would find the woman alluring. Here she felt only pity. The woman bugged her eyes, and Harriet realized she'd been caught staring too intensely. Embarrassed, she dropped her gaze and hurried past them toward the staircase, suddenly feeling desperate to be beyond the walls of the Ali Baba.

The night proved to be a delightful time for bicycle riding. Harriet discovered empty streets, stretching for blocks at a time. She playfully swerved from side to side, imagining herself a dolphin darting beneath the surf or a skier hurtling down an alpine slope.

Dearborn Avenue was home to many posh residents. The address where Johnny Bartlett lived was ten stories of handsome yellow brick. The imposing archway, guarded by an ornate high-gloss black wrought-iron gate, spoke to the residents' wealth. Harriet waited just beyond the sight of the entrance. When she heard the door open from the inside, she rushed around the corner, thanking the gentleman for holding the door, and entered before he could object or question her. Moments later, she stood in front of Apartment 8D.

The day before, she'd snatched the hefty skeleton key to Johnny's front door from Pearl's pegboard. She pulled it from the bottom of her handbag and slipped it into the lock. Giving her eyes time to adjust to the dark conditions, she stood just inside the doorway, noting the scent of leather and something sweet—vanilla perhaps? She blinked rapidly. The room's contours slowly emerged. Although she had seen window displays of Art Nouveau furnishings in expensive shops, never had she been in a home filled with such fabulous pieces. Johnny had tastefully composed the living room with polished wood and leather furniture, each piece featuring an unusual curve, swirl, or shape and accented with intricate inlays of gold or ebony. An enormous painting of a woman, her ruby red hair adorned with colorful flowers and wearing a flowing gown of yellow and gold patchwork, hung above the mantel in a beveled silver frame.

Johnny was about fifteen years older than Aubrey, but the fastidiousness on display was too extreme to be due solely to maturity. Harriet guessed that Johnny's desire for an immaculate environment was as natural as Aubrey's insistence on a bedroom of cluttered chaos. Harriet had always aspired to a clean and tidy house, but Johnny's apartment felt like a place to admire rather than live in.

After finding no sign or suggestion of Agnes in the living room or kitchen, Harriet tiptoed to the next room. An imposing arched headboard complemented sumptuous silk bedclothes and pillows in purples and gold. Johnny Bartlett lived well, which struck Harriet as patently unfair. She imagined the Wozniaks touring Johnny's home, wide-eyed and unbelieving that a young man with no job could live in such splendor free of worries about paying the rent or grocer. As fortunate as she was to have inherited her parents' apartment—and to have a job that paid more

than many women earned, especially at her young age—
she still struggled to make ends meet. She appraised Johnny
Bartlett's surroundings not so much with envy as with dismay at a society that fostered such disparity between the
haves and have-nots.

Harriet had not expected to find Agnes in the apartment
but was disappointed to discover nothing at all related to
the case. She opened a massive mahogany wardrobe and
was surprised to discover a lovely soft pink garment nestled among a dozen men's suits. Curious, she lifted the
hanger from the rod. A dress. Much too small for her. She
recalled the two blue uniforms in Agnes's closet. The gown
would be too roomy for the maid. Had Johnny bought the
dress for one of his women? Someone more high-class
than one of the prostitutes working the Ali Baba basement?

Harriet spent another ten minutes searching the apartment but found nothing that piqued her interest. Johnny
wasn't likely to return for hours, but it was foolish to
linger. The sooner she was safely out of the building, the
better. Passing through the living room, she took a final
moment to admire the large painting of the woman hanging above the fireplace. A white matchbox lay beside a silver candlestick; a trail of hardened red wax cascaded
down the candle's side and pooled on the marble mantle.
She held the matchbox to the window's scant light from
the streetlamp below. The image of a black rabbit had
been crudely printed onto the front. On the other side,
someone had scribbled the name *Mattie* in pencil.

We save that for the rabbit, Gloria had said.

Harriet pocketed the matchbox and slipped out of the
apartment.

Chapter 21

Harriet was ambivalent about finding Carl Somer in the office. He'd proven unpredictable, and she worried about which version of Carl she would encounter. Must she update him? She sighed, knowing the correct answer.

"Good morning, Mr. Somer. Might you spare five minutes?"

Frowning, he didn't look up from his paperwork. "For what?"

Five minutes, she told herself. *You can do anything for five minutes.* "The missing maid."

He muttered something undiscernible, sat back in his chair, and crossed his arms. "With dispatch, please. Some of us have real investigations to pursue."

Five minutes.

"Yes, of course. I appreciate your valuable time." Harriet hurriedly recapped the past day's events as if ticking items off a grocery list, concluding with her missing notebook and suitcase.

"Suitcase?" he said as if offended by the word.

Before considering the consequences, she answered, "It belonged to Pearl Bartlett's late husband."

"What on earth are you doing with her dead husband's suitcase?"

Speaking truthfully about the suitcase had run its course. Harriet wasn't about to share that she and Pearl had selected particular items for her from the late Horace Bartlett's wardrobe. She hadn't considered when she might wear them, only that the very idea of them delighted her immeasurably. The theft of the suitcase was disturbing, but losing its contents was devastating.

"It's related to my investigation," she finally answered.

"I can't imagine how."

She forced a smile, knowing it would look insincere. "I think the conversation has strayed from my original point. It appears that someone has taken things that don't belong to them. I have relayed this information to Mr. Prescott, but—"

"Whatever you think has gone missing will turn up in good time. When it does, your embarrassment will be nothing compared to the mortification you should feel at casting aspersions at those of us who work here."

She might be unable to convince Carl of her veracity, but she could deny him the argument he craved. "Well then, it would seem that in addition to finding the maid, a second mystery is mine alone to solve." Turning back from the doorway, she added, "When I identify the culprit, you shall be among the first to know."

Desiring a friendly conversation, she sought out Matthew McCabe. Minutes later, the elevator doors closed, and with just the two of them in the compartment, Matthew said, "Bravo, Miss Morrow. You managed to withstand Mr. Somer's rude remarks without issuing an insult of your own. I doubt I could have held my composure so admirably."

"I really must remember how thin the walls are," she replied.

"And you've still no idea who the thief might be?"

"None. The secretaries claim to have left the room for their coffee breaks, but one of them could be lying. The only other people I've met are the receptionist, Madelaine, Carl Somer, and you. I've not been introduced to the other detectives. As much as I detest suspecting those for whom I should have the most trust, what else can I possibly think?"

"You will meet the other detectives soon enough," he said, referring to the ten o'clock operatives meeting. "But first things first. You and I have some targets to murder."

After arriving at the gun club, Harriet was loaned the same derringer she had handled on the first visit. She liked how it fit in her hand and how its heft conveyed the assurance of a formidable weapon. Moreover, she appreciated the practicality of the pistol not being too heavy or oversized to carry in her handbag. Reciting the safety precautions to Matthew, she slid a bullet into each chamber.

Details—facts, figures, and formulas—Harriet easily remembered. Always a good student, she excelled in all subjects, especially math and science. What had made her a standout was not being top of her class but achieving academic success in a skirt. Harriet's mother had aspired for her daughter to attend college—specifically Oberlin, the first coed college in the nation. Although by 1895, the year Harriet would have enrolled, roughly half of the colleges in America admitted women. Harriet, however, had set her sights on a women-only school, such as Wellesley or Radcliffe. But it was not to be . . . no college was. Without her parents' income to pay her tuition, there was no way she could afford the cost. While her aunt and uncle had encouraged her ambitions, what extra money they had each month went to putting two additional plates on the dinner table. Still, Harriet kept the dream of going to college alive until the day she became her brother's guardian and the little hope she had left died out like embers in an unexpected rain.

"Remarkable!" Matthew exclaimed at her sharpshoot-

ing. "If you don't confess that you've been secretly practicing, I'm afraid I must think you're a terrible cheat and a
liar."

Harriet chuckled at the compliment. It felt good to be
good at something. She thought she could be a good detective as well, believing confidence was as essential as
smarts and courage. She'd been fortunate that her mother
had instilled in her a self-belief that caused her to question
society's parochial expectations of women.

The operatives' meeting was held in the agency's largest
space: the clerks' room. A dozen or so detectives stood,
backs to the wall, facing Theodore Prescott, who, despite
having the shortest stature—including Harriet—commanded
the room with an aura of unquestioned superiority. The
curious glances from everyone other than Carl Somer and
Matthew McCabe made it clear they weren't accustomed
to a woman attending the weekly operatives' meeting.

Pleasantries were not on the meeting's agenda, nor did
they ever seem to be. Prescott commenced proceedings on
the first of ten distant bongs from the lobby's grandfather
clock. Beginning with a summary of the agency's active investigations, interspersed with occasional questions to the
operative in charge, he moved from case to case in an
order everyone but she seemed to understand. She noted
that when a detective spoke, he did so with economy, citing facts and answering any query free of opinion unless
specifically asked.

Harriet learned that the Prescott Agency worked a variety of cases, more so than she'd imagined. A rotund senior
operative, Mr. Bonner—one of the several Charles—had
infiltrated a small group of socialist anarchists agitating
for a government overthrow. The eldest detective, Mr. Clem-
ens, was posing as a bank executive to root out another
who'd stolen secret documents from an unnamed holder
of a safety deposit box. Matthew McCabe was working

two cases: trailing the young wife of a real estate tycoon suspected of adultery and providing surveillance as part of a much larger agency investigation that Prescott referred to as "The Railroad Plot." Carl Somer was assigned to a complex legal matter involving the disputed patent ownership of a stolen invention related to the burgeoning automobile industry. Would Prescott call on her and ask about the search for Agnes Wozniak? She'd not anticipated having to speak in front of all the detectives. Nervous, she squeezed her handbag, realizing that had the possibility occurred to her, she would have gotten not a wink of sleep the night before.

At precisely 10:59, Prescott concluded the meeting by saying, "You gentleman will have noticed a new attendee at the meeting. She is the young woman I mentioned at last week's meeting. Miss Harriet Morrow."

Prescott gathered his papers as the men stared at her. Harriet experienced a mix of emotions. She was relieved to have escaped being put on the spot but bothered that Prescott had said nothing more about her. Attendee? Young woman? Nothing suggested her role as an operative. Stating her position wouldn't assure the men's welcome but would add to her credibility.

The men dispersed. Harriet raced down the hall after Prescott. "Excuse me, sir? Mr. Prescott?"

Brow furrowed, he turned back from his office doorway, waiting for her to approach. "What has you in a dither, Miss Morrow?"

"I'm curious, sir, why have you said so little about my employment here? It's . . . well, it's awkward, and I sense people are—"

"Skeptical?"

The abruptness of the word snatched her breath.

"Did you think being the first female operative at this agency would be easy, Miss Morrow? Did you expect . . . what? A cake? Balloons?"

"Of course not, sir. I just thought—"

"Every new man who came before you started as you are now. On a trial basis. You will receive no special accommodation or congratulations. On the contrary, even the suggestion that the bar has been lowered for you will affirm the opinion of those who don't believe a woman has any business doing the job. That doesn't mean you won't receive support. Prove yourself, Miss Morrow, and you will fully join the detective ranks. Until then, your attendance at the operatives' meeting is a courtesy . . . and incentive. By the way, I've decided that come Monday, you will work under the tutelage of Mr. Somer on the patent matter. There are many documents to catalog. Is there anything else?"

Harriet's stomach dropped. *Carl Somer?* "But, sir, isn't it customary for a junior operative to apprentice for a senior operative? Mr. Somer is a junior like myself."

"Mr. Somer has three years under his belt. You have four days. You will learn much from him. Follow his instructions as you would mine. He will report his thoughts on your progress to me directly."

That her professional fate was soon to be in Carl Somer's hands was most distressing. Harriet tried, "Perhaps Mr. McCabe might be a better—"

"Miss Morrow!" he snapped. "You are in no position to offer suggestions. That will be all. You may leave." Adding a heated look, he said, "Unless you have other ideas for how I might do my job?"

Scurrying away, she felt the weight of her mistake. She should have smiled demurely and replied, "Yes, sir . . . of course, sir . . . whatever you say, sir." Instead, she'd panicked. With Carl Somer as her mentor, would she even last until Tuesday? Maybe she could get her old bookkeeping job back. How would she explain her failure to Aubrey? She constantly lectured him to apply himself. What good had it done her?

In the lobby, Sandra Small leaned against the receptionist's desk. The women lowered their voices and sniggered as Harriet passed. Instead of causing her unease, the women's mockery and doubts fired her resolve. She wasn't finished yet. It was Friday. She had until Monday to solve the case, impress Prescott, and change his mind about assigning her to Carl Somer. The trajectory of her life would soon be decided. She needed only to do one thing. Find the dadgum maid.

Chapter 22

On Harriet's last birthday, Aubrey had surprised her with a small silver bell—made in England—purchased from Billy at the bicycle shop and now affixed to her handlebars. The gift was both practical and thoughtful. Despite its alarming *clang*, she couldn't suppress the urge to shout whenever a pedestrian was about to step into her path.

"Watch out!"

Harriet swerved to avoid a collision. Although the woman had been careless in pushing the baby carriage into her path, Harriet was pedaling too fast. She was anxious to get to the Wozniaks and find out whether the family had learned anything about Agnes's whereabouts. And there was a particular question she was eager to ask Barbara.

During her previous visit, Harriet had posed as an employee of Lakeshore Domestic Help, and the ruse had worked. But Harriet doubted Barbara would believe the service would send her again so soon to check on an absent maid. This time, Harriet would reveal her true identity and purpose, hoping Barbara wouldn't be too angry about being lied to and turn her away. A dismissal could be devastating to her investigation. Moreover, Harriet enjoyed Barbara's company and hoped they might become friends—perhaps more.

Heart pounding, Harriet coasted to a stop in front of the Wozniaks' building and chained her bicycle to a wooden porch railing sorely in need of paint. Standing in the dark, windowless hallway before the family's front door, she reached down, swept dust from the bottom of her skirt, and straightened her hat as if the adjustments might soften the blow of her revelation.

Moments later, Barbara took two steps back, taking in Harriet from a different angle. "You are a detective? But you are a woman. And so young."

This, Harriet knew, would be a blessing and a curse for years to come. While most people would never suspect she was a detective, they would be incredulous when she claimed to be one.

Harriet told Barbara everything—from Theodore Prescott's initial belief that Pearl Bartlett was mistaken about Agnes's disappearance to having only three days left to find her. She then held her breath, awaiting Barbara's reaction, hoping the truth would be enough to retain her trust. Barbara stood silently for a long moment, her expression giving nothing away. As much as Harriet longed to fill the void with reassurances about her honorable intentions and commitment, she kept silent. The woman deserved a few minutes to absorb the information and decide. It was, after all, her house, her family, her sister.

"I don't understand," she said, looking crestfallen. "Why did you lie before? What did you hope to gain?"

Harriet had taken Matthew McCabe's advice. She had accepted his rationale and even now, despite the awkwardness of confessing, had no regrets following it. "I didn't want to alarm you and your family unnecessarily. There might have been a perfectly innocent explanation for Agnes's disappearance. Her safe return could have been imminent. Unfortunately, enough time has passed that we both know that is not the case. I must adapt my approach."

The expression on Barbara's face telegraphed her misgivings. "That may be. But you had another reason, didn't you?" She held Harriet's gaze.

"I couldn't assume the innocence of everyone in your family. I had to allow for the possibility that someone close to her was involved, directly or indirectly. Revealing my true identity would have raised that person's guard and prevented me from learning something that might lead to Agnes's safe return."

"You considered us suspects? That one of us might have harmed Agnes? That *I* might have done something to my sister?"

"I don't believe that, Barbara."

"Perhaps not now," she scoffed. "But you did before, didn't you?"

"I couldn't know what to believe. But that's my job. I must presume the possibility of guilt until I can prove otherwise. You may disagree with my methods, and I understand that. From your perspective, I can see how you might take offense. But the only thing that matters is finding Agnes. Believe me when I say I am committed to doing that. That's been my only interest."

"We have heard nothing," Barbara finally said. "My father is now convinced something is wrong. You might think that is progress. It is not. He asked Bogdan Nowak to help find Agnes. Nowak already feels entitled to my sister. If she had any hope of escaping him before, my father is now obliged to give his blessing. Should that come to pass, I fear for Agnes's safety. Her misery is certain. The man is a brute."

"You need not convince me, Barbara. I've been to see Bogdan Nowak. I found him where you said he'd be—in an upstairs pool hall on Blackhawk Street."

Barbara's eyebrows jumped in surprise.

"My assessment of the man is no different from your own. But I need to ask you about something he said."

Barbara nodded, alarmed. "You spoke with Bogdan Nowak? Did he say anything about Agnes?"

"He said he had dinner here with your family a few Wednesdays back. He said the twins, Marek and Marcin, teased Agnes about a man she had seen while working at Pearl Bartlett's home. Nowak understood the ribbing was because Agnes was sweet on the man. He believed there was something to it. He didn't hear any name mentioned, which was fortunate for the man—he didn't like hearing that someone else had caught Agnes's eye. Can you confirm Nowak's story? If so, did you share his impression of that conversation?"

Barbara paced the room, seemingly too consternated to sit still. Eventually, she said, "The twins and Agnes are less than a year apart in age. They have always been close. Many people assume they are triplets. They seem to have a secret language, always joking, laughing, and causing a ruckus. I'm so used to it, I hardly pay them any mind. As for what was said that night, I don't recall hearing anything about Agnes noticing any man. But that doesn't mean it didn't happen. Though I'm not surprised Bogdan remembers. His eyes rarely stray from Agnes."

"Might Agnes have said something about the man on another occasion? Perhaps in confidence just to you?"

"No. Nothing. Agnes is close to Marek and Marcin, as I've said, but still, they are her brothers. She wouldn't talk to them about a boy. This is all very confusing. I am her sister. If she liked someone, why not confide in me?"

Hearing the desperation in Barbara's voice, Harriet wanted to comfort her. But how? What gesture might be welcome? Or was the very idea unprofessional? She knew Carl Somer would never consider it, but might someone like Matthew McCabe? Did guessing about a man's approach to the situation offer any benefit? Harriet had everything to learn about being a detective, but she didn't intend to do the job as would a man and deny herself what advantages being a woman might bring to the role. Perhaps an inclination toward empathy was one such strength.

Barbara slumped onto the sofa as if the subject of her sister had become too much to bear. "You don't know Agnes. She is strong-willed. Stubborn. If she believed that she'd be forced to marry Nowak, she would have done anything or gone anywhere to avoid him. She's been gone a week. In that time, for all we know, she could be well on her way back home to our village."

"Is that really a possibility? Has she ever mentioned any such intention?" That Agnes could have left the city, let alone the country, had never occurred to Harriet. But still, why go through the window? And why leave behind her personal belongings?

"And Damian Swiatek?" Harriet continued. "You said before that Agnes felt no attraction to him, but might she settle for him if he could save her from a life with Bogdan Nowak?"

Barbara shrugged. "I don't know. Perhaps. Damian is a good man. Solid, steady. Agnes recognized those qualities but wanted more. She wanted love." She laughed bitterly. "She and I are alike that way. It would seem love is to be neither of our fates."

"Surely a woman such as yourself will find love. Having too many admirers is more likely your challenge." The words spilled out before Harriet could consider whether they were too forward. Although she spoke honestly, after the odd conversation with Matthew McCabe and her strange encounters at the Ali Baba Theater, she realized she should be more circumspect about discussing personal matters.

Barbara's eyes flashed, conveying something Harriet didn't recognize. "That's a kind thing to say, Harriet. But if you knew me better, you'd know that is untrue. What about you? Am I to believe you have no sweetheart?"

Choosing her words carefully, she replied, "As it happens, there is no man I fancy."

The women held one another's gaze. A secret seemed to pass between them.

Harriet cleared her throat. "Returning to Agnes, I know we've been over this before, but I must ask again. Is there anyone else who had their eyes on your sister? A former beau? An admiring neighbor? Perhaps some friend of your brothers who might have been to the house and noticed her? A business associate of your father's or uncle's who may have taken an untoward interest?"

Life seemed to have drained from Barbara. She sat back on the sofa, dejected.

Harriet continued, "I have little time remaining to find Agnes, but you have my word that my every waking moment will be devoted to the task." She intended for the words to provide Barbara solace but knew that only her sister's safe return would do that.

"I must be going." Harriet stood.

Barbara climbed to her feet. As they emerged into the afternoon sunshine, Barbara touched Harriet's arm. "I'm sure you've done as much as anyone could, Harriet. Something is bound to turn up."

Harriet nodded, then blurted, "Wait! You don't, by chance, know of a place that uses the symbol of a black rabbit, do you? Perhaps a place here in the neighborhood? Somewhere that Agnes might have gone? A social establishment, perhaps, where young people go to meet one another?"

"No," Barbara drew out the word. "Not around here. Why do you ask?"

She rummaged in her handbag.

"Matches?" Barbara said, taking the small box offered by Harriet.

Harriet skipped over the part where she'd snuck into Johnny's apartment and snatched them, saying only that the matchbox had come from Pearl Bartlett's grandnephew, a notorious womanizer. While she spoke, Barbara had become flustered. She appeared to tremble, and the veins in her throat tightened.

"What is it?" Harriet said. "Do you recognize the name Johnny Bartlett? Did Agnes ever speak of him?"

"Where did you get these, Harriet?"

"From Johnny, Pearl's grandnephew. I'm unsure how seriously to take him as a suspect, but Agnes saw him several times at the mansion."

"No, no. That's not it." Looking at the image of the black rabbit printed on the matchbox, Barbara shook her head and flipped it over. "Who is Mattie?"

"I have no idea."

"This Johnny, he wouldn't have given you these." She paused. "Ah. But you didn't say that, did you? You took them?"

Harriet's heart nearly leaped from her chest, but not because she'd been found out; she sensed she was on to something. "Barbara, do you know Johnny Bartlett?"

"Why? Do you think he has something to do with my sister's disappearance?"

"As I say, I'm not sure. Truth be told, I have doubts. But Johnny knows your sister. And he's been inside the Bartlett mansion countless times. He must be familiar with the layout. Whoever took Agnes knew she lived there and which bedroom was hers. In addition to them seeing one another at the house, Pearl recently sent Agnes to Johnny's place to water the plants while he was out of town. Agnes's world is a small one. She spends six days of the week at the mansion and Wednesdays here at home. That leaves little opportunity for her to cross paths with others. Whoever took her must have met her here, where you or someone else in the family would know about them, or at Pearl's, where the list is quite short."

Barbara reached out again, this time squeezing Harriet's arm more forcefully. "You asked if I know Johnny Bartlett. I do not."

Crestfallen, Harriet said, "Then why didn't you say so?"

"I don't know the man, but I do know where those matches came from."

Eyes wide, Harriet reared back in surprise. "So I'm right? Whatever this place is, it's here in Polish Downtown?"

"No, no. It isn't. But I know of it. It is called the Black Rabbit."

"Please, Barbara." Harriet tried to hold steady, despite a nearly uncontrollable urge to shake the woman. "Please. Tell me what you know."

"The Black Rabbit is a large saloon, a hall really, that caters to a certain clientele. It's popular among the working class. Men mostly. But on special occasions, women also attend. That this Johnny would go there isn't entirely uncommon. High-class gentlemen like him find the freedoms of a place like the Black Rabbit liberating and arousing, depending on their inclinations. It's a place where men like him can escape the conservative society and enjoy a night of bawdy entertainment. The only way to find the Black Rabbit is to be taken there by someone who knows where it is. The location is never advertised or written down. It's not to be discussed. You'll notice there is no address on that matchbox. That's intentional. The members take precautions to keep the establishment out of the public eye."

"Is the Black Rabbit something to do with Bogdan Nowak? A secretive meeting place of criminals?"

Barbara snorted. "Depends on who you ask. But no. The Black Rabbit's clientele is not Nowak's kind. Far from it. The Black Rabbit is a club for queer men." She paused, holding Harriet's gaze. "And, on special nights, women who desire women."

Harriet's mouth gaped. In one fell swoop, Barbara had confirmed the existence of an establishment catering to queers and suggested that Johnny Bartlett had visited such a place. More shocking still, if Barbara knew of the place, did that mean what Harriet thought?

"Where?" Harriet asked breathlessly. "I need the address. Please, Barbara."

"As I say, giving out that information is forbidden." Seeming to sense Harriet's desperation, she raised a hand to stave off any further plea. "However, I can take you there. But it must be tomorrow night. The Black Rabbit usually operates on Friday nights, but this weekend is special. The club is closed tonight in preparation for tomorrow night."

"Why? What's tomorrow?"

"The Black Rabbit's annual ball is tomorrow night."

Harriet trembled with a mix of trepidation and excitement. "Ball? As in a fancy dress ball?"

Barbara chuckled. "Yes. Although it's not what you might expect and so much more than you can imagine."

A ball? Harriet had no dress suitable for such an occasion. She had yet to receive her first paycheck and had already accumulated various expenses while racing across the city in search of Agnes. Besides, she hated the idea of paying hard-earned money for a fancy gown she didn't want, wouldn't feel comfortable wearing, and would never wear again.

Barbara read her look of concern. "You don't want to go? You seemed eager only a moment ago."

"You're quite sure the hall won't be open tonight? Perhaps I could stop in and just take a look around? I don't plan on staying long."

"Impossible. Again, it's not in operation this evening. Besides, you can't possibly go alone."

"Yes, but a ball . . ." The words came out as a groan. Suddenly, Harriet wondered how Barbara could afford a proper dress.

As if reading her mind, Barbara asked, "You've nothing to wear?"

"I've only my mother's wedding dress in mothballs at the back of the closet. Even if I could fit into it, hardly would it do."

"Fortunately, for both of us, it's not a traditional ball."

"I don't understand. Dresses aren't worn?"

The question appeared to amuse Barbara. "They're worn—just not by us. Are you not familiar with the term 'drag'? It's a drag ball."

Harriet shook her head, confused.

"The men wear the dresses. The women wear men's formal attire, tuxedos for those lucky enough to get their hands on one. I don't suppose you have a man's suit lying around?"

The conversation was so disorienting that Harriet didn't think of the men's clothing that had, thanks to Pearl Bartlett, recently come into—and mysteriously gone from—her possession. Instead, she managed, "I'm to wear a man's suit of clothes?"

"Yes. But you should bring your attire with you. It's not advised that you wear your party dress in public. The men, especially, couldn't possibly. There are rooms at the club where you can change once you arrive and then change back before you leave."

"But how will I ever find it? You won't tell me where it is."

"Meet me at the corner of Polk and Dearborn. I'll show you the way from there. Nine o'clock. But Harriet, you must swear that you will tell no one. Do not mention the club's name or the location of our meeting place. These are club rules. They are sacrosanct."

"Yes, of course, Barbara. You have my word."

"There is one more thing."

"Yes?" Harriet's voice quivered from a mix of excitement and trepidation.

"I can only take you there if I'm sure. Do you understand what I'm asking?" She held Harriet's gaze. "I must be sure—*about you.*"

Sensing Harriet's distress, Barbara softened. "Just tell me if I'm wrong. Am I wrong about you, Harriet?"

Harriet gripped her bicycle's handlebars, unable to look Barbara in the eye. Pushing off, she said, "I shall see you at nine."

Chapter 23

Eager to make the most of her time in Polish Downtown, Harriet pedaled toward a nearby Milwaukee Avenue address she had found for W. Wozniak Badge and Banner Works. Standing outside the shop, Harriet's first thought was about how much Aubrey would delight in visiting. Two large windows, meticulously clean, flanked the entrance, displaying a broad assortment of badges, ribbons, flags, and certificates. Large religious banners—Catholic?—hung on either side of the door. Harriet recalled Barbara saying that her father was a supporter of the Polish Roman Catholic Union. By the looks of things, so was her uncle, the store's owner.

Harriet opened the screen door; its wooden frame with turned spindles gleamed with polish, further attesting to the owner's fastidiousness. Inside, the shop impressed with the number and variety of items for sale. Most dazzling was a wall of banners, most of which were approximately two by three feet, a few several times larger. Several photographs showed other similar banners used in parades, festivals, and celebrations. Flags, crosses, religious iconography, and other symbols for sports or businesses were prevalent.

A gray-whiskered man ambled from the back of the

shop to greet her. "Polish?" Whether his question was routine or because he suspected she was a stranger to the community, Harriet appreciated beginning the conversation with clarity.

"Thank you, sir. I'm afraid I only speak English."

Nodding, he said, "I will do my best," and then swept an arm through the air. "What you see are samples. Most of what we sell, we design for a particular occasion. What is it you're looking for?"

"Not so much a what as a who. You see, I wish to have a word with either Marek or Marcin Wozniak. I understand from their sister, Barbara, they are employed here."

The man nodded warily. "My nephews. What business do you have with them?"

So this was the uncle, Witold, and not Agnes's father. Harriet was past the ruse of posing as a fictitious character. Time was short. She explained her position and the reason for the visit.

"I don't understand," Mr. Wozniak said. "You are with the police?"

"No, sir. I am a detective with the Prescott Agency. We often work alongside the police, but we are a private company."

"Here in Chicago?"

"That's right. Our offices are downtown. While you may not be acquainted with the agency by name, I can assure you that the Prescott Agency is a most reputable firm. My employer, Theodore Prescott, is the next-door neighbor of your niece Agnes's employer, Mrs. Pearl Bartlett. I'm looking for Agnes at the request of Mrs. Bartlett."

The man stared hard at her. Harriet guessed he was deciding whether to believe a young woman could hold such a job. With an eventual shrug, he said. "The boys can't tell you anything you don't already know. If they knew where Agnes was, she wouldn't still be missing. But if you prefer to hear that from them directly, no harm in it, I suppose."

Halfway to the rear of the shop, he turned back. "Which one did you say you wanted to talk to?"

"Either will do. But if possible, I will gladly speak with both boys."

"Wait there."

Several minutes later, another man, similar in appearance to the first, hurried toward Harriet as if he suspected her of stealing. She presumed this was the father, Piotr, she'd heard so much about.

"You have no business here," he said tersely. "Leave."

The abrupt change of tone set her on her heels. "I'm sorry, sir. Perhaps you misunderstand—"

"My family's business is none of your concern. You are not welcome here."

Harriet's initial alarm by the man's anger was replaced by irritation. "I presume you are Agnes's father, yes? I am trying to find her. Nothing more, nothing less. Perhaps if I can state my case, you'll see that I'm only trying—"

"My family's affairs are private. Barbara told me some woman came snooping to the house the other day. If what my brother just told me is true, then you lied to her about who you are. Or you are lying now." He paused, examining her from bowler to toes. "You are no professional detective. I haven't time or interest in whatever game you're playing at. I will not ask you again. Go." He stepped toward her.

Harriet glanced over Piotr's broad shoulders at the back door. It appeared no other Wozniak would be intervening. She turned toward the door.

"We need the help of no one. God has a plan for Agnes," Piotr announced. "Who are we to question his will?"

The remark enraged Harriet, not the words themselves, but knowing that this man, Agnes's father, intended to force his daughter to marry Bogdan Nowak. Whether because of Nowak's financial support of the Catholic Union or his general wealth, Piotr treated his daughter as if she were chattel. Before she considered the wisdom of her action, she spun around. "I too have work to do. And that's to find your daughter. And I shall do it with or without your help." She let the lovely screen door slam shut behind her.

Harriet stood shaking on the sidewalk. She would never understand men like Piotr Wozniak. And yet, as a detective, she was bound to encounter men who were some version of him. She may dislike them, but she'd need to learn how to better deal with them. Stomping away in a huff accomplished nothing, leaving them with their minor victories.

She had taken a step in the direction of her bicycle when someone brushed past her and whispered, "Follow me." So suddenly had it happened that Harriet didn't get a look at the fellow's face. Judging by his lean frame and the looseness of his gait, he was young, either an adolescent or a man in his twenties, perhaps thirties. From behind, his size and hair color appeared similar to Tomasz Wozniak's. Presuming this to be one of the twins, she followed him down the block and around the corner into an alley.

Several steps into the narrow passageway, lined with trash bins and discarded crates, her eyes darted right, then left. He had vanished. She looked back over her shoulder. Had she made a mistake? Had she misheard him?

"In here," a voice beckoned.

Startled, she whirled around. A hand protruded from a nearby doorway, waving her inside. The previous day's altercation at the pool hall had her wary. The boy's size didn't make him an obvious threat, but he could have a weapon. And he might not be alone. Still, if she were right, this was either Marek or Marcin. She needed to speak with one of them. This could be her only chance.

Slipping inside the doorway, Harriet's hand flew up to cover her nose. "Where are we?"

Despite standing in shadow, she could make out the boy's features. He had the same broad nose, dark brown eyes, and thick hair as Tomasz and Barbara. With eyes adjusted to the dim conditions, she realized she'd seen him before, erasing all doubt about his identity. This was one of the boys pictured alongside Agnes in the family photograph left behind in the maid's third-floor bedroom.

"My friend works here," he replied. "This is his father's cheese shop. We can talk here. It's safe. But I don't have much time."

"Are you . . ."

"Marcin. My brother wanted to come, but it's less noticeable if only one of us is gone. My uncle told us you are looking for our sister. My father doesn't speak for all of us. What do you want to know?"

With haste, Harriet explained who she was and that she was particularly interested in the man Agnes had seen at the Bartlett mansion that had been the subject of the brothers' teasing.

"Marek and I don't know the fella's name, nothing like that. But we know Agnes. We put two and two together, that's all."

Harriet shook her head, confused. "I don't understand. What exactly did Agnes say that made you think she was smitten?"

"It wasn't what she said, but how she acted. She was in a silly mood, all smiles and absentminded. When we asked her why, she looked embarrassed, turned pink, and said, 'It's nothing.' That's when we guessed it must be a boy. Marek started singing, 'Agnes has a beau, she wants us not to know . . . Agnes has a beau . . .' That only made Agnes scream and run from the room. She jumped onto her bed and put a pillow over her head. She hollered for us to shut up and leave her be. Then we knew for sure."

Harriet didn't doubt Marcin. As a sibling, she often gleaned more about Aubrey's moods through observation than conversation, and they were five years apart. Considering what Barbara had said about the twins and Agnes being close in age and acting like triplets, she imagined they had an uncanny ability to communicate through expressions and gestures.

"This is vitally important, Marcin. Try to think. Did Agnes say anything about the man? Anything that might suggest his appearance? His job? His reason for being at Agnes's place of work? Or what your sister and the man might have said to one another?"

Marcin bunched his lips. "Not really. Maybe, though."

"Even if you are not one hundred percent sure, I still want very much to hear it."

"Marek and I both heard Agnes say something about his eyes, but we think she meant different things."

Harriet was ready to jump out of her skin with anticipation. "Go on."

"She said he had eyes like the choir master's."

"And what are his eyes like?"

"That's just it. I think Agnes meant the color gray. But Marek is sure Agnes meant how Choir Master Mallek always looks cross, like someone is singing the wrong note."

"So you know this Choir Master Mallek, do you? You've seen his eyes with your own?" If what she was hearing were true, this could be a significant finding. Having green eyes herself, she knew gray to be the other rarest eye color, along with hazel.

Marcin nodded confidently. "Mr. Mallek conducts the Chopin Choir at Holy Trinity Church. We see him every Sunday and at various holidays and concerts."

"And that's when Agnes would have seen him? She wasn't herself a member, was she?" Harriet asked, doubting the maid had free time for rehearsals and performances.

Marcin smiled. "It's a men's choir."

"Did you ask Agnes for the fellow's name?"

"Of course we did. We pestered her something awful." Adding a sheepish smile, he said, "She kept her head under her pillow and screamed for us to leave her alone. She never said more about him. Can't say I blame her. We probably made too much of it."

Given the twins' closeness to Agnes, Harriet was eager to hear Marcin's opinion about Agnes's two known suitors in the neighborhood. In reply, Marcin added nothing to what she'd already heard about Damian Swiatek—he was affable and reliable but didn't interest Agnes. When Harriet pointed out that Swiatek had pale blue eyes—possibly confused for gray—and was a member of the Chopin Choir, Marcin shrugged off the notion.

"Damian is a good man. My sister could do worse for herself. Damian has steady work at the sausage factory, doesn't drink or carouse. He's good company. But none of that matters. Agnes isn't interested. Marek and I feel a bit sorry for him, to tell you the truth. When Agnes was still living at home, he would come around with flowers and sweets or leave cards wishing her well on her birthday and holidays. He did everything properly. My mother and Barbara were impressed. And the rest of us—all but Father—like him well enough. But again, none of that matters. For whatever reason, Agnes never took to him."

"When did Damian relent, realizing his cause was lost?"

Marcin chuckled ruefully. "Poor fellow. I'm not sure he has or ever will. He's utterly besotted by Agnes. I think it will take her marrying someone else for him to finally understand they will never be together."

Satisfied that Damian Swiatek had not captured Agnes's attention, Harriet moved on to the other suitor. Marcin confirmed that Bogdan Nowak's wealth and generous contributions to the Polish Roman Catholic Union had earned his father's favor despite Bogdan being a notorious criminal.

"Since your father endorses Nowak's wish to marry Agnes, he doesn't seem to warrant suspicion in her disappearance. Moreover, your father asked his help to find her. So why would Nowak take the risk of snatching her?"

While Harriet spoke, Marcin's grew angry. "Marry? Where'd you get the notion that Nowak wants to marry my sister?"

The remark so surprised Harriet that she managed only to blink in reply. Eyes wide, she stared at him.

Marcin continued, "Nowak is interested in Agnes, all right. But not as a wife. Nowak is known to set his sights on pretty girls, one after the next. He puts them up at a house somewhere in the neighborhood until another girl he likes better comes along."

Harriet gasped, "But surely your father wouldn't allow that. Not his own daughter!"

"Father!" Marcin spat the word. "He cares about two things. Money and the Catholic Union. He pretends not to know Nowak's true intentions regarding Agnes. To him, she is nothing but a means to an end." Registering Harriet's shock, he added, "My father is not the first to use his daughter for his own gain. He has old, outdated ideas about the roles of men and women. You can't imagine the relief Marek and I felt when Agnes went to work for the old lady in the mansion. We thought she'd be safe there, well beyond his reach. Perhaps Nowak would forget about her. But Agnes arranged with her employer to come home one day a week. Nowak learned of her Wednesday visits and started showing up at the house for dinner on those nights. Still, we hoped he'd lose interest."

"But Barbara? Your mother? Surely they'd not allow it. It's inconceivable that they would stand by while Nowak forces Agnes into such a dreadful arrangement."

"They don't appreciate the threat," Marcin said. "They may detest Nowak and understand he's dangerous, but they live in a sheltered world. They can't imagine his true intentions and that he could get away with it—or that Father would look the other way while it happened."

Harriet hadn't met the Wozniak family matriarch, but Marcin's assessment of Barbara as being sheltered didn't square with her knowing about a place like the Black Rabbit. She marveled that even family members sharing the same roof could harbor such secrets from one another. Did

Aubrey keep secrets from her? Surely he must. After all, didn't she?

Marcin continued. "That's why Marek and I think Bogdan took Agnes. He avoids a nasty fight with the rest of the family. We would do anything—*anything*—to save Agnes from becoming his latest conquest. I hear that most women he takes have no family—no one to challenge him. But Agnes is exceptionally beautiful. He decided he must have her despite most of the family's opposition." Marcin sneered, "The monster thinks his power and wealth make him untouchable."

"Presuming that's all true, if your father suspects Nowak took your sister, it still makes no sense that he would ask for his help finding her."

"Don't you see? Father avoids war with the family. As it stands, he appears to be doing something when he does nothing. As long as Agnes remains missing, he is blameless. He bears no responsibility. Like Bogdan, he avoids a fight. All the while, Father is rewarded with continued financial support for the Catholic Union. I wouldn't be surprised if he slipped my father a private payment for keeping his suspicions to himself. That would more than compensate for Agnes's lost wages working as a maid."

"And your uncle? Might he intervene?"

Marcin shrugged. "Uncle Witold isn't as bad as my father, but he's also of a generation that believes the men decide everything, including what's best for the women in the family."

Marcin's revelation sent Harriet's head spinning. That a father could be so heartless seemed inconceivable. She recalled occasional spats with her father but nothing of such damning consequence. His desire for her happiness had been sincere. Growing up, she had been aware of and grateful for her parents' support but had not realized how fortunate she had been.

"Look, I got to go," Marcin said. "I've already been away too long."

"Thank you, Marcin. I am grateful you took a risk to talk with me. What you have shared is extremely helpful."

Marcin followed Harriet into the alley. Tipping his cap, he said, "I appreciate you trying to find our sister. But you best be careful, miss. Agnes may be missing, but as far as we know, she's still alive. No one has been killed. But get too close, and that could change in an instant."

Harriet had come for information. She'd not been disappointed. But rather than depart Polish Downtown with clarity, she had received conflicting clues, sending her in two opposing directions at the same time. Bogdan Nowak had reinserted himself onto her list of suspects, but he was not alone. A man with notable gray eyes had sparked Agnes's interest. Walking to retrieve her bicycle, she envisioned a man she had recently met whose eyes were a curious color—not quite blue, not quite hazel. She'd not thought to describe them as gray, but it fit. The revelation caused her to rush her steps. She knew this man. His matchbox was tucked inside her handbag.

Chapter 24

The pool hall where Bogdan Nowak conducted his nefarious business hadn't been on Harriet's itinerary when she set out that day. But that had changed. According to Marcin, Nowak kept a woman at a house somewhere in the city. She needed to find that house. But how? She ruled out trying to follow him. In addition to having no experience trailing a violent criminal, there was no telling if or when he would go there—assuming Marcin's information was even correct.

Her previous visit to the pool hall had ended by narrowly escaping a man's clutches, but she couldn't allow the possibility of danger to stop her. She wasn't a bookkeeper any longer.

Turning onto Blackhawk Street, Harriet smelled the bakery before she saw it. The name J. F. BYKOWSKI stretched across the storefront's awning. Sharing her brother's sweet tooth—although she preferred ice cream—she imagined Aubrey's delight when surprised with an exotic treat for dessert. Besides, she could use the few minutes delay to form a plan.

As a stout girl, Harriet had been encouraged by her mother to accept her thicker frame as natural and nothing for which she should ever feel ashamed. Mayre Morrow had been uncompromising in dismissing her daughter's self-criticism as unnatural. *I very much doubt the tree in the yard wishes itself to be shorter and thinner or the squirrel who calls it home to be taller and stronger*, she used to say, in many different versions. *Each of us is the size we were intended to be, Harriet. Yearning to be different is to deny the perfection that you already are.*

A tiny silver bell tied to the inside door handle announced Harriet's entrance. Hearing the incomprehensible chatter between the two patrons and the white-aproned man behind the counter, she realized her order would probably depend on a primitive form of sign language. Presuming the simpler-looking desserts cost less—and knowing Aubrey loved donuts—she pointed at the word PĄCZKI handwritten on a small placard next to a pile of golden-brown and chocolate-topped pastries. Guessing at the man's next question, she raised two fingers, then placed a quarter on the counter, hoping to receive change. When he handed her two dimes along with a white paper sack holding the treats, she thanked him in earnest before carefully tucking the purchase into her handbag.

She pushed open the door to the pool hall, not remembering its long squeak. Nor did she recall the first step—so warped it had pulled away from its riser, exposing the nails. The fist-sized hole in the plaster at shoulder height was new—she was sure of that. The loud *clack* of colliding billiard balls caused her to flinch. At least one table upstairs was in use.

The second-floor hall was enveloped in a thin haze of cigarette and cigar smoke. She drew a hand to the tip of her nose as if it might filter the acrid smell. A glance toward the back of the room confirmed Nowak wasn't at his desk. Good. Her minutes old plan required his absence. A large redheaded man—the one who had tried to grab her before—appeared and stood between her and the exit. As if some silent agreement had been made, the two men playing pool laid their cues onto the table and slowly turned toward her.

Fighting the instinct to run, she walked purposefully to Nowak's desk, sat in his chair, and laid her folded hands on the desktop with her back straight. She watched the men approach out of the corner of her eye.

"Bogdan won't take kindly to you sitting there," said one of the men who'd been playing pool. Harriet was surprised to hear him speak with no Polish accent. If anything, he sounded slightly British.

"Something tells me she won't be there when he gets back," said another, clearly Polish with a head as smooth as a billiard ball.

"Is that so?" Harriet tried for indignation. She raised the sleeve of her jacket to reveal the face of her wristwatch. "Two o'clock. That was the time Mr. Nowak and I agreed to meet. He said that I should make myself comfortable if I arrived before him. Are you suggesting that I not follow his instructions?"

The remark gave the men pause. They exchanged questioning looks.

Harriet pressed on, "I don't suppose there is a Barbara anywhere about?" Knowing few Polish women's names, she chose one she knew, hoping it might be apt. "Mr. Nowak said that if he was delayed, Barbara would ensure my comfort while I wait." Harriet leaned right and left, peering around the men. "Yes, well, seeing that she is not present, might I trouble one of you gentlemen for a cup of tea? Any kind will suit as long as it's hot."

Harriet's act flustered the men. They stared at her as if deciding whether to rough her up or ask if she required sugar. The redheaded man spoke, breaking the silence. "What's your business with Bogdan?"

This *was* in line with her recently formed plan. She figured that if Marcin had heard about the house where Nowak kept women, so had others—hopefully, "others" included at least one of these men. Getting them to reveal the address, if they knew it, would require trickery, but she had to try.

"I don't suppose you know what's keeping Mr. Nowak?" Adopting a scowl, she added, "Don't tell me he went straightaway to the house?" She searched the men's faces as if expecting them to have the answer. "Was I to have met him there?"

The men traded a fresh round of baffled looks.

Harriet explained matter-of-factly, "I manage a housekeeping business. Mr. Nowak is interested in hiring our service to give his home a vigorous weekly scrubbing." Harriet stopped abruptly and bit her lip, conveying a sudden thought. "I was here the other day to present my credentials, and I assumed we would meet here again. But I see my error—well, not *my* error, but my colleague's. She took Mr. Nowak's recent message and recorded the particulars. Alas, it wouldn't be the first time she didn't pay proper attention. She gets more wrong than right." She shook her head in disappointment. "It's really quite vexing."

"We got no idea what you're talking about," said the British-sounding man. The bald man with whom he'd been playing pool confirmed this with a shrug.

The redheaded man puffed up his chest. "Speak for yourselves."

Sensing an opportunity, Harriet said, "Of course, I understand that not all Mr. Nowak's associates would be entrusted with such information." Focusing her gaze on the redheaded man, she continued, "I could tell you might be the exception, someone Mr. Nowak confides in." She retrieved her notebook from her handbag, tore a sheet of paper, and pushed it across the desk with a pencil. "I shall relay your discretion to Mr. Nowak when I see him. I'm sure he will appreciate learning that you kept him from waiting for me while also safeguarding his information." She punctuated her remark with a smile.

Whether it was upstaging the two other men or the promise to have a good word said on his behalf, he didn't hesitate to scribble something onto the paper. He folded it and started to push it back toward Harriet.

She stopped him, saying, "If you'd like, please add your name to ensure you receive the proper credit."

"Thank you"—she stared at the words he'd scribbled next to the address: Leon Węgrzynkiewicz—"Leon."

After tucking the note into her handbag, she stood and smoothed her skirt. "Thank you, gentlemen. You've been most accommodating."

Walking to the exit, she fought the instinct to run. Her good luck might dry up any moment. Not only had her ruse worked, but Nowak hadn't arrived to spoil her performance. Once outside, she gulped fresh air, then sniffed her coat sleeve to assess how badly the smoke had permeated the fabric. She added another to her list of reasons for preferring to ride a bicycle—perhaps the wind would drive some of the stench from her clothes.

Carl Somer frowned as he read the address Harriet showed him on the paper. "Once again, Miss Morrow, you've demonstrated your lack of understanding the difference between grasping at straws and conducting a proper investigation. I very much doubt you will remain in the job long enough to learn it."

Harriet hadn't expected a pat on the head, but she'd hoped to encounter the pleasant version of Carl at least. Frustrated, she didn't doubt that had she delivered Agnes in the flesh, he would have found some fault with her actions, criticizing her approach or timing—perhaps renewing his argument that Agnes had never been missing in the first place. Still, she was taken aback by his vehemence.

"Surely you can't think this information is irrelevant?" Harriet emphasized the most pertinent points she had only moments before relayed in her full account: that Marcin, Agnes's brother, had told her about Nowak's secret house and that despite Piotr Wozniak's approval of Nowak, he still had reason to snatch her.

"You really must end this nonsense, Miss Morrow. Your tall tales continue growing in height, unburdened by the scantest evidence. You will write your final report and have it on my desk in an hour. I shall pass it along to Mr. Prescott if it meets my approval. Come Monday morning, we shall see if you're able to suppress your impertinence, follow orders, and make it to the day's end without giving me a reason to have you fired."

As much as Harriet thought she understood Carl's position, his intense opposition was shocking. That he struggled to accept Prescott's decision to hire her was one thing, but his attacks felt personal. It seemed not so much his intolerance of a woman in the role as it was *her* having the job. They were practically strangers. She had done nothing to earn his animosity. So what was it? Her attire? Her refusal to wilt under his harsh words? Or was it that he had decided he didn't like her and there was nothing more to it?

"Mr. Somer, I disagree that the information I have obtained through my investigation is meaningless. On the contrary, I should think another operative would see my discoveries as quite informative. Alas, that is for Mr. Prescott to judge. It is to him I will deliver my report. Although your unhelpful and disparaging remarks are disappointing, they will not stymie my investigation. Mr. Prescott has given me until Monday to find Agnes Wozniak. As you'll appreciate, my time is limited. I will devote what hours remain to pursuits that promise some progress toward my goal. As you've made abundantly clear that this conversation is not to be one of them, I shall leave you to your work, and I shall return to mine. Good day, Mr. Somer."

Before Carl could respond, Harriet spun on her heel, strode from the office, and closed the door behind her with more force than intended. She was halfway down the hall when Matthew McCabe sidled up beside her. "Meet me in the café in five minutes."

Chapter 25

Sitting on the same stool she'd occupied earlier that week, Harriet sipped soda water and watched passersby while anxiously awaiting Matthew McCabe's arrival. Just last week, she was a bookkeeper, traveling to and from work with little thought about what the job entailed. No task was unique or varied—precisely as management intended. Now, observing the unending stream of men and women scurry past the café's window, she wondered where everyone was rushing to with such vigor and determination. Was the man with a neatly trimmed mustache a lawyer on his way to the courthouse to make a final argument to the jury and save his client from the gallows? Was the older man with a shock of white hair a surgeon soon to snatch a scalpel from a silver tray and attempt to save a life? She had no trouble imagining men's wide-ranging vital professions. But sadly, when it came to doing the same for women, she could only envision them fetching fresh cups of tea for their bosses, typing correspondence, or ushering men into paneled offices to meet with other men while worrying whether their appearance was pleasing while also hoping they wouldn't attract unwelcomed advances.

Harriet didn't fit well into the world that whisked past.

She didn't want a life common to most women or to live as a man. She desired something in between: to do the same as men could—free of question or scrutiny—but unabashedly as a woman. And when returning home each night, she wanted to share her excitement and successes and her disappointments and challenges with a woman like Barbara Wozniak.

A tapping on the glass startled her, pulling her thoughts back to the present. Matthew had arrived. Although eager to share her newest discoveries with an ally, she had yet to type her report for Mr. Prescott and was desperate to visit the address the redheaded man had written on the paper. Compared to any other day in her twenty-one years of living, future events promised a new level of excitement. And still, there was more to anticipate. At nine o'clock the next evening she would meet Barbara and be taken to the secretive club known as the Black Rabbit.

"You won't sit?" she asked in response to Matthew standing beside the unoccupied stool.

"We've no time if we're to make it before closing. Come. I've got a buggy waiting for us around the corner."

Before she could object, he was heading for the door. Catching up to him on the sidewalk, she huffed, "Where are we going? I've got much to do. I've yet to complete my report."

"Strike while the iron is hot, Miss Morrow!" He strode to the far side of the buggy and climbed aboard.

Hoisting herself up, she met his eyes. "Mr. McCabe, where are you taking me?"

"I looked for you after the operatives' meeting, but you hightailed it out of the room, and I couldn't find you. No matter, I spoke with Mr. Prescott on my own. He agreed." Matthew beamed with delight, assuaging Harriet's apprehension, but only partially.

"I'm afraid I don't understand."

Matthew reached forward and tapped the driver's

shoulder. With a flick of the reins, the pair of horses clopped forward, and the buggy jerked into motion.

"Mr. McCabe, please."

"You're a detective now, Miss Morrow. You've proven in a short amount of time that you can handle the responsibility. And I don't mind saying I'll feel better once you have the means to protect yourself should you need it."

In an instant, she understood.

Still grinning, he confirmed it. "We're going to get you a gun."

En route to the shooting club, Harriet told Matthew about what she had learned about Bogdan Nowak and how she'd tricked a man at the pool hall into divulging the address of a house where he was rumored to keep a woman. However, honoring her promise to Barbara, she said nothing about the Black Rabbit.

"I can't allow you to go to the house alone," Matthew said. "I recognize I'm in no position to give you orders, but still. It's much too dangerous. I've no doubt that Mr. Prescott would agree."

"*Pfft*. You sound like Mr. Somer. Isn't the very reason for carrying a firearm to enable me to do precisely those things like going to the house? Hardly can I work as an operative if every man at the agency believes I need to be watched over like a toddler. More to my point, I don't suppose you would have these same concerns were I Harry and not Harriet."

She had never seen Matthew look perturbed; it was unsettling. "Miss Morrow, you being a woman has nothing to do with my opposition to you marching straight into danger. While your confidence likely contributed to winning the job, you don't seem to appreciate that you have been an operative for less than a week. I'm sorry to be so blunt, but you know next to nothing about how to be a detective. You should stop worrying about your success and give more attention to your learning—and survival."

Harriet bristled. She didn't need reminding of her inexperience and, despite what Matthew said, she didn't believe being a woman made no difference. And yet, by all accounts, Bogdan Nowak wasn't a man to go up against alone—gun or no gun.

"Perhaps you're correct," she said reluctantly.

"Perhaps?"

"Mr. Nowak is known to be violent."

"I take it you disagree with the rest of what I said?"

Harriet sighed heavily. "But don't you see? If I don't go to the house—"

"I never suggested you not follow your lead. I said that you shouldn't go alone."

Her head snapped around.

"As soon as we pick up the pistol, I'll go there with you straight away. I have just enough time to fit the journey between other commitments."

"But my report. I owe it to Mr. Prescott before the day's end."

"Right." He shot her a commiserating glance. "It must be turned in on time. Otherwise, Madelaine will ensure Mr. Prescott knows you submitted it late. Given that, we will return to the agency after our errand. I'm afraid visiting Nowak's house will have to wait until the morning. As I say, I have work commitments of my own." Registering her disappointment, he added, "It's actually for the best. You will find that surprising the suspect in the morning has advantages. The setting should be relatively quiet, and he may not expect visitors, giving you the element of surprise. Plus, he is not likely to be drunk, which tends to make any situation worse."

"I must object, Mr. McCabe. You say I'm not to go alone, yet you cannot accompany me until tomorrow. I can't be expected to sit on my hands while precious time passes."

"Your junior position gives you no license to object," he said curtly.

Harriet reared back, not appreciating his tone.

"Good heavens, Miss Morrow. It's admirable that an operative takes his—*her*—work seriously. But investigations have a rhythm of their own. Sometimes a case beats faster, sometimes slower than a detective would like. But forcing things rarely produces a positive result. You must work the case as it unfolds. Be vigilant, be aggressive. But never rush. It is the chief mistake made by new operatives who put impatience before prudence."

Overwhelmed by emotion, she looked away, fighting tears. One minute she was optimistic and self-assured; the next, she was sure that taking the job had been a horrible mistake. Matthew was on her side, and Prescott seemed supportive, although he wouldn't go out of his way to make anything easier on her. Everyone else in the agency viewed her with skepticism or outright derision. She liked to believe she was resilient enough to stand up to her naysayers, but the collective doubts had worn her down. If that weren't challenging enough, someone had snatched her notebook, knifed her bicycle tires, and stolen the suitcase. Were her parents alive, her father would envelop her in a tight hug and whisper encouraging words into her ear, and her mother would waggle a finger and tell her that progress wasn't easy, which was why she was proud to have raised a daughter who wasn't content taking the easy path. As it was, she would find only Aubrey at home, and if any sibling were to provide emotional support to the other, it would be her to him.

Nearly an hour later, Matthew and Harriet returned to the agency. As they were the only two people in the elevator, Matthew spoke freely. "Does the weight of the pistol in your handbag bother you? Perhaps we should have considered a holster of some kind?"

Harriet held out her bag, considering the additional heft of the pearl-handled double-barreled derringer and a small box of bullets. "If I didn't know better, I might forget it's there."

The doors to the sixth floor opened.

"Shall we say . . . eight o'clock tomorrow?" Matthew said. "Whatever building stands immediately east of the target address, I shall meet you there. Don't be early; do be prompt. A detective should never linger. You don't want to draw attention. We'll then go next door together."

"Agreed," Harriet added a decisive nod.

As she entered the room of secretaries, all three sets of eyes fastened upon her. Harriet looked at Sandra Small, the women's unofficial leader, for an indication of the reason. Sandra wore a smug look that fit her face as well as her shirtwaist complemented her bosom. Then Harriet saw it. The suitcase had reappeared. It sat beside her desk at the back of the room.

"Looks like you were worked up over nothing," Sandra said glibly.

Ignoring her, Harriet hurried past them, pulled the suitcase behind her desk where the others couldn't see it, snapped open the clasps, and peered inside. Upon a cursory glance, all of Pearl's late husband's clothing appeared to be there. She shook her head while examining the surrounding area for a note of explanation. There was none. She opened each desk drawer, saving the top for last. A single sheet of paper lay there.

You'll find what you are looking for at Swiatek's.

Harriet reread—and reread again—the note as if there were some hidden meaning she didn't comprehend. Swiatek's? That could only be Damian Swiatek's family's business. She had already been to the sausage factory. She had interviewed Swiatek. She had discussed his character and interest in Agnes with Barbara, Tomasz, and Marcin. The siblings were of one mind that Damian Swiatek was a good and decent man and that their sister had no romantic interest in him. Harriet had two solid suspects in Bogdan Nowak and Johnny Bartlett. The last thing she needed with just over two days left was a third.

Reading the note a fourth time, she noted the word "what" instead of "who." Could the exact words used be a simple error? Or did it suggest she would happen upon a clue that would subsequently lead to Agnes's whereabouts? Either way, the note couldn't be ignored. Nor could the question that had lodged her heart in her throat. Who had left it there?

Chapter 26

As Matthew McCabe had pointed out, Harriet had only five days of experience as an operative. A more seasoned detective would probably know which of several promising leads to pursue first. With the clock ticking, she would have to rely on reason alone. So where to next? Since the Black Rabbit would not be in operation until the following evening and a visit to Nowak's house must wait until the next morning's meeting with Matthew McCabe, that left one place—the Swiatek Sausage Factory.

After leaving her report with a sour-faced Madelaine, she considered what to do with the suitcase. Returning for it over the weekend would require access to the building and the office, neither of which was certain. The suitcase itself could wait until the following week, but not its contents; she required Pearl's late husband's clothes for Saturday night's drag ball at the Black Rabbit.

After a quick trip to a nearby hardware store, Harriet lashed the case onto her bicycle's rear rack with a stiff length of rope. Precarious as it was, she had transported other awkward items—a perfectly good cooking pot she'd found next to a trash bin, a small box of books a colleague at the grain elevator had given away, and, for Aubrey, a basketball she'd found abandoned in a park. With the suitcase deposited at the apartment, she would set off for Polish Downtown and, with luck, return home before the sun fully set. She told Aubrey he was responsible for making his own supper. His grumble was quickly replaced by a short intake of breath when she presented him with the pączki from the Polish bakery.

Between bites of the donut, Aubrey asked, "What's in there?" and pointed at the suitcase.

"Clothing."

"Are you leaving?"

The remark stopped her. "Leaving? And where would I be going?"

"St. Louis."

Harriet stared dumbfounded at her brother. The immediacy with which he offered a destination suggested that he had contemplated the possibility of her leaving before.

"Why would you think I'd go to St. Louis?"

He shrugged in the casual way natural to sixteen-year-old boys. "No reason. It's in another state."

"And why do you think I would want to travel to another state?"

"I don't know. No reason. Don't make a big deal of it, like you always do."

She held her tongue and lugged the suitcase the final few feet into her bedroom. She knew her brother well. Despite brushing aside the comment, she recognized there was something to it. The two of them living in the house once inhabited by all four of them had been a difficult adjustment. Every room, piece of furniture, and picture on the walls brought back memories of a happier time. Harriet suspected that Aubrey felt their parents had somehow abandoned him. Did he expect her to do the same eventually? If she were honest, she must admit she had wished to run away on multiple occasions. Playing mother to her often cranky brother plus the strain of keeping the house in order, the bills paid on time, food on the table, and clocking in at a tedious job five days a week had taken a toll. Aubrey couldn't see past his own loss and longings to recognize any of hers. Most days she tried to be understanding—what could reasonably be expected from a boy that age?—but today she was exhausted. She didn't have the energy to coddle and placate him. Besides, talking to him when he was in a mood usually made matters worse. A proper conversation couldn't be put off for long, but for now he needed to make himself a sandwich, and she had bloomers to change into for her bicycle ride to a sausage factory.

The wind off the lake stung her cheeks; her eyes teared. Worse, the cold air caused her nose to run, but she refused to drag a coat sleeve across her face as her brother would. She stopped several times to use a handkerchief and, on each occasion, cursed the chill that enveloped her ankles and numbed her fingers. After crossing the river on the Washington Street Bridge, she headed north to Milwaukee Avenue, which would take her straight into Polish Downtown. As expected, the factory was closed but surprisingly unlocked.

The dark and empty environs would have been more unsettling had she not been there just days before. Still, the silent machinery and off-putting smell cast an ominous pall. The note left in her desk drawer was anonymous and unspecific—she would find what she was looking for here. Given the note's secretive tone, she decided not to rouse anyone in the Swiatek residence in front. Instead, she would explore the place on her own.

Inside the factory, Harriet stumbled around for several minutes as her eyes slowly adjusted to the scant moonlight penetrating the grimy film coating the few windows. As best as she could see, there was nothing unusual to the factory's purpose or different from what she'd observed during her previous visit. Expelling a long breath, she scolded herself. What had she expected to discover? Agnes shackled to a meat grinder? Perhaps it was Agnes's abductor she was supposed to find? Could it be Damian Swiatek after all? Or another of the factory workers? She grumbled. Expanding the list of possible suspects didn't help. *Fitting that you're in the dark*, she chided herself. What she knew of Swiatek—that he was a good man besotted by Agnes— didn't square with snatching her from her bed. As for the other men at the factory, Tomasz was among them. If one of them had taken his sister, wouldn't he sense something amiss? She grumbled again, louder; she had been too eager to act on the note's contents.

A faint rustling met her ears. She froze. Cocked her head, listened intently. There it was again. A rat? She hoped for a cat. Regardless, she took the noise as an invitation to leave—quickly. She should have viewed the note, likely left by the same person who'd snatched her things, with more skepticism.

Like a bullet blast from her pistol, a large muscular dog burst into the room from some unseen spot in the darkness. It careened around the corner, its nails skidding on the slick hard floor. Harriet shrieked and made for the door. Realizing she wouldn't make it, she scrambled onto a tall butcher table, grateful she'd worn bloomers and not a long skirt. The dog lunged at her feet. She grabbed hold of a large steel hook dangling above her head and raised her legs beyond the reach of the dog's gnashing teeth. She couldn't hold the position for long.

Frantic, she looked for a way out. Above her, the hook slid along a track in the ceiling. She surmised its purpose was to move animal carcasses from one end of the floor to the other by pulling them through the air. If she could push away from the wall with enough force, she might slide to a spot by an open window. She had one chance. If she didn't travel far enough, she would end up clinging to the slippery hook in the middle of the room with nothing between her and the dog's snapping jaws. She took a few deep breaths and pushed off the wall with all her might. What happened next was not what she expected.

Instead of becoming stuck or moving jerkily in the track, she glided with ease and speed toward the window. Hoisting her knees to her chest, she punched her legs through the opening and scooted her rump onto the ledge, grateful her natural padding provided cushion against the rough, rigid frame. Her legs dangling against the outside wall, she peered down. Fortunately, the distance wasn't too far to jump.

Harriet estimated the drop was about eight feet. What lay below was dirt, hardened by the long winter months. The moment emphasized her substantial size; she would feel the impact. She recalled gymnastics lessons from high school. The physical education teacher with thick black hair on his arms had taught the girls to land with "soft knees" to absorb their weight better when landing. She never imagined the situation that would put that instruction to use.

Seconds later, Harriet was cursing that teacher. *Soft knees, my ass!* She climbed to her feet, brushing the dirt from her stockings and bloomers. Her hat, hugging her heap of hair, and handbag strapped to her shoulder, remained snugly in place. Now safe, she wondered why no one had been alerted by the dog's barking. While in peril, she was desperate for someone's intervention. Now, having escaped, she was relieved no one had come. How could she possibly explain herself?

Find what you are looking for at Swiatek's.

The message left in her drawer repeatedly played in her mind. Desperate to know its sender, she now questioned the motive. The author must have known she'd discover a closed factory, no indication of Agnes or her whereabouts, and a ferocious guard dog.

Stupid, stupid, stupid!

The missing notebook, slashed bicycle tires, the snatched suitcase, and now this. Someone at the Prescott Agency wasn't just meddling with her case—they were out to stop her for good.

Chapter 27

"What?" The word came out more aggressively than Harriet intended. But the look Aubrey gave her was similar to the ones she'd received earlier that day from Carl Somer and the secretaries. To return home and be greeted by a disapproving frown was too much to take. "You've something to say, say it, will you?"

Aubrey recoiled. "It's just that . . . well, you've torn your skirt and bloomers. You've also got an almighty gouge in your shoe."

"Oh." Harriet glanced down her front. "So it seems." Suddenly eager to change the topic, she said, "Did you fix yourself something to eat?"

Aubrey shrugged.

"Did you eat or not?" she snapped.

"Yes!"

She stomped across the living room and closed her bedroom door, suppressing the urge to slam it. She'd known the answer to her question before she'd asked. The donut crumbs on the counter, the mustard-coated knife, and bits of meat and cheese left on the plate beside the sink confirmed he'd had a sandwich after devouring the pączki—nothing made and saved for her. She wasn't in the mood for a quarrel, but her brother's laziness and thoughtlessness, like a furious itch, were impossible to ignore. After changing out of her soiled clothes, she reentered the living room in a nightgown. Aubrey lay across the sofa, Susan on his chest, reading a book. He made no effort to free space for her.

"We need to have a talk."

His eyes shifted slightly, confirming he'd heard her, but he said nothing. He didn't move. She lowered herself onto his outstretched legs.

"Get off!"

"Then make room!"

He tucked his knees with a dramatic groan. Susan padded over to Harriet and crawled onto her lap.

"I'm going to tell you a story," Harriet announced.

"I'm reading."

She snatched the book from his grasp.

"Stop it! Give it back!"

"I'm speaking. You will listen." She continued after another long groan. "There was once a seventeen-year-old girl. She was happy. She lived with her parents and younger brother. She had never considered that her life might change so dramatically, so terribly. But one day, in what seemed like a blink of an eye, her mother and father vanished from her life. The girl and her brother were forced to move from their home, their school, their friends—everything familiar and safe. The girl had planned to attend college, but that dream she shared with her mother was also taken from her. Still, the girl worked hard at school. She graduated and took a bookkeeping job to contribute to her uncle's and aunt's household income. They had taken her and her brother in. They were gracious and kind, but it was never the same as living with her parents. Not the same at all. But then, that would be impossible. Everyone knew that. And so they all did their best. When the girl turned twenty-one, she came into her inheritance. There was no money to speak of, but she did find herself the owner of the family's apartment and furnishings. The young girl was not her brother's guardian, nor did she presume to be. And yet, she was older and bore responsibility for the household. It was up to her to work and make money, do the shopping, the cooking, the cleaning, and provide for herself and her brother. The girl did this as best she could. But she was unhappy. She looked around and understood she was living a life she didn't want. And it didn't appear that it would ever change. She had a choice. Continue to be unhappy or do something about it. Then one day, she happened upon a newspaper advertisement. A downtown detective agency was seeking a junior operative. She knew she didn't stand a chance. The job would surely go to a man with a college education, who probably had some family connection to the firm's leader or at least one of its male operatives. But the girl, whether out of desperation or with what little hope she had left, presented her application."

Aubrey grinned. "She didn't like working at the grain elevator?"

"Despite the odds, the girl was given the position for a reason she may never fully understand. Although on a trial basis." She paused. "But it's not necessarily a happy ending."

"It's not?" Aubrey's amused expression turned wary.

"No. Not yet anyway. And it's hardly assured. The girl faces many challenges. She must find a missing girl by Monday, when she will begin work under the supervision of a man who is determined to see her fail. In addition, someone else inside the agency is secretly working to thwart her investigation. If she's fired, she must return to an income that's two-thirds of what she only just started earning. But more than that, she will have lost what she's quite sure is her one chance to make a rewarding and interesting life for herself."

She set her eyes on her brother's. "The girl is trying, Aubrey. She is truly trying her best. But she can't do it alone. She *can't*. She needs help from her colleagues at work."

She paused again. "And she needs help from her brother at home."

He stared back at her wordlessly. A victory, she sensed. He hadn't interrupted her with arguments. She transferred Susan from her lap to Aubrey's and went to the kitchen. Too tired to prepare a meal, she washed an apple, sliced some cheese, and tore the heel from a loaf of bread. Then despite her impulse to clean up after her brother, she went to bed.

The next morning she woke early. It was a big day. She would begin by meeting Matthew McCabe at Bogdan Nowak's house. She would end the day with Barbara at the mysterious Black Rabbit. In between, she would give Pearl Bartlett an update on the investigation.

The night before, Harriet had been too exhausted to unpack the suitcase. Now, with the men's clothing spread across the foot of her bed, she wondered where to store it. Should she be concerned about Aubrey seeing the suit and shirts hanging in her wardrobe or finding the smaller apparel items—socks, ties, and such—in her bureau drawers? Not thinking he snooped, she wouldn't put it past him either. But this was her house. Must she hide her things in her own home?

Harriet's preference for women had never been a topic of conversation with anyone, let alone her sixteen-year-old brother. Then most unexpectedly, in her first week at the Prescott Agency, the issue she kept buried had seemed inescapable. First, Pearl Bartlett divulged that she and her late husband had slept in different bedrooms and that she had a hunch that Harriet might have a use for his clothing. Matthew McCabe had seemed to hint at the topic in an awkwardly veiled conversation. And then, Barbara had talked of "queer men" and invited her to that night's annual drag ball, where men dressed as women and women as men. The whole thing was head-spinning. It was as if some unknown force had decided to surface another world—and just when the one she was familiar with was being upturned. Perhaps most extraordinary was finding herself with a wardrobe of fine men's clothing on a day that required her to wear them.

Recalling Barbara's instruction not to arrive in her ball attire, Harriet repacked the suitcase with a white shirt, a red bow tie, matching suspenders, and a dark wool suit. The remaining articles were hung or folded among her other clothing. Reluctantly, she dug an old pair of men's shoes from the back of her wardrobe. Aubrey had pointed out the damage done to her shoe by the sharp windowsill at the factory. A scratch might go unnoticed, but not the large gash that threatened to separate the entire toe from the rest of the shoe. Replacing them would be costly. She guessed her first opportunity to do so was at least three weeks' wages away.

She crept to the kitchen to avoid waking Aubrey in the other bedroom. It took a few moments before she realized he had cleaned up after she'd turned in the night before. She understood her delight was disproportionate to his modest achievement, but it was progress. He had heard the message of her story and done his part. Would it last? Probably before the day was done, she'd have some indication. But for the moment, she would butter toast and relish the small victory.

Chapter 28

No sooner had Harriet set off on her bicycle than she remembered why she had once retired the shoes she wore. The soles had worn smooth and slipped off the pedals. She would need to rethink her footwear. The pair of handsome leather lace-ups ruined in her ill-fated visit to the sausage factory had been a splurge. She had justified their nearly three-dollar price by foreseeing a long life, convincing herself it was worth less than a penny a day to enjoy such quality. However, the rigors of an operative's job had already taken a toll on her wardrobe. She wasn't sure if the rip in her skirt could be adequately repaired and anticipated scrubbing the dirt stains from her bloomers would be a time-consuming chore. Not for the first time, she considered swapping a skirt for trousers—a change certain to turn heads. But didn't she already?

The route to Polish Downtown was now familiar. She foresaw the largest depressions in the road and the busiest intersections. In the past few years, she had witnessed a dramatic change in riding a bicycle on the increasingly busy Chicago streets. The popularity of motorcars—with size, speed, and unforgiving steel—introduced an element of danger she'd not had to contend with as a child. The "own the road" attitude and poor driving skills of many drivers only made matters more precarious.

Harriet had examined a street map the night before. What she couldn't have anticipated was the closure of a particular block to accommodate an outdoor market. As it was Saturday morning, she presumed it was a weekly event. Fortunately, the detour added only a few minutes to her journey. Arriving at the address she'd obtained at the pool hall, she locked her bicycle several houses away from Bogdan Nowak's and strolled leisurely up the sidewalk. Matthew McCabe had been clear in his instruction not to be early; she understood the needless risk of loitering outside a known criminal's home. A glance at her wristwatch told her she had one minute. She slowed her pace.

As she approached the designated meeting spot—the house immediately east of Nowak's—Matthew appeared from around the opposite corner. He was dressed in the customary fashion of male operatives: simple dark suit, tie, and derby hat. She presumed the reason was to blend into a crowd. What unavoidably stood out, however, were Matthew's good looks. In the morning light, his eyes appeared a richer shade of blue, the hair below his hat redder. He was sure to be popular among women—and she didn't doubt certain men would also be charmed.

"Good morning, Miss Morrow." He smiled amiably and tipped his hat.

"Mr. McCabe."

"So here's what I'm thinking. We can't know who, if anyone, is inside the house. But prudence demands we plan for Nowak's presence. Given what you say about him, we must also presume he has a weapon and won't hesitate to use it if unduly surprised or feeling threatened. The man will recognize you from your visit to the pool hall. Moreover, he believes you to be associated with the domestic help service. Your presence will alarm him. For that reason alone, you should remain here and beyond sight from his doorway. I will go to the house and ring the bell. If Nowak is home, I'll try to determine if he is alone or if a woman is there too and, if so, what she looks like. I'll learn as much as I can. However, if a woman answers and Nowak isn't there, I'll summon you to join me. As you've seen a photograph of the missing woman, you can determine whether it is the maid you are looking for."

Harriet was disappointed not to accompany Matthew initially, but his plan made sense. There was no explaining her presence to Nowak. She repeated a description of Agnes and asked, "If Nowak is there, how will you explain yourself? Why are you knocking on his door?" Her interest was twofold—she was eager to learn a new strategy from a more experienced operative and was curious to know how Matthew planned to tailor the approach for the current moment.

"It was actually Carl Somer who taught me this trick." He straightened his shoulders and cleared his throat. "I'm sorry to disturb you, sir. I am looking for Helen." Matthew feigned fluster. "This *is* where she lives, isn't it?"

"Yes, but if Agnes is there and hidden away elsewhere in the house, you'll be turned away without confirming whether she is there."

"I won't leave so easily. I'm a determined suitor, don't you know. I'll say something like, 'But the young woman I saw the other day, you're saying that wasn't my Helen? I could swear it looked just like her. We lost touch, you see. And well, when I saw her enter the house the other day . . . you're quite sure there's no Helen inside?' "

Clever, Harriet thought. Were there any woman inside the house, the instinctive reply from most persons would be to say the woman inside was not Helen, thereby confirming the presence of *some* woman. If fortune were on Matthew's side, Nowak might even wish to conclusively prove that the woman present was not Helen by asking the woman who *was* there to show her face. However, if no woman were there, they would simply say that instead.

Matthew continued, "Of course, the best outcome is to

find only Agnes inside." He spread his hands. "Alas, seldom is an operative so fortunate."

"I wish you success," Harriet said. "I'll be watching and ready to join you at once if summoned."

Matthew gestured to her handbag. "Do me a favor and have that new pistol of yours in hand and at the ready. If Nowak's not around, you can return it to your bag on your way to the house."

Harriet nodded as a shiver ran through her. Fleeing the clutches of the redheaded man at the pool hall and then escaping the factory the night before had disabused her of any notion that detecting wasn't perilous. Matters were escalating rapidly. She feared she wasn't ready for gunplay with a man like Bogdan Nowak. But it would not be just her own life in peril; her colleague and one true ally at the agency could be endangered. If the moment demanded it, she would act. Was she prepared to shoot him? If it meant saving Matthew, yes.

Harriet held her breath while watching Matthew approach the house next door. He lifted his hand, apparently pressing a buzzer. He waited. Harriet noted that he didn't risk a glance in her direction. Another practice she would log in her memory—never assume you aren't being watched. She also admired Matthew's patience. A minute passed before he tried the buzzer again. A moment later, he stepped back. Someone had answered the door.

Given the distance, she couldn't make out the words, but the other voice belonged to a man. Matthew made a few gestures that, in Harriet's view, appeared disarming. She scrutinized Matthew's body movements for any indication of alarm or distress. There were none. She heard the door shut. Matthew turned and bounced down the steps. A moment later, he stood beside her.

Breathless, she managed, "Well?"

Matthew gripped her elbow and led her farther down the sidewalk away from the house. "I presume that was

Nowak. Big man, strong. Wild dark hair, unkempt beard, menacing eyes."

"Sounds like him," she confirmed.

"Regrettably, I didn't see or hear anyone else inside."

Her shoulders slumped.

"However, Nowak said I'd gotten it wrong. His exact words, 'She's not the woman you're looking for.' "

Harriet stopped and spun around to face Matthew. "It worked!"

Grinning, he replied, "Of course it worked. I've attempted that twice before and it worked both times. Now you must discover *who* is inside. That calls for the time-tested way among operatives. Watch and wait."

Again, Matthew's approach was wise. Nowak would eventually leave the house. When he did, they could return and see who was there. The challenge was timing. Nowak might leave any minute or not for hours—perhaps not for the entire day. The Monday deadline was looming. If Agnes were inside, waiting would be worth it. But if she weren't, valuable time would be wasted.

As if reading her mind, Matthew said, "As long as Nowak remains there, he's a threat. We have no way of knowing how long it will be before he departs. But when he does, be careful and wait five minutes before you approach the house and ring the bell. You want to make sure he hasn't forgotten something or stepped out for only a moment for some reason."

Harriet blinked rapidly, her mind making sense of his words.

"I'm sorry, Miss Morrow, but I've work of my own that demands attention. I will be at the agency should you need me. I'm confident you can handle matters on your own from here on. By the way, you'll be glad to know the window next to the door is ajar. If no one answers, enter through the window. Be discreet, and whatever you do, make it quick. You don't want to be caught inside when

Nowak returns. Any unease I have about leaving you is lessened by knowing you have that derringer in your handbag. Don't hesitate to use it. But remember, it's a close-range weapon. Keeping danger at a distance is a natural instinct, but you will only waste bullets. You need your target close."

Harriet didn't welcome the anxiety stirred by Matthew's leaving. But this was the job. She couldn't rely on others to protect her. Watching him disappear around the corner, she chuckled mockingly to herself. *You argued you could do a man's job . . . well, time to prove it.*

Her next thought was impatience—ten minutes later she was already restless. Why hadn't she suggested to Matthew that they summon the police and free the woman, whoever she was? If it were Agnes, the case would be solved immediately. And if it weren't, she could move on, knowing a woman had been rescued from a dire situation. Either way, Nowak would be arrested. Wouldn't he? She recalled Barbara, Tomasz, and Marcin all saying he contributed to the local political bosses to ensure his private business avoided police interference. But surely, kidnapping a woman was too significant a crime to ignore.

She thought of the women working in the Ali Baba's basement. They too were captives of a sort. After exhausting every other option to survive, they had turned to selling themselves. Over the past several years, the various forms of oppression had become a heightened topic in the newspapers and across kitchen tables. Women were paid scant wages and subjugated to the will of men. Children were employed in dangerous work. Immigrants and the poor toiled long hours in intolerable conditions and lived in squalor with little hope of improving their lot in life. Harriet's mother had done her part by working with the Illinois Equal Suffrage Association to someday win women the vote. Harriet had never questioned the righteousness of the cause and felt shame for her lack of involvement. She vowed to do more. If not her, then who?

She pulled back her sleeve and expelled a long breath. It had been six minutes since she last checked her watch. Over the next hour, she fell into a routine of sitting for five minutes, walking in a tight circle for five minutes, then repeating the cycle. She figured it would keep her alert, give her something to do, and ensure her joints didn't stiffen from sitting too long. Another hour passed, and she regretted not having brought along a snack. In the future, she determined to have an alternative plan when the first ground to a slow and maddening halt. If there was a way to lure Nowak out of the house, she couldn't conceive it. Besides, it wasn't enough to get him outside; he needed to stay away long enough for her to discover the identity of the woman inside. Muttering to herself, she wished she'd asked Matthew for advice on what to do should nothing happen. He had said she was to "wait and watch," but there must be a limit.

Completing what must be her tenth cycle, she heard a sound from next door. She spun around. Nowak lumbered down the stairs. She dashed for cover behind a shrub and watched him strut away in the opposite direction. He continued down the sidewalk until she lost sight of him two blocks in the distance. Another of Matthew's instructions had been to allow five minutes to pass before approaching the house. She might have done that two hours ago, but not now.

Hurrying to the door, she pressed the bell. The silence was maddening. She moved to the window—it was, as Matthew had said, slightly ajar. She glanced over each shoulder, ensuring no one was within sight, then slipped her fingers beneath the sash and lifted. Although sticky, the pane rose without much effort. After another look behind her, she pulled her handbag over her shoulder, arched a leg over the sill, and ducked inside the house.

Harriet was struck by the empty room's resemblance to the Wozniaks' front room: small, sparse, and undecorated. However, Agnes's family's home had been warm and smelled of cooking food. This place was dank. A moldy odor hung in the air. She shivered. If Agnes were in the next room, did the familiar surroundings remind her of all she'd lost? Harriet moved carefully but quickly into the narrow hallway. There were three doors. One narrower than the others suggested a closet. The widest with a substantial bolt must open to the backyard and the outhouse. The third door must lead to a bedroom.

Should she knock? The question released a cascade of others: what if someone besides the woman was in the room? What if she were armed and responded to Harriet as the intruder she was? What if Nowak suddenly reappeared? She quietly removed the loaded pistol from her handbag. Derringer in hand, she pushed open the door.

The room was still. A woman lay on the bed covered by a thin blanket. She appeared to be asleep, her long, dark-haired head was turned toward the wall. This could work in Harriet's favor. If the woman turned out not to be Agnes, Harriet could leave undiscovered. She moved cautiously around the bed, wishing for no squeaks from the floorboards. She held her breath and took the final step that would bring the woman's face into view.

Had the family photograph not clearly shown Agnes, Harriet might have convinced herself the woman could be her. But Agnes was an uncommon beauty. This woman, although attractive, was not her.

Two emotions competed for primacy—relief that Agnes wasn't being held there against her will and crushing disappointment that her search for the missing maid must continue. As Harriet lifted a foot in retreat, the woman's eyes popped open. They stared at one another in silence for several long seconds. Harriet could run, but something in the woman's gaze pinned her to the spot.

The woman—girl?—said, "You going to shoot me?"

Realizing she had the gun pointed at the woman, Harriet lowered her pistol and returned it to the handbag slung over her shoulder.

"What do you want?" the woman said.

The remark struck Harriet as forcefully as a fist. *What do you want?* Not *Have you come to save me?* or *Thank God, take me with you.* No shriek. No indication of alarm. Only resignation tinged with slight curiosity.

"I'm looking for a woman. Her name is Agnes Wozniak. I thought she might be here."

Fighting the urge to dash from the house, she said, "Miss, do you require help? Are you here against your will?"

The woman didn't move, didn't speak. Harriet glanced back at the doorway. Nowak might arrive any moment. But what if she were this woman's only chance to be rescued? She repeated her questions.

The woman bolted upright, startling Harriet. "Help? You come with an offer of help? What kind of help is that? A place to live? Money to buy food and clothes?" Angry, the woman thrust an accusing finger at Harriet. "You will protect me from him? Is that it? Is it? Tell me, how will you help me?"

Sputtering for a good answer, Harriet replied, "We can start by getting you out of here if that's what you want. I'm sure the rest can be arranged."

The woman sat up taller, infuriated by Harriet's reply. "You're sure? You know nothing. I can leave whenever I choose. You offer nothing." She spat the last word. "I've nowhere to go." She scoffed and shook her head. "Whoever you are, get out. Leave me be. You know nothing. Nothing!"

Ashamed to have offered the woman something she couldn't begin to deliver, Harriet nodded and turned to leave as the sound of heavy bootsteps clomped up the front steps. The front door opened.

Harriet didn't think. She ran. Skidding on the worn hallway floorboards, she lunged for the back door.

"Stop!" Bogdan shouted.

His bootsteps signaled he was closing in behind her. Frantic, she slid the bolt free and swung open the door.

Running from the building, she glanced right and left. A large broken crate lay against a stretch of fencing near the outhouse at the back of the property. She heard Nowak burst through the back door. Scrambling onto the crate, she felt a protruding nail puncture her palm. She swallowed a squeal of pain, jumped to her feet, and grabbed the top of the fence.

"Damn you! Stop!" Bogdan yelled.

She hoisted herself up but fell back, her hand protesting in pain and the slick underside of her shoes finding no traction on the vertical slats. She reset her grip, gritted her teeth, bent her knees and jumped, practically throwing herself over the fence—*halfway*. He was nearly upon her. She swung her legs up as he grabbed one of her shoes. She kicked hard. *Thwack*. He groaned. She heard him fall backward and off the crate onto the hard ground. She dropped to the other side of the fence and hobbled in one shoe toward a distant gate. Only when she'd reached the street did she risk looking back. There was no sight of Bogdan Nowak.

Chapter 29

Harriet stood in the middle of her bedroom looking down with a grimace. *At least both are black.* The shoe lost to Nowak's clutches had been the left. The night before, she'd irreparably damaged the right of her only other pair. Mismatched footwear was embarrassing; she wasn't a street urchin. Most bothersome were the heels' slight difference in height, enough to feel off-kilter. In addition to providing a progress report, she now had another reason to visit Pearl Bartlett. Perhaps a pair of her late husband's shoes might fit her.

Adding to her ragamuffin look, she wore a badly faded skirt with a frayed hem. She had no choice. While climbing over the fence, she had ripped her second skirt in as many days. She admonished herself again for not asking Mr. Prescott about expenses. Along with needing to replace several clothing items and shoes, she had incurred streetcar fares—a consequence of her ruined bicycle tires, which further depleted her pocketbook. And when would she be paid her wages? The bookkeeping job doled out pay at the end of each week. With several notices on the kitchen table and scant savings, she couldn't go longer than another week without paying the household bills.

With it being Saturday, Aubrey was still asleep. She envied his opportunity and ability to sleep until noon on weekends. Although she was naturally an early riser, the past week's anxiety had reset her internal alarm to a frustrating five o'clock, adding fatigue to her list of burdens. She glanced longingly at her bed and the kitten snuggled against the blanket but couldn't indulge in more sleep with less than forty-eight hours left to conclude her investigation.

She donned her hat.

Thirty minutes later, she leaned her bicycle against the back wall of Pearl's mansion. The music, a boisterous number featuring trombones, confirmed Pearl's presence. However, she didn't appear to be in the orangery or adjacent kitchen. A knock on the door wouldn't be heard over the marching band, so Harriet stepped inside the house to search for her client. No sooner had she closed the door behind her than Pearl, trailed by Toby, shuffled into the room, lugging a pail and shovel. She didn't seem surprised to find Harriet standing in her kitchen. She was, however, vexed.

"Harry! I've reached the end of my tether. I'm not one to flaunt my wealth, but the fact remains. I can more than afford a maid. Last I checked, I had one. Until I didn't. And it would appear that you have yet to find her."

She dropped the pail, sending up a plume of soot encircling her knees.

"It's been more than a week since Agnes disappeared. I take no enjoyment in replacing her, but I must. I don't have the energy or the time to keep this house up to snuff and tend to my plants and do my baking. So unless you've got Agnes hiding beneath your skirt . . ." She paused, appearing to assess the sorry state of Harriet's wardrobe. "Did you know you're wearing two different shoes?"

"Yes, Pearl. It's a long story. Speaking of which—"

"Must I do everything around here?" Shaking her head, she continued, "C'mon then. I'm a pretty good judge of sizes and portions—and character. Ha!" She abruptly left the room.

Harriet caught up with the fast-moving older woman and her white cat halfway up the main staircase. The home's enormity and grandeur never failed to impress, yet the kitchen was the only room Harriet had ever been comfortable in. Was that because of the smell of something always baking? The music from the adjacent orangery? Or simply that Pearl enlivened the room with her constant presence?

In the late Horace's bedroom, Harriet selected a fine pair of oxfords. She had admired such shoes in high-end store windows or the more exclusive section of Marshall Field's men's department, but never had she examined a pair up close or checked a price tag. She gulped at guessing their cost. Pearl nodded, her fists firmly planted at her bony hips.

"I knew it!" she crowed. "Like twelve cups of batter in a Bundt pan. There must be at least a half dozen other pairs at the bottom of the wardrobe, Harry. Take as many as you like. They're just taking up space."

Harriet didn't want to appear greedy, but the footwear collection was thrilling. She indulged by selecting three additional pairs. To carry them, Pearl provided a handsome canvas tote that Harriet imagined Horace had used for overnight stays in lavish country retreats. With the shoe issue resolved, Harriet turned to the topic of her investigation.

"I need until Monday morning, Pearl. Please. That is how long Mr. Prescott has allowed me. If I haven't found Agnes by then, then by all means, you should proceed to interview replacements."

Hands still on her hips, Pearl replied, "I might be persuaded, but you'll have to convince me there's reason for hope. Which is another way of asking if you've made progress that might actually lead to you finding her?"

Harriet recounted what she'd learned since she was last there, from the visit to the Ali Baba, the conversation with Marcin Wozniak at the back of the cheese shop, the cryptic note that led to the encounter at the sausage factory, and her narrow escape from Bogdan Nowak's house just that morning.

Looking more worried than satisfied, Pearl said, "Well, I've got to hand it to you, Harry. You're putting in a fair effort. So, all right. I'll continue to play the maid around this pile of bricks. But only for two more days. *Two days.* That's my limit."

"Thank you, Pearl. Thank you. I know being alone in this large house hasn't been easy."

The remark appeared to spark emotion in her host. "I'm going to tell you a story, Harry. But there isn't any story that doesn't go down better with a berry buckle."

"But Pearl, I haven't the time. Not now."

Pearl shot Harriet a stern look. "The kitchen. I gave you two days. You can give me a half hour. End of negotiation."

Harriet followed Pearl and Toby back downstairs and into the kitchen. With a generous slice of raspberry buckle before each of them, Pearl said, "How old would you say I am, Harry?"

Caught off guard by the question, Harriet scrambled for a polite reply. Shaving a decade from her guess, she replied, "Sixty?"

Pearl frowned. "Try again. And this time be honest."

"Seventy?"

"Closer. I've been an adult for more than a half century. That's a mighty long time. In all those years, I've wanted for nothing in the way of creature comforts. You can see that for yourself." She gestured broadly, sweeping a bony arm through the air. "But that doesn't mean I had a grand old time every minute. I eventually settled into a peaceable life here with Horace. But ours was a marriage of mutual convenience. Not love." She paused, caught in reflection.

"I suppose I came to love him in time but never as a husband. You see, Harry, I gave my heart to someone else when I was twenty-three years old. Her name was Bess."

Thankful for having just taken a bite of dessert, Harriet mumbled, "Oh."

"The year was 1851. I was, as I say, just twenty-three at the time. I suppose my privilege enabled my progressive beliefs. I could afford such thoughts, you see. I didn't have too much else to concern me. A friend of mine, Gladys, got wind of a gathering of women in her hometown of Akron, Ohio. The Ohio Women's Convention, it was called. It promised speeches from like-minded women who, to put it bluntly, were tired of men running everything. Gladys talked me into traveling with her to the event. Though truth be told, I was happy to go. I still remember the second day, May 29. But for two very different reasons. Did you know, Harry, that on that day, Sojourner Truth, the emancipated slave, delivered a rousing speech? No? Well, she did. It mightily affected the audience, all the women anyway. Now, I may not get her words just right, but she said something to the effect of, 'I am as muscled as any man and can do the same work.' Miss Truth went on to argue that men needn't be afraid to give women their rights. Many of her remarks were biblical in reference, which I don't give much credence to, but still, the forcefulness with which she spoke was mesmerizing. Here was a woman who had suffered unspeakable abuse and hardship. Yet she stood proudly on the steps, saying her piece. Her final words, I do recall. Gladys and I committed them to memory, writing them down shortly after the event. 'Man is in a tight place, the poor slave is on him, woman is coming on him, he is surely between a hawk and a buzzard.' Between a hawk and buzzard, Harry. Miss Truth wasn't one for mincing words."

Pearl followed a forkful of buckle with a swallow of milk. "The few men in attendance hooted and made appalling remarks, but they were far outnumbered. The courage of Miss Truth to say what she did affected Gladys and me profoundly. I vowed right then and there that I wouldn't live a life to satisfy society's expectations or live under the supervision of a man I didn't want.

"That evening, Gladys and I were invited to join several women to discuss Miss Truth's remarks in the home of a local leader of the convention. It was there that I met Bess. How does one describe such love, Harry? She was lovely. And witty. How she could make me laugh. I was in awe of her. And much to my surprise, she seemed to return my affection. The next week, Bess traveled to Chicago for a visit. She stayed here in the house, my parents' home at the time. We secretly spent private time together, as risky as that was. No one suspected that two silly girls could be more than friends. Two men, of course, would never get away with such an arrangement. But Bess and I could take walks while holding hands or offer one another displays of tenderness with no one batting an eye. For the next year, Bess visited once a month and stayed for a weekend, and we regularly exchanged correspondence. We conceived of a plan for how we might have a life together. The world would consider us spinsters. We knew that. But we'd not be suspected of anything untoward. We were to set up our home in Boston. I had the means to support us and had become restless living under my parents' constant gaze. I was in Boston searching for a suitable home for Bess and me when I received her final letter. She had accepted a marriage proposal from the son of a prominent Ohio banker."

Pearl stopped speaking abruptly, apparently lost in remembrance. Harriet waited. When it became apparent Pearl had concluded her story, Harriet said, "I'm sorry, Pearl." What more could she say? The woman had just shared her greatest sorrow. What words could she offer to provide solace? Their dessert finished, Pearl carried the empty plates to the sink. Much to Harriet's disapproval, Toby jumped onto the counter to attack the crumbs. Returning to the table, Pearl had regained her usual disposition. "You get the meaning of my story, Harry? Or do I need to spell it out for you?"

There was an answer Pearl desired, but Harriet wasn't sure what it was. "Love may be fleeting? That I'd do well to protect my heart?"

Pearl reared back as if slapped. "What? Good grief! No! That's precisely the opposite of my point. Embrace life, Harry! Embrace love, and don't let it go when you find it. Fight for it. Don't tuck your tail and whimper off into the corner. Do so, and you might still be there with your thumb stuck in your mouth fifty-one years later. Don't think you can't have or don't deserve what you truly want. Whatever that might be. Live your life for you, Harry. No one else."

Harriet sat silently, absorbing everything that Pearl had just said. Before she could reply, Pearl said, "Now. As you've made abundantly clear, time is of the essence. You best get on with finding my maid. I've got a monstrosity of a house that needs cleaning. I'm not sure if you noticed, but Toby is of little help when it comes to chores."

Surprising both of them, Harriet rushed to Pearl and enveloped her in her arms. "Thank you, Pearl."

Harriet held the hug until Pearl broke the moment, wriggling free of the embrace. "Good heavens, Harry. It was only cobbler."

Chapter 30

Harriet counted to ten. It was silly—she knew that. But the occasion called for ceremony—even if it had significance only to her. *Eight . . . nine . . . ten.* She opened her bedroom door and stepped into the living room.

Silence.

Aubrey lay on the sofa immersed in *The Boys with Old Hickory*, a book she'd given him on his last birthday. Susan slept nestled in the crook of his arm. After several long seconds, he became curious and glanced up from the page. The book fell to the floor with an emphatic *thud*. Susan gave a start before jumping down to trot over and greet Harriet.

"Why are you dressed like a man?"

"I am not dressed like a man," Harriet replied. "I am wearing clothing you're accustomed to seeing worn by men."

He shook his head, bewildered. "You're wearing a man's clothes."

"For years, you've heard me complain about the impracticality of skirts and shoes with unnecessarily high heels. Well, I've decided it's time I do something about it."

"But you already wear men's shoes."

"And now I've completed the look. There's no reason I

should continue to wear clothes that don't suit me. So? How do I look?"

"You look like you in men's clothes."

"Really?" She threw her hands in the air. "That's the best you can do? The simplest and most obvious observation possible?"

"You look . . . nice?"

She huffed loudly. "Never mind."

"Are you going outside like that?"

"No. Well, yes. I haven't quite decided."

"You just said you were done wearing clothes that don't suit you."

She pursed her lips, examining her brother's expression. Deciding he was sincere, she said, "I did, didn't I? But it's a big step. I'm considering this a trial."

"You look nice, Harriet. You look better in men's clothes."

The remark surprised her. Was he still being honest? Or saying what he thought she wanted to hear? Seeming to sense her uncertainty, he added, "You look more like you in trousers. Though people are sure to stare if you leave home dressed like that."

This Harriet knew. The anticipated scornful looks and whispered remarks had held her back for as long as she had understood her preference. The following year would be the same, and the year after and the year after that. Society wouldn't change on its own. It would take women like her to change it. Although her motivation wasn't to promote a cause, if her stepping out in a man's clothing emboldened other women to follow suit, then all the better. For the moment, however, Harriet would change into her usual attire and carry her clothes to her rendezvous with Barbara in the tote Pearl had given her. But that was still hours away.

"Do you want any help with dinner?" Aubrey asked.

The question, which might be common in other households, was so extraordinary coming from her brother that she first wondered whether she'd heard him right. "You want to help?"

He made a face. "I didn't say I wanted to help. I asked if you wanted help."

She couldn't help but smile. *Baby steps*, she thought.

"Yes. That would be appreciated. Let me change, and then you can peel the potatoes and carrots while I tend to the rest."

After dinner, Harriet explained to Aubrey that her work required her to leave for several hours. His concern for her safety was immediately supplanted with fascination when she revealed the derringer in her handbag. She wasn't comfortable having the gun at home with a curious adolescent boy, but it couldn't be helped. Deciding it was better to make him aware of its presence and discuss its danger rather than have him happen upon it himself, she said, "This gun has a singular purpose. Protection. Of course, a criminal might use a pistol with bad intentions, but mine is expressly to stop a threat as a last means of defense. I want you to know about it so we can be absolutely clear between us—this is not to be touched by you. It is not a toy, Aubrey. I understand you'll think it's exciting and be tempted to handle it, but you must promise to honor my request and leave it be."

Harriet knew her brother too well to rely on his word—not with such an alluring object within reach. And so she decided to strike a bargain that might actually win his compliance. "If you promise and abide by it, I will ask my colleague, Mr. McCabe, to take you to the shooting club and introduce you to the proper operation of a firearm. I would rather you approach a gun with responsibility and knowledge than act on curiosity alone."

He nodded enthusiastically. "Tomorrow?"

"No. I'm afraid I'm too busy with work, and as a courtesy to Mr. McCabe, we'll need to accommodate his schedule. Hopefully, we can arrange the outing for next weekend. That's the best I can offer. So. Do we have a deal?"

"Deal," Aubrey said, looking even more excited than when she'd surprised him with a donut from the Polish bakery.

With Horace Bartlett's hand-me-downs folded inside the tote bag, she strapped the bundle to the rear of her bicycle and ensured her hat was on tightly. Aubrey had continued on his path to improvement and offered to clean the dishes—though she suspected his motive was to remain in her good graces and not scuttle his opportunity to play Jesse James at the gun club.

The corner of Polk and Dearborn was just a short distance south of her home and yet a world away. Many establishments catered to various vices—gambling, prostitution, bawdy entertainment, and heavy drinking. Harriet hadn't thought to ask Barbara about the security of her bicycle. She hoped it would be possible to take the Victoria with them to the Black Rabbit, where there might be a safe place to store it. Lock or no lock, it wouldn't be wise to leave it outside in that part of the city. And she had only just replaced both tires.

Barbara's instruction had been precise—*meet at nine o'clock*. As Harriet had arrived several minutes early, she circled the surrounding blocks until the appointed time. Precisely on the hour, Barbara appeared holding a worn burlap bag. Harriet coasted to a stop.

"Hello," Barbara said, eyeing the tote strapped to the bicycle, "You've brought something to wear?"

"I have, yes." Harriet dismounted and wheeled the bicycle onto the sidewalk.

Barbara nodded. "This way, then. It's not far."

The moonlight added to Barbara's allure. The contours of her features and figure seemed more beguiling, more mysterious. She smelled lightly spicy, and her dark hair was still damp from a recent washing. They walked in silence as if required by their secretive purpose. Barbara surprised Harriet by abruptly turning into a narrow lane. Before she could ask, Barbara turned again into a passageway so narrow that Harriet struggled to fit through with her bicycle. They continued to the end and an unmarked door. Barbara knocked. A small panel at head height opened that Harriet hadn't noticed in the dark. A set of eyes peered out at them.

"Good evening, Albert," Barbara said.

The panel snapped shut. There was an odd scraping sound, and the door opened. They stepped inside; Harriet wheeled her bicycle alongside her. "Welcome to the ball," Albert said, removing his top hat and bowing with a flourish.

Harriet's gaze lowered to Albert, who wasn't over four feet tall, and suddenly understood the odd sound had been Albert moving a stool he had stood on to see through the panel in the door.

Over her shoulder, Barbara said, "Ready, Harriet? Once you step inside the Black Rabbit, there's no going back."

Harriet nodded nervously and followed Barbara down a short hallway through a curtained doorway into a large empty space. Gaining her bearings, Harriet understood they'd entered a vacant shop from the back.

"You can leave your bicycle here," Barbara said. "It will be as safe as we are."

Music, voices, and footsteps seeped through the ceiling. Harriet looked up with a mix of anticipation and trepidation.

"This way." Barbara gestured toward an open staircase against the wall. "Mind your step. It's a bit uneven in spots."

The sound steadily increased with their ascent. Harriet's pulse galloped. At the top of the steps was another hallway running the length of the building. Judging by the layout with several doors off the corridor, this had once been a large apartment above the store. Barbara ushered Harriet inside the first door.

A gas lamp illuminated what had once been a spacious bedroom. A simple chair or stool sat before two mirrored vanities. Various pieces of luggage lay here and there, cluttering the floor. All manner of women's clothing had been draped over the sparse furniture. The number of belongings shocked Harriet. At least two dozen women had passed through this room.

"I choose to arrive late," Barbara explained. "I've been to the club on a handful of occasions and only once before to the ball, but each time the dressing room was quite chaotic with all the ladies in here at once."

Harriet was grateful for Barbara's decision. Changing in front of a roomful of adult women was more exhibition than she was prepared for. Barbara didn't hesitate; she tugged off her jacket and began to unbutton her shirtwaist. Harriet abruptly turned away, aware her reaction might seem prudish. But whatever this place had to offer—whatever awaited her in the next room—pulsed with unfamiliar intensity. It would take some getting used to.

Harriet was pleased with herself for having tried on the late Horace's suit beforehand; it lessened her jitters. Once fully dressed, tie knotted, and shoes laced, she stood and turned toward Barbara.

Her heart leaped and lodged in her throat. A flood of emotion choked her ability to speak. Barbara filled the silence. "Well, well, well. Look at you, Miss Harriet Morrow. I must say, you look most handsome. Most handsome, indeed."

"And you," Harriet said softly. "You, Barbara, *yesh-tesh pee-enk-nah.*"

Barbara froze. The two women stared at one another for a long moment. "How do you know to say that?"

"Is it not correct?" Harriet said, suddenly worried she might have gotten the pronunciation wrong.

"*Jesteś piękna*," Barbara said. "You are beautiful." A smile took over her face. "Yes, I remember now. I said that to you the first day we met. I meant it."

"And I mean it now," Harriet said. Barbara wore a slightly too-large brown men's suit jacket and a grass-green silk tie. Notably, she had pulled her hair back into a tight chignon.

Barbara spread her hands wide to each side and turned slightly to the right and left. "The suit is a castoff from my uncle. He doesn't know I plucked it from the pile of clothes the family collected for a Union fundraiser. The tie belongs to my brother Tomasz." She put a finger to her lips. "He doesn't know I borrowed it. The shoes, however, are mine. I purchased them for the occasion. I had no choice. I'm not ashamed to say that my feet are bigger than any of my brothers." She grinned. "The shopkeeper presumed they were for my husband, though I said nothing to give him that idea." She shrugged. "And where did you come by such fine clothing?"

Harriet would tell Barbara about Pearl Bartlett and her late husband's wardrobe in good time. But the anticipation of arriving at the ball was too much to bear. "A story for later?"

Nodding, Barbara took Harriet's arm and led her from the dressing room. The music and sounds of conversation that had thrummed through the ceiling and wall burst into vivid clarity as they entered the Black Rabbit's main hall.

Harriet was dumbstruck. The room sparkled with laughter and convivial chatter. Golden light shimmered from hundreds of candles reflected by an ornate chandelier and a dozen mirrors lining the walls. Heavy black curtains covered all the windows. A piano player and bassist commanded a small stage in a corner opposite a polished mahogany bar. About fifty men and half as many women filled the space. The men wore dresses; many had rouged and powdered their faces. The few women who didn't wear a man's suit and tie—red, purple, and lavender, the most popular hues—wore a tuxedo. Champagne flutes were clutched in many hands, as were long-tipped, silver cigarette holders. That the event was clandestine added to its marvel; any passerby down on the street could never imagine what splendor awaited beyond the nondescript building's facade.

As Harriet had taken in the sights and sounds, Barbara had obtained two glasses of champagne. Handing one to Harriet, she said, "Welcome to the Black Rabbit, my lovely."

Chapter 31

Dazzled as she was, Harriet hadn't lost sight of her purpose for being there: to follow up on a suspect, Johnny Bartlett. The matchbox she had snatched from his home came from the Black Rabbit. If Marcin was right, Agnes had been smitten by a man with gray eyes who'd visited her place of employment. Johnny ticked both boxes. Moreover, Johnny frequently visited the Ali Baba Theater, where time with women was easily bought. His patronage there fit the reputation of a young lothario with money and time to spare. But not here. *Most definitely not here.*

Harriet recalled how the woman in the Ali Baba's basement had called Johnny "Mr. Money Bags" and said he could "afford whatever suits him. *We don't.*" Harriet had accepted the remark to mean his particular taste in women. When Harriet had clarified that Johnny never descended to the Depths, as the basement was known, the woman replied, "If you really knew Johnny, you wouldn't have to ask that." Could it be true? Was Johnny Bartlett a sexual invert? A queer? The notion confused Harriet. She wouldn't think less of him if he was, and yet she would be devastated—he would cease to be a likely suspect in Agnes's disappearance. Wouldn't he?

Turning to Barbara, Harriet said, "Besides Johnny

Bartlett, I'm eager to learn if anyone here is named Mattie." Registering Barbara's look, she reminded her, "The name scribbled on the back of the matchbox."

"Patience," Barbara advised. "I know you're anxious, Harriet. I appreciate that. We are both desperate to learn anything we can about Agnes. But this is a party—a once-a-year event. Everyone is here to have a good time and celebrate. You can't just interrupt a group and start interrogating them. Trust is in short supply among this crowd. They don't know you. A wrong first step, and they'll suspect you. Then you are done for. They'll tell you nothing. Tonight, you must first be Harriet, a detective second. It is the only way."

Barbara's counsel seemed correct but frustrating, nonetheless. Harriet's patience was worn thin. Bogdan Nowak didn't appear to have taken Agnes. Damian Swiatek seemed guilty of only pining for her. Gunther Clausen's wife had verified his alibi. That left only Johnny. As much as she doubted her lone remaining suspect had anything to do with Agnes's disappearance, she was determined to find out the truth.

The crowd's loud banter quieted to whispers. A handsome man in a black satin dress and a tiara took the stage. He addressed the audience. "Gentlemanly ladies and ladylike gentlemen . . ." He paused for the titters to subside. "Welcome to the Black Rabbit's Annual Ball. I need not emphasize to all in attendance what a special night it is. For tonight, Henry is Henrietta, William is Wilhelmina, Charlotte is Charles, and the rest of you are free to be whomever you wish." The crowd responded in applause and hoots of approval. After a long moment, the man shushed the crowd with a gesture of downturned hands. "As this is a once-a-year event, I won't take time from our revelry by stating the club's rules as we do at each gathering. Just know their strict abidance is required for us to continue. They are for our protection and continued existence. However, I must take a moment to thank . . ."

The man continued his remarks for several minutes, acknowledging several men and women in the crowd whose efforts culminated in the evening's success. He concluded, "And with that, join me in welcoming to the Black Rabbit, the incomparable Miss Gloria."

Appearing more glamorous than he had at the Ali Baba, Gloria took the stage wearing a contoured dusty rose dress and heavy silver necklace. The man at the piano played a short introduction. The song was a favorite among many, suitable for the festive occasion. Gloria sang:

> *A sweet Tuxedo girl you see,*
> *Queen of swell society*
> *Fond of fun as fond can be,*
> *When it's on the strict Q.T.*
> *I'm not too young, I'm not too old,*
> *Not too timid, not too bold,*
> *Just the kind you'd like to hold,*
> *Just the kind for sport, I'm told.*

The jubilance fostered by surroundings that accepted everyone for who they were was something Harriet had never experienced. The final chorus shook the chandelier as she joined in singing.

> *Ta-ra-ra Boom-de-ay, Ta-ra-ra Boom-de-ay,*
> *Ta-ra-ra Boom-de-ay, Ta-ra-ra Boom-de-ay,*
> *Ta-ra-ra Boom-de-ay, Ta-ra-ra Boom-de-ay*

Barbara had cautioned patience, but Harriet had met Gloria, who knew Johnny Bartlett. If he were there, Gloria would probably know. She excused herself from Barbara, saying, "I'll be back in a moment." Harriet desired a private word with Gloria and didn't want to explain to Barbara the circumstances of their first meeting.

"Good evening, Gloria," Harriet said, sidling up beside him as he descended the stage. "I enjoyed your number very much."

Gloria blinked several times, calling attention to his long lashes. "Harriet, isn't it?"

"Good memory."

"You remembered mine." He smiled wryly. "But then I'm not easily forgotten. I see you found your way to us. I'm not surprised. Though I am more than a little curious who sponsored your attendance." Gloria looked past Harriet assuming whoever had invited her was standing nearby. Harriet was unsure whether it was acceptable to name Barbara. The Black Rabbit emphasized secrecy. "I came with a woman. Is it permissible to say her name?"

Gloria nodded. The remark appeared well received. "Always safer to settle on discretion. Having a good time?"

Before, at the Ali Baba, Gloria had been circumspect and reluctant to talk to her. Here he was more relaxed, more amiable. She thought she understood. Whereas the Ali Baba crackled with an intensity that put one on guard, the Black Rabbit was a disarming and friendly environment.

Needing to move things along, Harriet stated her purpose: "I am wondering if Johnny Bartlett is here?"

Gloria cocked his head. "Didn't we just agree not to name names?"

"Johnny is different," Harriet tried.

"And how's that?"

"We both know him."

"Do we?" Gloria scoffed. "Then why do you keep asking if I know him or his whereabouts?"

Sharp, Harriet thought, nearly saying, *you should be the detective.* "Leaving names out of it, why would a man frequent the Ali Baba if the clientele here were more to his liking?"

Gloria appeared to ponder the question. Whether he was deciding if or how to answer was uncertain. Finally, he said, "Not one of us here doesn't worry about being found out. Men have it far worse, if you don't already know. Many of us must hide our natural mannerisms, lower the tenor of our laughs. We stride down the sidewalk with more authority than we might feel. And we never—*ever*—allow our eyes to linger too long on another man, regardless of any attraction. Given the need to stay hidden, one might envy someone like Johnny. He's convinced everyone that he is an incorrigible womanizer. He's the last person anyone would suspect of being a queer. Of course, the irony is that his false persona often requires him to castigate men like us—men like himself."

The seesaw of emotion was a jolt. One minute Harriet was enrapt in spirited singing; the next, she feared for the lives of those around her. And she was utterly confounded about her feelings for Johnny Bartlett. He had convinced even his great-aunt—a woman with an uncommonly supportive perspective on such matters—that he was a philanderer. Why go to such lengths when his efforts contributed to others' oppression? Had something occurred in his past that compelled what seemed extraordinary measures? Could anything justify his actions? More curious still was what the men in attendance thought of him. What Gloria described as envy might be considered betrayal. How much latitude did his handsome face and fit physique win him among this crowd?

"Very well," Harriet said. "Again, I enjoyed your singing. I hope to see you on stage another time soon."

Gloria chuckled. "You won't be waiting long. Every half hour I do another number."

As Harriet turned to rejoin Barbara, Gloria said, "By the way, Johnny's at the bar. He's the only one I know who can afford real pearls."

Suppressing the urge to rush the length of the hall to the bar, Harriet wove her way through the revelers in search of Barbara. Her companion had been kind to bring her along, and she risked appearing ill-mannered by leaving her alone too long. She needn't have worried; Barbara was merrily conversing with three other women. A tall redhead in a tuxedo with a small bosom and wide hips stood close to Barbara with a hand on her arm. The sight stung Harriet like a hot poker to the chest. Never mind that she'd been the one to leave Barbara's side; this wouldn't do. Approaching their tight huddle, Harriet noticed they each held a champagne flute. "Hello, I'm Harriet. I hope I'm not interrupting."

Barbara gave her an odd look. Harriet felt suddenly terrible. She *was* interrupting.

"I was wondering where you'd scampered off to," Barbara said, raising a brow. Slipping her arm out from under the redhead's, she linked arms with Harriet and announced to the group, "Ladies, this is my dear friend . . . *Harry*. She has done me the honor of accompanying me tonight. Harry, this is . . ." Working clockwise, Barbara introduced each woman—Sam, Laurence, and George. The redhead, George, shot Harriet a scathing look, bringing to mind an expression she'd come to expect from Madelaine at the agency. In reply, Harriet took Barbara's empty flute, saying, "Allow me to replenish your glass. I shan't be a moment." Walking away, Harriet felt their eyes, like pinpricks, on her back.

Had Gloria not identified Johnny Bartlett, Harriet doubted she would have recognized him—even with his distinctive gray eyes. Johnny's presence at the Black Rabbit Ball confirmed his preference for male companionship. As Harriet closed in on where Johnny stood at the bar, he turned to reveal the man standing beside him. Dressed in an elegant black gown with shimmering crystals sewn onto the neckline and sleeves, the man whispered in Johnny's ear, his eyes batting wickedly. Johnny laughed. Harriet gasped. She stopped, teetering in place as if the floor had started to shake. Despite the dress and the bit of rouge on his cheeks, there was no mistaking the man with Johnny. The matchbox. The name: *Mattie.* An avalanche of thoughts crashed into her brain. *Matthew McCabe.*

Chapter 32

Harriet didn't think. With animal instinct, she fled the hall. Had either Johnny or Matthew spotted her? Neither man would expect to see her in men's clothing, but she would otherwise be entirely recognizable. With the dressing room door closed behind her, she frantically paced the room. She had come there to verify Johnny's presence and eliminate him as a suspect. She had done that. But the appearance of her colleague, her one ally at the Prescott Agency, sent her reeling. Recalling the odd conversation with Matthew in his office, he had spoken of a reason that prevented them both from considering marriage. She had wondered if he were referring to a same-sex attraction, but he'd broken the suspense by saying he meant they both prioritized their work over domestic unions. Now she felt confident he had attempted to draw her out. But why raise such a fraught topic? He must appreciate the threat to his livelihood, well-being, and future if his true nature became public. Surely he would do anything to keep his secret?

Another thought crashed into her brain, nearly knocking her off her feet. Her missing notebook, slashed bicycle tires, the interference with the suitcase, and the note misleading her to the sausage factory. Someone within the agency was responsible for all of it. She had suspected Sandra Small or Madelaine. Now she wondered if her saboteur might be Matthew McCabe. Before tonight, he would have been her last guess. To throw off suspicion, had he taken a page from Johnny by portraying himself as the very opposite of who he truly was? If Matthew suspected Harriet was also queer, might he have feared their paths would inevitably cross outside of work, exposing him and threatening his position at the agency?

If that were true, it worked—her one friend was her secret enemy.

Harriet slumped onto a stool, hiding her face in her hands. She had mustered the resolve to withstand withering looks and snide remarks. She had screwed up her courage to pursue leads wherever they took her. She had tried her best. She had thought she wasn't entirely alone. But the reality could no longer be denied. *If Kate Warne could do it, why couldn't she?* The question had been answered. She was no Kate Warne.

Lifting her head, she wiped her cheeks and took in the room. The traditional clothing that each woman had shed represented their personal metamorphosis. If only for a few hours, they were free to be someone else—someone truer. How different she'd felt when arriving. The music. The shimmering light. The laughter and jovial banter. Barbara. The night had sparkled with magic and possibility. Now all she could see was the inevitability of each of them having to change back and return to a life of hiding in plain sight.

Harriet couldn't possibly enjoy the ball. Not now. Not with Matthew out there. The evening deserved revelry, and that was beyond her ability. She wouldn't ruin the night for anyone, especially not Barbara. Knowing that her escort would try to convince her to stay, she decided to leave a note.

My Dearest Barbara,

I'm sorry I was unsuccessful in finding your sister. It remains my greatest hope that she will reappear soon, safe and sound. You have shown me much kindness, and I am grateful for having had your companionship this evening. I regret that I must leave straight away. Please forgive me for not offering a farewell in person. I trust you will enjoy a lovely celebration among friends. The Black Rabbit was a revelation. I'll be forever grateful to you for sharing it with me.

Very sincerely yours,
Harriet

She tucked the folded note beneath the lapel of Barbara's jacket and hurried downstairs to retrieve her bicycle. Albert, who'd allowed them entry earlier, appraised her disapprovingly. "You forget something?" Registering her baffled expression, he gestured from her head to her toes.

"Oh!" She'd forgotten entirely about her clothes. "Thank you. I shan't be a moment." After leaning her bicycle against the wall, she raced back upstairs to the dressing room, gathered up her usual attire, and returned to the entrance. Instead of opening the door, Albert stepped in front of it, blocking her path. "Please, miss. Go back upstairs and change. I can't have you going out like that."

"But it's quite all right. It's dark, and I don't mind. Besides, I am in a terrible rush."

He shook his head. "I commend your boldness, miss, but you can't leave looking like that. It's a club rule. For everyone's safety as well as your own. We can't risk drawing the attention of anyone out on the street."

Although desperate to leave, she wouldn't put the club's members in jeopardy. "Yes, of course. I understand." Once more, she returned to the dressing room. There, framed in the moonlight, her silhouette illuminated by the full moon, Harriet discovered Barbara standing before the window reading her note.

Barbara looked up, clutching the slip of paper. "You were just going to leave?"

"I'm sorry, Barbara. You must trust me. It's for the best." Harriet turned away and began to change into her usual clothing.

Watching her, Barbara said, "For the best? I don't understand, Harriet. Why don't you tell me so I might?"

Harriet didn't look at her, sure that if their eyes met, she would start to cry and wouldn't stop. She had already upset what should be a joyous evening and wouldn't selfishly subject Barbara to hearing about her troubles. A hand fell on her shoulder as she buttoned her shirt. Barbara lowered herself snugly against Harriet's side. "You will stop this nonsense at once. Tell me. What has happened?"

Harriet started to stand, but Barbara held her back, gently turning Harriet's chin to face her. "Agnes is my sister. You can trust me, Harriet. You must trust someone. So tell me. Everything. I won't let you leave here until you do. You owe me that much."

And so, Harriet did.

A half hour later, with the Black Rabbit Ball in full stride on the other side of the wall, Harriet finished her story by saying, "And that is when I realized Matthew McCabe is likely not a friend at all, but my saboteur. And with Johnny's presence here, I've no more suspects."

Barbara sat quietly, apparently absorbing everything Harriet had just told her. The moment stretched to a point where Harriet started to worry that Barbara was angry, finding fault with her decisions and actions.

Finally, Barbara broke the silence. "You're quite sure that Marcin believes the man Agnes found attractive had gray eyes?"

"Yes. Well . . . not exactly." Harriet clarified, "He said she described the man's eyes as similar to the choir master's. Marcin believes she was referring to a Mr. Mallek."

"But not Mr. Mallek himself?"

"No. Merely his likeness. It was someone whom Agnes must have seen at the Bartlett mansion. That explains my focus on Johnny Bartlett, you see. Admittedly, he was an improbable abductor, but with so few suspects, I couldn't ignore anyone. But alas, now I feel certain. Whether Johnny was the man with gray eyes is irrelevant. Johnny prefers men. He has no interest in your sister."

"And the German handyman? You're quite certain it can't be him?"

Harriet nodded. "Quite sure. His wife confirms he was at their home when Agnes was taken."

"There must be someone else. The milkman? Newsboy? Other relatives? Visitors?"

"No," Harriet groaned the word. "Pearl was forthcoming and comprehensive in identifying all visitors to the house. Her mind is lucid, her memory sharp. Despite what Mr. Prescott and . . ." A jolt of adrenalin shot through Harriet.

Barbara felt her quiver. "Harriet? What is it?"

Harriet jumped to her feet and began quickly pacing the room. She'd been wrong about so many things. She needed a moment to think it through. She needed to be sure.

"Harriet?" Barbara repeated.

Harriet spun around. "Another man did go to Pearl's house. On two separate occasions. And both times after Agnes had started working there. A man with eyes the color of storm clouds. A man with access to my desk and the suitcase. The man who come Monday will be my supervisor."

Chapter 33

As a detective, Carl Somer worked on the right side of the law. Harriet barely knew him, but he didn't seem the type of man to scale the outside of a building, force an entry, and snatch a woman from her bed. But if Carl were involved in Agnes's disappearance, he wouldn't have liked learning that Mr. Prescott had assigned someone—even his newest and most inexperienced operative—to find her. Harriet's progress reports would have agitated him, possibly explaining his unpredictable reactions during their encounters and his constant argument that there was nothing to the case. But, like every other reason to believe it could be Carl, it was circumstantial at best. She didn't have a shred of evidence against him.

Harriet explained all that to Barbara. They sat in the dressing room, their silence a stark contrast to the sounds of music and laughter coming from the ball.

"What do you want to do?" Barbara said.

"I don't know." Harriet's words spilled out in a moan. "If I accuse Carl Somer and I'm wrong, I'll surely be fired. Carl himself scolded me for racing around town, led only by hunches. Although a junior operative, he still has several years of experience and, by all accounts, is a respected detective. I am unknown to everyone—an experiment.

Falsely accusing a fellow operative will be my undoing. Don't you see? I'll prove the naysayers right. Instead of working the case with clear-headed logic, as a woman I allowed my emotions to cloud my judgment."

"I understand, Harriet, truly I do. But if it's possible . . . if there is even the slightest chance your colleague is involved in my sister's disappearance, then . . . ?"

"Yes, yes. Of course, I must think of Agnes's plight and not myself. The possibility cannot be ignored. It must be pursued. But how? Unlike Bogdan Nowak or Damian, I can't go marching up to him with questions. I need to determine Carl's innocence or guilt without him knowing—without anyone else knowing. It's late, and tomorrow is Sunday. Besides him being an operative, I know next to nothing about the man."

"Yes, but you somehow managed to learn where Bogdan keeps a woman," Barbara encouraged, "and then you determined she was not Agnes. Why not do the same with this detective?"

"It's not at all the same. I can think of only two ways to learn where Carl lives. If I ask someone, they will demand my reason for wanting to know. I can't reveal the truth. No one will believe me. The accusation is too far-fetched. Nor can I conceive any other reason to explain myself. The other way is to find his address written on a document of some kind."

Barbara clapped. "So there's our answer! We find his home address in the directory. Provided he is the head of the household, he will be listed. Then we can . . ." Seeing Harriet's expression, she stopped. "What?"

"Carl Somer is a detective. I doubt he will be listed in the public directory." The comment made her wonder—with the inheritance of her parents' apartment, would her name be listed in the next edition of the city's public directory? If she still had a job next week, she should seek to prevent it.

Harriet considered by what other means she could find out where Carl lived. If he owned his home, it would be a matter of public record, but she couldn't wait until Monday when government offices would reopen. Then it struck her. When she joined the Prescott Agency, Madelaine had her complete several forms, one for tax and wage purposes, the other in case her immediate family needed to be contacted for some reason. Both forms required her home address. Carl must have similar documents on file somewhere in the agency. She didn't know if or how she could access the office at such an irregular hour, but she knew someone who would. And he happened to be there at the ball.

Harriet shared her thoughts with Barbara, along with her concern. "That my saboteur is Carl and not Matthew makes more sense—it's certainly my hope. But it could be neither of them."

"If everything were certain, what would there be for a detective to do?" Barbara said.

Although Harriet felt dejected, Barbara's words made her smile. "Quite right." Harriet leaned down to untie her shoelaces. "And now I must change clothing yet again."

Rejoining the festivities with Barbara, Harriet felt a pang of regret. They were missing a splendid evening. Men danced together as couples, as did the women. Mannerisms associated with the other sex were displayed without reservation, accentuated by the switch in attire and names. To Harriet's great delight, Gloria retook the stage and began singing the popular song "And the Band Played On." Reaching the familiar chorus, everyone joined in singing:

> *Casey would waltz with a strawberry blonde,*
> *And the band played on!*
> *He'd glide cross the floor with the girl he ador'd,*
> *And the band played on!*
> *But his brain was so loaded it nearly exploded,*

The poor girl would shake with alarm!
He'd ne'er leave the girl with the strawberry curl,
And the band played on!

Harriet spied Johnny Bartlett and Matthew McCabe among a group of six men absorbed in jovial conversation. Each of them held either a drink or a cigarette. Several had their arms draped over another's shoulder or around a waist. While their behavior was not unusual for the setting, Harriet continued to be amazed by their brazenness. She maneuvered through the crowd to where the men stood. Had Harriet been concerned that Matthew had spotted her before, she needn't have been. His evident shock confirmed he was seeing her for the first time that night.

As he sputtered for words, Harriet said, "Excuse the interruption, but I need a private word with Mattie."

Hearing her use that name, Matthew jerked in surprise. Johnny, who now recognized Harriet as the woman who had sought him out at the Ali Baba Theater, appeared baffled. Neither man appeared to know Barbara.

Harriet laid a hand on Matthew's arm and smiled. "Please. It's urgent. I must speak with you at once."

Amidst the men's confused expressions and mutterings, Matthew departed the group with a reassuring, "I shan't be gone but a moment," and followed Harriet and Barbara into the hallway. His tight smile vanished in an instant. He was livid.

"What in blazes are you doing here, Miss Morrow? Your recklessness is astonishing."

Harriet reared back, not appreciating his tone. "I'm here for the same reason as you, Mr. McCabe. And for the record, my presence is no more reckless than your own. My escort"—she gestured to Barbara—"informed me of all the precautions, which I've abided by. I'm sorry for pulling you away from the entertainment, but I have no choice. I need your help. I must get inside the Prescott Agency. Tonight. But I have no key, and should there be other means of security, I fear I'll be found out."

Matthew's angry look slid into curiosity. "What on earth do you need from inside the office? Surely, whatever it is can wait until Monday?"

She again gestured to Barbara. "This is Miss Barbara Wozniak, Agnes's sister. I'm here as Barbara's guest but primarily as part of my investigation."

Barbara and Matthew exchanged awkward nods.

Harriet continued, "I think I've figured out who took Agnes. But to be sure, I must first get inside the office. There is some information I need."

Matthew's expression of surprise had intensified to the point where he looked almost cartoonish, his brows threatening his hairline. "You do? Who? And what do you need from the office?"

Harriet and Barbara traded glances. There would be no going back. If she was right, she might find Agnes after all. If she were wrong, her dream of working as a detective would end less than a week after she'd started. She expelled a long breath and held Matthew's gaze. "I suspect Carl Somer."

For a long moment, it was as if time stopped. No one moved. No one even blinked. The sounds from the ball muted into an indistinguishable hum. Finally, Matthew said, "Tell me why."

Harriet started to speak but was cut off. "No. Not here. Come with me." He raised a hand to Barbara. "Please. I must speak with Miss Morrow alone."

"But this is Barbara Wozniak. I just told you that she's—"

"Miss Morrow! I'll hear you out. But I won't have this conversation in the company of others. This way."

Harriet whispered a quick apology to Barbara and hurried after Matthew, following him downstairs and into a storeroom at the back of the building. Entering, she realized how far they were from everyone in attendance. If Matthew wished to do her harm, this would be a good place. She regretted not having her derringer with her, yet the gun would never have come into her possession if it were not for him. She must trust him. What choice did she have?

Once inside the dimly lit room, Matthew shut the door behind them. "Now, Miss Morrow, explain yourself. And for your sake, I hope you are exceedingly convincing."

Chapter 34

Harriet observed Matthew's stoic expression as she laid out her case against Carl Somer. She found his inscrutability unnerving but also impressively effective—it kept her on tenterhooks. If she ever had the opportunity, she would try to replicate his demeanor in future discussions with suspects and witnesses.

"The truth is," Matthew finally said, "I don't know Carl Somer well enough to vouch for his innocence. But you are accusing a fellow operative of kidnapping. The gravity of what you're asserting is . . . well, let's just say if you're wrong, your employment won't survive it. And if I'm complicit in any way, neither will mine."

Harriet understood. Were their roles reversed, she would think no differently. Had she built her argument on evidence and not thin plausibility, he might be more willing to be involved. Then again, his assistance needn't be direct. Perhaps she could get what she needed without exposing him to undue risk.

Adopting a casual tone, she said, "I'm afraid, Mr. McCabe, that I've left some important case notes in my desk drawer at the office. Silly of me, I know. But I'm afraid I very much need them. It can't wait. I'm sure Madelaine intended to provide me with a key of my own, but as busy as she is . . . I'm sure it's just a simple oversight. If you'd be so kind as to allow me to borrow your key, I promise to return it to you first thing on Monday."

She waited as Matthew calculated the odds that lending her a key would get him into trouble. Like many of her actions the past week, the current plan was predicated on several assumptions. Her current scheme required that first, each operative had his own key, and second, that she could get inside the office, find Carl's address, and leave without being seen by anyone.

"Wait here," Matthew said.

Three seconds after he'd closed the storeroom door, she opened it slightly and peered through the crack. Matthew turned toward the staircase—the right direction. She guessed that if he had brought an office key with him, it would be tucked among his regular clothing in the men's dressing room upstairs. Fortunately for her frayed nerves, he returned quickly and held out a clenched fist. She offered an open palm.

"Whatever you might decide to do, Miss Morrow, do it before the morning. Although it will be Sunday, it's not uncommon for operatives to be present at any time. As you know, the job doesn't keep regular hours. As far as I'm concerned, our previous conversation about Mr. Somer never happened. Should I be confronted by him or Mr. Prescott or anyone else, I will deny that you ever shared your suspicions. If you challenge my position, it will be your word against mine. I hope you realize that given the weight of your allegation, you won't be believed." He paused, looking at once serious and empathetic. "There's an overnight guard stationed in the lobby. You'll need to get past him somehow. The rest, however, should be straightforward enough."

Harriet nodded.

Matthew dropped a gold key into her hand.

Before leaving the room, he turned back. "I do wish you well, Miss Morrow. I hope this turns out as you hope. And remember, you're not the only operative likely to be armed."

The temperature had dipped since Harriet arrived at the club, and she regretted having changed out of her men's trousers. Not only were they warmer, but they also made for easier pedaling. Although the Prescott Agency was closer than her home, she wouldn't go to the office immediately. She wasn't ready. Besides, delaying her arrival until the wee morning hours might lessen the chance of running into someone.

Harriet hadn't been truthful in telling Barbara why she left the party, allowing her to think it was concern for her brother being left alone in the apartment. As for her suspicions about Carl Somer, she explained that Matthew McCabe had agreed to meet and unlock the office early the next morning so she could search for Carl's home address. She didn't like withholding her true intention to sneak into the agency soon and alone but was concerned Barbara would insist on accompanying her. She placated her with a promise to meet at nine o'clock in the morning near Holy Trinity Church, just down the street from the Wozniaks' home. Only with that agreement did Barbara acquiesce and return to the ball. Harriet liked to believe she was a learner of lessons—entering the sausage factory and Nowak's house alone had put her in peril. Having Barbara nearby when she visited Carl Somer—provided she could discover his address—was a sensible precaution.

Hearing Harriet arrive, Susan dashed across the living room floor to greet her at the door. The kitten was an affectionate companion, but Harriet suspected the brushing against her ankles expressed a desire to be fed. The silence suggested Aubrey was asleep in his bedroom. She was glad not to have to explain that she still had work to do and would be going out later, not just dressed but disguised as a man. While on her bicycle, she'd devised a plan to circumvent the lobby guard, who would allow a detective entrance—all of whom were known to be men—but probably not a secretary. Presuming that her claim of being the former would be doubted, she would present herself as a more convincing version of Harry. Earlier in the school year, Aubrey had played the role of Sir Francis Chesney in the farce *Charley's Aunt*. He had pasted on a bushy mustache to portray the retired colonel. Thankfully, he had kept the false facial hair in a box in the hallway closet.

She didn't dare lie down for fear of falling asleep. Instead, she made a cup of strong coffee. Two hours later, at 1:30 a.m., she examined her whiskers in the mirror and chuckled, thinking she looked like Chicago Mayor Carter Henry Harrison. Satisfied that no glue was showing, she wriggled on her hat and pushed her bicycle into the hallway.

The wind had picked up since she was last out. Adding to the cold stinging her cheeks, she faced a most unusual sensation—the artificial hair above her lip tickled her nose. She gritted her teeth, fighting the urge to fiddle with her whiskers and risk loosening them. Reaching the office building, she made sure to stay beyond sight of the entrance. Her Victoria was made for a woman. She didn't want the guard to see how she'd arrived.

Harriet's stomach lurched as she entered the lobby. As Matthew had described, a podium that wasn't there during regular office hours had been positioned inside the door. A uniformed guard sat on a stool. He appeared to be asleep. Harriet had neglected to ask Matthew if there was a protocol to be followed. She'd have to hope for the best, which started with as little interaction with the guard as possible.

Harriet strode toward the elevator.

"Hold up, there," the guard said, suddenly very much awake.

She turned back. Was her disguise that obvious? Should she run? She might make it inside the elevator before he caught her, but he'd see which floor she had gone to. She approached, careful to stay at arm's length.

He tapped the ledger on the podium. "Need to sign in, sir."

Mumbling, "Right, right, of course," she scribbled *Harry Morrow, Prescott Agency*, and the time, *1:50 a.m.*, in the appropriate columns. Glancing up, she noticed with relief that the man's eyes were again closed. She returned her focus to the ledger and read up, then flipped to the previous page. The most recent visitor to the Prescott Agency had been the senior operative Charles Shoemaker at 9:10 that evening. The leftmost column where his time of departure would be logged was blank. She mumbled a low-throated "thank you" and hurried across the lobby.

A minute later, the elevator door opened to the sixth floor. She stood for a long moment while her eyes adjusted before digging inside her handbag and retrieving the key Matthew had loaned her. Inside the office was silent and darker still. Mr. Shoemaker was either present or had left the building without signing out. Madelaine's desk and file cabinet, where the personnel files were kept, were located outside Mr. Prescott's office to the right of the receptionist's station. The operatives' offices, including Charles Shoemaker's, were down the hallway to the left. She had a choice. She could sneak toward Charles's office to see if he were indeed there, or she could go the other direction and commence her search for Carl's address. Although she would proceed regardless, knowing that Charles had gone—if he had—would ease her mind considerably.

Passing by the clerk's area, she heard a sound. No sooner had she stopped than she heard it again. Then again. *Snoring*. It was coming from somewhere just ahead. She spun on her heel, hurried back the way she'd come, crossed the office lobby, and found herself behind Madelaine's desk before three large glass-fronted cabinets filled with files.

She now faced an unforeseen problem. In the dim conditions, she couldn't read what Madelaine had written on any of the folders. However, the moonlight through Prescott's window might allow her to read the labels. Did she dare enter his private office? If she carried them in batches, she could figure out which contained the employees' personal information and find Carl's file from there. Gripping the door handle, she hesitated but only for a moment. The entire evening's enterprise was tantamount to jumping off a cliff into unknown water. She had already leaped by falsifying her name in the guard's ledger. There was no way other than forward.

She gathered an armful of files and carried them to the credenza below the office window. They all appeared to be correspondence between the agency's principal and clients. She rushed them back to where she'd found them and collected another stack. These were various corporate filings to governmental agencies. She repeated the process four times before finding a folder marked "Marjorie Lancaster" and, beneath it, "Judith Middleton." None in the batch were Carl Somer's, but having narrowed her search, she now knew where to look. Minutes later, she found what she was looking for in Carl Somer's file: *852 West Argyle Street, Apartment 17.*

After recording his home address in her notebook, she had gathered the files when a nearby cough stopped her. Charles had woken, apparently, and was fast approaching. Still clutching the files, she dashed into Prescott's private lavatory and quietly closed the door behind her. Another cough, extremely close, told her Charles had entered Prescott's office. She didn't move. She concentrated all her faculties on listening. The rugs would dampen his footsteps, but still, shouldn't she hear something? Several long minutes passed, then a faint squeak. Harriet would have never remembered Prescott's chair making that sound, but hearing it was unmistakable. Charles had sat behind Prescott's desk. *The gall!* She envisioned the senior operative imagining himself as the principal detective of the famed Chicago agency. She mentally cataloged the man's ambition. One day the insight might prove beneficial. At the moment, she was trapped in the lavatory and could only hope Charles didn't want to assume another of Prescott's thrones.

Ten insufferable minutes ticked by. Harriet was nearing her wits' end when the snores reached her ears. She didn't hesitate. She gently opened the door and tiptoed across the room. The window framed Charles Shoemaker, backlit by the moonlight, his head tilted back and feet on Prescott's desk. If only she had the means to capture a photograph, there would be one senior operative she could rely on for a future favor of significant value.

Reassured by Charles's steady snoring, she returned the files to where she'd found them and shut the cabinet door. At the guard's podium in the building's lobby, she signed herself out—the time: 2:45 a.m. Sunrise was in less than four hours. Had a new day's dawning ever portended such consequence?

Chapter 35

Gazing up, Harriet admired Holy Trinity Church. The imposing entrance resembling Rome's famous Pantheon, which she'd seen pictured in *Life* magazine, was flanked by soaring towers with conical caps and steeples. As it was Sunday morning, the doors were propped open. A flow of parishioners, mostly adults clad in somber black dresses and suits, strolled past, making their way slowly up the steps and disappearing inside.

Harriet hadn't planned how she and Barbara would journey from the church to Carl's home a few miles north on Argyle Street. While it was possible to give a more petite person a lift on her bicycle by having them sit on the rack behind her seat, Barbara's size and the distance would require another means of travel.

She checked her watch. It had been over six hours since she left the Prescott Agency. Despite her attempt to sleep for a while, her too-active mind—and kitten—hadn't cooperated. Her fatigue was lessened by the two strong cups of coffee, eggs, and toast she'd consumed an hour ago. The caffeine, however, made her even more jittery, and she needed to use the toilet.

After securing her bicycle, musing that there might be no safer place than next to a church, she passed through the imposing entrance to Holy Trinity. The silence in the cavernous space was intermittently interrupted by footsteps on the hard polished floor, the creaking of a pew, or the echoing *plunk* of a dropped kneeler. Minutes later, she emerged from the building, shielding her eyes from the abrupt shift to brighter light. Barbara stood next to the Victoria and waved.

"Good morning," Harriet said. "I don't suppose you have acquired a buggy since I saw you last?"

The question had been in jest, so Harriet was surprised to learn that Barbara's uncle did in fact own a buggy and that her twin brothers, Marcin and Marek, were preparing the horses for a trip to Evanston to pick up supplies for the banner shop.

"They're traveling north as it is," Barbara said. "If we hurry, we can catch them before they set off. We can figure out our return later."

Harriet rode slowly beside Barbara as she walked quickly to the shop. "How do we explain what we're up to?" Harriet wondered aloud. "Surely, your brothers will be curious to know why you and I are traveling to a strange address so early on a Sunday morning. If we mention our purpose is related to Agnes, they'll want to be involved. While I appreciate their desire to help, I fear their presence will only complicate matters. Besides, Carl is an operative. He is acquainted with dangerous situations and will have access to a firearm. Despite my inexperience, this is my job. I won't have you or your brothers put in harm's way."

Barbara glanced at Harriet. "You don't expect *me* to wait outside, do you?"

Like their mode of transport to Carl's, what they would do when they arrived was another detail Harriet had not thought through. "Mr. McCabe saw fit to see that I obtained a gun. It's in my handbag. Should I become a target, I have the means to defend myself. But I can't protect you as well. So yes. I do expect you to wait outside the building."

Barbara grumbled her protest, but Harriet argued, "It's only pragmatic. The best way to ensure my safety is for you to be free to summon help if needed."

They arrived at the banner shop as the twins were climbing aboard the buggy. Noticing their sister's and Harriet's rapid approach, they stared with wide-eyed surprise. When asked to explain why they wanted a ride, Barbara did precisely what Harriet had asked her not to do. She said they were going to visit a man who might have taken their sister. Dismayed, Harriet emphasized that it was only a hunch and that no one should get overly excited. Moreover, she argued that she must go to the door alone. Her words had no effect. Animated by the possibility of finding Agnes, the twins refused. Instead, they decided to alert their brother, Tomasz, Damian Swiatek, and the other men at the sausage factory.

"Good heavens," Harriet lamented. "The last thing we need is a vigilante mob descending on my colleague. I will say again, I don't know for certain whether the man in question had anything to do with your sister's disappearance. Stirring up a posse is both premature and an overreaction."

Despite Harriet's protest, the siblings were adamant. Aghast, Harriet watched Marcin run toward home to fetch Tomasz while Marek headed toward the factory. She fumed at Barbara. As much as she understood her desperation, this wouldn't do. The situation was beyond control, and she sensed impending calamity. Something had to be done. And fast.

Without further thought, she rode away.

"Harriet! Where are you going? Harriet? Stop!"

Ignoring Barbara's shouts, she pedaled hard to increase the distance between her and Polish Downtown. Once out of sight, she knew the Wozniaks would never find her. She hadn't given anyone Carl's address.

Before, Harriet had been reassured knowing Barbara would be waiting for her outside Carl's apartment. Now, she would be on her own but didn't regret the decision. Not knowing if Carl was guilty, it was better not to arrive at his door with a half dozen angry young men.

The ride to the quiet north-side neighborhood was pleasant, considering. Perhaps no other daylight hour provided emptier streets, and the chilly temperature of the past evening had warmed to where she felt comfortable in her winter coat.

The apartment building at 852 West Argyle Street was a five-story simple but attractive building that stretched half the block. Harriet was relieved to find the main entrance unlocked. A directory hung on the wall inside. As there was no elevator, she climbed to the third floor and searched the quiet burgundy-carpeted hall for the door with a bronze *17* at nose height.

One of two things was about to happen. The first possibility was that Carl wasn't home. The relief of avoiding an encounter would be short-lived; she'd need to somehow get inside his apartment and search for evidence linking him to Agnes. The second possibility was that Carl answered the door. She would confront him, and he would deny any involvement. She would press her accusation, and he would call her insane. Moreover, he would demand to know how she learned where he lived. He would shout and threaten her, but that would be all he could do. If he were guilty, she could only hope that her unexpected appearance would so rattle him that he would slip up and admit something incriminating. Perhaps he would lash out—a violent reaction might persuade others to take her suspicions more seriously. Had she more time, she might devise a superior plan. *Wouldn't any plan be better?*

She raised a hand to the door, realizing that her one-week-old career as a professional detective was likely already over. Whatever was about to happen, she just wanted to get past the next ten minutes. She knocked.

Nothing.

She waited, knocked again, and pressed an ear to the

door. Silence. She tried the door. Locked. That Carl wouldn't be at home had been a possibility, but she'd thought it unlikely so early on a Sunday morning. Exhausted and defeated, she turned to go. As she neared the end of the hallway, she noticed a door slightly ajar and an eyeball spying on her. She stopped, stepped back.

"Hello?"

The door opened a few more inches to reveal an older woman in a heavy house dress with curlers rolled into her reddish-gray hair. "Curious, those two," she said, glancing down the hallway toward Apartment 17.

"I'm sorry, what?"

"I said they're curious."

Steady. Breathe, she told herself. The other resident could be a roommate, a brother, or even a parent. "I take it you are referring to the occupants of Apartment 17?"

"Who's asking?"

Harriet offered her hand. "Harriet Somer. Am I right? You know my brother, Carl?"

The woman didn't take her hand, but she did take the bait. "Comes and goes at all hours. Quiet, though. I'll give him that." She raised a brow. "What do you think of her?"

Harriet fought the urge to shake the woman and scream, *Who? Do you know her name? How long has she been living there? What does she look like?* Instead, she struggled to remain composed and played along as she suspected the woman wanted. Frowning, she said, "Pretty. But I think my brother can do better." She leaned closer, lowering her voice. "Terrible cook."

The woman cackled. "Unfriendly, too. I've only seen her a few times, and she hasn't the time for a single neighborly word. Just rushes in and out. Rude, if you ask me."

"I was supposed to meet them for breakfast. It's not like my brother to forget such a thing. I'm surprised they've already gone out."

"Him, yes. Her, no."

Now Harriet fought the urge to hug the woman and

give her a dollar for her service. "I must have just missed him. Tell me, did he just go out? Did you see Carl leave?"

She nodded. "A quarter hour ago. He won't be back for a while, though." Registering Harriet's questioning look, she explained, "Aftershave. A man doesn't put on aftershave to run to the store for milk. Not any man I know anyway."

Standing again before Apartment 17, Harriet knocked, this time longer and louder. Eventually, Harriet heard someone approach the door, then stop. After a long moment, she knocked again.

"Who is it?" The voice, cautious, perhaps even frightened, belonged to a young woman. Did she detect an accent?

"My name is Harriet Morrow."

"Carl stepped out."

"I've not come to see Carl. I've come to see you."

There was a long pause. "Who did you say you are, again?"

"My name is Harriet Morrow. I am a detective with the Prescott Agency. But you'll be more interested to know I just left your sister, Barbara, and brothers Marcin and Marek outside your uncle's shop. They're very worried about you. Now will you please open the door?"

The sound of a chain rattled; the door clicked open.

Harriet recognized the woman at once from the photograph she'd left behind on her bedside stand. Not only was she beautiful, but she looked unharmed and surprisingly well-rested.

"Hello, Agnes. I've been looking for you."

Chapter 36

Harriet had been wrong yet again. There hadn't been two possibilities but three. The third—so unlikely she'd not considered it—had been that she would find Agnes alone in Carl Somer's apartment. But even now, with the missing maid standing before her, Harriet found it hard to believe. It was one thing for a man like Bogdan Nowak to keep a woman, but for Carl Somer, a respectable operative with the Prescott Agency, to hold a woman in his private residence against her will seemed next to impossible. Yet there she was.

"Are you quite all right, Agnes?" Among the dozens of questions competing for primacy, Harriet chose the one most demanding of an answer.

"Yes. I'm quite well, thank you." Agnes's voice was soft, sweet. While the accent reminded Harriet of Barbara's, it was as if some of the harsher consonants had been ironed out. "You say you have seen my sister and brothers?"

"Yes. I left them not quite an hour ago. There is much to discuss, but there will be time for that later. We must hurry. We can't be certain when Carl will return. Have you anything to bring with you? If so, please collect it. But Agnes, you must be quick about it."

The urgent action Harriet expected from the young woman failed to materialize. Instead, she stood in the center of the living room, chewing her lip.

"Agnes?" Harriet stepped closer and looked into the woman's eyes. "Is there something wrong? Are you sure you're quite all right?"

Agnes nodded hesitantly. Something was off. Harriet felt a light shiver.

"Agnes, how did you come to be here in Carl Somer's home? Is he holding you here against your will?" Harriet wouldn't have imagined needing to ask the question, but Agnes showed neither sign of duress nor elation at being found. She appeared to be just as she claimed: quite well. The emotional rescue Harriet had anticipated had deflated into a stilted conversation.

"I cannot tell you that," Agnes replied. "I am sorry for your trouble, miss. But you shouldn't be here. No one must know where I am. Please, you mustn't tell my family. You don't understand. It's for the best." She moved to usher Harriet out; Harriet stepped sideways to block her path. "You should go."

"Go?" Harriet was dismayed by the suggestion.

"Please," Agnes said, her eyes flashing alarm. "You don't understand. But you must leave at once and tell no one where I am—especially not my family."

"No," Harriet said forcefully, leaving no doubt about her conviction. "Let me state the situation clearly so you appreciate *my* position. My superior, Mr. Theodore Prescott, lives next door to your employer, Pearl Bartlett. Pearl reported you missing more than a week ago. Mr. Prescott assigned me the task of finding you. After examining your third-floor bedroom, I discovered your personal belongings left behind, a bedside lamp overturned, and an open window. By all indications, someone came in through the bedroom window and snatched you. I've spent the past week desperately searching for you, Agnes. So you'll understand that to find you looking surprisingly well, even contented, here in my fellow operative's apartment is a shock. The idea that I will simply walk away is absurd. I'm not going anywhere until you explain what the blazes is going on."

In an instant, Agnes's resistance melted away. Her shoulders relaxed, her face softened. She appeared ready to unburden herself from whatever secret she was keeping.

"None of this is what you think," Agnes said.

"So I'm getting the idea."

"Perhaps we should sit. I just brewed a pot of coffee."

Still jittery from the strong cups she had earlier that morning, Harriet countered, "Water, perhaps?"

They moved to the kitchen and sat across from one another at a small, round table in Carl's tidy kitchen. Sunshine streamed through the window, cheerfully illuminating the scene. The moment was peaceful, the setting pleasant—nothing like Harriet had expected.

"How much do you know about my family?" Agnes said.

Harriet relayed what she had learned, emphasizing what she knew about Agnes's father, Piotr, and his endorsement of Bogdan Nowak as a suitor.

Agnes nodded along, confirming various aspects of Harriet's knowledge.

"My father is set in his ways. He lives life and commands my mother and the rest of us as if we were still in our small village back home. We may be in America now, but he refuses to accept a different way. He is stubborn. He won't listen. Everything must be his way. But I am not a cow to be sold off. I will not!" Agnes had become angry as she spoke. She took a sip from her cup to calm herself.

Allowing her another moment, Harriet said, "Am I right that you met Carl when he visited the Bartlett mansion to search for the missing silver? And that you both felt an attraction?"

Lowering her cup as she nodded, she replied, "Yes. Carl is so handsome. So charming. While Pearl was busy with her plants and baking downstairs, I assisted Carl in searching the second floor. I didn't believe in love at first sight. Not before, anyway. But from the moment he left the house, I could think only of him. It probably sounds ridiculous, I know. But that was his effect on me. I was desperate to see him again. To see if my feelings would be as strong. And, of course, I was eager to learn if he might return my interest. When I arranged for him to come to the house the second time to look for the missing jewelry, I knew."

Harriet jerked in realization. "You? You hid Pearl's jewelry so Carl would return?"

A sheepish grin spread across Agnes's face. "You must understand. I had to see him again. I simply had to."

"And then what? You two devised a plan to make it appear as though you'd been abducted?"

"We agreed it was the only way we could be together. My father and Nowak would never relent. Never."

"But why not just leave one day when Pearl wasn't paying attention? Why the elaborate hoax?"

"That was Carl's idea. He has experience with investigating missing persons. He said if it looked like I'd run off on my own, my father and Nowak would presume their ability to find me would outmatch my ability to stay hidden. It would be me versus them, and they would never let up. However, if someone else appeared responsible for my disappearance, that would be an altogether different situation. Carl worked it all out. He insisted I leave behind my things and that we overturn the lamp and open the window to give the appearance of a kidnapping. He was certain no one would find me because he is unknown to my family or anyone in the neighborhood. And he was right." She shot Harriet an annoyed look. "Until you proved him wrong."

Appreciating the compliment within the remark, Harriet changed topics. "You and Carl decided all this while searching for the jewelry you had hidden?"

Agnes smiled. "Pearl turns in early each night. Finding time to spend with Carl after she went to bed wasn't difficult. Pearl never knew."

Glancing around the kitchen, Harriet said, "So what? Will you spend the rest of your life hiding in this apartment? The woman down the hall said you never go out. Is that to be your future? I understand why you'd be reluctant to venture outdoors. There is no telling who might see you. But you can't go on like this forever, Agnes. Eventually, you'll need to get on with your life."

Another smile. "We plan to move out west to San Francisco. But Carl must first finish the case he is working on. He says his work is nearly completed, just another week or two. After a successful resolution, he will resign from his position at the Prescott Agency. He believes that by leaving on good terms, Mr. Prescott will provide him with a letter of recommendation so he can find suitable employment as an operative out there."

"And your family? I understand the problem with your father, but what about your mother? And your siblings? They are concerned about you."

"I miss them terribly. I know it seems cruel to have them worry so. But truly, there was no other way. Once we are safely beyond Bogdan's reach, I will write to Barbara, my mother, and my brothers. Perhaps they can visit me someday."

Agnes was alive, safe, and in love with a man who had gone to extraordinary lengths to protect her and engineer their future together. As far as finding Agnes went, Harriet couldn't conceive of a better outcome. However, the situation did little to help her professional standing. If she told Mr. Prescott she'd solved the case, she would likely doom

Carl's opportunity to leave the agency on good terms and, by extension, his prospects out west. Mr. Prescott would be furious to learn that one of his operatives had frittered away the time of another operative—even the most junior— in pursuit of the supposed crime he had orchestrated. Nor could she tell Barbara or Agnes's brothers that their sister had been found—they'd never relent until she told them Agnes's whereabouts. The only positive outcome would be that she could count on Carl Somer's goodwill as long as he remained at the agency. Understanding that his previous animosity toward her was motivated by a desire that Agnes not be found now gave Harriet the upper hand. Although denied any credit or praise from Mr. Prescott for solving the case, she'd at least keep her job.

Among the many emotions Harriet felt, disappointment was the strongest. There would be no satisfaction in rescuing Agnes. No punishment meted out for an abductor. No pride in recounting her success to Mr. Prescott and Mr. McCabe. No joyous reunion between Agnes and her family. No tearful thanks from Barbara. Even Pearl would be vexed to learn that her maid would never return. Still, Harriet realized the situation could end no other way. She wouldn't ruin the life Agnes and Carl had ahead of them.

Hearing Harriet's promise to keep her secret, Agnes reached across the table for Harriet's hands. "Thank you, Miss Morrow. Thank you."

With nothing more to discuss or be gained, Harriet started to stand.

Suddenly, both women froze. Someone had just opened the front door. Agnes's eyes widened. "I wasn't expecting Carl back for several hours."

Harriet grimaced. Most every encounter with Carl had been unpleasant. Although this one promised to be quite different, she was exhausted, with no energy for an argument.

Beaming, Agnes stood in anticipation of her sweetheart's return. Had Harriet had any remaining doubt about her decision, it was erased by seeing the pure joy in the young woman's eyes. The next instant, Agnes's face fell. She gasped and stumbled back against the wall.

"There you are."

Recognizing the voice, Harriet twisted around in her chair.

Bogdan Nowak stood grinning in the kitchen doorway.

Chapter 37

Nowak's broad shoulders filled the doorway. He appeared at ease, as if this were his house and the two women seated at the table were family. *Smug*, Harriet thought. Agnes cowered in the corner, terrified. Her single greatest fear—one she'd thought she'd escaped—had come to life in the form of the notorious criminal.

He told Agnes, "Go on and get whatever you want to bring with you. I'll give you two minutes. Then we're leaving." To Harriet, he said, "You stay put till we're good and gone."

Agnes didn't move. Stunned by the man's appearance, she couldn't.

Nowak shrugged. "I was just being courteous. If you don't have anything worth taking, no skin off my back. I'm sure your housemate won't mind keeping it for herself."

Baffled, Harriet wondered whether Nowak believed Harriet and Agnes lived there together. Then it dawned on her. He didn't know about Carl Somer. But if he hadn't found Agnes through Carl, then how?

Aiming his cold stare at Harriet, he said, "I don't know what you were playing at, coming by the pool hall or breaking into my house. Had I not more important things to focus on at present, I'd be interested to find out." He spread his hands wide. "The mind of woman . . . such a mystery. A bit of advice. You'll do well to stay clear of me from now on. In fact, you'd better make sure I never lay eyes on you again. If I do, mark my word, you'll not see the next sunrise." Returning his attention to Agnes, he pointed a thumb over his shoulder. "Let's go. I'm done playing hide-and-seek."

Harriet found Nowak at once revolting and fascinating. Like the dog in the sausage factory, he was ruled by a single objective. In his case: to acquire Agnes. He had no immediate interest in learning why Agnes was there or, as he apparently thought, living with Harriet. Perhaps later, when he was safely away with his prize, his curiosity would be piqued. Was this an insight into the criminal mind? Allow for no unnecessary distractions? Let nothing stand in your way? Harriet wondered. While such unwavering focus might lead to results, it could also produce blind spots.

Harriet reached for her handbag and, stalling for time, said, "How? How did you find this place?"

He wagged a meaty finger. "You got only yourself to thank for that. All the ruckus out front of Wozniak's store caught my attention. I had a hunch and followed you here."

Harriet struggled to breathe; her throat went dry. The revelation made her want to scream. After everything she'd been through and accomplished, in the end she had led him straight to Agnes. She reached for her handbag.

"Whatever you're thinking, don't be stupid," he warned.

Harriet froze. Nowak moved with unexpected speed and agility for his size. He grabbed Agnes roughly by the arm and dragged her from the kitchen. Harriet fumbled for her handbag and jumped to her feet. She reached the living room as the front door slammed shut. Derringer in hand, she dashed from the apartment, catching a glimpse of Nowak's coattail as he descended the staircase. Nowak would surely have a weapon of his own. Moreover, he would be an expert with a gun and wouldn't hesitate to use it. Was she prepared to shoot him? Could she get close enough? And if so, was her aim good enough not to hit Agnes by mistake?

Harriet stumbled, nearly falling, racing down the steps. Nowak and Agnes were already a full flight ahead and increasing their distance. By the time she reached the main floor, Nowak had tossed Agnes into a buggy and climbed aboard. Harriet burst through the doorway as he snapped the reins. He was never within range. She started to run after them, but on foot, she'd not catch the horses at a canter. But on her Victoria, she might.

Not a minute later, pedaling as fast as she could, Harriet turned south. She'd lost sight of the buggy but guessed that Nowak would be headed toward Polish Downtown. A lifelong Chicagoan, she was familiar with the city's grid-like layout. Nowak would likely take a main street, either Clark or Ashland. She chose Ashland, one of the two that provided a straight path into the heart of the neighborhood. She had started to fear she'd chosen wrongly or that he'd pushed the horses to a faster pace when she saw the buggy two blocks ahead. Legs already hot with pain, she pedaled even harder. She told herself she could let up when she'd closed the distance to a single block. That would keep the buggy within sight while staying far enough back that her pursuit would not be noticed.

The ride gave her time to consider what she would do when Nowak reached his destination. To attempt a rescue herself was foolish. Knowing her location, if she left Agnes there, she could alert Agnes's brothers, Barbara, and Carl Somer—together, they would stand better odds against

Nowak. The downsides were that the moment of surprise would be lost, and involving the others would put them in peril. Regardless, presuming Agnes could be freed, how could anyone ensure her continued safety?

Harriet couldn't have been more right about Nowak's choice of Ashland Avenue. He continued straight into the heart of Polish Downtown, finally turning onto Blackhawk Street. *The pool hall.*

Whatever his plan, it was probably improvised. He hadn't woken that morning knowing Harriet would suddenly appear and lead him to Agnes. The pool hall must be a temporary stop while he considered his options. Harriet's mind raced along with her heavy legs. She considered the advantages and disadvantages of the location. She was familiar with the space, and it was unlikely to be busy, possibly empty at that hour. However, she knew of only one way in and out—the front staircase.

Harriet pedaled and fumed, her worries and fears mutating into angry determination. If she didn't act immediately, Nowak would take Agnes somewhere else, and she'd have to renew her search. But the second time around, she wouldn't have the resources and support of the Prescott Agency. Tomorrow was Monday. Her time would be up.

Harriet braked a block from the pool hall and watched Nowak hitch the horses and carry Agnes over his shoulder as if she were a rolled carpet. They disappeared inside the building. She drew her gun from her handbag, cocked it, and opened the door.

Mindful that the slightest squeak might alert Nowak to her presence, she crept up the stairs. Her advantage was the element of surprise. It couldn't be squandered because of a rushed misstep. Halfway up the staircase, she heard Nowak's voice but at such a distance she couldn't discern his words. She continued up. Reaching the second floor, she stopped short of turning the corner and revealing herself to anyone in the pool hall.

Now what? Threaten to shoot him unless he released Agnes? Gun or no gun, she wasn't likely to get far. Her derringer was a close-range pistol. Given Nowak's reputation, his weapon would be more powerful. By any measure, he possessed greater strength. She listened for voices that would indicate where they were in the room.

"*Nie!*" Agnes shouted. "*Przestań!*"

Harriet peered around the corner. She could see only Nowak's broad back; he blocked the view of Agnes on the other side of him. He appeared to be holding her wrists.

"*Nie, nie!*" Agnes's shouts and struggle with Nowak masked Harriet's fast-approaching footsteps.

Nowak froze as she pressed the cold pistol barrel against the back of his neck.

"Let. Her. Go," Harriet said, holding at least her voice steady.

Released, Agnes stumbled backward a safe distance.

"You are making a very big mistake," Nowak hissed.

Harriet locked eyes with Agnes and tilted her head toward the exit. She hesitated. Harriet repeated the gesture more forcefully. Agnes ran toward the staircase.

"So what?" Nowak scoffed. "You're going to shoot me?"

Harriet hadn't intended to put herself in this predicament. Acting impulsively, she knew no other way of stopping him from assaulting Agnes. She struggled to steady her hand.

"You going to fire your little gun?" he taunted. "Just like a woman. No control of your emotions. Maybe you kill me. Maybe not. One thing's certain. You will hang. I can imagine the headline. *Respectable business owner gunned down in his own place of business by insane lesbian.*"

The remark might as well have been a slap across the face. She stepped back—beyond his reach but still within range of a lethal shot. He spun around, revealing a long-barreled pistol. Seeing her derringer, he threw his head back and laughed. "It's even smaller than I imagined. To think I had any worry about your little toy. You will give it to me. Now." He reached out his free hand.

Pulse galloping, Harriet squared her shoulders. "I am an operative with the Prescott Detective Agency. Mr. Prescott won't take kindly to having one of his operatives shot while conducting an investigation. Agnes will attest to my saving her. Whatever protections you have arranged with the local authorities won't withstand a charge of murder. So I ask you, Bogdan Nowak, are *you* prepared to rot in prison?"

He shrugged. "I'll take my chances."

She examined the face of her enemy. He operated according to a different code—one that met obstacles with violence and dealt with the consequences later. She wouldn't succeed by appealing to reason. As frightened as she was, the visible quiver was manufactured. "And . . . and you will allow me to leave?"

"Yeah, sure. Now hand it over."

She feigned hesitation. "You promise? I have your word as a gentleman?"

He grinned, flashing his yellowed teeth. "You're not worth my trouble."

Lowering her gun, she noted the glint in his eye and knew he would shoot her.

Pop!

He didn't scream. He didn't flinch. The look on his face didn't change, not even a wince. He looked down at the hole in his boot with astonishment. Head lowered, he said, "Now I'm angry."

Harriet turned and ran. *Crack!* The bullet yanked her hat, pulling her hair. Crouching behind the pool tables, she frantically zigzagged her way to the top of the staircase.

Crack! The wooden doorframe splintered inches from her ear. She careened around the corner. Taking the steps two at a time, she stumbled down toward the exit. Another bullet struck the door ahead of her, shattering the glass pane. She fired a second bullet over her shoulder. Nowak yowled. A crash followed. She glanced back. He tumbled toward her down the staircase, a cartwheeling frenzy of arms and legs. She threw open the door, started running, and didn't stop.

Chapter 38

A hand to her heaving chest, Harriet stood before Barbara, gulping air. She had run the eight blocks from the pool hall to the Wozniaks' home. Only now did her thoughts clear enough for her to realize she could have taken her bicycle.

"Harriet!" Barbara exclaimed. "Are you all right?"

"Yes, yes," she blurted. "I've much to tell you."

"But you've been shot! Are you sure you're all right? You're not bleeding anywhere?"

Harriet jerked in surprise and gave herself a quick examination. "No. I don't think so. It was much too close a call, but I'm fine."

Barbara pointed to her head. "The same cannot be said for your hat."

Harriet removed her bowler. Two holes, front and back, marked the entry and exit of Nowak's first bullet. "As I say, much too close a call."

Barbara's bewilderment at seeing Harriet in such a state was mixed with anger at being left behind when Harriet had ridden off alone to Carl Somer's apartment. Barbara didn't know that Agnes had been found or that Nowak had subsequently taken her. With haste, Harriet informed her of all that had happened, concluding with the most recent event that had left her panting and desperate.

"Where is he now?" Barbara exclaimed.

"I can't say for certain." Harriet spun in a circle, too distraught to stand still. "The shot to his foot didn't do him much harm. It didn't slow him down. I don't know if the second bullet hit him or not. Regardless, he took a terrible tumble down the stairs. If he is alive, he'll be hopping mad. I fear for whoever crosses his path."

"And my sister?" Barbara said, her voice verging on panic. "Where is Agnes?"

Harriet's eyes flashed alarm. "She's not here?"

A look of dread washed over Barbara's face. "No."

"Perhaps she went to summon help? She knew I was in danger. Would she go to the police?"

Barbara slapped a hand to her forehead. "This is not good. Bogdan Nowak has an arrangement with the authorities. Everyone knows they're in cahoots. They're more likely to arrest Agnes than send someone to help." Barbara raised a finger, said, "One moment," and hurried inside the house. She reemerged less than a minute later wearing a coat and hat. Tomasz was beside her.

"The twins haven't returned from Evanston. Otherwise, they'd come, too."

Harriet traded nods with Tomasz. They started jogging back to Blackhawk Street. After her race to the house, Harriet doubted she could keep up for a block, let alone the entire distance. But three blocks later, she'd gotten a second wind and managed to match their pace. When they turned the corner to the pool hall, they stopped. There was no sign of the police. No Agnes. No Nowak. Several pedestrians strolled the sidewalk, seemingly oblivious to the shootout not fifteen minutes before. They proceeded cautiously to the entrance. From the sidewalk, Harriet pointed to the bullet hole in the pane. Although frantic when she'd escaped, she knew she hadn't closed the door. Someone had.

Tomasz didn't hesitate. He gripped the handle and pushed. The area just inside the doorway was empty, as were the steps. There was, however, a trail of blood.

"Where is he?" Harriet said, her voice nearly a whisper.

Tomasz started up the stairs; Barbara grabbed her brother's arm, holding him back. "No. He could be up there." Turning back to Harriet, she said, "Bogdan still has his gun, yes?"

"We must assume so," Harriet confirmed. "But he's not up there. Look." She pointed to the drops of blood. "Had he returned upstairs, there would be a second trail."

Barbara and Tomasz appeared to share her thought. They stepped back outside and examined the sidewalk. In their race to arrive, they hadn't noticed the dark red splotches leading in the direction opposite from where they came.

"Had my second bullet hit him," Harriet said, "I would expect more blood. I may have slowed him, but I most certainly didn't stop him."

"Where's he going?" Tomasz said.

"Where would he think Agnes would go?" Harriet replied.

"To our house?" he wondered aloud.

"No," Harriet answered. "I don't think so. He's not there. At least not yet. Besides, the trail doesn't lead in that direction. And as much as Agnes wants to see you, I don't think she'd go there now for the same reason she was hiding out at Carl Somer's. She's not safe—not even at home—as long as Nowak is on the loose and your father doesn't oppose him."

Barbara's eyes flashed with excitement. "The house up north where she's been staying! At Carl Somer's, then." Seeing Harriet's grimace, she said, "What? You don't agree?"

"It's too far to travel on foot. Agnes has no money for the elevated train or trolley, let alone a private buggy. Nowak gave her no time to collect any belongings, including her handbag. Now that Nowak knows where she's been hiding out, that is the most likely place for him to look. He mistakenly believes that Agnes has been living there with me. Nowak doesn't know about Carl Somer. Agnes must know that. She won't want to draw danger to Carl's door by returning there. I think she'd do anything to protect him."

"Yes, but it's only a matter of time," Barbara said.

She made a good point. Carl was in mortal danger. Harriet said, "I must find Carl and warn him. But that still leaves Agnes. Presuming she did go to the police, if she had successfully rallied them to action"—she swept a hand through the air—"they would be here by now. She could still be at the station, but where else might she go for help? Someplace nearby. Think like your sister. Where would you go if you were her?"

"Damian's," the siblings said in unison.

"Damian would do anything for her," Tomasz explained. "Agnes also knows he has brothers, and his father is a leader of the Polish National Alliance. Bogdan and our father are Unionists, fierce rivals. They'd be eager to help for that reason alone."

Harriet pointed down at the splatters. "Let's hope you're right and she did go there. The blood doesn't lead toward the Swiateks' house either."

They agreed that Barbara and Tomasz would search for Agnes—first, at the police station and then at Damian's—while Harriet warned Carl. They would regroup at the sausage factory in an hour.

Harriet recalled from the weekly operatives' meeting that Carl was assigned to a legal matter involving a disputed patent and the automobile industry. That sounded like desk work. Also, his nosy neighbor had noted his clean-shaven appearance that morning. Although it was Sunday, Matthew McCabe had cautioned her that it was common for operatives to be in the office at all hours. She'd learn if her hunch was correct when she arrived at the agency.

The lobby guard was different from the sleepy fellow who had been on duty earlier that morning. A younger and more alert man had replaced him. Harriet drew a finger down the ledger on the podium and sighed with relief. Carl Somer had signed in earlier and had yet to sign out. Without the benefit of disguise, Harriet wouldn't pass as Harry. She inked her true name and the other required information onto the page, turned, and strode toward the elevators as if she'd performed the routine a hundred times.

"Hold on there," the guard said as he hurried from behind his station to block her path. "You're not on the list."

"And what list is that?" Harriet said.

"The list of Prescott's detectives. Only those gentlemen on the list are allowed to enter during irregular hours."

"But I am a detective." Uttering the words, she knew she would be denied entrance. Even if she had been on his list, being a woman would trigger a challenge she'd not likely win. But the moment called for action. She wouldn't be turned away because of a clerical omission or a young man's ignorance. She pushed past him and pressed the button for the elevator.

"Now see here, miss. I can't let you go up." He jumped in front of her and held out his hands to hold her back if she didn't relent.

In reply, Harriet threw her hands in the air. "Fine. You win." She whirled around and took a few tentative steps toward the exit. Sensing the guard's return to his station, she awaited the familiar chime announcing the elevator's arrival. With her sixth step, it sounded. She spun around, dashed into the open compartment, and pressed 6 several times rapidly.

"Hey, now!" The guard raced back toward the elevator, but he was too late. The doors closed, nearly pinching his nose. He would know her destination from the ledger entry or by watching the floor location indicator at the top of the elevator doors. But once she found Carl, his interference wouldn't matter. She readied Matthew's key.

Although on a serious mission, she couldn't suppress her smile at first hearing, then seeing Charles Shoemaker sawing logs in his office. Five doors down, she found Carl at his desk, sharpening a pencil. Several tall stacks of documents nearly hid him from view. Hearing her approach, he looked up.

"Mr. Somer—"

"What the blazes!" He jumped to his feet.

She raised a hand. "I know."

Despite the long odds, he appeared to understand her meaning from just those two words. He dropped his shoulders, relaxed the tension in his furrowed brow.

"I know about you and Agnes. But you must come with me at once. Time is of the essence. I'm afraid Agnes may be in peril."

Carl didn't leap to his feet as expected. Instead, he sat back. "I can assure you, Miss Morrow, she's quite safe."

"No, she certainly is not!" Harriet blurted, aghast at his disbelief. "And neither are you. I will explain everything. But we must go. Now! This very instant. I've been to your home. I found Agnes. But I was followed by Bogdan Nowak and—"

"Agnes!" Carl jumped to his feet, grabbed his coat and hat, and raced from the office. Harriet caught up to him as the elevator doors opened, revealing the guard. The guard didn't hesitate. He grabbed Harriet by the arm and pulled her inside the compartment with him. Baffled, Carl jumped in alongside them. "What's going on?" Carl said to the guard as the door closed. "Unhand her."

"Sorry, sir," the guard said, "but this woman is a trespasser."

"She's no such thing. This is Miss Harriet Morrow. She is an operative with the Prescott Agency. I won't tell you again to unhand her at once."

The guard, responding to Carl's insistence more than believing his claim, released her.

"Tell me," Carl said to Harriet, his voice urgent. "What has happened?"

As they dashed from the building in search of a buggy, Harriet recounted the morning's events. Carl's curiosity about how Harriet had found Agnes was eclipsed by his singular concern for Agnes's safety. Harriet reassured him that, as far as she knew, Nowak didn't have her. The whereabouts of both Agnes and Nowak were unknown, though she suspected Nowak had gone to Carl's home to look for her. Barbara and Tomasz believed their sister had taken refuge with Damian Swiatek's family.

"So you see, I had to stop you from returning home," Harriet explained. "I feared you'd be walking into a trap."

Carl nodded. "I appreciate that, Miss Morrow. Let's first confirm that Agnes is indeed at Damian's home. Once we know she is all right, we can turn our attention to Nowak."

Harriet squeezed her handbag as if the strength of her grip could quell her anxiety. Agnes would still be safely hidden if she had not gone to Carl's that morning. She expected that Carl would be furious with her. But he wasn't. At least, he didn't appear to be.

"I owe you an apology, Miss Morrow. I have been an ass. But I was right to have been." Seeing her frown, he smiled, but it appeared strained. "I feared your success. I figured if I made things rough on you, you'd turn tail and leave. But you didn't. Then when I meddled in your work, I thought you'd surely give it up. Again, you didn't. Not only did you stick it out, you seemed more determined than ever. And despite all the obstacles thrown in your path, you did it. You solved your case."

Harriet appreciated Carl's words. But she couldn't accept them—not yet.

"I think you'll agree we have some mighty frayed loose ends to tie up before we can honestly say I've solved anything."

"Your assignment was to find a missing maid, not to conquer a man like Bogdan Nowak."

Harriet nodded but wondered. What was the better measure of a detective? Achieving a specific and expected result? Or resolving a matter with a thoroughness that ensured it wouldn't reoccur and continue to cause hardship and heartache? Perhaps the latter notion was too grandiose. But if Harriet was going to be a detective—and she was—she aspired to solve a case once and for all.

The buggy neared the sausage factory. The driver slowed the horses and said over his shoulder, "Looks like some sort of trouble up ahead."

Harriet and Carl leaned past the driver and horses. Dread sank Harriet's spirits. Suddenly tense, Carl opened his coat and withdrew a seven-inch-barrel pistol, its size falling between her derringer and Nowak's firearm.

"What do you want me to do?" the driver asked, clearly apprehensive about continuing.

"Stop here," Carl instructed. "We will walk the rest of the way."

The driver pinched his hat's brim in appreciation for the understanding and generous tip. Harriet understood the driver's concern. She shared it, as she knew Carl did.

"What do you propose we do?" Harriet asked as they marched toward the Wozniaks.

"There's no more hiding. No more skirting the issue. We sort this out as men." He shot her a glance. "Manner of speaking, sorry. You'll take some getting used to, Miss Morrow."

The remark would have delighted Harriet on any other occasion. But the present moment was too ominous to allow it. Standing before the Wozniaks' home were two men, Piotr Wozniak and Bogdan Nowak, each holding a rifle.

Chapter 39

As they neared the Wozniak's house, Carl said, "You've no gun, I presume?"

"I do, actually," Harriet said, surprising herself nearly as much as Carl. "But I'm afraid it won't do me much good. I've no bullets." Forestalling his admonishment, she added, "I never imagined needing more than the two in the chambers when I set out this morning. I won't make that mistake again."

The plan—such as it was—had Harriet sneaking into the narrow corridor leading to the sausage factory and entering the Wozniaks' home from the back. She expected to find Agnes, Barbara, Tomasz, Damian, and his family inside. If they weren't aware they had visitors out front, she would inform them. It was then up to her to somehow focus Piotr's and Bogdan's attention on the house. Neither man knew Carl, who, acting as a passing stranger, would surprise them from behind. Harriet wasn't entirely comfortable with Carl working alone against two armed men, but he was confident that with his Remington six-shooter pointed at their backs, they would drop their weapons. At that point, whoever was inside could safely come out. The rest would be resolved once the men were disarmed.

Reaching the rear of the house, Harriet froze. The guard dog stood in the opening of a small shelter at the opposite end of the yard. Ears at attention, his dark eyes fixed on her. She glanced at the back door to the house and judged the distance at about twenty feet. The dog was about fifty feet away. The odds? She guessed she could make it inside before the dog sank his teeth into her leg. However, if the door were locked, she'd be in serious trouble. Not for the first time that week, she wished for a better alternative plan. She didn't have much time. Carl would be strolling up the sidewalk soon. And any second, the dog could decide to attack.

Rushing back into the passageway, she dumped out the contents of a large metal trash can. Empty, it was heavy but still manageable. She couldn't run at full stride while carrying it, but it promised to be an effective shield, provided she could keep it between her and the dog. She figured that even if the door were locked, she could fend off the animal with the can while pounding on the door for help.

At the back of the house, the dog hadn't moved, nor had he shifted his attention from the backyard intruder. With nothing to be gained by waiting, she lifted the can and raced for the door. The dog's reaction was immediate—he bolted from the doghouse. As he rapidly closed the distance, she saw something entirely unexpected. The dog was uncoiling a leash as it ran. Five feet from the door, her foot caught. She fell, losing hold of the can. *No, no, no.* The dog would be on her in seconds. She scrambled backward as the dog abruptly stopped, their noses no more than a foot apart. He snarled and strained against the taut leash. Saliva from his gnashing jaws spattered her face. She crawled a safe distance away before climbing to her feet and hurrying into the unlocked house.

Catching her breath, she looked down and groaned. She had ripped a two-foot tear in her last good skirt during the fall or while scrambling on all fours.

The kitchen was cluttered with wooden furniture worn smooth with use, standard appliances and dishware, and a half dozen cast iron pots and skillets hanging from a suspended rack. The smell of cooked cabbage filled the room. Frantic voices came from an adjacent parlor.

Several heads snapped in Harriet's direction as she appeared in the doorway.

"Harriet!" Barbara rushed to her and embraced her tightly. Over her shoulder, Harriet noted those present: Agnes, Damian, a woman she presumed to be Mrs. Swiatek, and four men, one of whom must be the father, and the others, Damian's brothers. She quickly learned they were quite aware that Piotr Wozniak and Bogdan Nowak were outside.

"Then what?" Tomasz said after hearing Harriet tell of Carl's plan to disarm Nowak and Piotr. "They won't just go home and forget about this. Especially Nowak. Agnes will never be safe. By standing up to them, neither will the rest of us."

Aware she was making it up as she went, Harriet replied. "Well . . . we secure their guns. That's first. Then . . ."

Damian spoke up for the first time, addressing Agnes. "You deserve to be happy, Agnes. If it's this Carl fellow you want, then I wish you well. It's time someone stands up to Bogdan Nowak and your father. I suppose that time has come."

Mr. Swiatek said, "That's all well and good, son, but I need to protect this family. Piotr Wozniak I can handle. But Bogdan Nowak won't stop coming for us if he decides we are his enemy."

"You are not anyone's enemy," Barbara declared. "You are decent and kind people—all of you. None of us should suffer because of a couple of arrogant, backward-thinking men. Enough! My sister will not be that beast's possession. This ends here. Now!"

To a room of dropped jaws, Barbara swung open the front door and marched outside. Harriet rushed to stop her but was too late. Everyone in the house scurried to the window or the open doorway.

"Father!" Barbara shouted as she approached him and Nowak. "Go home!" She shooed him away like a pesky fly. "You've caused enough trouble."

Harriet gasped. This was not the plan.

Barbara pointed and shouted at her father. "You do nothing while this monster destroys your family! You have no shame, Father. How could you give such a man your blessing to take Agnes? You say it's in service to the Catholic Union and the church." She spat. "No, Father. The truth is you're a coward." She shifted her finger toward Nowak. "You fear him. And you stand there beside him. Beside him! Not us. You have chosen this monster over your own family!"

Expressionless, Bogdan raised his rifle and aimed it at Barbara.

Tomasz dashed outside and stood beside his sister. "You'll have to shoot both of us."

The next instant, Agnes ran out to join her sister and brother. "And me!" she shouted defiantly.

"Well, there's my little Agnes," Bogdan said. "I knew you'd come around."

"Now! Do it now!" Agnes howled. "I won't go on like this. I won't be given away like a lame donkey. I refuse! I'd rather you shoot me."

"Suit yourself," Bogdan said, shifting the barrel of his rifle from Barbara to her.

"No!" Agnes screamed. "Not you." She thrust a finger at her father. "You do it! You've been slowly killing me for the past year. So get it over with. Do it. Do it now!"

Barbara and Tomasz stepped in front of their sister. Agnes struggled, but together they held her back. Then Harriet and the entire Swiatek family rushed from the house and stood beside the three Wozniak children.

Piotr looked utterly confused. Furious at the unfolding scene, Bogdan cocked his rifle. Everyone had been so focused on Bogdan and his rifle that no one noticed the man fast approaching up the sidewalk. Suddenly, Agnes did.

"Carl!" Agnes broke free of her siblings and ran toward Carl. For an instant, Carl shifted his attention from the armed men to Agnes. Bogdan swung around and with the barrel of his rifle, knocked the pistol from Carl's hand. It skittered into the street.

"You?" Bogdan sneered. "You're less than I imagined."

The gunshot made Harriet jump. Time seemed to stop. Everyone stood gape-mouthed in shock. The horror of witnessing a man's chest exploding in front of them overwhelmed all the senses. He lay sprawled on the sidewalk, blood painting a crude crimson silhouette of his torso.

Looking up at Piotr, Bogdan sneered. "You son of a bitch."

Chapter 40

Madelaine was so befuddled that it took both shaking hands to steady her cup and sip her tea. Her usually uneventful Monday morning routine of settling into the week ahead had been disrupted first by Carl Somer and Harriet hovering by her desk and then by Theodore Prescott's shouting soon after he arrived and they followed him into his office.

Carl and Harriet informed their boss about the events that had culminated in a notorious criminal named Bogdan Nowak being shot and killed outside a sausage factory in Polish Downtown by the missing maid's father. Prescott had been most incensed to learn that one of his operatives was responsible for the entire ordeal. Harriet developed heightened respect for Carl; she doubted she could withstand such scathing criticism with such fortitude. Most surprising was that the primary reason Prescott was so angry was not wasting the agency's time and resources.

"You put Miss Morrow here in a perilous situation," Prescott admonished. "I sent this woman out on what appeared to be a harmless inquiry. All the while, you"—he thrust an accusing finger toward Carl—"knew full well the dangers that lurked. You went to the appalling extreme of fabricating the maid's abduction for those very reasons. You knew how dangerous the situation was. That a man has been killed leaves no doubt about the severity of the threat. There is no explanation for your reprehensible behavior, Mr. Somer. None."

That Mr. Prescott was most upset at Carl because he had put her in harm's way was astonishing. She didn't doubt Prescott preferred his operatives alive and able-bodied to conduct their assigned business. Still, the intensity of his ire reflected a different emotion: he genuinely cared about her. Stopping short of sentimentality, he turned his interest to the facts of the case.

"The father was arrested, you say?"

"He turned himself over to the police," Carl said. "He admits everything."

Prescott raised a hand, signaling him to stop. "As you no longer work for this agency, I'll appreciate your silence on this matter." He turned his gaze on Harriet. "You will answer."

Although Harriet understood the reasons for Prescott's harsh treatment of Carl, she wasn't entirely unsympathetic. Carl had acted out of love and longing. Upon reflection, his choices had been ill-considered at best, but his motive—a desire to protect and be with Agnes—was understandable, and he'd not meant for harm to come to anyone. At least that was his plan before Harriet joined the agency and started looking into the matter.

"Miss Morrow?" Prescott said, flashing impatience.

Her thoughts pulled back to the moment, she answered, "As Mr. Somer says, Mr. Piotr Wozniak, the father of Agnes, is in police custody. There is no question of his guilt in shooting dead Bogdan Nowak. Mr. Wozniak admits he pulled the trigger, and there are several witnesses to the fact, including Mr. Somer and myself."

"Piotr saved my life," Carl said. "Had he waited another second, I'd have been the one lying dead on the sidewalk."

Prescott shot Carl a stern look but didn't reprimand him for speaking. Addressing Harriet, he asked, "The maid? Where is she now? I don't need to remind you that this whole business started because my wife believes our next-door neighbor is missing her servant."

"She is at home with her family." Harriet glanced at Carl. "However, as for her longer-term plans . . ."

Carl nodded, seemingly thankful for Harriet's encouragement. "Agnes and I are moving out West. San Francisco. It has been our plan all along."

Prescott appeared intrigued; his anger subsided. "But why? Now that the father and Nowak aren't standing in your way, why travel so far? Do you know anyone out there? Any prospects?"

"Perhaps it's a romantic notion, sir, but the idea has taken hold of us," Carl said. "The move promises Agnes and me a fresh beginning. Everything will be new and exciting. Such a change will doubtlessly present challenges and setbacks, but we will experience them together."

"You will marry, then?" Prescott asked.

"That is our intention, yes. It was impossible to consider a wedding in Chicago while Agnes's father and Nowak stood in the way. But now? I don't know. The Wozniaks are Catholic, and I am not. Our marriage may still be opposed. I expect a justice of the peace will officiate our union once we arrive in California."

Prescott's eyes flashed, signaling a new thought. "Your missing notebook," he said to Harriet. "Your assertion that someone here was meddling in your work. Am I to understand that was you?" he shifted his gaze again to Carl.

"I'm not proud to admit it, but yes. It was me, sir. And Miss Morrow, I owe you whatever expense you incurred for replacing your bicycle tires."

"That was also you?" Prescott didn't hide his surprise.

"I couldn't have Miss Morrow getting close to the truth. I just needed another week or two to conclude my current investigation and collect my final wages. I had hoped to journey west with a letter of recommendation attesting to my service here. Though I don't imagine I should be so fortunate now . . . given the circumstances."

"Absolutely not," Prescott barked. "You have acted most egregiously and recklessly. Frankly, I'm astonished you would dare to mention such a courtesy."

"Yes, of course, sir," Carl said, properly cowed.

Harriet's eyes darted from Carl to Prescott and back. They had reached a gentlemen's understanding, an appropriate conclusion—and she disagreed.

"Is it not true that Mr. Somer has been a dutiful and competent operative for several years? Surely that must account for something. No one, including Mr. Somer himself, will argue that his recent actions were acceptable, but he feared for his beloved. Having encountered Bogdan Nowak, I can attest to his despicable nature. Had I been in Mr. Somer's shoes, I can't say to what lengths I might have gone to protect the one I loved from such a beast."

Prescott appeared to bristle at her words. "I am intimately acquainted with the darkest nature of men, Miss Morrow. But confronting wrongdoing by doing wrong yourself is never permissible. A professional detective must refuse equivocation. Lawful versus criminal. Right versus wrong. Honorable versus dishonorable. The line delineating one from the other is bright, broad, and straight. Blur it at your peril."

Harriet remained unconvinced. While such clarity earned mutterings of agreement from a church congregation or political rally, it too neatly ignored human nature, which seemed to endlessly scurry from good to bad depending on the circumstance, never able to plant feet firmly on one side.

"Perhaps a letter simply conveying Mr. Somer's period of service might be possible?" Harriet suggested. "Understanding that a favorable endorsement might be too much to ask."

Prescott's indignation forced him to his feet. "Miss Morrow! You will speak no further on Mr. Somer's behalf. I haven't asked for your opinion, nor do I want it. You may both leave my office. This untoward business has already taken up too much of my morning. Moreover, I must smooth any misunderstandings with the local authorities about two of my operatives being present at a murder. Even though 'involvement' is more apt to describe your roles. Mr. Somer, you will wait in your office until I determine how best to transfer your current casework. Miss Morrow, you will wait at your desk until I decide what in blazes to do with you."

Harriet opened Prescott's door as Madelaine, who'd apparently had her ear pressed to the other side, shuffled back to her desk. Carl followed Harriet down the hallway. Her usual instinct to walk beside a person and offer a collegial word was preempted by having nothing to say to Carl that hadn't been said. She understood why he did what he did, but she didn't condone it. He had been reckless, nearly getting himself and others—possibly her— killed. Despite all he had done to upend her first week as a detective, his gravest affront had been one she wasn't ready to forgive. Carl had dared to damage her bicycle.

Chapter 41

"I'm going to slice you another piece," Pearl said, removing Harriet's plate of crumbs. "You need to help me eat this carrot cake. It's best fresh. I made it for Johnny, but he hasn't come by the past few days. And its presence torments poor Toby. He can smell the cream frosting."

"Pearl, please," Harriet pleaded, "I really can't."

"Pish-posh, Harry. You can't say it's not delicious, and I won't abide any word of you watching your waist. We both know that ship has sailed."

Had anyone else said such a thing, Harriet would have been aghast. But Pearl meant no slight by it. She spoke her mind, and the observation was undeniable.

Harriet had come to announce that Agnes had been found. The news had pleased Pearl until she heard about Agnes's plan to move to San Francisco with the operative Prescott had sent to her house on two previous occasions.

"You're telling me I've endured ten days of inconvenience with no maid because I asked for Teddy's help?" Pearl slid a second piece of cake across the table at Harriet. "I never suspected any attraction between that detective fellow and Agnes. But then I suppose I was too worried I was losing my marbles. First the silver, then my jewelry. I'm ashamed to say I suspected Agnes at first. As soon as the new girl arrives, my valuables start disappearing. Truth be told, I asked Teddy for help to find them as much to clear Agnes from suspicion as anything else."

Harriet was happy to relieve Pearl's mind about the misplaced jewelry by telling her that Agnes had hidden it, creating a reason for Carl's return. As for the silver, Harriet wanted to believe it was anything other than a sign of Pearl's deteriorating faculties.

"I don't suppose you're interested in a job as a maid?" Pearl poked a fork in her direction.

Nearly choking on a mouthful of cake, Harriet shook her head.

"It wasn't a serious question, Harry. Though I do need to find a new housekeeper. Had you said yes, I'd have been inclined to give you a swift kick in the rump. You're not maid material. You're a detective. How many girls can say that?"

Harriet swallowed, mumbled. "Not many."

"Teddy seems to think you've got it in you. And that's saying something. The man's not one for dispensing praise willy-nilly. It's got to be earned. And even then you might be unsure whether you're being praised or scolded. You want more milk?"

"What was that?"

"Milk. Your glass is empty." Pearl sprang to her feet and headed toward the icebox.

"No, not the milk. What did you mean by 'Teddy thinks I've got it in me?' "

Returning to the table with a fresh bottle, Pearl said, "He came by after work, told me more or less the same story you just did about what happened with Agnes. Though Teddy's partial to brevity. Case in point, he left out the fact that Agnes won't be coming back. Still, he went out of his way to commend your work."

Stunned by Pearl's comment, Harriet could only blink in reply.

"He said you were headstrong, with more courage than good sense."

"That doesn't sound like a compliment."

"*Pfft*. I've known Teddy Prescott for thirty years. Trust me, it is. He likes you. Though I don't doubt you remind him of his Jennie." Registering Harriet's baffled look, Pearl continued. "Jennie was Theodore's and Winnifred's daughter. She would have been about your age now. I imagine she might have looked something like you, too. Jennie wasn't destined to be a slender beauty, but she was strong-willed and fearless. How that girl raced around the neighborhood on that bicycle of hers. She was always more comfortable around the boys than the girls. She had spunk."

Harriet's thoughts swirled. "What happened to her?"

"Drowned in the lake. Took a dare she could swim farther out than she could. Teddy's never gotten over it. Not that coming to terms with such a tragedy should be expected. Having no children of my own, I can only imagine the loss."

"Are there other children?"

Pearl nodded. "Two boys. One twelve, the other fourteen. Fine boys. Well-behaved. Smart. Teddy loves them as any father would. But the boys are Winnifred's pride and joy, whereas Jennie was the apple of Teddy's eye. The man simply adored her."

The revelation that Harriet resembled Jennie, both in stature and personality, helped explain why Theodore Prescott had taken a chance on employing a young woman with no college degree, experience, or evidence to suggest she might succeed in the job. Harriet had presumed her confidence—her boldness—in applying for the position had impressed Prescott. Could it have been something else entirely? Something not to do with recognizing her brimming potential but rather her tugging at the heartstrings of a still-grieving father? Although the reason she was hired didn't change things, the realization nonetheless disappointed her.

Pearl said, "Now don't you go getting all sad-sack, Harry. As women, when given an opportunity, it does us no good to dissect the reason. Take it! Be grateful. And do something with it. I was only telling you a story. Who is to say whether the memory of Jennie figured into Teddy's decision to hire you? Either way, one thing is certain. What happens from here on out is up to you. As much as I believe that to be true, it's also the case that it is not only about you. Your position might help the next young woman who dares to want more for herself than serving a husband, tending children, and making a pot roast on Sunday. When you succeed as a detective, you not only prove yourself, you prove the capabilities of all women. You're not just a girl to whom Teddy gave a chance. You, Harry, are a blazer of trails.

"I may no longer be your client, but I remain an interested party. If you like, you may even consider me a friend. You're always welcome here. Though it's best you not come around again for a few days. This house is in a dreadful state to host company. Once I have a new maid in place, it will take several days just to set things right. How about dinner this Sunday?"

Harriet had thought this visit with Pearl Bartlett would be the last. Never had she imagined returning for dinner, let alone as a friend. Yet she couldn't have been more delighted by the prospect of either.

"And my brother, Aubrey? May he come along?"

"Depends. How does he feel about dancing?"

"Well . . . I suppose . . ."

"Don't worry. I can teach him the basics. Six o'clock work for you?"

Harriet strapped a bag containing more of Horace's clothes to the back of her bicycle. Pearl had insisted she take them, and Harriet hadn't refused. Dressing as a man at the drag ball had felt marvelous. She recalled Aubrey's words before she had stepped out for the evening: *You look more like you in trousers.* Harriet agreed. Plus there was the indisputable practicality of a man's clothing for bicycle riding, escaping a guard dog, and scrambling over a fence to avoid the clutches of a fearsome criminal. Would she be so bold as to trade her skirts for trousers for good?

Settling onto her Victoria's seat, she nodded decisively. She didn't need an excuse for dressing as she'd always wanted—being who she always was. What mattered was that she was true to herself. That, and being a good detective.

Chapter 42

It would take some getting used to. For years, whenever Harriet looked down, only the toes of her shoes peeked out from below her long skirt. Now, the narrow legged men's trousers—among the hand-me-downs from the late Horace Bartlett—revealed the topmost eyelets of her handsome oxfords. She was accustomed to dressing in a masculine way, but the trousers were a bold advance. She imagined many passersby would mistake her for a man. The ability to pass as Harry—or another male alias— might benefit her future as a detective. However, proving that a woman could perform the duties of a professional operative required that she be seen first and foremost as Miss Harriet Morrow.

She stepped out of her bedroom. Aubrey, finishing his bowl of cereal, glanced up.

"I like it," he said. Since he was not one for long conversations, let alone with his sister in the morning, she accepted his remark as high praise.

"And what does your day hold in store?" she asked.

He shrugged. "School."

"And that business with Sherman Truss and Louisa Klopsberger?"

Another shrug. "It's fine."

"You would tell me if he were bothering you?"

"Yes," he groaned. "It's fine. Sherman's afraid of Louisa's brothers."

"As much as I might be interested in Louisa, my primary concern is you."

"Geez, Harriet, I said it's fine."

She couldn't help but smile. There was comfort in such moments: her acting as the overprotective older sibling, him as the short-on-words adolescent boy. It was an expected and welcome change to the tumult of the past ten days.

"I don't anticipate working late this evening," she said, wheeling her bicycle to the door. "I'll pick up groceries for supper on my way home."

"Can I have a dollar?"

She stopped, turned back. "Whatever for? I've yet to be paid my wages. The food money is nearly gone."

"Okay, never mind."

Considering how seldom he asked for money, she asked, "Is it truly necessary?"

"I was thinking I could do the shopping, save you the trouble. But I only have twenty cents."

"Oh. Well." Never had Aubrey offered to take on additional responsibilities. The gesture, albeit modest, overwhelmed her. She dug into her change purse and handed him four quarters.

"What should I buy?"

"Surprise me. But no one knows better my limited skills in the kitchen, so please don't bring home anything so exotic that I won't have the foggiest idea what to do with it."

He smiled mischievously. "Eggplant and pig knuckles?"

"And milk, please. You might suffer through dry cereal, but we can't have Susan with an empty saucer."

"Good morning, Miss Morrow." The receptionist's greeting was perfunctory, yet Harriet appreciated the progress made since her first day. The other woman, along with everyone else at the agency, knew her name and that she was there as a detective. Even Madelaine had softened her gruffness—she didn't offer a smile but didn't appear constipated whenever Harriet was in her presence.

In the room of secretaries, she stopped halfway to the back. A pretty woman about her own age sat at her desk, head down and typing up a storm. Harriet felt her breakfast threaten to come up. She visually swept the room for any indication from the other women—a smirk, a sideways glance, a titter—that she'd been dismissed midway through her second week on the job. Not even Sandra Small seemed to notice her looking utterly forlorn.

Harriet approached the woman in her chair. "Excuse me, miss. I am wondering if there might not be a mistake. I am Harriet Morrow, and this is my desk."

The announcement surprised the woman, whose lips formed a perfect circle, rendering any utterance redundant. Determined to "sort things out," Harriet marched from the room. As she approached Madelaine's desk, Prescott emerged from his office.

"Oh, good. Miss Morrow. I'm saved the trouble of finding you. Come in. I need a word." He ushered her inside.

Harriet's heart was in her throat. She had found the missing maid. She had done all she could. And still, she was about to be fired. Had this been Prescott's plan all along? He had said she was his "experiment." How had she failed?

Prescott sat behind his desk and riffled through papers. "Ah, yes. Here we are." Glancing up, he said, "Sit, Miss Morrow."

Indignant by what she perceived as gross unfairness, she said, "Thank you, sir, but I prefer to stand, short as the conversation will undoubtedly be."

The look on Prescott's face was extraordinary. Harriet was quite sure she'd never seen the agency principal look so bewildered. "What's gotten into you, Miss Morrow? I don't take well to insubordination. I said, sit!"

Squeezing her handbag, she restrained her anger. "To sit as a child while you berate me and then fire me seems cruel. I shall stand. It may seem a trivial gesture to you, but it preserves what dignity I have while still within these walls."

"Good God, woman. I'm not firing you. I'm making official your role here as an operative. But keep up this impertinent behavior, and you will have it your way after all."

"But . . . I don't understand."

"Clearly."

Harriet pointed behind her. "The woman . . . she's sitting at my desk . . . I assumed—"

"What the blazes are you blathering on about? What woman?"

"Madelaine put another woman in my chair this morning. When I arrived, I found her sitting there. I . . . I thought you had replaced me."

"If you had been replaced, Miss Morrow, I can assure you it would be for a good reason. Moreover, you would have heard about it from me directly. I would like to believe you might have that expectation. As for the woman you speak of, I believe she is our newest secretary. Why you would be alarmed by a secretary sitting among the secretaries is the real question."

Harriet closed her eyes momentarily, wishing she could hide entirely. "I'm sorry, Mr. Prescott. This is most embarrassing. But I had been sitting with the secretaries while not being one. So I thought—"

"Did you or did you not solve your first case?"

Sensing a test, Harriet answered carefully to avoid any further missteps. "Yes, I was tasked with finding Pearl's missing maid. And I did."

"Right then, it seems we finally agree on something this morning. Perhaps you haven't noticed, but the operatives, even juniors such as yourself, have private offices."

"But again, you had me sitting with the secretaries. I assumed—"

"You must stop assuming, Miss Morrow. You sat where you did because there were no offices available. With Mr. Somer moving to San Francisco, you will take his office. I believe Madelaine has it ready for you, such as it is. Now sit. And listen. Unless you object to having your own office or being assigned this agency's most senior man as your direct supervisor."

Harriet had arrived at the agency not a quarter hour ago and had already experienced the lowest and highest emotions. Feeling a bit light-headed, she was only too happy to sit.

Thirty minutes later, Harriet left Prescott's office. Pausing at his secretary's desk, she said, "I wish you a most pleasant day, Madelaine."

"That's . . ." Madelaine sputtered. "Thank you. I shall do my best."

"As you always do."

Leaving the woman baffled, Harriet determined to treat the women in the office with kindness and respect, regardless of whether it was reciprocated. She might not make friends with everyone, and some might not like her despite her efforts, but she'd not give anyone a reason to consider her an enemy.

Carl Somer's name was still stenciled on the door. Aside from the customary sparse furnishings, the office was empty, with one notable exception. A pretty bouquet of pale pink and yellow roses sat on the corner of the desk. She removed her coat and hat and hung them on the stand. Hearing a knock, she turned.

"Remember, Miss Morrow," Matthew said with a wide smile, "the walls are thin. So don't say too many nice things about me. You'll give me a swelled head." Looking surprised, he said, "Those are new."

"You don't think they are too much?" She stepped forward to provide a fuller view of her trousers.

He closed the door and sat in the chair before the desk. "Not at all." He lowered his voice and cupped a hand around his mouth. "But you've met Mattie, so . . . But I was actually referring to the flowers. The Prescott Agency doesn't extend such pleasantries, and I don't suppose Mr. Somer left them behind."

"I've honestly no idea who sent them, but I'm quite sure they're not for me."

"No? What does the card say?"

She looked closer at the arrangement.

Matthew plucked a small white envelope hidden among the buds and handed it to her. It read: *Miss Harriet Morrow, The Prescott Detective Agency.*

"*Tsk-tsk*, Miss Morrow. Someday you will learn to greet the unknown with more curiosity and less certainty. A lesson for both detecting and life."

Her fingers trembled as she peeled back the flap. Whoever had sent the arrangement was not someone within the agency. She removed a card.

"Well?" Matthew said.

Harriet swallowed. "They're from Barbara."

Matthew extended his hand. She handed him the note.

> *Dearest Harriet,*
>
> *Thank you for returning our Agnes to us. Although she will soon journey far away, to know she is safe and loved is a blessing beyond measure. I hope these flowers brighten your days as you have brightened mine. Jesteś piękna.*
>
> *Yours most truly, Barbara Wozniak*

He placed the note by the vase, removed a handkerchief from his jacket pocket, and offered it to her. She nodded her gratitude.

After a long but comfortable silence, he said, "I need to ask you . . . the other night. My position here. I can't have—"

"Mr. McCabe—"

"Please. When it's just the two of us, call me Matthew."

"Agreed, provided you call me Harriet. I understand your request, Matthew. And I appreciate your need to ask it. But never"—she held his gaze—"will I betray your confidence. Yes, we share an uncommon preference, which binds us in an irregular allegiance. But that's not the primary reason you can trust my word. I believe you're a good man, Matthew McCabe, and if I may be so bold, I would like to count you as a friend."

"You? Bold?" Matthew chuckled. "I believe we understand one another perfectly, Harriet Morrow. I am honored to be your friend and colleague." His expression changed abruptly, signaling a new thought. "I still haven't heard. What happened at Bogdan Nowak's house after I left? At the Black Rabbit, with all the focus on Carl Somer, I didn't think to ask."

Harriet told Matthew about sneaking into the house, finding the woman, and Nowak returning to catch her in the act. Matthew seemed most surprised to learn that she had since returned to the house with Barbara, who convinced the woman to take shelter in a small group home supported by the Polish Women's Alliance. Employment had been arranged for her at a local bakery. Barbara had been so astonished when Harriet asked if the baker might be Mr. Bykowski, her favorite *pączki* maker, that she jokingly proclaimed Harriet an honorary resident of Polish Downtown. Impressed by the Polish Women's Alliance's work, Harriet inquired about joining herself, but learning that meetings were conducted primarily in Polish disabused her of the idea. Instead, she contacted a close friend of her late mother's to learn more about the Illinois Equal Suffrage Association. The next meeting was a week from Thursday. Harriet planned to attend.

"With all your good works, how have you any time for us here at the agency?" Matthew said with a wink in his voice. "Speaking of which, with Mr. Somer's departure, has Mr. Prescott named a new supervisor for you?"

Harriet couldn't hide her grin. "Indeed he has. I met with Mr. Prescott just moments ago. He will serve as my direct supervisor."

"Prescott?" Matthew drew out the word, emphasizing each syllable. "An operative can work for years before getting the opportunity to work directly with the principal."

"I share your surprise. But I stand alone among agency operatives as possessing a particular quality."

"*Hmm.*" Matthew cocked his head. "Let me guess. Bravery? Resilience? No?" He chuckled. "Then surely it must be your sharpshooting."

"Jest if you must, but the matter is of great consequence." As Matthew's expression turned serious, she said, "Mr. Prescott said if he is to have a woman operative, he will be 'damn sure to show Pinkerton how it's done.'"

His smile returned. "Might it not be considered cheating if she wears trousers?"

"I may be a dutiful detective, but I have my limits."

Author's Note

Much of the fun of reading a historical novel is immersing yourself in a different time. To accurately bring 1898 Chicago to life, I researched those persons, places, and things referenced within the book. When certainty for some detail remained beyond reach—or demanded more research acumen or tools than I possess—I reset my goal from precision to something within the range of plausibility. I hope any inaccuracies I have made aren't so glaring as to be a distraction.

One particular aspect of the book—a main character who is a lesbian in 1898 Chicago—required finesse. Just landing on the correct term for a woman like Harriet proved challenging. The word *lesbian* wasn't widely used beyond medical or academic circles, as the notion of a sexual relationship between two "normal" women had yet to enter the broad social consciousness. Romantic friendships—close relationships among women that might entail holding hands, other light expressions of affection, or prolonged time together—were considered innocent among young women. "Boston marriages"—two unmarried women (commonly referred to as "spinsters") living together—were mainly accepted because of the perceived practicality.

However, sexual relationships between women were usually associated with either a masculine woman perverting a weak-minded one or prostitutes performing acts for men's entertainment. Interestingly, a woman's sexual activity—*lesbian or straight*—could only be imagined when a man or a masculine woman was involved.

It's widely accepted that the gay rights movement in America started with the Stonewall Riots in 1969. While much is known about the struggles for LGBTQ+ rights from that time forward, far less is known about what life was like for gay and lesbian persons several decades earlier. From historical accounts around the time of the story, we know homosexuals or queers (two terms of the time referring predominately to gay men) took great risks when congregating, whether in underground clubs or secretive out-of-the-way spaces. The difference between society's prevailing ignorance of lesbian relationships and the absolute intolerance of homosexual men is both fascinating and deplorable. I touch on this profound difference through Harriet's friendship with her gay (certainly not out) fellow detective, Matthew McCabe.

If there is a definitive book on what an active social life would have been like for a queer woman like Harriet in the late nineteenth century, please point me to it! However, I am fortunate that several excellent books about queer life in late nineteenth-century America exist. I particularly benefited from the scholarship within the pages of *Gay American History: Lesbians and Gay Men in the U.S.A* by Jonathan Katz; *Gay New York: Gender, Urban Culture, and the Making of the Gay Male World, 1890–1940* by George Chauncey; *Chicago Whispers: A History of LGBT Chicago before Stonewall* by St. Sukie De La Croix; and *Odd Girls and Twilight Lovers: A History of Lesbian Life in Twentieth-Century America* by Lillian Faderman. Any disagreement between these books' deeply researched content and this story is either my exercising creative license or my mistake.

Despite limited documentation on gay bars in major American cities in the late nineteenth century, such places existed. New York City's Black Rabbit was one of them. Liking the name, I borrowed it for the Chicago queer bar in the book. Descriptions of the Black Rabbit have been informed by the relevant literature but are largely imagined. The particulars of the annual drag ball are an invention, as is the event's bringing together men and women. While it's conceivable that a club might have regularly catered to both gays and lesbians, I didn't find a specific reference to one at the time—most *known* bars served a male clientele. Also, such clubs were primarily segmented by class. For the story, I took the liberty of having Johnny Bartlett, a wealthy man, frequent the Black Rabbit, a working-class establishment in an undesirable neighborhood. I justify this because bars like the Black Rabbit allowed patrons across classes to escape from conservative societal conventions—the term *to slum* was used at the time, retaining its original meaning today.

Professional detective agencies—the Pinkerton Detective Agency being the most heralded—existed long before the Prescott Detective Agency, which is fictitious. And so, Theodore Prescott's agency never occupied the sixth floor at 30 North LaSalle Street. Today, a forty-four-floor office tower, completed in 1975, stands at that address. Speaking of the agency's offices, could Mr. Prescott have really had a private lavatory? Whatever the answer, I wanted him to have one, so he does. This is one of many details throughout the book—not all itemized in this note—where I embraced the freedom of writing fiction.

Kate Warne was a real female detective working for the Pinkerton Agency in Chicago, professionally active decades before Harriet was born. There are many terrific books on detective agencies and female detectives in the late nineteenth and early twentieth centuries. These include *Pinkerton's First Lady: Kate Warne—United States First Female Detective* by John Derrig; *Girl in Disguise* (a novel) by Greer Macallister; *Pinkerton's Great Detective: The Amazing Life and Times of James McParland* by Beau Riffenburg; and *Pistols and Petticoats: 175 Years of Lady Detectives in Fact and Fiction* by Erika Janik.

America's Progressive Era (1890–1920), defined a period in which swelling immigration, urbanization, and industrialization fueled optimism that the country was moving in the right direction. However, that progress left much of the population behind. Social and economic justice issues—suffrage, child labor, poverty and gross wage disparity; dangerous working conditions; tenement housing; and political corruption—energized many middle-class Americans. On this topic, I relied heavily on the slim but information-packed *The Progressive Era: A History from Beginning to End* by Hourly History.

An excellent example of the Progressive Era in action was Hull House, the social settlement founded by Jane Addams and Ellen Gates Starr on Chicago's Near West Side in 1889. You can learn, as I did, about this organization's noble works serving the immigrant community at the museum's website: https://www.hullhousemuseum.org/about-jane-addams. The Illinois Equal Suffrage Association, to which Harriet's mother is said to have belonged, and the Ohio Women's Convention, which Pearl Bartlett attended, are reflections of women collectively working toward social justice, specifically the right to vote.

At the time, and arguably still today, the undisputed heart of Polonia (people of Polish descent living outside their historical lands—at the time of the story, the country of Poland, as we know it today, didn't exist) was Chicago. Moreover, Chicago claimed the second-greatest concentration of Polish people in its compact northwest neighborhood called Polish Downtown. For knowledge of this area, I am grateful for two books in particular: *American Warsaw: The Rise, Fall, and Rebirth of Polish Chicago* by Dominic A. Pacyga; and *Chicago's Polish Downtown* by Victoria Granacki, in Association with the Polish Museum of America. Also helpful were "The Poles of Chicago, 1837–1937: A History of One Century of Polish Contribution to the City of Chicago, Illinois," https://ia904705.us. archive.org/35/items/polesofchicago1800zgle/polesofchicago1800zgle.pdf; and "A Brief History of the Polish Community in Chicago," https://theculturetrip.com/northamerica/usa/illinois/articles/a-history-of-polish-americansin-chicago/.

As mentioned in the book, the location of Polish Downtown is accurate, as are the two Catholic churches, St. Stanislaus Kostka and Holy Trinity. Also factual are the references to the Polish Roman Catholic Union of America, the Polish National Alliance, and the Polish Women's Alliance.

Wages and prices are an area where I set a reasonable rather than precise goal. For example, a woman bookkeeper's weekly wage at Chicago's Rock Island Grain Elevator was estimated by referencing price and wage statistics on the voluminous online site of the University of Missouri Library at https://libraryguides.missouri.edu/pricesandwages/1890-1899#occupation and the National Bureau of Economic Research at https://www.nber.org/system/files/chapters/c2486/c2486.pdf.

Harriet's pay at the Prescott Agency is harder to estimate because female detectives were rare at the time. Again I relied on historical wage data to triangulate a reasonable figure. The same approach was taken to estimate other costs, such as the price of a sandwich at a downtown café and a derringer pistol.

Other historical resources on specific topics for which I'm grateful:

Chicago "L" elevated train:
Block Club Chicago—
    https://blockclubchicago.org/2019/03/12/the-l-
    through-the-years-in-maps-including-the-loop-conne
    ctor-that-never-happened/;
Chicago Loop Alliance—https://loopchicago.com/
    in-the-loop/then-and-now-a-brief-history-of-the-
    chicago-l/.
Streetcars: Smithsonian National Museum of American
    History, Streetcar City: The Trolley and American
    Life—https://americanhistory.si.edu/america-on-the-
    move/streetcar-city.
    https://chicagoinmaps.com/chicagostreetcars.html.
Bicycle map;
    https://luna.lib.uchicago.edu/luna/servlet/view/.
Harriet's beloved Victoria bicycle:
Online Bicycle Museum—
    https://onlinebicyclemuseum.co.uk/1893-overman-
    victoria-single-tube-ladies-bicycle/;
Smithsonian National Museum of American History—
    https://americanhistory.si.edu/collections/search/
    object/nmah_843087.
Prairie Avenue:
Chicagology—https://chicagology.com/chicagostreets/
    prairieavenue/;
Chicago Detours—https://chicagodetours.com/prairie-
    avenue/.
Women's college attendance:
A History of Women in Higher Education—
    https://www.bestcolleges.com/news/analysis/2021/03
    /21/history-women-higher-education/.
Derringer pistol operation:
PyramydAir: The .41 caliber Remington Double
    Derringer: Part 1—

309 AUTHOR'S NOTE 309

https://www.pyramydair.com/blog/2022/07/the-41-
caliber-remington-double-derringer-part-1/;
Duelist1954: "Western Double Barrel Derringer—
https://www.youtube.com/watch?v=CJy6IoODdg8.
Miscellaneous product pricing and information:
Chicago Blue Book, 1898, University of Illinois
Library Collection—
https://libsysdigi.library.illinois.edu/oca/Books2007-
10/chicagobluebook0/chicagobluebook01898chic/
"1908 Sears, Roebuck Catalogue No. 117: A
Treasured Replica from the Archives of History,"
edited by Joseph J. Schroeder, Jr.

In closing, I am compelled to note that while Harriet could live today as an out lesbian without fear of complete societal ostracism, hardly would she enjoy universal acceptance or equal treatment. Instead, she would see what hard-won rights she has gained as an LGBTQ+ person under constant threat while subject to bias in myriad pockets of society. As a woman, Harriet would still be paid on average less than a man for the same work, face skepticism in her ability to perform a role traditionally held by men, and be outnumbered by men in her chosen profession—especially as she ascends the ranks.

Also consider that progressives in Harriet's time worked to improve many of the same ills that continue to plague the United States 125 years later: corporate opposition to the formation and bargaining power of unions, poor (often dangerous) working conditions for low-paid workers, child labor, a criminal justice system that punishes people of color and the poor more harshly than others, abusive treatment of immigrants, and threats to one's right to vote.

That said, there's reason to end this note on an upbeat. Despite society not fully fixing itself, most Americans haven't given up trying. America's Progressive Era may be defined by the three decades ending in 1920, but in reality, the issues, ideas, and goals most associated with that movement are still pursued in ways large and small by countless citizens in every community across this country. Harriet's pursuit of social justice during the Progressive Era in America offers readers an interesting lens through which to view the advances of that movement—how far we've come and have yet to go.